COOKIE CUTTER

COOKIE CUTTER

STERLING ANTHONY

ONE WORLD

BALLANTINE BOOKS | NEW YORK

A One World Book
Published by The Ballantine Publishing Group

Copyright © 1999 by Sterling Anthony

www.randomhouse.com/BB/

Library of Congress Cataloging-in-Publication Data

Anthony, Sterling, 1949–
Cookie cutter / Sterling Anthony.
p.   cm.
ISBN: 0-345-42604-5 (alk. paper)
1. Afro-Americans—Michigan—Detroit Fiction.   I. Title.
PS3551.N736C66   1999
813'.54—dc21   99-42027

Manufactured in the United States of America

First Edition: November 1999
10   9   8   7   6   5   4   3   2   1

*Dedicated in loving memory to my
father, Sterling, Sr.; my sister,
Dilcie; and my brother, Steve.*

ACKNOWLEDGMENTS

I'm grateful to some female Detroit homicide investigators who provided valuable glimpses into their line of work: Officer Carrie Russell, Officer Barbara Simon, and the inimitable Officer Monica Childs, known throughout the ranks as "Sassy."

I'm indebted to Donald Calloway, an internationally celebrated artist, for supplying insights into the art world.

My thanks goes to Camille Brewer, curator, Detroit Institute of Arts, Department of African, Oceanic, and New World Cultures, for information about museums, and for our warm friendship.

I'm obliged to Rachal V. Gehrls, who has studied dance all her life and was generous with her knowledge.

I extend gratitude to several friends, who by coincidence are in the field of law, although their contributions didn't necessarily deal with that capacity. They are attorney Elizabeth A. Stafford and her husband, attorney Carl F. Stafford, attorney Reginald Turner, and James K. Robinson, assistant attorney general, Criminal Division, U.S. Department of Justice.

I owe a ton of appreciation to my editor, Cheryl D. Woodruff. She was my taskmaster and guardian angel. She extracted the best I had to offer, then demanded more; but in exchange she championed my cause and shepherded me through the ordeal of a first novel. I also thank editor Gary Brozek and the rest of the staff at One World.

My most special acknowledgment, however, is reserved for my love and best friend, Victoria A. Roberts, U.S. district judge. From the start, her belief, enthusiasm, and promotion never waivered. She sustained me and renewed me.

PROLOGUE

1967 | BENT FORK, ALABAMA

"I'm pregnant," stammered Annie Parsons. She attempted a smile, but her facial muscles, tight from crying spells, only twitched crookedly. Isaac Shaw did a quick, worried study of her extended belly and heavy breasts before she shot him with the other barrel: "It's yours." They were in the office of the Shaw Funeral Home in Bent Fork, Alabama. The year was 1967. She was fifteen years old and white. He was twenty-eight and black.

"How do you—" Isaac began.

"That one time was my first," she said. "There ain't been nobody else." She was lanky, with a firestorm of curly red hair. Her eyes were translucent jade. She looked too pale to bleed, despite the soaked handkerchief wrapped around her left wrist.

Isaac had met Annie nine months before at the wake of Hattie Mae Jones, a stump of a woman with huge upper arms. After the other mourners left, the white girl who had sat quietly but not unnoticed in the back of the parlor went to the coffin. Isaac observed from a distance as Annie whispered to Hattie in between sobs, kissed her forehead, and with a quivering finger smoothed Hattie's bushy eyebrows, accidentally tilting the woman's wig. Isaac approached and in the ensuing conversation learned that Hattie had been Annie's family's maid and that Annie had sneaked in to attend the wake. Annie professed her love for Hattie, who had practically raised her, and asked Isaac why race had to color everything in life, as if he were the guru who could explain it.

Even if Isaac had an answer, it might have been drowned out, for Annie lapsed into loud wails that her hands cupped over her face couldn't muffle. When his professional tendencies kicked in and he tried to console her with a gentle hand on the shoulder, she whirled and buried her face in his chest, her runny nose wiping across his lapel. She nudged closer, seeking only to be held firmer to lessen the spasms. A pulsing erection grew as they stood flattened against each other. He was certain that she felt it, and he interpreted her failure to back away as acquiescence, despite her slack, vacant expression.

Isaac sent one hand roaming over Annie's rear as his other hand grabbed her between the legs, but a probing finger discovered no lubrication. Undaunted, he moved frantically: swept her up, scurried to the front door and locked it, then side-skipped to his office, where he settled her onto his desk. Maintaining the pace, he unzipped, took himself out, retrieved a condom from a drawer, rolled it on, and plopped on the girl. He pulled back the panty crotch and poked himself around until her squeal signaled he was at the spot. A stab—a scream—a dozen strokes at most—and done. He withdrew immediately and the condom was missing, maybe pulled off by the girl's tightness. He inched her back down as she tried to sit up. The condom sounded a snap as he extracted it.

During it all she hadn't spoken, just a series of suppressed grunts. She remained silent as he let her out the door. He went straight to a window, but as he peered, she already had dissolved into the ink of a country night.

At Hattie's funeral, when the family thanked absent Samuel Parsons for paying for his employee's funeral, Isaac realized that Annie was the daughter of one of the most powerful men in Green County—cotton, banking, and some miscellaneous. How was Isaac to have known, having lived most of the previous ten years in Detroit, where he had relatives and where he attended mortuary college? After graduation, he had stayed in the Motor City instead of working at the family's funeral business for his taskmaster father. After the elder Shaw died from a stroke, his only son, Isaac, returned to take the reins. Almost two years later, there were details about local white society that he hadn't bothered to learn. And, in this instance, it seemed certain that it would cost him big.

The months after Hattie's wake had been marked by anxiety attacks, cold sweats, and occasional nightmares, but there had been no arrest warrants, and better yet, no vigilante mob. Isaac had begun to ease into a sense of having dodged a bullet fired at point-blank range, but that was all shattered when Annie waddled back onto the scene.

The Shaw Funeral Home was isolated just past the outskirts of the black folks' end of town, on a winding dirt road, like a knot in a string. Ranch-style with a basement, it was what the Shaws had to show for three generations in the business. Now a girl with the figure of a python that has swallowed a boulder might destroy it all. And, as much as anything else, the complete uncertainty surrounding her reappearance caused his anxiety to spread like a swarm of ants. Wildly in need of a stalling tactic as he fought to recompose himself, he resumed speaking to the girl. "Where have you been all this time? Who have you told?"

"Birmingham. Daddy sent me to stay with my uncle Silas when I started to show." She placed an emphasizing hand on her belly. "I'm supposed to give the baby up for adoption, then come back." Defiance marked her voice as she added, "But I'm keeping this baby."

Annie's words implied that her family didn't know about Isaac. Still, with masked impatience he asked, "Who have you told that I'm the father, girl?"

"Nobody. Daddy thinks it's this boy I used to like, though Billy denies it. But when the baby comes out colored, some way or other Daddy will make me tell." She was speaking quickly, her glance ricocheting like a pinball, as if frightened that her father could appear genie-fashion. With a now-that-you-know-the-situation look in her eye, she said, "That's why we got to go away, me and you."

"Did you tell anybody that you were coming here?"

"No. I took the Greyhound back. Uncle Silas don't know where I am, and I ain't gone to my parents'. Wait—I did stop at my friend's, but I didn't tell her I was coming here. I swear."

"A white girl out this way by herself," said Isaac, "somebody had to notice."

"Nobody seen me. I made sure of that. I didn't want nobody telling Daddy. So I waited 'til dark. And those times I seen headlights, I ducked in the woods." Then, with hope in her voice, she asked, "All these questions mean you hatching us a getaway plan?"

He didn't answer. An evil weed of a thought was being watered and fertilized by Annie's assertions that no one knew her whereabouts. His mind's sickle could only whack off the top of that weed, leaving the roots intact, and it kept regenerating. It was too late to entrust her to Miss Lucy, a whiz with a coat hanger, although several times he'd provided funerals to Lucy's clients. Nonetheless, he couldn't deny Annie's childlike innocence, and it made him take a last-ditch pull at the weed. "Where did you have in mind for us to go?" he asked.

Her face gladdened, and she clasped her hands prayerfully. "We could go up north. Things are different up there. My folks say all the time that niggers—I mean, colored—live like whites in places like New York and Chicago."

He cut her off. "You don't watch much news, do you, girl? Right now, race riots are happening in Detroit, where I used to live. There are no havens, so give up that fantasy."

Her spirits plunged like a stalled jet, and her belly shifted forcefully, followed by a pain that momentarily delayed her panicked words. "You're wrong. You don't know what you're talking about, 'cause you're just some country nigger who ain't never been outside Alabama." Her arms were crossed, palms clasping shoulders, chin pressed against her chest, eyes clinched. As she quivered and rocked, her head swung like a pendulum, in insistent denial.

"Let me think this north idea some more," Isaac said. He feared that she might snap out of her trance and bolt into the night. He feared where she might go and what she might say once there. The weed swayed in growth as he thought about the convenience of the basement's embalming room, a place designed for making a messy cleanup easy.

His last comment pierced her haze and she said slowly and unblinkingly, "Anywhere would be better than around here, if Daddy ever learns the truth."

"You're right," he said, but it was more a concession to the weed than to her. "You can stay with my relatives in Detroit. Come with me to the basement. A safe is down there. I'll give you money for train fare and to live on."

"But what about—"

"I'll join you later, after I've sold the business."

She closed in for a hug and kiss. That's when she noticed a wedding portrait on the desk. "You're married!" she screamed in accusation.

His expression confessed before the words did. "Yes, but—"

"You been lying. Probably about having folks up north, too." She was shaking as though she had cerebral palsy.

"Just wait a minute," he said, palms patting the air.

Dazed, she took a couple of steps backward, and when he quickened toward her she grabbed a letter opener off the desk. "I'll kill myself. Don't think I won't." She held the opener above her head at a point from where she could make good her threat as well as defend against him. "You'll get the blame. I lied about not telling nobody I was coming here. My best friend, she knows. She'll know what to do when I don't show up."

Isaac's instincts said the girl was lying about her friend; they also said that the situation was irretrievable. He had to get her to the basement. He feinted at her raised arm to test her reflexes. She missed with her first stab, but surprised him with a cobra-quick arc that sliced the back of his left hand, opening a canal that soon overflowed with blood. He snared her attack hand, twisting her wrist until she dropped the letter opener. He spun her, locked her arm behind her, and placed his other arm about her neck, like a cop subduing a belligerent drunk. She fought ferociously but was simply overmatched. He dragged her to the doorway, where she suddenly reared into him, leapt, planted her feet at the sides of the doorway, and pushed like an Olympic rower, sending the two of them sprawling to the floor. They rolled about for a few seconds, and he ended on top of her. He got to his feet and, holding her by both wrists, started pulling her up. Then his feet flew from under him. He had slipped in something. The floor was wet. Her water had broken.

Annie screamed in the throes of childbirth. Isaac released her wrists and her head thudded against the floor. She panted rapidly, mouth wide open, tongue folded down. Pain bulged her eyes. Unable to speak, she begged for his help with a terrified, beseeching stare. He was transfixed. Possessed by contractions, she yanked at her panties, able to get them only to midthigh. The baby's feet had appeared: a breech birth. The screams became wrenching, as if she were birthing a truck. She was propped on an elbow, her head thrown back in agony. A lightning bolt of a pain struck her and she jerked into a frozen pose. Then she collapsed out of it, like a released string puppet. She lay as still and silent as one of Miss Lucy's mishaps.

Isaac checked her pulse, a formality because an undertaker knows death when he sees it. He saw that the baby was a boy, fully emerged except for the head. The boy was motionless, and if alive, was being deprived of oxygen. Isaac wanted to see the face. Additional precious seconds elapsed before Isaac pulled him free. The boy was at least eight and a half pounds and could pass for white—not too surprising, since Isaac was rather fair-skinned. The nose, however, might play tattletale; the nostrils were flared in the Shaw tradition. Isaac looked at the peach fuzz covering the head and wondered whether it would turn kinky later, in further betrayal. Immediately he wanted to kick himself in the ass for even thinking in terms of later. Isaac placed his palm over the tiny Shaw nose and Parsons mouth and was about to apply deadly pressure. But he hesitated. Then, as if compelled, he opened the baby's mouth, covered it and the nose with his own mouth, and blew repeatedly. The room became noisy as the baby's pale face turned ruddy from the strain of his angry cries. Little arms and legs became uncoordinated tentacles. Isaac rose.

In the basement waited the body of Bernard Lincoln, a numbers runner. The scuttlebutt was that his missing head was courtesy of a 12-gauge shotgun blast, retribution for skimming the take. A closed-casket funeral, for sure. Bernard could not complain about sharing his top-of-the-line casket with Annie.

Finally, Isaac took a sheet of paper and, in the imagined style of the person he was about to invent, wrote:

> *Dear folks,*
> *I am a Negro woman who been raped by a white man. I cann't love this baby but he deserve a life. Please find him a good home. If he die please give him a good funeral.*
> *the mother*

ONE

1997 | DETROIT, MICHIGAN

Thomas Kincaid heard the click in his headphones, the usual signal that his sound engineer was about to cut in for a station identification break followed by a commercial. When the engineer held up three fingers from behind the glass wall that separated them, Kincaid knew that the break could wait. He pressed a flashing button on his control panel. The host of the Motor City's newest talk-radio show, Kincaid adjusted his microphone and, using his signature greeting, he said, "Caller, identify yourself."

The caller had been so preoccupied that he'd forgotten about the greeting, even though this wasn't the first time that day that he and Kincaid had spoken—more like sparred—over the airwaves. The caller was about to give a new alias, but kept the old one, out of reverence for the dead. "Larkin."

The quick Kincaid processed the short utterance, and confidently said, "So, you're back again." And without benefit of a response, he added, "What's on your mind this go 'round?"

First, the caller voiced a complaint. "You hung up on me."

"You wouldn't stay on today's topic."

"What color is black? That's supposed to be a topic?"

"If you ever get your own radio talk show, then you can choose the topic. Until then—"

"Until then," interrupted the caller, "I call into shows like yours, and battle the misdirection you're perpetrating."

"Listen to yourself, Larkin, sounding like a graduate from a prison library, throwing around a few big words." What Kincaid wasn't admitting was that he was willing to stay with this caller for a while because the several previous callers had been completely unprovocative, in contradiction to the reputation that Kincaid was trying to build for his fledgling talk show that was a month old. "Flaunt your intelligence by proving that you can stay on a subject."

Accepting the challenge, the caller said, "There's only one color of black, and a person either is or he ain't."

"An interesting, if ignorant, viewpoint. And who decides that *oneness*? You?"

"I'm qualified." With an indicting tone, the caller said, "I'm proud to be black."

"You still haven't defined what it is to be black. Is it behavior? Thinking? How about color? I'm light-skinned—"

Again, the caller interrupted. "So what? It's all about the color inside, anyway. We don't have a choice about our color on the outside, but we do about our color on the inside. That's why it's possible to be black on the outside but white on the inside."

"Are you calling me an Uncle Tom? Not an imaginative insult since my name is Thomas."

The caller cryptically replied, "A term that's a bit more colorful comes to mind. Anyway, I didn't call back to insult you, Brother Kincaid. That's not good negotiating strategy."

Intrigued, Kincaid asked, "What are we supposed to be negotiating?"

"A new format. Your show insults blacks while you shuffle for whites." Then, despite his earlier pledge to diplomacy, the caller began to speak with increasing animosity. "Take today's topic for example. Whites shouldn't even be calling in. Yet you've given them more airtime than us."

"What do you propose I do with the white callers?"

"Tell them to call back on another topic. We've got to have something for ourselves."

"Do I ask whether they're white or assume their race from their voices, like I can with you?"

"I'm not ashamed of my voice."

"I didn't say you should be. But you do sound like the typical angry black man, seeing everything in black and white."

"Better than seeing everything in only white," countered the caller.

"I'm an equal-opportunity ass-kicker—black and white. To paraphrase Mark Twain, who once said that reports of his death have been greatly exaggerated, that's how I feel about bigotry. It's alive and kicking and I'll argue any white who claims otherwise. Still, I offer no shoulder to cry on to any black who uses bigotry as an excuse for lack of individual initiative."

Unmoved, the caller accused, "You don't ridicule white culture like you do black culture. Like earlier in the week, when you ridiculed the new Museum of Afro-American History."

"You're misrepresenting, pal. What I said was that blacks are quick to slap ethnic labels on things—Black Miss America, Black National Anthem, Afro-American Museum—but cry foul over anything labeled white."

"You just don't get it." Now the caller's breathing was audible. "They don't have to label something white because it goes without saying. You talk like things are equal between the races. When you do, you give whites a greater advantage and put blacks at a greater disadvantage."

Kincaid felt that the caller had scored a point at his expense. Rather than an acknowledgment, what Kincaid gave was, "Time's up, Larkin, and I've been more than generous. If you have more to say, get back in line."

"If I were you, I wouldn't—" but the caller wasn't allowed to finish.

"You're not me," was the curt reminder. "As for labels applied to me, the only one that matters is my own, which is a person who opposes lies and hypocrisy, without regard to race, creed, gender, religion, or any other category. This city needs me. The Detroit area is the most segregated metropolis in the nation, with its black inner city and lily-white suburbs, each wallowing in self-serving myopia."

"Now who's sounding like a prison library graduate?"

"But I'm the graduate with the microphone and I control the phone lines. And my advice to you and your kind who have a problem with me is to get over it, because I plan on being around for a long time. This summer, there's the mayor's race, the thirtieth anniversary of the 1967 riots, and a boatload of other issues that will be my topics. Not that my topics will always be local. In fact, I look to go syndicated someday. I'm a man on a mission."

With a slow, frigid delivery, the caller said, "I also have a mission. Unfortunately, ours can't coexist." Then he slammed the phone, with errant aim, because there was a clank followed by raking before the receiver hooked into place, triggering a dial tone.

"Aw heck, he hung up before I could ask him to send me some of his blackness pills to turn me the right color inside and out," Kincaid told his listeners. Yet his bravado couldn't dismiss the unsettledness he felt over that last caller. He took an unscheduled break and played a public affairs announcement.

Radio station WDMT was housed on the top floor of a six-story commercial building on Mack Avenue, on Detroit's eastside, close to the tony suburb of Grosse Pointe. The building was deeply set in from curbside, and the parking lot was in back. In the main, the building obstructed a view of the parking lot from the street. Except for WDMT, the other occupants maintained conventional business hours; so the lot never contained many cars when Kincaid finished his 6:00–8:00 A.M. show.

Kincaid walked out into the promise of a warm, sunny June 1997 morning. He got into his late model Cadillac and backed out of his space. He heard, "flub, flub, flub," felt the misalignment in his seating and knew that he had a flat tire. He pulled back into the space. While inspecting the obvious, Kincaid was startled by a sudden voice in back of him.

"You're not going far on that flat," said the man who had materialized. He wore a broad smile.

Kincaid looked him over then sarcastically said, "You must be an expert on cars."

The smile remained and the man said, "I have my own car problem, or will have if I don't do something."

Kincaid dryly remarked, "Hope yours is as easily solved as mine." He took off his suit coat in preparation for changing the tire.

"We can help each other. I drove my girlfriend to work but forgot my wallet. I noticed after she got out that the gas gauge was past empty. I live outside Detroit, too far to make it on what's in the tank. I was on my way into the building to get some money from her, but I'm not exactly dressed presentably. If you give me five bucks, I'll change the tire and have you rolling in a jiffy. No reason for you to get your suit dirty if you don't have to. Is it a deal?"

"You got yourself a deal," agreed Kincaid, not bothering to shake hands. He liked the idea of underpaying a white guy to do dirty work. He activated the remote key and the trunk yawned. He pushed the lid upward, too forcefully, causing it to bounce on its hinges. The trunk was junky. He slid aside two boxes that were covering the spare tire. He went digging under a pile of clothes until he found the jack. The tire iron was entangled in battery cables and he fumbled for seconds freeing the iron from the snaky coils. All this while, Kincaid's back was turned; therefore, he didn't see when the man's eyes lowered to half-mast, nor did he see when the man's head dropped and his neck rolled as if succumbing to hypnosis.

Now that all the necessary items had been uncovered, Kincaid was about to step aside when he heard a faint puncturing sound. He did a quick, involuntary jerk. Then came crippling pain in his side. Then a similar sound, of flesh and cloth being ripped by the rapid withdrawal of something lethally sharp. Another jerk. He staggered around to face his assailant. He bobbed back and forth, back and forth, in reaction to puncture and withdrawal, puncture and withdrawal.

The pain peaked then started to ebb. Kincaid couldn't feel his own hands clamped against his wounds. Other senses began to go on the blink: his vision blurred and his taste wouldn't register the blood welling in his mouth. But his sense of smell worked well enough to detect the smell of his spilling blood, and his hearing was functioning well enough to record his assailant's mocking words, "Permit this caller to identify himself." And Kincaid's dimming consciousness discerned that his assailant's voice was now different. Different but familiar.

With his dying breath, and even as he was being pushed into his trunk, he made a last, defiant, blood-gurgled utterance to let his killer know that he knew his identity.

TWO

Sergeant Mary Cunningham exited the interrogation room, leaving the murder suspect, a white male, seated at the table. "We've got our guy," she told Detectives Paul Nitkowski and Frank Corleone, who had been watching from the other side of the one-way mirror.

"Forgive me if I prefer a confession over your certainty," said Frank, thirty-five. He was tall, athletically built, and dressed like a *Gentleman's Quarterly* model. He had oil-black hair with waves that crested inches above his scalp. His swagger was complemented by a constant smiling sneer.

Mary's wide-set eyes narrowed combatively. She was thirty-nine years old, five feet six, 140 pounds, with a short Afro. She was the color of a pound cake. Out of long habit, and to give her some time to compose herself, she traced the outline of a prominent scar above her full mouth. The scar was shaped like Nike's "swoosh" logo. "I'll be happy to butt out, Frank. I have my own work to do. Remember, you asked for *my* help."

Frank corrected her. "Paul asked. I didn't."

"Because we were making about as much progress as a Polack trying to change a lightbulb by himself," Nitkowski said in self-deprecation. A couple of years from retirement, he was shaped like a pear: droop-shouldered, barrel-chested, and beer-bellied. The frayed waistband of his powder-blue polyester slacks was clamped by suspenders. In the Homicide Unit, he and his partner, Frank, were called the Odd Couple. "What's next, Mary?"

Mary scrutinized the suspect for a few moments, as though she were looking at an intricately laid trail of dominoes before deciding to tip that all-important first one. "Give me a little longer with him."

Frank grunted in annoyance. Pointing at the suspect, he asked Mary, "How long do you plan to waltz with that punk, like you're in one of those dance contests of yours?"

Mary returned the favor by correcting Frank. "The tango is my dance, not the waltz, thank you."

Frank appealed directly to his partner. "Paul, I say we sweat this guy hard, and he'll break down like a cheap used car."

"The only tactic you know, Frank," Mary said. "That's why you couldn't get the Pope to confess that he's Catholic."

Nitkowski crushed a half-smoked cigarette on the sole of his shoe, then flicked the snuffed cigarette across the room. He met Mary's inquisitive gaze. "Trying to cut down." Then to Frank he said, "Have a little patience. Nobody has a better record than Mary's for extracting confessions."

Frank said, "I tell you, Paul, we can do this ourselves."

"Then proceed with my blessings," Mary said. She turned to walk away.

Nitkowski grabbed her by the hand. "I'm surprised at you, Mary. You know not to take Frank seriously." He released her, then wrapped his arm around Frank's neck in a fake choke hold and told Mary, "Go back in there and handle it."

Mary nodded toward the suspect, who sat with his legs bouncing and his eyes darting around the small interrogation room. "I really think that I'm close to getting him to roll over, Paul."

Nitkowski pulled out a cigarette but shoved it back into the pack. Then willpower yielded to a nicotine craving and he snatched that same cigarette free, flipped it to his lips, lit it, and took a long drag. He blew a long stream of smoke through his nostrils. "These cases when somebody prominent gets murdered are always a pain in the ass because of the added pressure to get them solved, so I appreciate your help. So does my knucklehead partner. He's just too stubborn to admit it."

Mary reentered the interrogation room, a dingy cubicle inside the catacomb of squad rooms that comprised Homicide on the fifth floor of headquarters. "I'm baaack," she sang. She tried to push the door closed, but a stronger force pushed back.

"Excuse me," Frank said, shouldering his way through the opening.

He went straight to the scratched-up metal table and four metal chairs that were the room's only furnishings. He twirled a chair around, then straddled it.

Mary, still at the door, let a false smile spread, then strolled to the table. When she sat, she completed an arrangement with the suspect at the head of the table, Frank to the left, she to the right. The suspect wore plaid shorts on which he periodically wiped his sweating palms. Mary had on beige slacks, a maroon T-shirt underneath a black vest, and white sneakers.

Over the next hour of interrogation, the suspect shifted in his seat, fiddled with his collar, and continued wiping those sweaty palms. When he asked for coffee, Mary left the room and returned with a pot and foam cups. When he asked for a cigarette, Nitkowski rushed in, held out his pack, gave him a light, then left to resume his position behind the one-way mirror.

Frank, who had been silent throughout, sneered, "Want anything else, like maybe a goddamn pizza?"

"Officer Corleone moonlights as a stand-up comedian," said Mary. She didn't want the suspect to tighten up, since he had been giving signals that he might be edging toward a confession or a deal. Still, she had to maintain the pressure. "I'm going to ask you some questions about a weapon."

That statement seemed to stir the suspect. "Can I be alone for a minute to think? I'll let you know when I'm ready to talk some more," he said.

To Mary the request was a railroad crossing signal, flashing and clanging. Depending on her deft touch at the switch, the results could vary from a smooth glide into the station to derailment. "Sure thing," she said, and rose immediately.

Frank, however, stayed planted for long seconds, glaring at the suspect who nervously reached for the coffeepot with an unsteady and sweat-slick hand. The pot dropped and toppled on the table. The steaming flood coursed toward Frank, who sprang from his seat. The smooth leather soles of Frank's fashionable wing tips proved too slippery for quick footwork, and he tumbled backward, his pratfall ending with him on his back and his legs stuck in the air.

"Motherfuck!" he spewed. He was on his feet in an instant. He briskly brushed the dirt from his clothes, all the while cursing.

Mary held her breath, hoping that would stifle the laughter swelling inside. She spasmed, as if under a seizure of hiccups. Then it broke: the Mary Cunningham laugh, a reverberating, raucous laugh well known to family, friends, and coworkers. Bad enough, but when the suspect let a chuckle escape, Frank became livid. "What are you laughing at, cocksucker?"

The suspect sobered quickly. "I'm sorry. I didn't mean to—"

"Fuck you," Frank shouted. "Laugh about this, shithead: we got your prints on the murder weapon. You weren't as neat as you thought."

Recognizing that anger was controlling Frank's mouth, Mary said, "Frank, let's talk outside."

"No! This is my goddamn case. No deals, no—"

The suspect broke in. "What did you say about the murder weapon?" He leisurely leaned back and folded his arms behind his head. "You don't have anything on me. You've been bluffing."

Frank lapsed into silence. The suspect's smug grin communicated that he knew that Frank had blurted out the wrong thing. Mary scowled at Frank and then stormed out of the room. Frank followed in chagrin, leaving Mary and Nitkowski to discuss the fiasco without him.

After a detour to a candy machine, Mary returned to her squad room. Homicide consisted of seven squads, located in rooms barely large enough to contain the desks. The squad room names—Felony Murder, Narcotics Related, Child & Juvenile—did not automatically determine case assignments, except for Mary's squad. Although Special Assignments handled all types of investigations, it was the only squad that handled cases involving shootings of or by officers. The Special Assignments squad room was a pallid yellow, as if painted with diluted bile. The eight desks and four tables formed a maze that Mary had to negotiate to get to her desk. She pulled back her chair and plopped down. Something wet and cold penetrated her slacks. She shot up and turned to inspect. It was a tampon soaked in tomato juice. The color, size, and location of the stain on her pants fulfilled the prankster's intentions.

And despite whether the prankster intended it, the tampon was a hated symbol. Police work is still male dominated, with many subscribing to the notion that a woman's behavior is hormone-driven. And on more than a few occasions, Mary had it expressed to her as crudely as, "You must be on the rag this week."

She had been dubbed "Bloody Mary," shortly after the second time she killed in the line of duty. In a separate incident, she had been shot, adding to her legendary exploits. The three incidents took place when she worked in Vice, before she transferred to Homicide. Whereas most cops were grateful that they'd never had to fire their weapons in the line of duty or been shot at, an insecure and mis-guidedly envious few resented Mary. The harassment she endured was infrequent and mostly verbal—comments such as "How's it go-ing, Bloody Mary?"—which typically earned the reply "Kiss my Bloody Mary ass." This latest bit of sport was akin to a drawing that had appeared on the wall of the women's rest room a year before: a naked female with male genitals. The artist had made sure to name his creation, although he himself remained anonymous.

Nothing anyone could say could torture her any worse than she'd tortured herself. Both of her kills had been black men. Though both shootings were absolutely clean, there'd been the usual cries of po-lice brutality and excessive force. What angered Mary was that no community leader stood up to defend her. No one on the force went out of his way to let the public know that she was a good cop. When Mary bled, it was all internal.

The only other person in the room was Ellery Tarver, her partner and squad leader. His desk was at the front of the room, and he sat scratching notes onto a legal pad. She knew he wasn't the prankster, but she'd been peeved at him for quite a while for other reasons. She said to the back of his head, "I wonder what it would be like to have a partner that watched my back."

Ellery drew a weary breath and stopped writing. He didn't swivel around to face her but said, "Mary, whatever you're about to go off about, I'm not in the mood for any shit."

Mary ripped several tissues from the box on her desk, then picked up the tampon. She stomped to Ellery and stood in front of him, refusing to be ignored. She held out her hand. In a tone that she knew would rouse her partner from his apathetic state, she said, "Some pencil-dick, cowardly bastard put this in my chair. And you mean to tell me that you don't know anything about it?"

Ellery rubbed a finger up and down his unshaven cheek. He'd re-cently turned fifty. Despite her anger, Mary was worried about him. The raccoonlike circles under his eyes were conspicuous even against his dark skin. She noticed the lint in his uncombed hair. His rumpled shirt was well past due for a laundering. Mary knew that though he'd been married for only a short time, things were not going well. His child bride was a slut who delighted in flaunting her infidelities and thought nothing of staying away for days on end. It hurt her just to look at Ellery, to remember the kind of cop and the kind of friend he'd once been.

"Some of these guys are assholes, Mary. There's no denying that. They love to tick you off with that 'Bloody Mary' stuff. But if I'd seen somebody trying to put that in your chair I wouldn't have allowed it."

Ellery's vacant tone concerned Mary. She believed him, but she felt she had to press the issue, just to keep fanning the spark, hoping that he'd catch fire again. Maybe by taking it out on her, he'd release some of the pressure she knew was building inside of him. Besides, she needed him to carry his share of the load. She persisted, saying, "Have your powers of observation gotten so bad that somebody can march in here and you not see them?"

Ellery blew a long sigh. Gas mushroomed in his belly. He raised his shoulders as it shot upward. He tried to cork it with a swallow, but it backtracked and came through his nose. "You're mistaken if you think I'm going to spend all day listening to this." Mary hid her pleasure, but she recognized all the unmistakable signs: it was time for Lieutenant Ellery Tarver to pull rank. "What's-his-name from Squad Four was in here for a second. I barely looked up. He went toward the back, but I didn't see him carrying anything and I don't know whether he went to your desk. The hothead."

"Frank Corleone?" Mary's concern for Ellery now took a backseat to her anger.

"Right. I don't know why his name didn't come to me."

But Mary already was going through the door. In seconds she was in Squad Four, where she intercepted Frank on his way out to lunch. There were two other men in the room. She threw the tampon, striking Frank in the chest. "Stick it up your ass, bitch."

The tampon had been swaddled in tissues when she threw it, but upon hitting the floor the bundle separated, revealing its contents. Frank looked at it, then angrily kicked it out of his way. He pointed a finger in Mary's face and said, "Are you out of your goddamn mind? I ought to—"

Mary didn't let him finish. She slapped his finger away and stepped to him, totally in his face. "You ought to what, big, bad man? Here I am. Do something."

"You're crazy. Absolutely nuts. And I don't hit women."

"Oh, the perfect gentleman. What you do is done behind the back. You're a pussy, Frank."

She hadn't taken a step back, but neither had he. They were practically nose-to-nose. Frank flung an arm out to the side in punctuation as he said, "I don't know what the fuck your crazy ass is talking about."

"You left that tampon in my chair."

"I don't do off-the-wall shit like that. Is that blood?"

"You know that it's not."

"I didn't know because I didn't do it. That's why I got so mad. I thought you threw a bloody tampon at me."

"I have more class than that, even though you deserve it."

"What reason would I have for doing it, Mary?"

"You were pissed off about what went down in the interrogation room. And you were mad that I laughed at you." Incredibly, she found herself having to purse her lips to keep from giggling as she recalled the incident.

The other two guys were staying out of the fray, but their attentions were riveted. Frank didn't want them to know about his spill. "I apologized to Paul for my mistake and I let it go at that. I didn't even give you a thought. Not everything that goes on here revolves around you. Your ego is unbelievable."

"I don't believe you." Mary, no longer certain that Frank was the culprit, nonetheless said, "And no one's ego is more unbelievable than yours, Frank. You were made to look foolish and you wanted payback."

Frank's smiling sneer returned. "The way you busted in here, you must have sat square on that thing. Probably you're the one who's looking foolish. Turn around and let's see."

"Go flush your head." She took a self-conscious step back.

"So you did sit on it." He tried to walk around her for a rear view.

Mary countercircled, denying him the view. "Stop it," she demanded. When they once again stood stationary, she threatened, "I'll get even. Somehow or another. Better believe it."

"For the last time, it wasn't me. But if you want a war, I certainly won't run from you." Frank looked past her toward the door. Mary refused to turn around to see who had entered.

"Ellery, do us a favor and take your partner out of here. She needs to see the department psychiatrist, man."

Ellery said to Mary, "We have a run to make. It just came in."

Frank said, "You look like hell, Ellery. Don't let being Mary's partner wear you down."

"Even if Ellery were in twice as bad shape as he is now, he could still kick your ass, you sissy, you." Immediately she realized that she had slighted Ellery. She grinned at him sheepishly and shrugged her shoulders. "Sorry. You know what I mean, Ellery."

Ellery merely asked, "You coming or not, Mary?"

Mary backed through the door as Frank watched and snickered.

"Remember, Frank. Payback is a dog." Actually, it was more bluster than threat. She felt that her outburst of laughter had been unprofessional, try as she had to stifle it. She had contributed to botching an interview of a murder suspect. She regretted that, but smart-mouth Frank had cheated himself out of any possibility that she would apologize to him.

En route back to their squad room, they passed a Neanderthal, who noticed Mary's stain and wolf whistled.

Ellery snickered and shook his head. Mary was heartened by the first sign of good humor in her partner in weeks. Donning her blazer to cover her stained pants, she asked, "What do you know so far?"

Ellery grabbed his jacket. "A radio personality was found stuffed in the trunk of his car. Officer on the scene said it looked like someone caught him in the middle of a snack."

"What the hell does that mean?"

THREE

"Oh, honey, I'm so sorry," Mary said to her husband, Cliff, after her right heel had hit perilously high against his left thigh. "You're not hurt, are you?"

El Gancho, a kick between the man's legs, was a move that Mary usually performed flawlessly, but this evening both her timing and her aim were off. While angled to his left side, she was supposed to straddle his left leg and bend her right knee, hooking her lower leg backward and wrapping it around his calf. Cliff referred to the move as the mustard applied to the hot dog of any combination. But since it had no count of its own, it had to be spread quickly and unerringly.

"I'm not sure," answered Cliff. "Does my voice sound several pitches higher?"

"It's as deep, manly, and sexy as ever," she said.

"Then I guess I'm okay. For now at least." He started toward the CD player to turn off the music, en route asking, "What is it with you tonight?"

"I'm having an off night. Simple as that." She folded her arms across her chest and feigned a petulant pout.

The finished basement of their four-bedroom home doubled as their practice studio. The home was located in Detroit's New Center area, a gentrified community of Victorian houses, condos, and apartment buildings situated on tree-lined boulevards flanked by decorative lampposts, with flower beds planted in the medians.

He returned to her side and pecked a kiss onto her pouting mouth, hugged her, and delivered a single spank on her butt. "I love you," he confessed, "but you're spoiled rotten."

"I am not," she replied. "Let me go." She shrugged and side-stepped her way out of his embrace.

"Stubborn, too," he added.

"I am not," she muttered under her breath.

Cliff's voice became somber. "We haven't had a decent practice in some time, Mary. There's a reason, despite whether you want to admit it."

Mary turned to face him, hoping that her smile would produce the desired effect. "Cliff, don't overdo this. You're the big sports fan. Baseball players have batting slumps, basketball players have shooting slumps, football players have . . ." She paused, not knowing how to extend the analogy, then said, "Whatever they have. I'm in a slump. I'll work my way out."

Directly signaling that he wasn't buying her explanation, Cliff said, "It has to do with the dance studio, doesn't it?"

Her pulse quickened and uneasiness flashed in her eyes, reactions she attempted to mask with a casually tossed off "What has that got to do with the price of ice water in hell?"

"The further matters progress, the more distant you become," said Mary's third husband. Tight-bodied at forty-five years of age, he lied two inches' worth every time he claimed to be six feet. He was dark-complexioned, with a receding hairline counterbalanced by a full beard. Usually he dressed in the casual style typical of the college professor that he was. "It started weeks ago when the business plan was completed, and it's worsened since the loan application was submitted to the Small Business Administration last week."

"Ever think that maybe it could have something to do with me working all day and being tired when I come home?" Cliff was on summer break until the start of fall semester. If she could play on his male pride—make him feel guilty about staying in bed while she rose for work—she could steer the conversation away from troubled waters. "Anyway, lately, me and Ellery—"

"Ellery and I."

Mary dipped her head and began anew with, "Ellery and I—" then abruptly switched to "I hate it when you do that. I'm not your student anymore." They'd met when Mary had taken his English night class in the finishing stages of her bachelor's degree.

Shortly after they were married Mary had asked Cliff to correct her grammar, but to do it privately. She told him grammatical correctness would make her police reports more polished. What she hadn't told him was that it would ease her insecurities when they socialized with his colleagues. Now she was complaining about something she'd requested, and Cliff saw through the smoke screen.

"Sorry I interrupted," he said.

"As I was saying, Ellery and I have been running ourselves ragged working the Kincaid case. Be thankful you don't have to work with a partner who breaks down and cries whenever he has a few spare moments to think about how his wife is raking him over the coals. The man is slowly disintegrating before my eyes, and it's not a pretty sight, Cliff. Between police work and trying to keep Ellery stable, it's to my credit that I have the energy to drag my feet at the end of the day, let alone dance." She thought this was one of her better rejoinders, of the type most dangerous to Cliff when he was debating her: based in truth, emotionally delivered, but not connected to the topic.

"You can put all of that behind you once the studio is operating. You're the one who said you'd like to get out of police work."

"What I said was that owning my own dance studio was what I'd like to do *if* I wasn't a cop."

Cliff knew that this was not the time to tell her that the proper wording is "if I *weren't* a cop." He made sure to make eye contact, because he knew what he was about to say would be tantamount to calling her a liar. "You said outright that you wanted a career change, and you've said it numerous times until lately. And if I'm wrong, why have you let me put gears in motion as I have?"

Mary sat down on the sectional sofa to take off her high heels. She massaged her bowling-pin calves while she reentered the battle. "It wasn't like you kept me informed about every little development. So don't blame me for anything you've done on your own. I *never* promised that I would leave police work, and I *never* told you to make the studio happen. And you can't deny that long before I ever made mention of a studio you were riding me to quit the force. Maybe you heard what you wanted to hear." She patted the couch to urge him to take a seat beside her.

Cliff sat, but not cozily close. "I don't deny that I want you off the force. Any man who loves his wife wouldn't want her in a hazardous line of work."

Mary leaned toward him, propping herself up on her hands. Her soulful gaze softened the harshness of her words. "Don't talk about love, Cliff. Fight fair. I'm good at being a cop. It's important work. It matters."

"You'd be just as good at running a business."

Mary shook a chastising finger at Cliff and said, smiling, "You know better than to push me too hard. The more you do, the more I'll resist."

"The extreme of that is called cutting off your nose to spite your face."

Mary pushed herself back against the sofa's arm. She didn't have a good rejoinder at the ready, so she resorted to being a bit conciliatory. "Homicide work sounds more dangerous than it is, Cliff. By the time I come on stage, the danger is over. I've never run into any danger on a murder investigation. Tell you one thing, those assholes wouldn't call me Bloody Mary if I'd been in Homicide all my career."

"Still, it's not an impossibility that you'll be forced to use your weapon. How can you be sure that— Let me see your hands, Mary."

"Why?" She hid them behind her back. "You know I don't like how they look."

"Arthritis can be a dangerous thing for a cop."

During the course of the last year, the condition had worsened. Her medication helped combat the pain and stiffness. And over the months, the thousands of times that she'd performed her flexibility exercises—clenching and opening, clenching and opening—had made the veins show prominently in the back of her hands, infusing strength at the price of unsightliness. Yet there still were times when her hands operated like those of the Tin Man after he'd been caught in a downpour.

"I'm ambidextrous," she said, but she knew that it wasn't the perfect comeback, because both hands were afflicted.

Cliff slid next to Mary. He stretched out his legs, rested his laced fingers on his belly, and arched his neck to rest his head against the top of the sofa. As if conversing with the ceiling that he was staring at, he said wearily, "If you've made up your mind to stay a cop, say so, and say it without hedging. I don't want to spin my wheels chasing a dance studio that you don't want. Just give the word and it's dead forever."

All she needed to say was that she'd decided to remain in the serve-and-protect business. After all, she knew that Cliff was a man of his word. Instead she said, "I haven't decided. And I don't want to tonight. I know we have the SBA loan application in and all that, but even when it's approved, we don't have to take it. I will have decided by then."

"So be it." Cliff spent some moments in contemplation, then sat up straight and spoke to his wife. "Could be part of the problem is we're putting too much importance on the dance contest. Sure, it would be great to win it. Would be a hell of a promotion tool for a studio. But practice still should be fun. Remember how it used to be?"

"Yeah, I do."

Cliff placed his arm around her shoulders and she leaned in and rested her head on his chest as he continued to reminisce. "The flirting. The passion. The going upstairs to bed afterward."

"Sometimes not even making it upstairs," she said.

"Let's go upstairs," said Cliff, his intentions evident in his tone.

"You go up, honey. I need a few moments to collect my thoughts. I won't be long." To accentuate what she was about to add, she cut him a glance out of bedroom eyes. "And when I come up, you will not have the right or the will to remain silent."

"Is that a threat?"

"That's a promise."

Dance and police work would seem to have little in common—the siren call of the dance, the screech of the police siren; the feather-footed choreography of the dance, the flatfooted trudging of investigations; the dance a ritual of life, homicide an act of death. For Mary, however, they were linked by tragedy and for the past thirty years had been a constant source of emotional upheaval. It had been a knotty dilemma, a tragedy so personal that she'd been unable to exclude both from her life, and so intertwined that she'd been unable to choose one exclusively.

Alone after Cliff had ascended the stairs, she battled guilt for leading him in circles. She was feeding him a diet of false hopes. She hadn't even disclosed that her real reason for staying downstairs was that she wanted to catch the ten P.M. news on television. There would be a feature about the Kincaid murder. Larkin's voice would be played, and viewers informed that the speaker was sought for questioning; the plea would be for him or anyone suspecting who he was to contact the authorities—sort of an audio version of *America's Most Wanted*. Mary and Ellery had sold the idea to their higher-ups as a chance to resuscitate a case that had gone flatline. It wasn't that Mary was trying to spare herself the hassle of Cliff's fretting over the feature; rather, she didn't know whether the reporter would refer to her by rank. Her new rank, that is. Cliff was unaware that she had taken the promotion exam, that the scores had been posted just days ago, and that now he was married to Lieutenant Mary Cunningham.

FOUR

The first rule of Homicide Investigation is to reconstruct the last twenty-four hours of the victim's life. As part of that pursuit, Mary repeatedly listened to the tape of Kincaid's last broadcast. The calls from Larkin stuck to her instincts like flypaper, not just because of their content and tone, but their connection to an item of evidence at the murder scene: an Oreo cookie in Kincaid's hand. From first sight, Mary believed that it had been placed by the killer. Larkin became a suspect from his own words: *"A term that's a bit more colorful comes to mind; . . . black on the outside, but white on the inside, . . . ours can't coexist."*

Ellery had an alternative theory: the cookie was planted to lay a false trail to a caller. Mary attacked it as improbable. The killer would have had to hatch the murder plot a mere hour before enactment. He would have had to be sure that the homicide investigators would make the connection between the cookie and the caller (obviously, he wasn't counting on the likes of Ellery). But Ellery had dug in his heels and insisted that his theory was at least as probable as Mary's, and as squad leader, he had the authority to direct the investigation in any direction he chose.

Having dealt so long with overblown male egos, Mary suspected that Ellery's stubbornness was due in part to his initial, amateurish assessment of the cookie as a piece of evidence. Whatever his reasons, she found herself in a familiar predicament, having to waste time investigating the stupid theory of a male superior in order to gain permission to investigate her own. It was the equivalent of working double duty.

The fact that Larkin had made telephone calls automatically gave Mary an initial avenue of pursuit. A search warrant for the telephone company's records would provide her with a copy of their Auto Message Accounting for Kincaid's number at the station for the day of his murder. From the tapes of the show the station had been asked to provide, Mary would be able to pin down to the second when the suspiciously threatening call came in.

But when the Auto Message Accounting came back, the information it provided was not as specific as she had hoped: the calls had been made from various public telephones, all located in Detroit's Warehouse District.

Now she knew that the killer had an association with a particular section of town, but she didn't know why. By itself that information was of little immediate value; it was just another piece of the puzzle she would have to assemble. And there were other things that she now knew: the killer was a planner; the killer was smart; the killer was careful. Maybe he knew about AMAs, or maybe he didn't and was just damn calculating.

Mary had considered using a Trap and Trace Search, another capability of the phone company. TTS identifies the source of an incoming call while it's in progress, but the mechanism must be installed in advance at the receiving end. She would have had to get Larkin to call the station again, even though Kincaid was dead. She thought that an appeal to listeners to call in and express their feelings about the murder might entice Larkin to jump on the horn one more time. The problem with the plan was that it would require the staking out of every public phone in the Warehouse District, after which Larkin might not even call or might call from another area. She wasn't too surprised when Homicide brass killed the plan.

So she came back at them with her plan to play Larkin's voice on television news in hopes of recruiting a snitch. Since, unlike her radio brainstorm, this one didn't require manpower, the brass let her run with it. The public responded, for what it was worth. Mary eliminated most of the tips after only brief conversation. It comes with experience, the ability to know what to ask and how to size up the answers. Some tips she did investigate. More work. No results.

Mary had been at murder scenes where she knew immediately that the chances of nabbing the killer were nil—well-executed professional hits, for example. Too, she'd investigated plenty of scenes where the killer's sloppiness made her work short. And she'd seen just about everything in between those extremes, cases that, to varying degrees, stretched her mentally, emotionally, and physically. Still, there was an unsettling newness to the Kincaid murder that she felt burrowing into her psyche. She had a murky sense, an intuition that transcended all her training and experience, that she had some connection with the killer; but trying to turn that disquieting sensation into something tangible was like grabbing fog. She resolved to fight against being distracted by such gut feelings, for she knew enlightenment would come only when she apprehended the killer.

This was the first time that Mary had hunted a voice, and gradually she was being forced to examine certain of her own attitudes related to race. It was likely that the caller used a fake voice, but certain qualities of it were genuine—its pitch, inflection, and timbre. She felt liberal and superior by criticizing Ellery's theory that a voice such as Larkin's—that deep, that brooding—went with a dark-skinned, braided-Afro, militant appearance. She wondered if her criticism was self-serving, supporting her belief that Larkin was able to get close to Kincaid because he didn't have a menacing look; for she found it difficult to mentally match the voice with this look. It caused her some discomfort to realize how much she might be infected with the stereotyping virus.

And she was reluctant to share aspects of her investigation with Ellery, who had enough burdens related to his personal life. In one sense, she was grateful that that was the case. Additionally, she knew that she was disappointing Cliff, that being consumed with her work made their plans for the studio recede into the distance. But in some strange way, she blamed him, too: Knowing how he felt about her work, at home she was unable to set down her load of worries and rest. She simply had to keep her mouth shut and her feet moving.

The Kincaid case so consumed her—intruding into her thoughts even during her off-hours—that she felt as if she was being haunted. She'd visualize an enormous face, like the one that the Wizard of Oz conned on Dorothy; except this face was a constantly changing arrangement of light and shadow. And whenever she tried to fine-tune the image, the killer scrambled the signal as if by remote control. But every once in a while it seemed as if the face would freeze-frame just long enough for her to make out a mouth jeering at her.

This case had gotten past her professional detachment. And on the most visceral level, she suspected why. It was that inexplicable feeling of connection operating—the feeling that a reckoning between her and the killer was inevitable. But most disturbingly, it probably meant that the killer had not struck for the last time.

Of course, she couldn't present theories of fate and destiny to her fellow Homicide officers; for while they acknowledged that there is such a thing as cop's intuition, what she had conjured exceeded even its most elastic definition. Unfortunately her thoughts would have to remain unexpressed, despite how convinced she was that events would bear them out.

Meanwhile, in that awful interim, the clock was racing. She feared that all the effort she was pouring into the case merely amounted to waiting for the other shoe to drop. And in her line of work, that shoe usually ended up on the foot of a corpse.

FIVE

At almost 8:30 P.M., daylight was dwindling into dusk as the young man made a right-hand turn off the main strip and onto the wooden bridge that arched across a creek. Lit like a runway for its annual mid-July Weekend Bash, the private Detroit Yacht Club was located on public Belle Isle, an island park in the Detroit River.

He lowered his driver's-side power window, creating a miniature weather front as intruding hot, muggy air collided with escaping fan-cooled air. He flashed a disarming smile at the white man, a generation-Xer, perched on a long-legged stool. "How you doing, guy? They tell me there's a party going on around here this weekend."

"That's the rumor," said the attendant from inside his enclosure. "Would you be a member or guest?"

"Guest. The Fitzgeralds." He knew the name from a newspaper article about the Bash. Archibald Fitzgerald was an organizer.

"I need your name." The attendant was lifting pages on a clipboard, hunting for the Fitzgerald guest list. Having apparently found it, he stared at the page, waiting for the driver's response.

"John Kelly."

"Kelly . . . Kelly," recited the attendant, running an index finger down the page. "You're not here."

"Shit." The man remained smiling. "That's what I get for waiting until the last minute before accepting the invitation. I thought I was going to be out of town. Didn't give them enough time to add me to the list. When is that list made up?"

"Hey, you're asking the wrong guy," said the attendant. "But I'd guess at least a couple days ago."

Building on the budding rapport he sensed, the man continued, "I know you have rules, but I drove in from way out in the suburbs to party. Isn't there a way to call them, page them, or something?"

"Not really." Then the attendant said, "I know you're legit. Don't sweat it. Party extra hard for me."

"Thanks." He shifted from park to drive.

"Pull up a bit, though," said the attendant, "so I can write down your license-plate number. At least we can follow that much of the rules."

"You bet." Instead of going forward, he closed his eyes and slapped the heel of his palm against his forehead and held it there for a second. "Damn," he said. "Here I am with not even a bottle of wine to offer when I go aboard my boss's yacht. I have to hit a party store or else my ass is going to look tacky." His back-up lights told the driver behind him to give room so that he could swing around. Moments later he was crossing the creek bridge again, the live outdoor music bidding him good-bye.

SIX

Xavier Livingstone's yacht, the *Rising Son,* was nestled at the end of the marina, sandwiched between the *Sea No Evil* and the *Wave Your Troubles Good-bye.* Both neighboring yachts were covered and unoccupied. Livingstone stood on the stern, checking the lines that tethered the *Rising Son* in the slip. He noted that the crowds had thinned considerably from earlier in the day, then stood admiring the many party lights strung around the marina glowing like fireflies. He spotted the dusky silhouette of a man walking along the docks.

"Looking for a particular boat?" Livingstone asked.

"Not really," the stranger answered. "Just roaming, trying to see how the other half lives."

"More like the other five percent," said Livingstone, unable to take the boastful edge off his words.

The stranger stepped casually to the rear. "The *Rising Son,* huh?" he said as if that were the first time he'd read it. "Witty. Do you suppose I could take a tour? She sure is something from the outside."

Xavier Livingstone, age fifty, was the color of India ink. He was dressed all in white: skipper's hat, boat shoes, pants, and polo shirt. Matching the attire were the veinless whites of his eyes, and teeth like fine porcelain. His face had no entrenched lines, and his six-foot-three frame packed a svelte 215 pounds. In a tone that was friendly but not apologetic, he said, "Bad timing. I'm going to the club in a minute."

"And even if you weren't," the stranger said, "you're probably fed up having people tracking through your boat." Then he told another in a series of well-rehearsed lies: "I don't know how my uncle puts up with it like he does. Maybe you know him. Alex Latimer?"

Livingstone raised his eyebrows in surprise. "Alex sponsored my membership in the DYC," he said. Livingstone made a quick mental weighing, the way a person with meager funds ponders whether to spend some on an overdue debt. Then he told the man, "Come on aboard."

"I appreciate it," the stranger said. The yacht was bobbing slightly, but enough that his leap onto the deck caused him to stumble after landing. "Whoa," he said sheepishly as Livingstone steadied him by the arm. "It's obvious that I'm no Jacques Cousteau."

"I'm not much better," assured Livingstone. "I bought the boat last year. Before that, I couldn't paddle a canoe."

The stranger served up a handshake and another lie: "The name's Jerry."

"Glad to meet you. Call me Xavier. Let's start at the bridge," he said, ascending the steps. "That's where the yacht is steered."

They spent about ten minutes on the bridge. Livingstone explained the bells and whistles of the control panel, but his guest was tuning in and out. At one point the newcomer folded his arms, then unfolded them as quickly as if he had hugged some broken ribs. Livingstone noted this but kept talking. "This computer-looking thing is a global positioning satellite. It'll give you your location no matter where you are at sea."

"What's this yacht's top speed?"

"Thirty-six knots." Livingstone thought about explaining how knots converted to land miles per hour, but didn't, disappointed over the unimaginative question. And taking into account the man's sometimes poorly disguised inattentiveness, Livingstone considered cutting the tour short.

"So how about we see the rest of her," the stranger asked, as if he sensed Livingstone's intentions.

"Okay," Livingstone replied blandly.

From the bridge, the uppermost of three levels, they could see the Detroit Yacht Club. It was the size of a royal-family estate and anchored the east end of Belle Isle. The stranger gazed out across the water toward Windsor, Canada. Guests splashed in the outdoor pool, while others reveled to live music, food, and conversation in the outdoor restaurant. Ground-level floodlights bathed the building, but the lighting around the pool and in the restaurant was subdued. In the marina, lampposts cast a pale yellow light just bright enough to prevent pedestrians from falling into the water.

Livingstone conducted the rest of the tour as a quick walk-through. The aft deck sported a couch, table and chairs, and an entertainment/sound system—TV, CDs, tapes, records, AM/FM radio—housed within a wall unit. In the lower quarters was the dining area, which included a fully appointed kitchen. The smaller of two bedrooms contained a bed, closet, dresser of drawers, and an adjoining bathroom. The main bedroom boasted a queen-size bed, strategically located mirrors, generous closet and storage space, and a bathroom with a shower stall. Throughout, the yacht was appointed with cherrywood paneling and plush marine carpet.

Livingstone wound the tour back to the aft deck, glad to be through. Standing at the rail that his guest had leapt over to come aboard, Livingstone said, "You've seen her all."

But the man pretended he couldn't take a hint, his hands in his pockets, glancing about, nodding approval. "Not half bad," he said.

"Thanks. Be careful clearing the rail."

The stranger could pretend no longer. He shook hands with Livingstone, then turned and gripped the rail with both hands, readying himself to leap over. He rocked, so as to time his leap, as a child does before leaping between rotating double-Dutch jump ropes. But, after planting one foot on the rail, he halted and looked over his shoulder at Livingstone. "Mind if I ask you one last question?"

"What?" Livingstone hoped his curtness spoke for itself.

The stranger stepped down from the rail and faced Livingstone. "The pictures of you and the Chinese . . ."

"Japanese."

"Japanese, then. It looks like they were giving you an award or something."

"That was exactly the case." A faint smile curled one corner of Livingstone's mouth. "Those pictures were taken in Japan at the headquarters of Hitasundi Motors. I work for them."

"No fooling. So, what's it like living over there?"

"I don't. I work in Detroit. I'm assistant vice president of sales and marketing for minority programs for North American operations." It was a mouthful of a job title, but it tumbled forth as if he always kept it balanced on the tip of his tongue.

"I have a friend who bought a new Climax. Loves it."

"That Climax is a honey. We're coming out with a convertible next year."

The stranger waved an accusing finger at Livingstone and said, "I bet you're a car junkie."

"I got motor oil in my veins," Livingstone bragged. "Been fascinated with cars since I was a boy in Mississippi. Say, how 'bout a cold one?" He strutted to the galley and opened the fridge. First he took out a bucket of chicken. Then he fished out a six-pack and plucked two cans free from the plastic holder. He made an underhand toss to his guest, who was being rewarded for broaching Livingstone's favorite topic.

He made the catch and opened the pull tab. "Sounds like air being let out a tire, don't it?"

"Help yourself to some bird," Livingstone offered, pointing with a drumstick.

"You must have heard my stomach growling," the other man responded before claiming a breast. "So, about the awards . . ."

"One award. This picture," Livingstone said, resting his hand on top of the frame sitting on the kitchen counter, "is me with the minister of commerce. In the bedroom is me with Mr. Hitasundi." He opened his beer.

"What was the award and what did you have to do?"

"The Impact Award. Only about a half-dozen get it each year, worldwide. Bottom line: I earned the company a lot of yen."

Livingstone's guest snapped his fingers. "Wait a minute. You're that dude who's been in the news over that black boycott against Hitasundi."

The history of that incident dated back six years, when Mr. Hitasundi told a British reporter that one of Japan's advantages in car manufacturing was its homogeneous society, which lacked the racial problems of the United States, where supposedly less-qualified blacks were forced upon industry by federal policies.

With tongues like Samurai swords, black civil rights activists attacked Hitasundi. After U.S. politicians and the domestic car industry self-servingly piled on, Hitasundi's spin doctors explained that something had been lost in the translation and he had meant to say that black workers were disadvantaged by institutionalized racism and not by innate inferiority.

Matters didn't settle, however, until Hitasundi Motors agreed to a five-year plan to increase black representation in all phases of its North American operations, and to establish a scholarship fund for black engineering students. Now, five years later, differences over the assessment of gains and the apparent need for another five-year plan had degenerated into a call for boycott. Xavier Livingstone was Hitasundi's point man.

"There is no black boycott," insisted Livingstone, his love of debate taking precedence over the drumstick, which he had laid on the counter after two bites.

"Then what do you call it?"

"Some blacks are stuck in reverse, but they don't represent the whole race, like they claim to."

The stranger tilted his head apologetically and said, "I didn't mean to start talking about race. It can be a taboo subject."

"Not with me," said Livingstone. "Race can't be dismissed. You notice my race, I notice yours. We can never literally be a color-blind society. I don't want advantages because of my color—just opportunity, despite it."

The stranger wiped his fingers with a napkin, then said, "But isn't it true that too many don't have that opportunity?"

"It's more true that too many don't take advantage of what opportunity they have."

"Some might consider you a—I mean, a . . ."

"Uncle Tom? I've been called that, mostly by people with a vested interest in race baiting."

"How's that?"

"Nobody appreciates the gains of the civil rights movement more than I do. But, even today, civil rights leaders won't admit to those gains. Damnedest thing. If things are as bad as ever, those leaders are failures and why should blacks still follow them?"

"And what about—" he began, but Livingstone wasn't finished.

"Hitasundi increased the number of black dealerships, managers, and suppliers—by good numbers, too. Still, blacks in the race business harp about the manufacturing facility, even though hardly any blacks live in that area. That aside, the company relocated a black guy and promoted him to assistant plant manager. Only, he didn't stay because his wife preferred city life. What a martyr. Now, what were you about to say?"

"I forgot." He had heard enough. He had been fair to Livingstone, given him an opportunity at redemption. Livingstone had failed. The mission dictated what had to be done. The time had come.

The stranger began to take long, slow breaths. He bent at the waist, head down, right hand on chest as though he were pledging allegiance to the flag. Then he looked up at Livingstone. "Aw, hell, I'm feeling queasy from the rocking of the boat. I need to go to the john."

Livingstone chuckled. "Use the one off the main bedroom. The toilet is bigger."

After he closed the bathroom door, the stranger stood in front of the medicine cabinet's mirror. Slowly, trancelike, he placed his hands on the sink for support and leaned until he was nose-to-nose with his reflection. He began a mumbling, rambling soliloquy: questioning, answering, stating, affirming, denying. Minutes passed.

Livingstone, hearing no telltale heaves, went to the bathroom door. "You all right in there?" No response. Livingstone rapped the door. "Hey, I said are you all right?"

"I'm okay. . . . I feel like a pansy."

"It happens," said Livingstone, his ear close to the door. "Get yourself together and come up front." He stepped from the door and started toward the aft deck.

"I don't believe this," the guest shouted. "Now the damn door is stuck." As he spoke, he reached under his shirt and freed something taped to his waist.

Annoyed, Livingstone returned. "Move back," he instructed as he grabbed the knob. It turned obediently, and he pushed the door open.

The stranger's arm was raised high in the air. Livingstone saw a glint from the instrument before it drove deep into his chest. With speed and precision, the man stabbed repeatedly. Livingstone reeled back on his heels, arms extended to the sides. Motor controls short-circuited, Livingstone spun into the dresser, bounced off, and stumbled forward a few steps. Two collapsing lungs denied him the breath to scream. The man pounced again. Two more strikes, these in the back. Livingstone fell facedown. On the way he hit the corner of the bed, flipped over, and landed on his back. He pulled on the bed's comforter until his grip relaxed in death, his white attire now a canvas of scarlet.

The killer used an unstained area of the dead man's pant leg to wipe the instrument. His head felt so pressurized that he held it tightly in his hands as if to contain an imminent explosion. His mouth was as dry as dust, and each swallow hurt. Cold and clammy perspiration wet his forehead, underarms, and groin. He fought off panic as he tried to think. First he replaced the instrument; the tape still held. Next he threw his beer can overboard. Then he took a towel from the bathroom and wiped any prints from the sink and door. Then he draped the towel over the area of the rail he would have to touch getting off the yacht.

Returning to Livingstone, he reached into his own pants pocket and withdrew an item. A satisfied smile spread when he saw that it hadn't been broken during the action. He placed it into Livingstone's palm, then, one by one, folded the dead man's ebony fingers around it.

A shining sliver of new moon watched as he leaped over the rail. A breeze stirred, and he wondered whether the smell of blood would hop a ride and waft through the area. The raven sky was an inverted bowl, the stars like winking pinholes. In the distance, the baleful bellow of a freighter warned a sailboat to get out of its path.

Walking toward the Yacht Club, he was struck by a runaway kid, six years old, blond, blue eyes, sprinting in one direction, looking in another. The collision would have been worse had the man not reached down to slow the youngster. He hoisted him by the underarms and looked into an impish face. The boy's prosperous-looking mother, who had been pursuing the child and now stood just a few feet away, showed no alarm over her dangling son.

"Nicholas," she said, "you apologize to this nice man."

SEVEN

Inspector Warren Newberry, head of Homicide, greeted Mary gruffly. "Where is Ellery?" Newberry, late forties, was dark-skinned and muscular. And quite short. The nickname whispered behind his back was "Napoleon."

Showing more manners than Newberry, she first said, "Good morning, Inspector." Cornelius Upton also was in the room, and she acknowledged him with "And good morning to you, Chief."

"Good morning, Lieutenant Cunningham." Chief Upton nodded curtly.

Newberry cut back in with "I'll ask more slowly this time. Where's Ellery?"

"I don't know," she admitted. "After I got your call, I had no more luck reaching him than you did. I left a message on his voice mail. Plus I tried paging him." It was a Saturday morning, shortly after six o'clock. Neither Mary nor Ellery was scheduled to work.

"Get on with it, Inspector." The chief's impatience was legendary, but even he seemed more wound up than usual.

Newberry walked to the spot Mary had been shooting glances at from the time she entered the room. "This is Xavier Livingstone," he said of the dead body. "He owned this boat. Take a look at him. You'll recognize some things."

Mary knew to what Newberry was referring. She just knew. She'd known that there would be other victims, but her pulse raced just as wildly as if she'd been taken by surprise. As she approached, she experienced the mixed sensations familiar to hunters of deadly game: exhilaration and fear from closing in on the prey. Dried blood made stiff folds and creases in portions of Livingstone's shirt. Wet blood around the stab wounds was thick and black, and his shirt clung to his torso around those areas. She saw the cookie—more accurately, a part of it—in Livingstone's palm.

"The boat hadn't been tied down good enough," Newberry told Mary, "and it was knocking around in its . . . uh—Hey, Smitty, what do you call the parking space for one of these boats?"

One of several crime-scene technicians, who was milling around snapping photographs, making drawings, and collecting evidence, Smitty responded, "Like I own one."

"It's called a slip," said Mary.

Without acknowledging her input, Newberry continued. "According to the statement of the guy who discovered the body, he got suspicious because the boat looked occupied since it didn't have its covers on. Said he shouted out a number of times before boarding."

Mary wondered aloud, "Why did the killer think Livingstone was an Oreo?"

"An Oreo?" Chief Upton asked without embarrassment. He was a tall, medium-built Caucasian. He had a large mole at the top of the bridge of a ski-slope nose, and Mary often had been distracted with imaginings of the mole detaching, rolling down, and taking flight. He had no lips to speak of, despite a wide mouth. Aging had turned his full head of once golden hair flaxen. His eyebrows were even paler, and from a distance, hardly detectable against his sallow skin. His celestial blue eyes betrayed his almost albino appearance.

Newberry explained, "An Oreo is a black person who sides with whites against other black people. In other words, black, but white at the core."

"In other words," said Upton, now educated, "an Uncle Tom."

Newberry's lower lip jutted out like a diving board, and he had the unsightly habit of manually folding it down toward his chin when he was absorbed in thought. He released it and said to Upton, "Mary has believed from the beginning that Kincaid was murdered because the killer branded him an Oreo. Ellery Tarver isn't so sure. He believes the killer might have known that Kincaid had been threatened over the radio by a person who in so many words called him an Oreo."

"And that the killer left the cookie on Kincaid to divert suspicion to the radio caller?" asked Upton.

"That's correct," said Newberry. "But this second body seems to give Mary's theory some real legs. Looks like we have a crusader out there."

Surprisingly, Upton said, "Let's not be alarmists. Don't prematurely toss away any feasible theories."

Detroit politics forges a symbiotic relationship between the mayor and the police chief. The mayor appoints the police chief, and when a new mayor takes office a new chief is a foregone conclusion. And in any Detroit mayoral race, crime is a key campaign issue, because it affects the city's quality of life, its image, and its ability to attract industry. With intertwined fates, the current mayor and chief had devised a policy designed to control the perception of crime in Detroit.

The policy called for the chief to be notified of major crimes involving a high-profile person, and of major crimes occurring in high-profile locations or events. The Detroit Yacht Club and its annual Weekend Bash fell into the latter category. Certain locations have the power to lure suburbanites: Greektown, the sports stadiums, and the theater district; so have certain events: the Thanksgiving Day Parade, the North American Auto Show, the Grand Prix, and the July Fourth fireworks. But skittish suburbanites have to be kept confident that the sojourn is safe.

"This is the second murder with this m.o.," Mary said to the chief. "It's clear that we're dealing with a serial killer who's targeting black people for being Oreos."

"Don't be reckless with such talk, Lieutenant Cunningham," cautioned Chief Upton, well aware of the incendiary nature of her theory, especially with a mayoral election months away.

Newberry read insubordination in Mary's eyes and said, "Pay attention to the chief, Mary. You might be right, but for now, don't get rash with any public statements."

"I'll say it clearer," said Upton. "It's not up to you to make any public statements of any nature." His dressing-down of Mary was consistent with his purpose in being there: damage control, spin doctoring. Already the media had descended, but were being kept off the yacht by uniformed officers. "Is that clear, Officer

Cunningham?" That he didn't address her by rank underscored his resolve.

"Couldn't be clearer, Chief." Mary decided to take a different tack: "What's been learned so far about the victim's life?"

Newberry saw through her question; however, because he knew it was a legitimate inquiry in any murder investigation, he was compelled to respond. "Livingstone was the spokesman for Hitasundi Motors in its fight with some black groups."

Incredulity and defiance showed on her face, but her tone was respectful. "Doesn't that support my theory?"

"Support, but not prove, Cunningham." Now Upton's voice was sterner, to go along with the impersonal addressing of her by her last name.

And Mary was skating on melting ice when she said, "There should be a public announcement, or else people are going to needlessly die."

"When did you start making policy?" the chief said, his pale face having gone crimson.

"No disrespect intended," she said, "but the public deserves to be put on notice."

"That'll be enough from you." The chief noticed that the crime-scene technicians were tuning in, and he lowered his voice. "More than enough."

Heavy footsteps announced that someone was bounding down the stairs. "Sorry I'm late," said Frank. "I was at a friend's."

"And she's probably feeling better for it," quipped Newberry in an attempt to thaw the atmosphere.

"What the hell is he doing here?" Mary asked.

"Your partner's AWOL. We need backup. Corleone's on." Newberry stepped aside to let Corleone join their circle.

Mary said, "The chief was in the middle of explaining why we should put innocent people at risk."

Upton almost growled before he said, "You're bucking to be demoted, Cunningham."

Newberry quickly interceded. "Mary, I want you to go to the main deck and talk to the man who reported the murder. He claims he didn't touch anything, but take him over his story again. And while you're up there, interview the officers who were first on the scene. Nose around to your heart's content. But it's best that you leave for now."

Mary swallowed hard. She was being dismissed, sent out of the room, like a misbehaving little girl. It might be that Chief Upton would have reacted in the same manner were she a male, that there was no sexism operating here, but she was unconvinced. She exited, almost colliding with the medical examiner, who'd just arrived. Frank had started to follow her, but Upton said, "You stay down here, Detective Corleone. We'll update you. I'm interested in hearing your thoughts." It was an additional slap at Mary, seeking the input of a junior investigator after banishing her. Would Upton have resorted to such measures to squash the same challenge from a male?

After Mary had interviewed the officers and the man who reported the murder, she continued to poke around, and she was eventually joined by the crime-scene technicians. Something caught Mary's eye, and she said to one of them, "Watch out, don't step on that."

"What?" asked the tech.

"There," she said, pointing to what appeared to be a bit of wind-blown debris from the nearby grounds.

"That's nothing to be bothered with. I'm not a damned groundskeeper."

"You can't say for sure it's not important. I don't see any lying around anywhere else. There might be a reason why it's at that particular spot." Then she applied a little charm. Smiling sweetly, she said, "Come on, Sam. How much trouble would it be to collect it, huh?"

Sam snorted and looked at her a few seconds for effect, then he went to the spot carrying tweezers and a small plastic bag. "Just like at home. Always a woman to tell me that I missed a spot."

EIGHT

Summer had run a high fever the day Mary was called to the Livingstone murder scene, and after more than twelve hours of sweaty investigating, she'd returned home funky in body and attitude. A long, bubbly soak in the bathtub corrected only one of the conditions. As she stepped dripping onto the floor mat, Cliff came into the bathroom.

"What are you fussing to yourself about?" he asked. "I could hear you all the way from the bedroom."

Mary yanked a folded towel from the shelf. "It's those damn assholes I have to answer to at work."

Cliff took the towel from Mary and started rubbing her shampooed hair with it. "What did they do?" He began drying her neck and shoulders, simultaneously massaging those tense areas through the towel. "I'm listening."

"I'm fed up with their sexist attitudes and their stupid decisions." She switched to personalized invectives. "That Newberry. So short they won't let him on amusement rides. And Upton . . . if he ever has an intelligent thought, it'll die of loneliness."

By now Cliff had dabbed her dry to the waist. He dropped to his knees to do her lower body, and as he dried her legs he inhaled her scrubbed scent. He draped the towel over his shoulder and, still kneading her tight muscles, began probing the cleft between her legs with his tongue. What started as teasing increased in ardor when he heard his wife's soft moans and sharp exhalations.

"Don't start a fire unless you're going to take the time to douse it," she instructed, mindful that she and Cliff were to attend a dinner party hosted by one of his fellow professors. But even as she spoke, she slyly eased her pelvis forward, further encouraging him.

Cliff spoke, punctuating each word with a flick or a languid lap of his tongue. "You . . . wouldn't have to . . . endure those hassles . . . if you . . . left . . . the force . . . for the . . . dance . . . studio."

Mary stepped back, at the same time snatching the towel from Cliff. While she hurriedly finished drying herself off, she said, "I don't need that from you, Cliff."

"What?" he asked, perplexed. "You've worked all day—not to mention you were supposed to have the day off—and come home mad over treatment from your bosses. All I'm saying is—"

Mary cut in. "Whenever you start a sentence with 'All I'm saying,' I know that's not *all* you're saying. I know exactly what you're saying. And what you're doing. You're taking advantage. Trying to pressure me."

"How? I didn't bring it up out of the blue."

Mary crossed and uncrossed her arms like a baseball umpire signaling safe, only she announced what her gesture meant with "Cut it, Cliff." She ignored the hamper and flung the towel onto the floor. "I don't feel up to fighting with you over my own damn career. Not tonight." In a huff, she left and went into the bedroom.

A minute later Cliff stood watching her don her underwear: black silk bikini panties accented in gold, matching bra—too delicate and pretty to be tugged and pulled as she was doing. Cliff said, "You're in no mood for a dinner party. I'll call the Furmans and cancel."

"Don't do it on my account," said Mary. "The last thing I want to do is give you reason to blame something else on my job. Instead of giving me grief, why don't you start getting dressed yourself."

"What's the use in—"

"And for once," she interrupted, "wear something with some style to it. I'm sick of the jeans and sport coat bit."

"You're in a foul mood, Mary. Why don't you admit it?"

Mary walked to Cliff's closet, still on the attack. "Every time we go around your white associates, you act like you're scared to dress like a black man." She pulled something out and asked, "What's wrong with this outfit I bought you for Father's Day?"

Cliff's patience showed the first signs of wear. Intentionally not looking at the white slacks and knit shirt, he said with forced calm,

"Explain to me how a black man is supposed to dress." Then he immediately said, "No, no, before you do, first explain how it is that you can tell me what to wear but I can't breathe a word about your job."

"You're right," she said. But the concession was spoiled by "You're a big boy. Wear what you want." She returned the outfit to the rack with a force that almost straightened the curved top of the hanger.

Cliff shook his head and shut his eyes momentarily. "I say we stay home and fight in the comfort of familiar surroundings. It's better than going somewhere and embarrassing ourselves."

Mary had crossed the room to her closet and retrieved an olive pantsuit. She stepped one unshaven leg through, then the other. A hair caught in the pants' fabric. Damn Cliff and his fetish for hairy legs. Mary continued, "What you really mean is you don't want to go somewhere and be embarrassed by me. Right?" She knew she was being unreasonable, but on top of everything else the thought of one more night spent worrying if she measured up to the standards of her husband's Ph.D. friends had set her teeth on edge. "I promise not to split too many infinitives, or to have too many disagreements between subject and verb. Besides, if we stay at home, you won't get to see 'Ms. Thang.' "

"Who?"

Mary had to give him credit: his ignorance seemed almost genuine. "The one who wears her necklines to her navel. Never shows up with a man, but is always grinning in your face. You know the yellow heifer I'm speaking of." Somewhat surprised that her last comment had escaped from her lips, she said, "I take it back. I wouldn't care if she was plaid with polka dots. She better keep her distance from you. I don't want to have to beat her ass."

Cliff scratched the back of his head. "That kind of talk is way beneath you, Mary. And it's not feminine."

Mary slumped onto the bed and held her head in her hands. Her husband had just practically called her a man. The locker-room drawing of a naked Bloody Mary with a big penis flashed in her mind. As a survival technique in the male-dominated, macho world of law enforcement, she had learned how to talk the talk and walk the walk. But cops are always on duty, and they vary in their ability to switch into domestic mode. Mary's unexpressed anxieties about how well she fit in with Cliff's colleagues affected her interpretation of his words. "I'm not feminine enough for you, Cliff? You're calling me a man?" Cliff could only stare in wide-eyed amazement over her questions. But she had one more, and it was anything but feminine. "Did you think you were sucking on my dick back there in the bathroom?"

"You're doing it again," accused Cliff. "Trying to run me in circles. You know as sure as you're standing there that you don't want to go to this affair. But you're going about it the dishonest way by picking a fight over every silly thing you can think of."

"I don't know what you're talking about," Mary claimed with a straight face. "I'm practically dressed and ready. You're going to be the holdup."

"Don't give me that." Cliff's voice was raised, and he was verging on anger. He took several deep breaths. Then he again tried to inject reason into their discussion. "Before the conversation spun out of control, you were talking about what happened today with your bosses. Am I right?"

"Yes."

"So let's rewind to that part and take it from there. Something is really eating at you, Mary. Tell me what it is."

Cliff's simple, honest request took some of the edge off. She could feel her claws retract. Still, she felt conflicted: she wanted to confide in Cliff about what was bothering her, but she didn't want to give him another excuse to lobby for her resignation. Mary's combative behavior had been a defense mechanism against the intrusion of a certain truth, but the present cease-fire with Cliff allowed it to charge in. That truth was this: she was scared, and the fear was palpable and annoying, like someone insistently tapping her on her shoulder. And before she even had acknowledged to herself how she would respond to Cliff's request, she found herself telling him, "I'm tracking a serial killer."

The words slammed Cliff to the body, and he tensed to absorb the blow. "How many murders so far?" He tried to sound clinical, but his stomach was doing flip-flops. He sat down on the bed beside her.

"Two that I know of."

"That's what the call this morning was about? A second victim?"

"Yes. Xavier Livingstone was murdered last night on his yacht at the DYC."

"The automotive guy?"

"Correct."

"And the other one?"

"Thomas Kincaid. I told you about him."

"Right. So Livingstone's body had an Oreo cookie, stab wounds, and everything?"

"Exactly."

Cliff had done a good job of interrogation, and he knew his conclusion was way off target, but out of hope he launched his theory anyway. "And you're mad at your bosses because they want you off the case. Is that it? I agree with them, Mary. Let the men chase this psychopath. It's too dangerous a case for you."

Mary examined her sleeve and sat twisting the brass buttons that decorated the cuff.

"I haven't been taken off the case." A thin smile spread across her mouth, and she looked at Cliff. "You think you've already seen some antics from me? Nothing compared to how I would have reacted if they had done some shit like that. No, what I'm mad at them about—actually, it's the chief's decision—is that all this is to be kept hush-hush."

"From the public, you mean?"

"Yeah. Meanwhile, people that the killer might decide are Oreos are blissfully going about their business, unaware that they could be in danger. It's not fair." Mary punched both her thighs before standing up and returning to the dresser. She rifled noisily through a jewelry box.

"What do you think is behind the chief's decision?"

"Damn politics. The media might sensationalize it in a way that costs the mayor votes." Mary fumbled with a necklace, but her afflicted hands refused to let her undo the clasp. She dropped the necklace and kicked at it in frustration.

"My top concern is for your safety, sweetheart." Cliff stooped to pick up the necklace and then placed it around her neck. He kissed both of her cheeks. Mary felt undeserving of the sensitivity that he was showering on her. She felt her throat tighten and the sting of tears welling in her eyes. She turned her head away from Cliff, pretending to primp her hair in the mirror.

Cliff continued. "Alerting the public gives you that many more sources of tips. Could get this maniac off the streets faster. Maybe you can leak the story."

Mary shook her head, her voice barely above a whisper. "No. I can't."

Gathering herself again, she cleared her throat. Her voice picked up strength as she proceeded. "Rather, I won't. But I'm going to keep trying to win headquarters over to my side."

"And your chances?"

Mary shrugged. "Slim to none, probably. But I have to try."

"And you prefer this type of life to the one you'd have with the dance studio." It wasn't a question; it was a reopening salvo.

"Cliff—" Mary paused. "Right now I just really need your support."

"I thought that's what I was doing."

"I know you think that's how you sound, but I'm hearing a different tune. I need you with me on this one, Cliff. More than any other, because . . ." Mary took a deep breath and forged ahead, "I'm scared."

Neither of them was able to hide surprise at Mary's admission. The rest flowed out of her: "I have a sixth sense about this killer. It tells me that he's not through killing. It also tells me that he and I share something that is going to make our paths cross. It's an eerie, spooky feeling, honey. You're the only one I can hope to talk to about it. Don't make me turn away from you, Cliff."

"I love you without limits, Mary. Being protective of you is part of that love. I can't help it. But I never want you to feel that you can't turn to me in any time of need. I just wish you'd get over this foolishness."

"Foolishness? You think what I do for a living is foolishness?"

Cliff tried to wave her off, but Mary plowed ahead. "You want to talk about foolishness. It's pretty damn easy for you to sit up there in your ivory-tower throne and play 'send me the cream of the crop so I can uplift them that don't need uplifting.' "

"Mary, let's not do this. You know the value that I put on education."

"I know you do, Cliff, but how can I make you understand how much what I do matters to me? Black people especially don't trust the police. And I'm not saying that opinion is without foundation. But do you think that I like the idea that nearly every black face I see on the job looks at me with suspicion? I need to make a difference."

"There are other ways to contribute."

"Cliff, I sometimes see our people at their worst, I'll admit that. And that isn't easy. But I'll be damned if I'm going to step aside just because it's hard. How do you think some things went so far wrong?"

"You're right. My head tells me that you're right, but my heart just won't agree. I don't want you to get hurt."

Mary put her arms around Cliff's neck and pulled him toward her. They stood with foreheads touching. "Cliff, I know you mean that, and I do believe you. I'm sorry that I haven't said anything about these feelings sooner. Sometimes I get so used to shutting that part of myself off that I forget how to open the valve again."

"It's okay, Mary. That's what we're supposed to do for one another. I'm sorry, too. I can't promise you that my feelings are going to change, but I am going to try to be there for you."

Mary tilted her head back and shook it rapidly, as though she could rid herself of whatever negative thoughts had collected in her head. "Yeah, well, I guess I take advantage of you, expecting that you'll always understand."

"I do, baby."

Mary kissed him and caressed his cheek with the back of her hand. "Thank you, honey."

"Feel better?"

"I do. I feel loads better. And I'm hungry, too. Are we going to dinner or not?"

"Sure." He went to his closet, took out his Father's Day gift, and laid it on the bed. "I'm going to take a quick shower." But before starting for the bathroom he said, "About your sixth sense that you and the killer are going to cross paths—do you see yourself alone in that encounter, or is Ellery or somebody else with you?" Before she could answer, he asked, "And is that the source of your fear?"

"Maybe I made it sound like I have clear images playing in my head. That's not the case. There's no scenario. No characters. Just feelings. So I can't say how Ellery or others figure in. And I'm not so sure that the fear is just for myself."

"You're also worried about future victims."

"I am, but that's not what I was referring to. I can't shake the feeling that I have a connection with the killer. That possibility is a big part of my fear. It might sound strange, but I'd be less fearful if I were sure that I was the only one at risk. After all, I do carry a gun.

But I have this hollow feeling that someone close to me might be involved." Then, almost under her breath, she said, "Maybe even you."

"How?"

"Your English proficiency exam comes to mind."

Cliff had made a proposal two years before to his department head that passing an English proficiency exam should be mandatory in the pursuit of a degree. It went through channels, ultimately being approved by the president and the board of regents, but not without stirring some controversy. Detractors—some from the black community—claimed cultural and racial bias. It became university policy anyway. Throughout the process Cliff received media coverage, and some of the more ardent critics of the proposal leveled unflattering remarks at him personally. Cliff and Mary both knew that harsh feeling might be rekindled when the policy went into effect in the coming fall semester.

Earlier, Mary's sensitivities had seemed to affect her hearing. Now it was Cliff's turn. His next words dripped with accusation. "You're saying I'm a target for your Oreo killer?"

"Don't twist my words, Cliff. I wasn't calling you an Oreo. But who the hell knows what a demented killer uses as his criteria. That's all I was trying to say."

But Mary's disclaimer didn't lessen Cliff's sarcasm. "Dress like a black man. That's what you told me minutes ago. Was it for my own protection, Mary? What else should I do? I know—I'll propose a curriculum that leads to a bachelor's degree in black English. That should put me in good stead with the killer, you think?"

It pained Mary to see Cliff so bruised. She said, "Baby, why don't we just let this rest and go have us a good time."

"I'm not in the mood anymore. To paraphrase that old song, Mary— it's my party and I'll cancel if I want to." As he walked to the phone he recited his next line: "You would cancel, too, if it happened to you."

NINE

Detroit's mayor, Randal Clay, had a habit of turning his back, literally, on what he didn't like. Consequently, his reelection team, seated around the conference table, knew what it meant when they saw him standing, back turned, staring out a window. The four eyed one another beseechingly, in silent recruit of a brave soul to break the silence. But there was no sound except a few nervous taps of a pencil eraser. And after losing a bet with himself over which of two pigeons perched on the ledge outside the window would fly off first, Clay turned and switched from body language to the spoken word.

"This is one hell of a time to change advice about whether I should commemorate the anniversary. The thing is next week, for Christ's sake. And need I mention that the August primary is just days after that?"

In addition to being a mayoral election year, 1997 would see the thirtieth anniversary of the weeklong riot that ignited on July 23, 1967. The official toll was 43 killed, 350 injured, 4,000 arrested, 1,300 buildings torched, and 2,700 businesses looted. Property damage was estimated at over half a billion dollars. But many a pundit would later argue that the greater damage was to the city's future: the flight of whites, capital, and businesses would leave Detroit isolated and embattled.

"If the wind never shifted, one wouldn't need all those arrows on a weather vane, now would one?" said Birdie Monahan, a white woman in her mid-fifties whose legs perfectly suited her name. A political pollster from Atlanta, she spoke with a distinctly southern accent and her upper lip twitched whenever she spoke, as though she were about to sneeze.

"We need to talk damage control," said Jordan Ashford, vice president of community relations at Michigan Natural Gas. He and Clay had been basketball teammates in college. Clay went on to play professionally with the Detroit Pistons and Ashford pursued a business career.

Clay strolled back to the table and folded his six-foot-six frame into his seat. Facially, he resembled Sidney Poitier. "Ideas, people," he said. He clapped his large hands commandingly. "Let's have 'em."

"Makes sense to start with why opinion shifted," said Saul Eden, a partner in Detroit's largest minority law firm. Eden, Whitman, & Sanders handled a good chunk of the city's municipal bond business.

"We know why," insisted Clay. "That group that picketed last week."

"The Survivors' Network," added Eden, a pudgy fellow. Recently divorced, Eden quietly endured his clients' whispers about his midlife affectations—a ponytail and a pierced ear.

"Maybe there was a better way to deal with them, Randal," Ashford said as he adjusted his signature bow tie.

"Like what?" returned Clay. "They want a plaque in City Hall honoring those who died in the riot and they want me to preside over a memorial ceremony."

Clay felt that such a commemoration would alienate whites, particularly the financial backers of the megaprojects that he was relying on to revitalize downtown. He feared that a commemoration might sabotage his four-year campaign to reverse the perception that the city was hostile toward white people. After Clay denied the request, the Network took to picketing City Hall. The media showed up. And before Clay could see it coming, scurrilous talk was circulating throughout the neighborhoods, claiming that he wasn't black enough to identify with the riots.

"We have time for damage control if we act fast," said Carol Givens, the mayor's press secretary. She was sixtyish, with blue-silver hair and the body and face of a not too badly faded fashion model. She gave a sheet of paper to each of the others. "I've prepared these comments for the Sunday newspapers."

Clay read to himself, then spoke: "Basically, this has me coming off as sympathetic to members of the Survivors' Network who lost loved ones during the riots. But it emphasizes the improvements in the quality of life since then, and directs our focus to the future. I like it."

"Good," said Givens. She took the next few minutes to outline the strategy for polishing the mayor's image through the upcoming electronic media coverage of the anniversary.

Birdie Monahan sounded a caution. "In the South, we've had to deal with race-sensitive issues for generations—from the Confederate flag to every conceivable anniversary except General Robert E. Lee losing his virginity." Her upper lip was back in motion. "Y'all need to maintain the lowest possible profile on these types of matters. Give festering sores time to heal and don't keep picking at the scabs."

"Detroit's black majority makes this situation a different animal," said Ashford.

"Let me explain to you the first law of politics in Detroit," said Clay to Monahan. "There's no such thing as a small race issue in this city. An entire generation has grown up that wasn't even born at the time of the riots. And I believe that the graybeards of my generation don't want to dwell on the past. Yet and still, in this town people are as interested in me proving that I'm black as they are in me proving that I can deliver municipal services."

"There wasn't this fuss over the tenth anniversary or even the twentieth," reminded Monahan. "And conditions are better now than back then."

"Has a lot to do with who was sitting in this chair then," answered Clay. "The old man never organized a parade or nothing like that. In fact, we're following his example of speaking at the Rebirth Commons, the housing project built at the location where the riots started. But remember, he was the city's living, breathing symbol of black empowerment. Had he stayed in bed each anniversary, no one would have questioned whether he was black enough."

The "old man" was Nigel Bradfield, the tough, cuss-you-out-in-a-second, first black mayor of Detroit. The black majority that developed after the riots swept Bradfield to victory in 1973. Bradfield's "Who the hell needs 'em" bravado regarding the whites who fled the city instilled pride and inspired loyalty throughout the black population, most of whom didn't foresee the lean times ahead.

Bradfield built a political machine that successfully branded any black opponent as the "white man's candidate."

Eden said, "We can add a historical angle to our position. Detroit has had four major racial disturbances. For example, in 1943, on Belle Isle, there was an outbreak between black youths and white sailors. Twenty-five blacks and nine whites were killed."

"I didn't know anything about a 1943 riot," admitted Clay. The lack of response from the others suggested that he wasn't alone. "How do I use it?"

"You say something along the lines that the race divide has scarred this city too long. That the best way to honor those who died victims of racial hatred is to work tirelessly against it. That we should regard the past as a source of lessons and not as a justification for looking back in anger and mistrust."

"Preach, Saul, preach," said Clay.

"Should I put a speechwriter on Mr. Eden's suggestion?" Givens asked the mayor.

"Yeah, only don't assign this one to Webber. Lately some of his phrasing has been about as original as an echo." Clay took in a long breath through his nose and quickly expelled it through his mouth. "We've put something together here. Now we have to shake our kernels over the heat and see how well they pop."

Four years earlier, when Randal Clay ran for mayor, he was dubbed "the Garbageman." As unflattering as the name sounded, he used it to great advantage. When Mayor Nigel Bradfield privatized trash pickup during his third term in 1981, Clay's start-up firm was awarded the contract, which included the purchase of Detroit's incinerator plant. Clay expanded into recycling, hazardous-materials disposal, and environmental engineering. By 1990, The Clay Companies was listed among the top ten in *The Black Capitalist* magazine's list of the largest black-owned businesses.

When Clay ran against incumbent Sheila Roundtree, he promised "to haul the garbage from government." It was an impromptu utterance, and he would later explain that by "garbage" he meant practices and not people. But that didn't placate Roundtree. Fortunately for him, her term had been rocked by ethical charges, which undercut her claims of mudslinging. So "the Garbageman" became an epithet with crusader overtones.

Clay's victory was lopsided. "The right alternative to Brad-field's combativeness and Roundtree's ineffectiveness," read one national publication. "Should put the Motor City back in gear," read another.

The business sector was heartened by Clay's election. It regarded him as one of its own; it felt that he understood the importance of tax breaks and other incentives for business as the path to jobs creation and economic growth. Slowly, tentatively at first, the inquiries began, which led to discussions, which led to agreements, which led to projects, which led to investments in the city.

At fifty-four years of age, Clay was riding a set of statistics that made him a most formidable candidate for reelection: major crimes, down; unemployment, down; housing values, up; voters' confidence about the future, up. But for every Goliath there's a David somewhere out there taking slingshot practice; for every Superman there's someone willing to try to put a Kryptonite boot in his butt.

"What's the latest on the sweepstakes for who wins the privilege of getting his ass kicked next month?" Clay said.

"That's quite a change in rhetoric from when you were fretting a minute ago about losing votes over the riot anniversary," said Ashford.

"The only thing I fret is the margin of victory. I like to win big. I want the advantage of playing an opponent in the finals who I've already stomped in the preliminaries."

"Isaac Shaw seems a lock," said Monahan.

"Even with Galliger in?" Clay asked. Congressman Andrew Galliger, of the 13th U.S. Congressional District, was an eleventh-hour entry.

"Yes, surprisingly," said Monahan.

"Roll call, then," said Clay. "Kalabrosos."

"People don't take him seriously," Monahan said of the Greek businessman and three-time loser in mayoral races.

"Watts."

"Too young. No experience. No money."

"Dudley."

"Communist. Enough said."

"Arnold."

"Too closely associated with Roundtree."

"Colson."

"People don't even think that he was a good school superintendent."

"And those are the ones I've heard of before," said Clay. "The others . . ."

"The others aren't even a blip on the screen," assured Monahan.

"How did Shaw break out of the pack?" asked Eden.

"He's been organizing for years," Givens said.

"He supported me in '93," Clay said.

"And he has a network," Ashford said.

"Not that word again," said Clay.

"Sorry, Randal, but it's true. When it comes to the poor, he's buried a lot of people practically free. Good, decent burials, from what I understand. That type of word of mouth pays dividends."

"Funerals for votes. Is that legal? Sounds like a bribe to me." Clay winked playfully and adjusted his cuff links.

"Joke if you want, Randal," warned Ashford. "But I wouldn't play this guy cheap if I were you. He's a lot like you. Good businessman. He's in good with the black churches, too."

"How?"

"Reverend Charles Moody is his cousin," answered Ashford, "and Shaw gives the congregation a discount. And it doesn't stop there. Moody heads the Greater Council of Detroit Baptist Churches, and they all get discounts."

"Hey, this is getting a bit interesting," Clay said.

"And I've yet to tell you about the unions," said Ashford. "Anybody on strike faced with funeral expenses gets special considerations. I found that out from a gas meter reader whose mother died while he was on strike. These are not matters that automatically make the news. So who can say how many unions he's in good with. People's memories can be long when you help them in their saddest hour."

"Church, labor, working class—he's certainly going after the key constituencies," Clay said. "Maybe somewhere down the line we might have ourselves a ball game. That means scouting reports."

"So far we don't have any dirt on the undertaker." Ashford looked around the room to be sure his pun had registered before resuming. "This guy's pretty solid. Longtime Detroiter and all."

"What do you mean, 'longtime'? Where's he from?" Clay leaned forward and rested his elbows on his desk, his interest piqued.

"Down south somewhere." Arnold began flipping through a file folder.

"Find out the shack he was born in. Could be he wasn't so solid down there. Family?"

"Lives with his wife."

"Anything about her a liability?"

Arnold fumbled with a sheaf of papers before shaking his head and mumbling, "Don't know."

"Married before?"

"Don't know."

"What about kids?"

"Don't know."

"I hate to interrupt you, Jordan, when you're on a roll, but off-hand I'd say that there are a number of gaps we need to fill in on our knowledge of our opponent."

"One son," said Eden. "I remember reading that he has a grown adopted son."

"Do you want the usual people on this?" asked Givens.

"No, no, too close. I want a couple of layers between them and us, just in case they come up with something nasty that has to be handled with tongs."

"Glad you're taking this seriously," said Ashford.

"Oh, but I am. The Garbageman versus the Undertaker. Ironic, though."

"In what way?" Eden flicked his earring.

"Both of us coming from the disposal business."

Clay's secretary came into the room at that moment and went to his side. She bent toward him and whispered something in his ear. Clay inclined his head toward her and then nodded briskly. Clay excused himself from the room. After a brief meeting with Chief Cornelius Upton, he returned to his staff meeting. Without retaking his seat, he clapped those big hands again, his previously bright expression having turned dour. "Meeting over, folks."

Clay left immediately to rejoin the chief and learn more of the serial killer who'd chosen this most inopportune time to stalk the city.

TEN

Ellery Tarver entered the squad room, dragging his feet like the zombie he resembled. It was more than an hour past the start of the shift, and he was seldom late for work. He sleepwalked to his desk, but he only stood there, looking confused, as if he'd forgotten how to bend his knees to sit. This was his worst entrance ever. Respectfully, the others in the room didn't speak, pretending that they didn't notice him; but Mary looked on, her face a mix of sympathy and disgust. Ellery returned her gaze. He went to her. The trek was slow and sad to watch.

"Where the hell have you been, Ellery?"

In a weak, quivering voice, Ellery said, "I need to tell you something. Not in here."

"Will the hallway do?"

"Yes."

In the hallway, Mary waited until some passersby were out of earshot before asking, "What is it, Ellery?"

"I settled things with Beverly. You won't have to worry about that no more."

"Good. I'm glad to hear that." Mary put her hand on Ellery's forearm and squeezed it.

"She won't be going behind my back anymore." He tilted his head back and exhaled heavily. He looked back at Mary and then quickly averted his eyes.

Something in Ellery's tone, the glazed look in his eyes, sent a chill down Mary's spine.

"Oh, God, Ellery. You didn't."

He nodded mutely.

While Mary struggled to speak, Ellery dropped another bomb-shell. "I killed her boyfriend, too."

"Where are they, Ellery?"

"Fucker had it coming, Mary."

Mary choked back a sob before whispering, "Where, Ellery?"

"They're at his place, Eldridge Court Apartments, 2A."

Mary was trembling. "We have to go talk to the inspector," she said, and took him by the elbow to lead him to Newberry's office.

Ellery took her hand off his elbow and softly squeezed it. "Okay. Just let me duck into the men's room and work on my appearance. I don't want him to see me looking like this."

It seemed a strange concern, but Mary let him go.

A minute after Ellery disappeared into the men's room, a single gunshot sounded.

ELEVEN

Najah Harlan's keys jangled as she fumbled with them, finally nabbing the one to the dead bolt. Anxiously she poked the key at the lock, failing the first couple of tries before making the insertion. Good name, "dead bolt": a person could end up dead trying to unlock it in a crisis. She turned the key sharply. Now she had to repeat the process, with another key, for the lock in the doorknob. It all was taking too long. Someone had followed her home, and Najah wanted in—badly. Once inside, she leaned her back against the door, breathing deeply. Then, with excitement playing in her voice, she said, "Welcome to my apartment."

Her pursuer stood before her as silently as he had stood behind her when she was battling the locks. He stayed silent while she placed her hand on his crotch. She didn't have to pat searchingly, and she smiled with wicked satisfaction. The difference in their heights was such that she only had to wrap her arms around his neck and rise on tiptoes to grind against him. Then they kissed, their tongues thrusting and parrying like sabers during a fencing duel. The next minute she was holding on to his shoulder with one hand while she used the other to pull off her panties from under a long, white, African-style dress—steadying herself on just one leg, then the other, with the balance of a high-wire artist in heat. Sans undies, she spun and faced the door, slapping her hands against it in the manner of one about to be frisked. Well, almost, since the procedure usually doesn't require one to bend sharply, dress flipped to expose a gorgeous ass, and say, "Do me doggy-style."

"Is the fire department on its way and we have to do this before the place burns down?" he quipped. So that his words would be interpreted without sting, he squeezed her buttocks, then reached between her legs for a handful of vulva. Her chocolate-rich skin contrasted as starkly against his hand as it did against her dress. He pressed his groin against her so that she could feel his arousal, then leaned his chest against her back and spoke into her ear: "I'm willing to take as long as necessary to do the job right. Know what I'm saying?"

"I like the sound of that," said Najah. She turned to face him and playfully bit his nose. "Want some wine?"

"Have any cranberry juice?"

"Yeah, as a matter of fact." She flicked a light switch and sashayed to the kitchen.

He walked around her apartment inspecting his surroundings. The sprawling front room sported a pink S-shaped suede sofa, a glass coffee table, an entertainment center, furnishings for a home office, and an exercise bike; however, what most caught his eye were the pictures on the walls, the carvings, the throw rugs—all of African or African American themes. It didn't surprise him. Actually, he congratulated himself on how accurately he had sized her up.

He had known she was a self-aware woman the moment she strutted proudly past him hours earlier at the Ethnic Festival in downtown Detroit. A longtime Motor City tradition, the summer-long outdoor festivals devote each weekend to a particular ethnic group. Detroit's predominant ethnic group, the African American population, turned out in force for its culture's mix of music, food, and vendors. The festivals, however, pride themselves on diversity, since many attendees are not members of the featured ethnic group. This evening—as was always the case with the African American Festival—the "sisters" had turned out in numbers: every shape, size, and shade, dressed and undressed in every way imaginable.

Over the past months he had become skilled at studying a person inconspicuously and was much better at it than was Najah. So the various stakeout points from where she had watched him and the several times that she had just happened to cross his field of vision all had been transparently obvious to him. He had always received attention from women, although he seldom returned it in kind. But there was something singular about Najah. He felt it viscerally.

And, later, when he had taken a seat in the Hart Plaza outdoor amphitheater, he had known that she had followed at a strategic distance, although he didn't let on when she sweetly cooed, "Is this seat taken?" During the free concert, they connected, so much so that, afterward, it became a matter of "your place or mine?" Then it had been his turn to follow her, and he gunned his Mustang to keep up with her Corvette on the freeway to the suburb of Farmington.

He was still standing when Najah emerged from the kitchen carrying a serving tray. After they were seated on the sofa, she poured her wine and his cranberry juice, then asked, "Ice?"

"Is it already cold?"

"Yes."

"No ice."

"I want you to have some ice," she urged.

From her coquettish smile he knew that he stood to gain more than a colder drink, so he held out the glass to her and said, "Load me up."

Najah reached into the ice bucket and withdrew a single cube. She popped it into her mouth, held it there for a few seconds, then let it drop into the juice. She did it three times. "There you are," she said.

He swirled his drink. The ice cubes chimed. "You made it colder and sweeter," he said. He emptied the glass.

His reaction to the ice put Najah even more on fire. She gulped her wine, eager to resume the preliminaries.

Inevitably they ended up in the bedroom, where the naked Najah went to her dresser of drawers, rummaged a moment, then flung silk scarves over her shoulder. The scarves drifted down to the king-size brass bed. From a standing position, Najah flopped onto the bed, landing on her butt. Then she lay on her back and, grasping the bars of the headboard, told him, "I want you to tie me up."

He shrugged his shoulders. "You want it, you got it." He straddled her chest and began making like a Boy Scout, tying slipknots that he slid over her wrists. "Tell me if I draw them too tightly," he said.

She didn't say anything in response; instead she nodded her head up and down more rapidly on the erect penis in her mouth. Her lips smacked as he withdrew to lie next to her. He took one of her nipples in his mouth. She still smelled of apricots from shower gel, but she tasted slightly salty.

The connection he had felt at the Ethnic Festival was proving to be prophetic.

"Najah, gal, you are something else, and I am so glad that you chose me to be something else with tonight."

She bit her lip and exhaled sharply in response.

No doubt she saw in him the same traits he saw in her. Soul mates they were destined to be.

There came a time, of course, when he was on top of her and about to penetrate. "Now for some A-1, prime diggidy." Translation: great sex.

Najah chuckled, but not completely from amusement. "You don't have to talk that black jive for my sake," she said. "Be yourself. Opposites attract. That's what this is all about."

She read the confusion in his eyes even before he said, "I don't know if I get where you're coming from."

"Sure you do," she insisted. "Jungle fever, baby. There's nothing wrong with it. You want a taste of chocolate, I want a taste of vanilla. It's an old tale."

He felt his erection dying. His eyelids suddenly felt heavy, and he lowered them as if to feed more energy to his hearing, which he hoped was not functioning properly. But when he reopened his eyes he saw how Najah viewed him, how she had viewed him from the start. There was nothing wrong with his hearing. "You're saying you chose me because I'm a white guy?"

Najah corrected him. "Because you're one *fine* white guy. Makes a difference." Sensing that her compliment was lost on him, she said, "What's your problem, sweety? I like white men. Prefer them, if you want to know the truth. I knew you were at the Ethnic Festival prowling for some black nookie. Now, let's cut the noise and get back to business."

He swung his leg around and sat on the edge of the bed before pushing himself up. He began pacing, tapping his fist against his chin, trying to sort it all out. It didn't add up: her attire, her looks, her apartment. Even the name, *Najah*—although he'd never before encountered it—conjured ethnic and cultural images. A proud, self-aware black woman? Anything but! He felt foolish, like an impostor. But as he pondered further, he realized that *she* was the impostor. Now he felt angry.

"Look," Najah said, trying to sound authoritative yet unthreatening, "somewhere we seem to have miscommunicated. I'd like you to leave. Untie me, please."

He stopped pacing. He gave her a long, malignant stare. Najah struggled against the restraints. All the while, he watched in abject silence.

"You're scaring me." Najah stopped thrashing for a moment and tried to quell her panic. "Untie me, please."

"Shut up, you damn Oreo. I have to think."

What was there to think about? Her rising anxiety tightened her chest. She resumed struggling, but her arms were angled too widely away from her body for her to have any leverage, and the knots were tied too well. Conceding the futility of those efforts, she pleaded, "Listen to me. As far as I'm concerned, nothing reportable has happened so far. Untie me, and all's forgotten."

When he still said nothing, made no attempt to free her, and when his stare seemed to have gotten stonier, she filled her lungs—she knew this first attempt had to be good, because it might be her only one—and screamed, "Help! Help me! Help me, somebod—"

The last syllable was muffled by his hand clamped against her mouth. He stretched and with his free hand grabbed one of the scarves he hadn't used. In short order he had it tied so tightly around her mouth that she felt her pulse drumming against her temples. He was lying full-press on her, and he said, "Prefer white, do you? Maybe that's what you should be." He began sliding his body up and down hers, harshly, chafingly, and not for sexual gratification. When he paused he said, "Looks like white doesn't rub off. Too bad, because such beautiful black skin is wasted on someone like you." That last statement forced a realization: Najah resembled dearly departed Carol, she of skin as dark as deep space. How dare Najah resemble her, yet be so offensively her opposite. Such mockery must not go unpunished. He pushed up off Najah, got out of bed and left the room.

Crying had swollen Najah's eyes into slits, but they sprang open in horror at the clatter that came from the kitchen. He had pulled a drawer too far out and it had fallen to the floor, sending spoons, forks, and knives colliding. When he returned, he was brandishing the biggest and sharpest of her cutlery. She bucked wildly, kicking at him, trying to thwart his attempts to jump into the bed. But his timing was too good and he ended up on top of her, blade to her throat. She froze and lay perfectly still, except that she was shivering so violently he felt as if he were on a vibrating bed.

There were certain factors to be considered. For one thing, she was essentially a nobody, hardly a suitable candidate for the full treatment. Besides, he hadn't come with his tools of the trade. He'd have to improvise.

He yanked off the band that directed her medium-length braids toward the back of her head. He gathered a bunch in his fist and pulled it vertical, so hard that Najah grimaced. It was all her natural hair, thick and strong. With the blade held horizontally and scraping her scalp, he sawed jaggedly through, then slung the Medusa-like braids against the wall. He hacked at another bunch. And another. And another. She had no right to wear her hair that way.

But what could he do about her lovely dark skin, short of drenching it in red? He knew that a message had to be sent. Najah had a well-stocked vanity, and in the next minute he was smearing lotions and creams all over her body. When he'd covered every inch of her flesh, he stood above her, contemplating a suitable finishing touch. He bent over and picked up a bottle of baby powder, tore off the top, and dumped the contents on her. He scooped up a couple of handfuls and soon had her completely dusted.

"Good." He sat down in a chair across the room from the bed and admired his ghastly creation in white. "Now you're the same color inside and out."

He dressed, slowly and methodically. He sat for a few minutes on the couch, all the while thinking about what cover-up was needed to protect the mission. He was glad that he'd given her only his first name. By the time he was about to leave, he had wiped everything he could remember having touched. The glass that had held his cranberry juice he smashed against the wall. He remembered the bit about the ice cubes and felt a gagging disgust. Her behavior that he had found so exciting, so bewitching, he now considered tawdry and crass. He raked his forearm across his mouth.

In a parting gesture of compassion, he left her door wide open, figuring that before long, it would attract some curious passerby.

TWELVE

For the better part of the late afternoon, while his wife, Gertrude, busied herself in the kitchen, Isaac Shaw had sat in the family room preparing a campaign speech. Throughout, Isaac had known better than to invade her province. Over the sound of the clacking keys of his laptop he'd heard a succession of sounds: the cushioned closings of the refrigerator, the creaky openings of the oven, the whir of appliances, and the clang of pots and pans. But even if he had been deaf, the smells would have made it evident that his wife was whipping up something special for their dinner guest.

The Shaws lived in Indian Village, a stately neighborhood on Detroit's East Side. Like the other homes on the block, their house sat on an immaculately maintained property, from the manicured landscaping to the impressive stonework of the porte cochere that guarded the driveway's entrance. The home's interior was equally impressive. All fourteen rooms seemed torn from the pages of *House Beautiful*. Counting the luxury cars in the driveway, the second home in South Carolina, and the investment portfolio, the Shaws had done well for themselves since they relocated from Bent Fork in 1975.

The four Shaw Funeral Homes were the foundation of Isaac's empire and made him the most successful funeral director in the city. He had bought the first one the same year he arrived in Detroit. Allen Waldman no longer could buck the white flight to the suburbs that had continued unabated since the 1967 riots, and had sold his funeral home to Isaac at a bargain price.

On this Sunday, the scar on Isaac's left hand was bothering him. The gash that Annie Parsons had put there had been stitched that same night at the hospital. The doctor had found no reason to question his claim that the self-inflicted wound was the result of an accident suffered while embalming a body. Lots of cutting involved in that procedure anyway. Typical of the suturing of thirty years before, the wound had healed into a scar resembling a football's laces. Isaac preferred to think of it as a zipper, one that held closed his wretched secret. The scar seemed to have a life of its own, subject to its own set of influences, like an injury or ailment aggravated by the weather. In this case, though, it was the flashes of memory he couldn't suppress that seemed to give it a pulse and make it feel as though a long, fat nightcrawler lay beneath his skin.

Fitting Annie into the casket with Bernard Lincoln had not been difficult: remove the interior lining, not pack Lincoln's chest cavity, and angle Annie just so on top of Lincoln, and it was done. But Isaac would have buried the pair in an inferior casket had he been able to pull off the switch. The reason would not have been to pocket the difference in cost, however. A lesser casket would have permitted water seepage, would have permitted worms to dine, would have hastened "from ashes to ashes, dust to dust." Even thirty years later, Isaac occasionally had to fight distraction when selling the bereaved on the advantages of a sealed casket. He wondered if there was enough of Annie left to hang him if the casket ever were exhumed. Quality and craftsmanship can have their drawbacks.

A crash in the kitchen snapped Isaac from his preoccupation with his scar. He heard Gertrude swear—or rather what, for her, passed for swearing. Whatever the mishap, he knew that she would make sure that the dinner would be a success. She was a homemaker par excellence who had not held a job since moving to Detroit. It was her choice. She believed that Isaac owed it to her, that it was the least he could do.

As his wife, she had a stake in all their assets; however, she had insisted on a separate legal agreement that gave her sole ownership of the works of the artist who'd generously supplied her over the years. The collection, worth a modest fortune, was hung throughout the home.

Gertrude popped into the family room, hurriedly wiping her hands on her apron. She shot an unapproving look at Isaac. "Why are you sitting there like a bump on a log? Wasn't that the doorbell?"

"No, Gertrude."

"Sure sounded like it."

"Relax," advised Isaac.

"Listen to you. Earlier, you were the one anxiously puttering around here."

Isaac said, "Well, that can happen when you know who you're expecting but don't know who's going to show up."

His words were no riddle to Gertrude, who said, "I wouldn't speak negatives if I were you. Don't get me started."

"Heaven forbid."

"Because," said Gertrude, "we can have ourselves a good little discussion about a good many things."

Isaac adopted a conciliatory posture. "And if we do, it'll be for the one millionth time. Look, let's just try to get through this evening without incident. For everyone's sake."

"Exclude yourself from 'everyone's sake,' and I'd be willing to make a go of this evening," she said.

"Then consider me excluded."

"For you have no right to expect me to hold you in consideration."

Conscious of the impending arrival of their guest, Isaac tried to steer Gertrude's thoughts back to the dinner. "What was that crash in the kitchen?"

"A cake pan fell from my hand while I was taking it from the oven. No tragedy, because I always bake an extra layer just in case something happens." Gertrude was average height, slender, and a few shades darker than Isaac. She had long hair, grayed past the halfway point, and she wore it in a bun. Her choice of outfits was generally as matronly as her hairstyle. She hadn't always been that way. During their courtship she was as vivacious and alluring as any woman Isaac had ever dated. In their second year of marriage, and after a number of failed attempts at pregnancy, she was diagnosed as infertile. Isaac could point to that discovery as the beginning of her transformation and the seeds of his lone betrayal.

As though he could overcome his wife's stodginess, Isaac was something of a fashion plate. Despite the paunch he had acquired, he was otherwise in good shape and health. For a man who'd been surrounded by the deceased most of his life, Isaac was surprisingly queasy about matters pertaining to his own aging and mortality. Thanks to dyeing, his hair had no gray. Isaac lived in suits, dress shirts, and ties, even at home, so that if death should catch him unaware, he'd at least be dressed properly. Gertrude complained that he dressed too much like the fathers in those old situation comedies on television.

But there was very little that was lighthearted about the Shaw household. At best, an uneasy truce marked by cold formalities reigned. The sturdiest walls in the house were not those composed of plaster.

The sound of a car door closing put an end to their conversation.

Isaac stated the obvious. "We have company, Gertrude."

She was out of the apron like a quick-change artist, wiping her hands on it again before hanging it on a kitchen hook before hurriedly making her way to the front door. She grasped the doorknob with one hand and smoothed nonexistent wrinkles from her dress with the other. A few quick pats on her bun. She glanced back at Isaac. "Is my hair in place?"

"Yes, Gertrude. Open the door."

But she waited for the ring. Then she opened it. Their guest entered.

"Eugene, Eugene," she exclaimed, her eyes starting to water. She clamped his face between her hands and smacked kisses on each cheek. Next she held him by the shoulders and took a step back. She looked him up and down. "You look great. Doesn't he took great, Isaac?"

"He looks great." Isaac embraced him, then released him and asked, "How are you?"

"Like I look, I guess, great." He stood before them dressed in denim coveralls and sneakers. He wore an athletic undershirt, and his exposed arms and shoulders were just as ghostly as his face, despite its being July. His pallor was a result not of ill health but of genetics.

Gertrude said, "Boy, I should take a belt and give you the whipping of your life. You been back for months and this is the first time you've seen fit to visit us. If I wasn't so glad to see you, I'd give you what for."

"I have good excuses," said Eugene, feigning fear by raising his arms to shield his face. He put his arm around Gertrude's shoulder and led her into the house. "Relocating is a monster in itself, plus I made a couple of overseas trips. And don't forget that I have the thing going with the Museum of Afro-American History. I'm juggling lots of balls at the same time, and I wouldn't be here now if I hadn't said to myself, 'Hey, swamped or not, I'm going to take time out and visit my parents.' "

"You're forgiven," said Gertrude, always the soft touch when it came to Eugene. "Isn't he, Isaac?"

"As far as I'm concerned, he is," said Isaac. He was studying Eugene, trying not to be obvious. So far, so good. But it was still early.

Gertrude said, "Let's go to the family room, Eugene, baby, so we can sit and talk before dinner."

"I almost forgot my surprise," he said. He started walking backward toward the front door, still looking at Isaac and Gertrude. He kept watching them as he opened the door and grabbed what he had left on the porch. He hid it behind his back, though. As he walked toward the Shaws, his eyes darted and he smiled knowingly. Then he presented what he had to Isaac. It was a campaign sign, the lawn display variety.

"It's you, Isaac," said Gertrude of the likeness on the sign.

She was half right. It was Isaac's head, but the photo had been superimposed on a torso that was clad in African garb, replete with beads. And the sign was bordered with an African pattern. One would have thought that Isaac himself had posed for the sign, it looked so lifelike. Then again, it hadn't been much of a challenge for someone with Eugene's artistic talents, as his pieces throughout the Shaws' home testified to.

"And check out the slogan," enthused Eugene. It read, "Isaac Shaw for Mayor: A Real Brother for the People." He looked at Isaac, who was taken aback, and said, "It sure beats those lame signs that your campaign manager came up with. The primary election is next month. Time to pull out all the stops."

"The . . . eh, the . . . the budget is tight at this point," Isaac stammered. "What's left is earmarked for media spending." He could hear Gertrude's silent laughter. "The money's not there to reproduce this in any real numbers."

"Not to worry. Not to worry," beamed Eugene. "I took care of that end of it. I have cases and cases of these babies. And if we need more, I'll pay for them, too."

"Fine. Deliver them here and the staffers will take care of the distribution." It was the only strategy Isaac could devise on the spot. Later he'd be able to decide how to dispose of the signs.

"Sure, I'll give you what's left."

"What do you mean?" asked Isaac.

"I got the jump start on you. I've been going around like Johnny Appleseed, planting them everywhere."

"Oh, really," commented Gertrude. Her smile was borderline malicious.

"Yep. You'll love what I did in your own neighborhood before coming here. Put one on everybody's lawn. I let your old signs stay but added the new one. And—you're going to love this—where there was someone else's sign, I pulled it up, threw it in the street, and replaced it with yours."

Eugene had left the inside door open. Through the screen door Isaac watched as a patrol car stopped in front of the house and two uniformed officers got out. He didn't have to guess why they had come.

THIRTEEN

When Isaac Shaw proposed marriage to Gertrude Allen, she already had decided that their first son would be named Eugene. Once, when it seemed that Isaac's workload would interfere with a date, she pitched in and wrote some obituaries, then was embarrassed when he told her that she had misspelled "eulogy." She consulted a dictionary and learned that the Greek prefix *eu* means "good," and there, among the various words that utilize it, was *Eugene*. She thought it appropriate: *"A male's name meaning having good hereditary traits."* Decision made.

An increased vocabulary, however, seemed the only benefit that she'd ever derive from the name after her infertility was diagnosed. But she knew that God had other plans the day that Isaac came home with the newborn and the letter and asked her the unnecessary question "What should we do?" For Gertrude, no greater proof was possible that God works in mysterious ways than sending her a baby conceived through rape, when she had the perfect healing name already selected for him. And there was a bonus godsend: the baby's color.

For generations, the Shaws had based their marriage decisions on the likelihood of producing light-skinned, straight-haired, and keen-featured offspring, a perverse natural selection that took into consideration the advantage of those traits in American society. When it became apparent that Isaac was serious about the darker Gertrude, some of his relatives tried to torpedo the courtship in ways meant to be obvious to her. After the marriage her in-laws were spoilsports, unwilling to admit to having lost unfair and unsquare. And when Gertrude's infertility eliminated nightmares of pickaninnies, her in-laws scorned her for being a knot on the family tree instead of a branch. Damned either way.

But Gertrude knew that the color-struck Shaws would obsess over Eugene. And, deliciously, he and she were a package deal. No more barbs and icy treatment from her in-laws; otherwise, she would restrict their access to him. It was the ace she held during the early years. Gertrude's maternal instincts made her lie to Eugene to protect him from knowledge of his mother's rape. With Isaac's complicity, she told the boy that his black mother and white father gave him up for adoption because they couldn't endure the pressures of bigotry. He was also told that his parents wanted their identities kept secret. This was the South during the civil rights era, and children learned early the impact of race. Eugene swallowed the story whole and loved his parents even more for being such humanitarians.

But the lies Isaac had so carefully knitted had a few loose strands, at which the years slowly tugged, unraveling them like an old sock. The boy's nose which from the beginning had whispered "Shaw," developed into a shout. Baby teeth were replaced by a double set of bottom center teeth, which was another Shaw trait. Worse still, Eugene developed the same pigeon-toed stride as Isaac.

What had become a topic of snickering gossip came to a head one night when Eugene, almost eight years old, was awakened by the thud of a skillet striking a wall. Isaac had escaped a creased skull by nimbly dodging, not through Gertrude's faulty aim. Sitting up in his bed in the middle of the night, Eugene heard an exchange that altered his life.

"Admit you fathered Eugene, or so help me—"

"Lower your voice, woman, or you'll wake him."

"Then you better talk fast, or my voice will raise this roof. You've made me the town fool, and I won't stand for it any longer."

"I was drunk that night, Gertrude. It happened one time, in my car. Never laid eyes on her again until she showed up at the funeral home with a baby she claimed was mine. She refused to discuss it. Just walked out and left him."

"Who is she, Isaac? Does she live in Bent Fork?"

"Millie, is all I know. Said she's from Montgomery and was here visiting—her sister, I think. I was coming out of Ruby's Lounge when I saw her. My first thought was that she was lost and needed directions."

"Like how to lie on her back."

"Turned out she knew exactly the side of town she was in, and like I said, I was drunk. She was tipsy also."

"That's a cockamamie story."

"Every word's the truth. And after things progressed to a certain point, I went the rest of the way, scared she might go to the sheriff and claim rape if I didn't give her what she wanted."

"You give scared stiff a new meaning."

"Give me credit, Gertrude, for doing the Christian thing and wanting the boy to have a home. But I never wanted it to come to this."

"I knew about your rooster days before I married you, but you swore to me they were over."

"They are, Gertrude. That's the only time I've been unfaithful. It'll never happen again."

"I thought you were special, Isaac Shaw. But you're just another stupid nigger who'll risk anything for a white woman. I bet she was as ugly as a warthog, too. May God forgive me for saying it, but families would be stronger if Negroes were still guaranteed a lynching for looking at white women."

"You love the boy, Gertrude. And he loves you. That's the one good thing that's come of this. The one thing we can build on. Please, please, Gertrude, don't make him pay for my sins."

"I'm too much a Christian woman for that. I'll ask God to keep my heart pure toward Eugene. But you're another story, Isaac Shaw. All I feel for you is disgust."

"I understand. But time heals all wounds."

"I don't need your clichés. My wounds are the reopening kind. Whenever I look at Eugene, I'll have to fight the Devil to keep from thinking of him as the bastard you fathered with some white trash."

"I'll make it up to you, Gertrude. If it takes the rest of my life."

"It'll take at least that long. And I'm not sure I want to give you the chance."

"Name your terms. I'll do anything."

"It has to begin with abandoning the lies, Isaac. A public confession that you're Eugene's father. He has a right to know. Afterward, maybe the three of us can stand united against the small-minded busybodies in this town."

"That's the one thing I can't do. I just can't."

Gertrude was out the door before Isaac could elaborate. He knew that he could never confess that Annie Parsons was the mother. And he couldn't go public with the Millie lie, either; the incurably nosy might search for her and ultimately conclude that she was a fiction.

The young Eugene didn't know why Isaac had refused to comply with Gertrude's demands. It had to have had something to do with him. He blamed himself for being the source of his father's shame. It was understandable, being ashamed of someone whom the other children constantly tormented with taunts of "zebra," "half-breed," "white bread," and "Casper." And who was to blame except he that after Gertrude's huffy departure, she stayed gone for weeks?

Gertrude eventually returned to raise her son, doubtful that she would win a custody battle if she divorced Isaac. The wealthy, influential Shaws had a reputation for putting aside differences and uniting against any external threat. So she stayed and remained silent about Isaac's paternity. In time, her silence became self-perpetuating, because she didn't know how to justify to Eugene her participation in the deception. And on many days and nights of painful introspection, she questioned the purity of her love for Eugene. She wondered whether she was exploiting him as a way to prove her worthiness to the Shaws. After all, before that fateful confrontation she had been an avid user of bleaching creams in pursuit of becoming incrementally lighter skinned. *Eugene: A male's name meaning having good hereditary traits.* She used to laugh at the irony of it all: what if Eugene developed the kind of narrow-mindedness and mean-spiritedness that characterized the Shaws' treatment of her? Plus, she knew nothing about what he might have inherited from that strumpet Millie.

Isaac by then had unsettling knowledge about what Eugene might have inherited from his mother's side. In retrospect, the facts that came to light—during the trial of the man who was convicted and sent to prison for her murder—explained a lot about Annie.

There truly was no shortage of deception among the three of them. Eugene was complicit as well: he never revealed to Isaac and Gertrude that he had overheard them that night.

Thus was their kinship a forgery of loyalty and lechery, blood and betrayal, love and lies. And on the evening that Eugene came to visit, and after Isaac had convinced the police officers that there would be no further complaints about unauthorized planting of campaign signs, they sat down to dinner, Gertrude beginning grace with "Dear Lord, please keep and bless this family."

FOURTEEN

Joe Kingsley squinted at what Mary had handed him, patting his shirt pocket for his eyeglasses. His daughter stood waiting. Her arms were behind her, one hand cuffing the other wrist, and she twisted slightly back and forth at the waist, weight shifting alternatingly between right foot and left. She wasn't aware of the fidgeting, so ingrained had these habits become. It almost was a throwback to thirty years before, when she used to anxiously await Joe's evaluation of her report card.

Joe read aloud the rank on his daughter's newly minted ID, "Lieutenant." He turned his head to the side and out of danger of eye contact, stirred a finger in an itching ear canal, and said in a tone that was anything but celebratory, "I suppose congratulations are in order."

A starving Mary snatched the crumb and smiled gratefully. "Thank you, Daddy."

Dispirited, Joe added, "I never even made detective."

Mary chastised herself for hoping that the reception would be warmer. She'd even foolishly hoped that Joe would identify with her mourning over Ellery, although she was angry that Ellery killed his wife as if she were his property, a head of livestock. Joe didn't mention the tragedy, although it made headlines.

A double homicide/suicide tends to disqualify a cop from burial with departmental honors. But Mary was among a small contingent of police who attended Ellery's funeral. She'd been surprised to see Frank Corleone there.

The day of Ellery's funeral had been awash in sunshine, in contrast with the overcast moods. All funerals, however, were difficult for Mary, reminding her as they did of a particular one she attended a lifetime ago.

As Mary stood before Joe, there in the house in which she'd spent her childhood, a sense of timelessness swept over her. There was the vinyl-enshrouded sofa—which on many an occasion she had used as a trampoline—preserved as reliably as if in a hermetic tomb. There was the wallpaper, although seamless and intact, dated by tiny tulips. There was the lingering smell of meat loaf that—as sure as any calendar—announced that it was Wednesday. Yet Mary felt no sense of warm nostalgia, only a deep sadness, as though she was mourning a loss that defied the concept of time.

The photographs along the mantel, and others crowding a lamp table, were all part of the preservation process. Their chronology was evident: the sepia portraits of Joe in the Army, and of nubile Sophie Guthrie, his future bride; a family portrait of them and their children, rangy Joe Jr. and toddler Mary; and all the other photographs, whether of a single subject or more, reflecting the parade of years. Conspicuous by their absence were photos of Mary's later life—her graduation from the police academy, her weddings. It was as if the timeline stopped not long after the most recent photo of Joe Jr. was taken. It captured him as a sixteen-year-old junior police cadet, posing next to his beaming, uniform-clad father.

Joe Kingsley had dark skin that radiated with a natural sheen. His short, tight curls had turned gray. To Mary, who'd always considered him dashing, he'd grown more handsome over the years. Although he was still imposing, now Joe Kingsley seemed shorter, his stooped posture likely due to the heavy load of memories he carried on his shoulders all the time.

Joe gave Mary back her ID. "Before it's over," he said, "you'll likely make police chief." To Mary his words sounded like anything but a hopeful prediction.

Mary said, "Wouldn't that be something," but the smile was forced.

Given Joe's reaction to her having made lieutenant, she decided not to mention her other promotion. Mary had asked Inspector Newberry to appoint her squad leader in replacement of Ellery. Newberry had hemmed and hawed, portraying the position as being a lot of paper pushing in addition to regular duties. Mary wouldn't be dissuaded and Newberry grudgingly gave in. However, since Paul Nitkowski recently had been diagnosed with lung cancer and had retired, Newberry made it a package deal—squad leader and Frank Corleone as her partner.

She tapped her ID card against her palm several times, ticking off some awkward seconds of silence. Then she sighed and said, "Well, Daddy, guess I'll be going." She hugged his neck warmly in exchange for several tepid pats on her back.

As he walked her to the door, he commented, "I suppose Cliff is happy for you."

Mary still hadn't told Cliff about her promotions, but she responded, "Very happy." She immediately felt the anxiety she had as a girl, fretting about the expiration date on a lie. But she was in such need of this one that she would have had to clamp her hands over her mouth to prevent its escape. Otherwise, she would have had to acknowledge aloud that the men she loved most were the same side of two coins, neither one supportive of her career.

Mary was leaving disheartened, but she had herself to blame; for there had been a bunch of promotions between beat cop and lieutenant, each serving as a stage for the same one-act tragedy. She'd come over that evening presumably to learn new stitching techniques from her mother. For a year, Mary had been learning to quilt as a means to keep her arthritic fingers nimble. After the sewing, she should have packed up and left without a word to her father about her career.

But Mary would rather be hurt than ignored, a peculiar aspect of her personality that time and again manifested itself with the men in her life. Joe sowed the seeds with the attention he used to lavish on "snookums," his pet name for her. At the time of Junior's death, Joe had so convinced nine-year-old Mary that she was the center of the universe that the tiniest retraction of that theory would have been as noticeable as an exploding galaxy. That his theory was debunked overnight was catastrophic. By her midteens she had become promiscuous. At seventeen she was pregnant by a man ten years her senior. Now, still relatively young, she was on her third marriage.

As a young girl Mary had always associated a police uniform with goodness. One of her warmest memories was when her father spoke to her class on Career Day and his presentation sparked more interest and questions than any other parent's. Police were the good guys. That all changed with Junior's death. After that, the uniform came to represent something vile. And every day she saw Joe in one. Repulsion being an attraction in its own right, she became a cop herself.

When Joe, now retired, had joined the force, it was overwhelmingly white, and African Americans summarized community relations as blue vs. blacks. And within the department, discriminatory practices frustrated the ambitions of Joe and other black officers. Joe, however, was sustained by the belief that he was making a difference, paving a smoother road for those who would come later. It's an old thread in the American fabric. Junior would have far more opportunities. Son following in father's footsteps, establishing a family tradition: old-fashioned and time-honored. It was Joe's dream. Okay, Mary was family. Maybe if she joined . . .

It hadn't worked.

How could she ever have hoped to fulfill Joe's dream when it was her dreams that caused his nightmare?

FIFTEEN

For years, the scar above Mary's mouth had been a source of much curiosity and speculation. The old-timers on the police force knew that she had had the scar before she became a cop; yet it didn't prevent the growth of a kind of lore—colorful, if not always complimentary, accounts—about how Bloody Mary got her beauty mark in the line of duty.

Mary was a minimalist when it came to wearing makeup. She wore the most when she competed in dance contests, and even then she considered it part of the costume. Her mouth, however, was an exception. Daily, she lavished attention on it. The ritual involved the application of luminously red lipstick followed by the outlining of her mouth with black lip liner. The effect against her skin tone was like neon.

Was it a badge celebrating something prideful, or a brand masochistically conspicuous and remindful? Or some of both? Mary, herself, couldn't say definitely. When asked, her stock reply was that it was personal.

Mary had been eight years old when she contracted dance fever one wintry Saturday afternoon. While walking along a neighborhood commercial block with some friends, she noticed a new business storefront. The frost prevented her from seeing through the big plate window, and it presented just enough mystery for the inquisitive Mary to covet a peek. She put a mittened hand against the glass and rubbed circles, only to discover that the other side was clouded. Placing her hands on the sides of her head like blinders, she pressed her nose against the glass, attempting to peer through. Her friends and the biting wind coaxed her to move along, but for minutes she was transfixed, marveling at bodies displaying the flexibility of invertebrates, the leaping ability of kangaroos, and the spirit of woodland fairies. Instant fever.

The Bigelow Ballet Studio was on Grand River, a street that slashes a diagonal clear across Detroit's West Side on a discourteous shortcut into downtown. The studio was within walking distance of Mary's home, along a strip that she visited frequently. The nearby Rialto movie theater, for example, was where she and her girlfriends, giddy with fright, would watch monster movies through fingers spread across faces. The corner candy store was where her week's allowance could spend like an inheritance. And Maggie's Beauty Shop was where, every other week, her hair was pressed and curled. And it was among those ritual stops that Polly and Frances Bigelow had chosen to relocate their studio.

When Mary first ventured inside the school, she already had her father's permission to take lessons. She was to bring him information about cost and enrollment. Joe Kingsley usually relented whenever his daughter pleaded with those big, wide-set eyes of hers, for Joe delighted in providing for his children. But Polly Bigelow didn't want Mary for a student. Told her that the school was full. Told her to go somewhere else.

The Bigelow Studio had black students, so Polly's refusal had nothing to do with race. Polly had determined that Mary's big butt, big legs, and sprouting chest didn't combine for a ballerina's body. Mary was built for modern dance, jazz dance, or any of those other bastardized forms, but not classical ballet. Not the incomparable art form to which Polly had devoted her life. And even a casual observer would be struck by the similarity of build among Polly's chosen: flat butts, flat chests, long legs, spidery arms, swan necks.

When Joe came through the door with his red-eyed daughter, Polly repeated her claim that the school presently wasn't accepting new students and recommended another school. But none of that satisfied Joe. Out of the corner of his eye, he had monitored Mary as Polly Bigelow spoke. No show of heartening from the girl. Joe knew that Mary had matured out of her childhood belief that Daddy could fix any situation. But a father does not welcome the end of such worship and forever seeks the opportunity to prove that he still possesses some of the old magic. That's why he had overruled Mary's request to drop the matter and had taken her back to the school.

Joe Kingsley and Polly Bigelow were like members of the United Nations Assembly without their translation headphones: they just were not speaking the same language. Joe's offer to pay tuition months in advance did nothing to change Polly's mind. Nor did his assurance that Mary would not be a discipline problem. It was a wonder that shouts didn't ring out sooner than they did.

Frances decided the matter. Stepping between Polly and Joe, she placed her hands on Mary's shoulders and congratulated her on being the school's newest student. Frances's assertiveness was so untypical that Polly was taken aback; however, Polly considered it gauche to argue in front of others, so the two retreated to the office. Only Frances returned to speak to Joe and Mary. Mary was in. Frances, a polio survivor who was physically incapable of dancing ballet, could not tolerate the injustice of denying a perfectly healthy person the opportunity to learn to dance. So Polly begrudgingly relented, mostly because Frances had asked so little over the years. First and last, the Bigelows were twins, and no chunky black girl and her father were going to drive a wedge between them.

From the beginning Polly Bigelow was a taskmaster with Mary, constantly carping. Mary's *pirouettes* weren't whirled gracefully enough, her *pliés* weren't dipped deeply enough, her *sautés* weren't leapt high enough—forever something wrong. It was easier to get change for a penny than to pry a compliment from patrician Polly. But the more she rode Mary in an attempt to break her, the more the girl buckled down.

Throughout those first weeks, there was nowhere that Mary didn't ache. She toddled on complaining calves and throbbing thighs; her knees ached as though they had undergone surgery; her feet cramped like angry fists; her waist was a wrung washcloth; her shoulders were leaden cannonballs; and her buttocks spasmed as though poked by a cattle prod. Despite it all, she was happy, motivated, and determined.

Joe was Mary's cheerleader. Upon coming home from work, he would head straight for his recliner, kissing or hugging anyone in his path. From his throne—shoes off, feet up—he would shed his concerns. Mary would entertain Joe with her dancing. Joe gave his unsplintered attention, always selectively blind to her stumbles, no matter how much they were made obvious by her gestures of vexation.

By the summer of 1967, Mary had been studying dance for a year, and Polly assigned her a starring role in one of the dances in the school's annual recital. She was to dance as a butterfly, fluttering among leotard-clad flowers. The choreography called for the flowers to scatter at first and to withhold their nectar, then for an individual flower to join her in step and to lift her in symbolic drink. That flower was to then spin her to the next blossom, who would repeat the ritual with stylized variations. And so it was to go until each flower had been paired with the butterfly. As far as Mary was concerned, this terpsichorean fluff was the equivalent of *The Nutcracker*.

Mary's costume was a chiffon gown that draped almost to the ankles and was the color of a dandelion in May. But as a butterfly costume, it was missing one essential—*the* essential: wings. Frances Bigelow would correct that defect. She kept a sewing machine on the premises just for such recurring needs. She took some fabric that was gossamer and iridescent, and sewed it between the armpits and waist of the gown. When Mary donned it for tryout, it responded to her movements in gentle, breeze-stirred, undulating flappings, imitative of the flight of a butterfly.

Mary had been more than satisfied and was ready to take her costume home, but Frances decided on an additional artistic touch as she watched her handiwork in motion. Frances wanted the wings to be spotted. So after Mary took off the costume, Frances hung it in the closet. And that's why, hours later, early Sunday morning, July 23, 1967, Mary's gown was at the Bigelow School of Dance when the riots started.

The catalyst had been the cops' raid of an after-hours joint on Twelfth Street, notorious then as a haven for prostitution and drugs. A restive group had assembled, drawn by the fleet of police cars. The details of how the riot started will forever vary, but taunts flew, then rocks, bottles, and other missiles. Anger, despair, disdain, frustration, and whatever other emotions the crowd internalized, all combined in a brew that flowed through the area as if from an overturned cauldron. Soon it wouldn't be the dawn that would chase away the night's darkness but the deadly illumination from buildings aflame.

Mary learned from her mother, Sophie, that the family would not be going to church that morning. "A riot is going on," she explained.

"What's a riot, Mama?" Mary asked.

"Girl, must you have a question for everything?" Sophie responded irritably, worried over the safety of her husband, who had been called back to work in the middle of the night. Then she composed herself and gave Mary a proper explanation. She and the children spent the morning watching live TV coverage. At times the sirens and gunfire heard from the television were joined by what the family heard right there in the neighborhood.

Two days later, Sophie released the children from house confinement and told them that they were not to leave the yard. Like the overwhelming majority of Detroiters, the Kingsleys had played no part in the disturbances. "Unless you want your hides tanned, you'll do like you been told," warned Sophie.

"Yes, Mama," said Junior.

"I'm waiting to hear from you, Mary."

"Yes, Mama."

"And if I told you once, I told you a hundred times not to clean your brush and leave the hair lying around. Didn't I, young lady?"

"Uh-huh."

"One of these days a bird is going to get hold of some and make a nest with it. Then you'll have splitting headaches, like nobody's business." Sophie was a bit superstitious.

"Sorry, Mama."

"Now get your butts outside. Your daddy and me want some peace and quiet." Joe, who had been working double shifts since the start of the riots, had the day off.

Perched on the front steps, Mary and Junior watched looters carrying food, clothing, appliances—you name it—from area establishments. On the other side of the street, Valerie Boswell, the sun reflecting off a bald spot from a recent hair-pulling fight with Mary, was quick-footing it to her house along with her mother. Both had armfuls of clothes. Valerie tripped on a dangling sleeve and almost fell. As she reclaimed her balance, she was rankled by Mary's laughter. Seizing upon the first revengeful thing that she could think of, Valerie gave the news to Mary with mean-spirited delight.

"They did a number on your stupid old dance school, and I hope they burn it down."

The costume! From all of Mary's colliding thoughts, that one came to the forefront. She reasoned that neither the Bigelows nor the students were in danger because the school wasn't open in the morning. But the costume was in peril and had to be rescued. It was representative of Polly Bigelow's long-withheld acceptance, was emblematic of hundreds of hours of practice to become accomplished enough to star in her own dance, and was a token of the backing she had received from her family, especially her father.

Mary sprang from the steps in preparation for an all-out sprint, but Junior grabbed her arm. She tussled against his grip and resisted the urge to kick him in the shins. Junior, meanwhile, was hurriedly reminding Mary of the punishment she would receive for disobeying their parents. He was suckered into believing it had worked when Mary ceased struggling. He released her. She shot down the street, legs moving like pistons.

Junior's first instinct was to shout out after Mary, who already had a sizable head start, but that could bring their mother rushing to investigate the commotion, and Junior was no tattletale. Mary always had been fleet-footed; Junior was more so, but it took him a block and a half to catch her.

She cried buckets as he began to pull her back toward the house. Her tears weakened his resolve. They were away from the house and probably already in big-time trouble. And from their present location, they could be at the school in a little while. What to do?

Junior signaled his surrender with a look, and they began a fast jog in the direction of the Bigelow School of Dance, or what might be left of it.

He went in through the large storefront window, which had been busted out by looters. Those who had come before him had ransacked the place and made off with everything of any real value. He had found the dress lying crumpled and trampled on the floor of the small closet where Mary had told him it would be. Upon being surprised by the cops, Junior halted when ordered, dropped the dress when ordered, made no menacing gestures; still, he was blown off his feet by a shotgun blast.

Mary, who'd been on lookout, had heard the screeching brakes and had seen the four cops pour out of the squad car, but there had been no time to warn her brother. She had dropped to her knees, cradled Junior's head in her arms, and hysterically begged the corpse not to die. Her pleadings were interrupted when the cop who had shot Junior slammed the butt of his shotgun into her face, opening it above the lip. She keeled over unconscious.

She was revived by her father, who was kneeling over her, wiping her face with a wet cloth supplied by a neighborhood resident. She managed "I'm sorry, Daddy," but her grogginess and opened lip made her speech unintelligible. The killer cop stood over father and daughter. Mary's blurred vision couldn't make out his gloat, and registered him only as a hulkish apparition. Seconds later, his tossed blond hair came into focus and thereafter his name badge: "R. Carson." Another cop pulled the rookie away and said, "Don't fret it, Reed. These people got what they deserved."

SIXTEEN

Eugene Shaw raised the freshly painted canvas overhead and slammed it to the floor. He stomped it repeatedly, his foot slipping in the wet paint. With a violent jerk, he tore the canvas off its frame. His jaws shimmied as he expelled anguished yelps through clenched teeth. He ripped the canvas in two. Crumpling the halves into a ball, he hurled it.

Eugene scanned wild-eyed about his studio. There were other works that deserved the same fate. His criterion for choosing them was harshly simple: whatever didn't measure up to his established excellence had to go. That meant most of what he'd painted the last several months. Some, although still in his possession, already had been sold at hefty prices. Anyone not satisfied with a refund could see him in court.

One offending painting remained hanging on a wall. He rushed to it and with a scraping sweep of his arms sent it cartwheeling. Running, he caught up to it and launched it with a kick. Other paintings, as if to escape, cowered interspersed among stacks that contained "real" art. He rifled stack after stack, extracting the pretenders and slinging them over his shoulder, unconcerned with whatever they crashed against. And the ones hiding draped on easels fared no better after he yanked their covers.

It was a frenzied and nonstop roundup, and most of the victims suffered further defacing before being dumped into a single pile in the middle of the floor.

Reality had stormed Eugene's fortress of denial, and present measures were meant to stem the invasion. Almost like the physical laws that prevent two objects from occupying the same space at the same time, the denied and the undeniable can't peacefully coexist. So destroy the undeniable. Destroy the evidence.

Eugene Shaw, artist, had achieved fame' and fortune because of what he had come to think of as his third eye. It visualized colors with vividness and inventiveness that shocked some and delighted others but never failed to elicit a strong response. It did so with kaleidoscopic virtuosity and computerlike quickness. And it imprinted its visualizations and creations on Eugene's memory so reliably that he easily reproduced them. This third eye, remarkably wired for color, was Eugene's mind's eye. And, to his horror, he was certain that it had developed a cataract, spreading and hardening, blurring his vision.

What used to be effortless now triggered migraines that made him wish he had a second pair of hands to hold both a throbbing head and a spasmodic stomach. The pain, pressure, and nausea left him weakened and drained. And for all that suffering, the images that came forth were anemic. They weren't the stuff of the hue, tint, shade, and tone that he could harmonize with his signature mastery. His human figures weren't the reds, bronzes, golds, purples, and blues that so many times he had melded to convey something as subtle as a blush, or that tempted viewers to touch the canvas expecting the depicted person to register a beating pulse. What he could summon now was better suited to a different type of painter, one who slops a flat coat on a wall.

It perplexed him that no one else seemed aware of his affliction. Maybe it was a testament to how great his talent was that it could erode as it had and still his works were in demand. Eugene suspected that part of the explanation could be that most people were ignorant about art. But the ignorant are just slower. Eventually even they would see him as the has-been he was quickly turning into. Time for a strategy.

Eugene decided that until he could attach a cause and cure to his deterioration, he would not paint, would not subject himself to its wracking effects. His third eye was indispensable. He would never sink to re-creating merely through the lens of his other two eyes. That would be about as artistic as snapping a Polaroid. He would turn to other artistic endeavors—sketching, for example. He was a highly talented sketch artist anyway. It required only visualizations in shades of black and white, an ability that seemed to have sharpened in direct proportion to his fading ability with colors. And consistent with shades of black and white, there was a silver lining to this gray cloud: he could have more time to devote to the mission.

But first there was the matter of the evidence. As he studied the hateful, mangled pile of paintings, his mind a jumble, his chest heaving from his hyperventilation, his dominant thought was to set a roaring bonfire.

SEVENTEEN

Larkin O'Neal had been Eugene's best—and only—childhood friend. Eugene's protected and pampered life changed abruptly when he started school, and it would have been insufferable had it not been for Larkin.

Back then segregation ruled in Bent Fork, and busing was something done by restaurant workers clearing tables. Black students attended all-black schools in all-black neighborhoods. Eugene had been no exception, and was the only child at the recently renamed Martin Luther King Elementary School whose birth certificate read "Father: Unknown Caucasian."

Throughout his earliest school years, Eugene had been jerked by the continuing intraracial backlash against fair-skinned blacks, as mantras such as "Black Is Beautiful" and "I'm Black and I'm Proud" elevated the status of darker skin, coarser hair, and fuller features. Nor did it help matters that connotations of the terms "sister" and "brother" could be as much about color as about race. In Bent Fork one had to go to a white school to find a child who looked like Eugene. And he caught hell for that. From all sides. He couldn't even find acceptance among the other fair-skinned children, many of whom struggled with their own problems of color consciousness and didn't need the complication of his friendship. But for a time there was always Larkin.

In the summer of 1975 the eavesdropping Eugene discovered that Isaac was his biological father, so he started the third grade that fall loaded down with more than his customary baggage. The relationship between Isaac and Gertrude had turned arctic, and as children of warring parents are known to do, Eugene blamed himself. And it made the hurtful barbs—"Yo' daddy was a cracker and yo' mama blackberry jam"—salt the already painful wounds. Eugene felt more isolated than ever. Thank goodness for Larkin.

On a sun-splashed Saturday morning, he and Larkin were having a rock-skipping contest at Olsen Pond. The youngsters worked up a thirst and took a time-out to chug Larkin's soda. Larkin took the first swig, long and guzzling. He handed the bottle to Eugene, who reduced the contents to a corner. The bottle was passed back to Larkin for last takes.

The boys' first awareness of the presence of Jimmy Lee Polk and his son, Bubba, was when the elder Polk descended upon them like sudden nightfall, knocking the bottle from Larkin's lips before slinging the boy to the ground. Then Polk glared at Eugene, whose momentary indecision had cost him any opportunity to outrun the burly redneck. Polk stomped to him, and Eugene readied himself for similar mistreatment.

"Boy, didn't your folks learn you no better than to drink behind niggers? I'd sooner see you lap from the same dish as my hounds," scolded Polk. He and Bubba had been running a pair of bird dogs.

"I am not a nigger," protested Larkin, still on the ground. He got up and, with pride and defiance, added, "I'm black." He was short for a ten-year-old, but husky.

"Hear that, Bubba? This here spearchucker wants to be addressed just so." His smile made all the more ugly by snuff-stained teeth, Polk started toward Larkin, but Polk's every step forward was matched by a backward one by Larkin. The dogs, tails going like high-speed windshield wipers and their noses sniffing the ground, crossed in front of Polk. "I got half a mind," he said—a true statement of itself—"to see whether my hounds like the taste of coon."

"I got him, Daddy." Bubba, sixteen, his face pockmarked with acne, had sneaked up from behind and trapped Larkin in a bear hug.

"Good work, Bubba," said Polk. He grabbed Larkin by his large Afro. "You listen to me, jungle bunny. You speak with respect to your superiors, or else keep your trap shut." He yanked Larkin's hair for punctuation.

Larkin bleated in pain, then gained his release with a swift kick to Polk's shin. But almost immediately he was back in Polk's clutches, large dirty hands clamped against the sides of his head. Polk's mouth was contorted into a growl as bestial as any ever flashed by the dogs. He gave Larkin's head a sharp twist to the left. It made the sound of a twig being broken underfoot. The boy went limp, and Polk let him slump to the ground.

"Round up them hounds, Bubba, and git to the truck." Polk sounded scared. "Have a rush about you, boy."

"Come on, Daddy," the running Bubba called urgently.

"Be with you directly," shouted Polk. His hands were trembling and sweat trickled down his spine, but first he had to attend to Eugene, who was so traumatized that he couldn't summon his voice to plead for his life. But Eugene was not in the danger he feared. "Let this be a lesson to you, boy. Stay with your own kind." Polk gripped Eugene by the shoulders, lowered himself to eye level, and, emitting whiskey fumes, resumed speaking. "As far as that thing over there," he said, referring to Larkin, "you ain't seen nothin' and you don't know nothin'."

Eugene, watching the Polks' rusting truck barrel down the road, tailpipe farting soot, stood shivering in the sun, surely from terror, but also from having wet his pants. He crept over to Larkin, and it was as if he were viewing death for the first time, despite all he'd seen of Isaac's business. For this was different: no peaceful, sleep-like, dignified repose. Larkin lay facedown in dirt, limbs sprawled, eyes open. The image seared onto Eugene's brain. Eugene's legs refused to support him any longer, and he dropped to his knees on his way down to pressing his face against Larkin's. Then came the torrent of tears.

No child should ever have to feel guilt over being alive, but it was survivor's guilt that gripped Eugene, squeezing tightly, restricting blood flow to his brain, disabling him from sorting his tangled thoughts.

He'd been spared because Polk believed him to be white, but gratitude felt so indecent. And in his bowels he felt a dishonorable sense of advantage. Credit his relatives—the Shaws—and their words and behavior. Give Gertrude credit, also, for such loving comments as "Pay no mind to those mean, nappy-headed children. They're just jealous of your good hair."

Did he believe himself to be better than the others? Better than Larkin, even? If not, why hadn't he spoken? He'd had time to append an "I'm black, too" to Larkin's declaration. He would have known how to explain that he had one black parent. Would have made all the difference to Polk, would have meant two of a kind drinking from the same bottle. Under those circumstances, Polk wouldn't have cared if he had caught the boys kissing. Eugene knew men like Polk subscribed to the ridiculous theory that one drop of black blood makes one black. Biracial was a contradiction; it was as impossible to be half-white as it was to end up with half-clean water by mixing distilled and swamp varieties. Eugene had been a Judas to Isaac's preachings that he should be proud of his black heritage, and his silence had caused his best friend's death.

When Sheriff Hershel Boone came calling on Jimmy Lee, based on Eugene's descriptions of the Polks, their dogs, and their truck, he advised Lee to take the charges seriously, as one good ol' boy to another. The phone calls warning Isaac that the same thing could happen to Eugene were nightmarish. He began taking his son to school and bringing him home. In between, Eugene was virtually under house arrest. It lasted less than two weeks, until the Shaws' house was gutted by firebombs. The next month, Isaac moved his family to Detroit.

Although he has never been told, Eugene knew the reason for the sudden relocation.

More than twenty years later, he made his first and only return trip to Bent Fork. It happened several months before the murder of Thomas Kincaid. His homecoming was surreal. He didn't visit any of the few Shaws who still lived in Bent Fork. Didn't trust himself not to reveal that he was one of them by blood. He walked the streets of downtown, studying white faces, searching for resemblances, wondering whether any were related to his mother, Millie. After all, he had heard Isaac confess that Millie claimed to have a sister who lived in town. Meanwhile, he passed by Parsons Realty, Parsons Hardware Store, and the National Bank of Bent Fork, where the Parsons family were majority owners—all without attaching any significance to it.

He wandered the streets of the black side of town, endured the stares and incredulous looks of the women out hanging wash who pulled their children toward them and shielded them behind a thrust hip and leg. Eugene walked until he found what he was looking for—a weed-choked lot and the collapsed foundation of his burnt-out childhood home.

Eugene had come back to Bent Fork weeks too late. But having suffered so long and traveled so far, he wasn't going to accept the disappointing discovery without proof. He had gotten it earlier with a trip to the cemetery. Jimmy Lee Polk had died and gone to hell. Cirrhosis of the liver, most likely; Eugene hoped that Jimmy had suffered before dying. Eugene wouldn't be able to exact the revenge that he had come for. He would have to settle for second best.

Through quiet inquiry, Eugene learned the address of a lawyer who had a reputation for championing the rights of the underrepresented and the downtrodden. He walked into the ramshackle storefront office that stood alongside a long-abandoned hardware store and a luncheonette that hadn't survived the fast-food chains out on the bypass. Eugene was greeted by a middle-aged man, a behemoth in a cheap, frumpy suit, with a face etched by laugh lines.

"Howdy. Name's Charlie."

After the handshake, Eugene identified himself. "John White."

"What can I do for y'all?" asked Charlie as he motioned Eugene to go around a partition and have a seat across from his desk. "Coffee? My secretary is out to lunch."

"I saw her leave," said Eugene. "No coffee. I come to discuss a hate crime."

Charlie's eyes narrowed in interest. "Tell me about it."

Eugene said, "A black kid was murdered by a racist." Then he fell silent.

On his desk Charlie kept a small American flag that was mounted on a round stand. He reached across and slid it to the side in order to get an unobstructed view of Eugene. "I'm waiting for the details, Mr. White. And might you not be better served at the sheriff's office or the prosecuting attorney?"

Eugene responded by whisking the American flag from the desk and driving the pointed end of the staff repeatedly into the heart of Charlie "Bubba" Polk.

EIGHTEEN

The week after the Livingstone murder, Inspector Newberry called Mary and Frank into his office. "Brief me on the Oreo killings. I'm sure Upton will be shining a flashlight up our asses until it's solved." Newberry weighed his next comments before speaking. "I'm just as sure Upton is telling the mayor every detail. This thing can lose votes. Goddamn politics." Newberry's voice and facial expression registered the disdain he felt.

Mary said, "First, Inspector, let me tell you my name for this case. Cookie Cutter." Newberry seemed neither impressed nor curious. She went on to explain the name. "Cookie as in Oreo. Cutter as in knifing."

Newberry remained impassive. "Yeah, that's real creative."

Mary said, "Give me a second, Inspector. I had another reason for that name. Think about what a real cookie cutter does. It makes identical shapes out of dough. If Kincaid and Livingstone were killed because they didn't think and behave—quote, unquote—black . . ."

Newberry beat her to the conclusion, not confident that she would be as brief as he was about to be. "Then their killer has a cookie-cutter mentality. Got it. Now brief me."

Chancing Newberry's wrath with something short of a direct response, Mary said, "Please don't blow up, but there's something that I must say first." She spoke fast when she said, "I think the public ought to be informed about this one, Inspector."

"Makes no difference what you think," Newberry countered.

"You don't violate policy. Hurry up and solve the damn case, and that'll take care of the public's right to know. And even if you were given the green light, we might not have enough to stuff into a meaningful statement anyway."

Mary's expression turned into a half-pout. "Police warn about a serial rapist so possible victims can take precautions. I was thinking that the same thing should be done here, that's all."

"What should we say?" Newberry asked. He rose from his chair, stuffed his hands into his back pockets, and arched his back. "All Uncle Toms be on the lookout? Who's to say who's an Oreo? There's a lot of subjectivity involved."

"I agree," Frank said. "Take Livingstone, for example. Solid family man, according to his wife. Good provider. Good father. Kids in college. Big house in the suburbs. The wife said that in no way was he ashamed of being black. Even Kincaid's family and friends claim that he was totally different from how he came across on the radio."

"I don't want the conversation to be all editorial," Newberry said. He pulled out his chair and sat down again. "Let the next words I hear be my briefing."

Mary said, "I think the killer is someone who looks like he swims in the mainstream. Someone who doesn't look threatening."

"Why?" asked Newberry.

"Let's start with the fact that he was able to get to Kincaid without alarming him."

"But Ellery's theory was—"

"I know what his theory was," injected Mary with polite assertiveness. "With all due respect, Inspector, is Ellery going to head this investigation from his grave, or am I going to conduct it?"

"Point taken," said Newberry. "What else are you going on?"

"There's Livingstone." Mary's voice rose in volume and speed. "He bought a bucket of chicken from the joint across from the Belle Isle Bridge—the girl at the drive-through remembered him. But the bones in the garbage didn't coincide with the amount of food found in his stomach. I say the killer ate with him."

"The killer could have eaten afterward," Newberry said. "Maybe killing worked up his appetite."

"Then consider Livingstone's size. Why no signs of a struggle to subdue such a large person?" she queried.

"The killer could have taken him by surprise," countered Newberry.

Mary wasn't finished. "He was killed in the lower quarters. What are the odds that the killer surprised him there and Livingstone never knew he was aboard?"

"Livingstone could have been asleep just before being awakened. Maybe the killer wore boat shoes. I understand they're quiet," said Newberry.

Mary warmed to the challenge of Newberry playing devil's advocate. "Wrap all of your could-haves into one theory and you have one improbable theory. And you know that."

"Fine," said Newberry. "Let's say, for the time being, that the killer is somebody who doesn't look the part. That narrows it down to ninety-eight percent of the population."

"This might narrow it further: Every black person that anyone remembers at the Yacht Club that night has been accounted for, either as an employee, member, guest, or whatever. And all of them can account for their time. Hey, let's face it, a black person can sneak into the White House easier than he can get past the Yacht Club gate without proving he's supposed to be there."

"Wait a minute, Mary," Frank said. He tugged at the cuffs of his shirt and pulled at his shirt collar as if to ready himself. "Are you saying you think that the killer is white?" He turned to Newberry. "I shouldn't be blindsided by my partner. She had me believing that we were hunting a black suspect. She was holding out on me."

"No, I wasn't. It's possible that the killer is white, but that fit doesn't feel right."

"So we're back to a black suspect?" asked Frank.

"Never left," said Mary. "Even though a black person would have had to materialize out of air, then escape back into it, not to have been noticed by anybody."

Newberry coughed and cleared his throat. "This is not the same question, but you totally reject the possibility that the Oreo cookie is a trick to send us chasing a bogus motive?"

Mary looked at each man in turn before responding. "I'm convinced that both murders were planned. If Kincaid and Livingstone weren't killed for being Oreos, then they were killed because they had something else in common. But so far no link between them has surfaced, except that they'd both been criticized for selling out."

Newberry asked, "Do you think the killer will strike again?"

"I don't think he's through, Inspector. That's my short answer."

She thought that she saw an opening, and she tried to barge through it. "And if I'm right, the public ought to be warned."

"That's a nonsubject," said Newberry.

Frank tried to hide his smug grin, and averted his eyes from Mary's. "There's a back door to the Yacht Club. A ferry that operates from the Jefferson Avenue Marina. Some Yacht Club members dock at Jefferson because no slips are available at Belle Isle, and ferry over. Though I don't understand what sense it makes to restrict entry from the island when anybody can enter by ferry."

"The DYC probably thinks that the riffraff is more likely to crash by gate than by boat," theorized Newberry.

Without knowing that they were discussing the way that Eugene actually had gotten to the DYC, Frank said, "But guess what, nobody interviewed remembers a black person taking the ferry that night."

Mary said, "That's the wall we keep butting our heads against, Inspector. Black men are not invisible. If anything, they're conspicuous, menacing-looking or not. But I don't have to preach that to you, of all people."

"Don't try to talk over my head," said Frank.

"We wouldn't do that, would we, Mary?" For the first time in weeks, Newberry's tone was light, his speech closer to banter than directive.

"Not me, Inspector." Mary shrank back in mock horror.

"Mary's your first black female partner, Frank?"

"My first black partner, period. But, hey, it don't bother me none. I'm just trying to do my job."

"So far, Mary, has Frank been a help or a hindrance?"

Mary studied her partner for a few seconds, then asked Newberry, "Are those my only two choices?"

NINETEEN

An all-white jury had taken only forty minutes to convict Porter Jones of Annie Parsons's murder. The judge sentenced him to life. Porter's wife, Hattie, had died of diabetes four months prior. And at eleven years of age, their only child, little Precious Jones—shy, thin, pigtailed—began a hellish odyssey that, thirty years later, had created a felon with a long rap sheet.

Her downward spiral started when a Greyhound bus driver identified the picture of Annie shown to him by Sheriff Boone and confirmed that she had ridden from Montgomery to Bent Fork. Later, young Billy Owens, who Sam Parsons believed had impregnated Annie, swore to the sheriff that he didn't know her whereabouts. Eventually Boone came knocking at the home of Porter Jones. It was widely known that Porter's daughter, Precious, was Annie's best friend.

Porter hadn't known about Annie's visit. He had been working the cotton fields, his daily dawn-to-dusk routine, and Annie had left before his return. He also was in the fields the day after, when Boone interrogated Precious. Innocently, Precious told Boone that Annie, indeed, had paid a visit. The information sent Boone sniffing around like a hunting dog with cleared sinuses.

Under Precious's bed he found the straight razor that Porter used once a week before church. And it had blood on it. As did the floor. Not much. Drops. Also under the bed was a bloodstained handkerchief. It was one of a three-piece set that Precious got for Christmas. Boone grabbed Precious by her willowy arms and roughly examined her for cuts, even under her dress. There were none. He swung her around to face him, pointed a knobby-knuckled finger in her face, and demanded an explanation for the blood. She couldn't give one.

How could she when she had been in the kitchen, preparing sugar water and a mayonnaise sandwich for a hungry, wailing Annie, whom she'd left in the bedroom? Annie went to use the bathroom and found the razor. She brought it back to the bedroom and made several hesitant slashes on her wrist before the pain and sight of blood made her abandon further attempts. She wrapped her wrist with one of Precious's handkerchiefs. It quickly became soaked, and she hid it and wrapped her wrist with a second from the set.

By the time Precious returned, Annie had climbed out the window. She saw Annie angling across the yard. When Precious called to her, Annie extended an arm, palm up, like a traffic cop, pleading with her friend not to follow. And off the other palm, she blew a kiss good-bye.

Standing stiff under Boone's glowering gaze, Precious was too scared to lie and too naive to foresee the consequences from telling the truth. Her tears began to roll, but Boone was unmoved. She told him what she remembered about Annie's visit, including something he was unprepared for: Annie had said that the man who made her pregnant was a Negro. Precious didn't know his name, only that Annie had said that he was an older man.

Porter Jones was one good meal past skinny. His weathered forehead was as furrowed as a newly plowed field. Because of a bad back, he couldn't stand completely erect. His speech was slow and simple. When he looked up from his tilling and saw Boone approaching, he pulled a rag from his coveralls and wiped his hands, even though the possibility was remote that Boone would offer a handshake.

Boone took Porter to town for questioning. Porter denied any knowledge about Annie being at his home, and was released that night. Days later, he was arrested and charged with the murder of Annie Parsons.

The State's evidence was that the blood was Annie's type and not that of either Porter or Precious. The State charged that Porter's motive was to avoid prison for statutory rape. The Green County prosecutor would have insisted on a much stronger case if it hadn't been made clear to him that Sam Parsons was willing to cash in every one of his many political chips to get the case to trial speedily. Parsons might have been spurred, in part, by the growing criticism that he was partially responsible for what happened to Annie for having permitted his daughter to socialize with the Jones family as if they were equals. According to those minds, equality wasn't possible, since Hattie had been Parsons's maid and Porter one of his sharecroppers. Then again, Sam Parsons wasn't the type who'd publicly admit that the slightly slow-witted Precious was the ideal playmate for his daughter, for reasons embedded in guilt and shame.

In Bent Fork, Jimmy Collins was a criminal attorney, in more than one meaning of that phrase. Soon after the court appointed him to defend Porter, Collins was mailed a bank receipt stating that his mortgage had been paid off. It was an incidental that Collins didn't disclose to the court. Nor did he disclose that he hadn't made such a payment. Nor that the bank was controlled by the Parsons family. Collins, however, wouldn't be around long enough to provide the bank a return on its investment; while preening before the cameras, he lost his footing, fell down the courthouse steps, and sustained a paralyzing injury to the spine.

Buford McManus, from the town of Boligee, was appointed to replace Collins. He was elderly, bald on top with a ring of long white locks, in the style of Benjamin Franklin. And unlike Collins, it mattered to him that Porter be given a competent defense. McManus received contributions from collections taken in the black community, but, together, they paled against the $10,000 guilt money that Isaac Shaw donated anonymously.

It was too late for McManus to do anything about the jury. The racial makeup wasn't the whole problem. He had successfully defended blacks before all-white juries. What he didn't know, in this instance, was that all but three of the jurors had present or past business associations with the Parsons family.

During cross-examination McManus got Sam Parsons to admit that Annie was an independent-minded, often rebellious child. He got Parsons to admit that for two years and up to the time she was sent to live with her uncle Silas, Annie was seeing a psychiatrist, and that her school files spoke of sometimes fanciful and disassociative behavior. However, the judge sustained all of the prosecutor's objections to questions about the Parsons family's mental health history. So McManus had to settle for calling a shrink from Mobile who testified that Annie's claim of being impregnated by a Negro could have been the result of a disturbed imagination, and that her disappearance could have been an intentional act of defiance. Another expert for the defense testified about what portion of the population had Annie's blood type and that there was no scientifically based proof that the evidence was her blood. None of it mattered to the jury.

Precious first went to live with Hattie's youngest sister, Carla, in Selma. That lasted a year, after which Precious was sent packing to Porter's brother, Harold, in Tuscaloosa. That lasted even less time, because Harold went to jail for selling phony insurance, leaving Precious to an orphanage. Dolly Hawthorne, the headmaster of the orphanage, developed a fondness for Precious that she liked to express during late-night visits to the girl's room. By the time Precious was fifteen, she was regularly being penetrated with various objects and being forced to administer orally on Hawthorne.

The debilitatingly shy Precious remained at the orphanage until, at age seventeen, she received word that Porter had been strangled in his prison cell. No more letter writing between father and daughter, which, over the years, had been her lone tenuous grip on sanity. She had written many letters to him asking for his forgiveness for whatever contribution she might have made to his imprisonment. He had written even more letters back, telling her that she was not to blame for anything. She was never fully convinced, and with his death the unfinished job came completely undone. She ran away from the orphanage.

Sonny Hudson, wearing a red jumpsuit with a collar as wide as the wingspan of a jumbo jet, was scouting the Birmingham bus station for new talent when he saw Precious. As a hyena recognizes wounded prey and then pounces, Hudson went after Precious. That night he took her to an apartment shared by two of his "associates," where she was fed, given a change of clothes, permitted to bathe, and provided a sofa to sleep on.

Three days later, Precious turned her first trick. The middle-aged white man was clumsy, but most important, he was quick. Five years she would be with Sonny, until he was shot dead by a competitor. By then she was a junkie. Precious took to drugs readily because they stole her sensibilities, allowed her to endure the unnatural acts and abuse, whether from the johns or Sonny.

After Sonny's death she tried to freelance, only to find out that without the protection of being known as "somebody's property," other pimps and whores felt free to whip her ass anytime they caught her trespassing on their territory. So throughout her twenties, she went through a string of "managers." That period also was marked by a series of arrests for solicitation, possession, and passing bad checks. They netted her a series of jail terms, the longest being fifteen months.

When she was thirty-two, she looked more than a decade older. She had once had a missing front tooth that she replaced with a gold one, but had ended up swallowing it when her pimp slapped it down her throat. Her arms and legs were pocked with needle tracks. Hygiene had become a distant memory. She had been dumped by her last pimp because too many johns passed her up for better-looking whores. It was at that low point that she met Charlie Beamon, who would show her that the bottom was yet to come.

Charlie wasn't one of those prissy, choosy types. He walked right up to Precious, as though she was the high-priced spread, and asked how much. The two addicts began an association that led to their living together in a roach-infested rat trap. Charlie stole anything that wasn't nailed down. Precious, wearing a pound of makeup and avoiding well-lit areas, did a low but steady volume of whoring. Charlie would lurk nearby as her protector.

They combined their professions one night, and it resulted in a man getting his skull bashed in. Precious lured him into an alley, having agreed to a five-dollar blow job. Charlie, who was to roll him, was too heavy-handed with the metal pipe.

Had they examined the slain man's jewelry more carefully before pawning it, they would have noticed that his wedding band had his initials engraved on the inside, a fact that his wife told the police. The cops were working the possibility that the crime was committed to support a drug habit, so it was textbook procedure to canvass area pawnshops. They found the one where Charlie and Precious had taken their business. When they returned days later to pawn a radio, the pawnbroker stalled them while he went in the back and called the police.

The offer to Precious for her testimony against Charlie was a rap less than first-degree murder. She felt that compared to what her father was convicted on, the cops had an ironclad case. She hadn't seen Charlie since their arrest, and didn't know whether the cops were telling the truth about his stories implicating her. Her attorney told her that a trial, all things considered, would be dicey. She took the offer and received fifteen to twenty.

Nine years later, in the summer of 1997, Precious was released. The parole board was impressed with how she had served the time without incident—"a model prisoner" was the cliché used. Her parole officer got her a dishwashing job in Montgomery.

In prison, withdrawal from heroin had almost killed her. Detoxification had been long and torturous, as though her millions of brain cells were being liberated at the rate of one a day. And as each one was freed, she assigned it to unraveling her memories of that last visit from Annie Parsons. It wasn't until the year before her release, during a fitful sleep, that her recall came stampeding back. Up until then, details—sketchy and out of sequence—had come to her. They tumbled about in her head like socks in a dryer. But when clear recall finally struck, Precious remembered that she had not been the only one Annie had told about the mystery father, and most likely this other confidant had been told far more than she. Her memory as to the whereabouts of that other confidant had also come to her.

TWENTY

Mocha Springwell was examining the instrument, holding it between thumbs and forefingers, slowly rotating it at close eye level, her initial curiosity replaced by admiration for the fine craftsmanship. Then Eugene approached her silently from behind and snatched it, startling Mocha.

She recoiled and then relaxed. "Damn, Gene. I wasn't hurting the thing."

"Sorry if I scared you, Moe, but this is no toy. I shouldn't have had it lying out in the open like that."

"You could have cut yourself, mister."

"I'm fine."

"I've never seen a knife like that."

"It's a dagger."

"Where did you get it?"

Eugene held it in the palms of both hands as though it were a sacrificial offering. "I brought it back from my last trip to Africa. This is a replica. There's an interesting history attached to the original. You see, long ago—"

Mocha, recognizing the signs that Eugene was about to launch into one of his narratives, said, "Is this going to take long, Gene? Because I'm not up for another lecture about Africa. Can't we just get down to business?"

"There used to be this tribal king," resumed Eugene, ignoring Mocha's plea, "who personally executed traitors with a dagger like this one to send a message." He held the dagger outstretched, in illustration of his next comments. "The top of the handle is carved in the shape of a snake's head, and the wavy blade represents the snake's body. Get it?"

Mocha made no attempt to hide the exasperation in her voice. "Get what, Gene?"

With venom suited to the subject, Eugene said, "Traitors are two-legged snakes. Now do you see the justice?"

"What I see is a beautifully made dagger. Too bad it has an ugly history." She again tried to switch the focus to the reason she was there. Wedging out of her sandals, she said, "Can I undress now?"

"I'll even help you." He unbuttoned the back of her minidress and slipped it off her shoulders. It glided down her body and pooled on the wooden floor. She wasn't wearing a stitch of underwear.

The curves that ran wild over her dark body gave her the appearance of motion, even when she was stationary. She was twenty-four years old, and tall, with legs that seemed to go up past her waist and arms that seemed to go down past her knees. She was firm all over; gravity hadn't claimed anything yet. Her pubic area was neatly trimmed except for the lowermost hair, which hung like a hermit's beard. She had a coin slot of a navel, deeply recessed, that winked come-hither with every movement of her torso.

Her features crowded her face, as if that face originally had been a liquid surface and each feature had been a droplet that spread upon contact, barely escaping overlap. The bushy, naturally arched eyebrows almost met at center forehead. Her eyes were saucers, her nose long with valentine-shaped nostrils. Her wide, plump mouth was as lush as peak-of-the-season fruit, and looked as if it would squirt juice if kissed hard. Eugene liked it when she wore her thick, crinkled lion's mane pulled back, but she seldom did, fearing that her ears were too large.

Mocha had posed nude for Eugene scores of times, and he had kept—hoarded, actually—every painting of her, although he wouldn't acknowledge to himself why he refused to part with them, why he valued them so. All were in the building he owned that housed his studio and living quarters in Detroit's Warehouse District, a riverfront community of former industrial buildings that had been converted to lofts, restaurants, and nightspots.

Eugene's brick building was one of the most conspicuous in the area. It had two floors, but because of its twenty-foot ceilings, the building was as tall as four stories; it was nearly as wide as three side-by-side bungalows. The first floor was used for storage; otherwise it was merely a site of entrance. There were a front door, a side door, and a large sectional door covering the loading dock. The second floor could be reached by a freight elevator or by one of three stairways. The only windows were on the second floor. Two months prior, Eugene had had the entire exterior of the building painted black.

The apartment on the second floor consisted of a kitchen, bathroom, living room, and bedroom, and consumed roughly a third of the floor space. The rest served as a studio. The place was never without the smells of oils and acrylics, although faint because of the building's spaciousness.

A half-dozen easels stood about the place, a couple of them concealed by drapes. The floor, stools, and tables in the studio were stained and spotted, as though a rainbow had dripped on them. The place was a gallery of Eugene's depictions of black people: urban, rural, U.S., African, Caribbean, contemporary, historic, happy, sad, angry, solitary, assembled. What weren't Eugene's creations dealt mostly with black repression. There were, for example, announcements of slave auctions, photos of Ku Klux Klan lynchings, signs reading "Whites Only" and "Colored Only," and various Jim Crow–era product ads ("Ask any pickaninny: ain't our watermelons the juiciest"). Included among the memorabilia—sort of a collaboration—was a black lawn jockey that Eugene had outfitted with an Uncle Sam hat.

"For a while, I thought you had kicked me to the curb," said Mocha as she walked to the refrigerator and opened it.

"My favorite model?" Eugene asked incredulously. "Never."

"Then why the stretch since the last time you called?" She bent at the waist and stuck her head into the refrigerator. She stood again and put one hand on her hip and wagged her finger at him exaggeratedly. "Is this your imitation of the starving-artist routine?"

"I'm hardly starving. Just been too busy to go to the store. I take it the pizza didn't tempt you."

"That's what that is?" said Mocha, closing the refrigerator. "I couldn't tell for all the fuzzy mold." She turned her search to the cabinets, then spotted something on top of the shelf. She edged up on her toes to retrieve the package of cookies.

"No!" commanded Eugene. He sprinted to her, accidentally brushing her roughly as he slammed shut the cabinet.

It took Mocha a few seconds to collect herself. "That's twice," she said, referring to the dagger incident as well. "You're spooking me. I'm going to get dressed and leave."

"You don't want to do that, Moe." Now his demeanor was collected, his voice calm. He gently led her by the hand away from the cabinets. "Those things are so stale you would have broken a tooth. If you're hungry, I'll have something delivered. What do you have a taste for?"

She gazed at him warily but soon relented, despite his increasingly familiar pattern of outbursts and mood swings. Besides, she told herself, they never lasted for long and always were followed by a chivalrous gesture.

An hour later, Mocha, still naked, sat patting her full stomach. "A girl can work behind a meal like that," she said. "Where do you want me?"

He struggled with indecision. "Should I have you stand, sit, or lie? You see, I want to sketch just your genitals."

Mocha spoke her concern immediately. "You into porn now?"

"You know better." Then Eugene explained what he had in mind. "I want to do a series of sketches in tribute to the black female's vagina, which spawned mankind itself."

"Is this on the up-and-up?" Mocha searched his expression. No signs that he was joking.

"Completely. The white man's own science admits that we are the original race. I'll want you to sit for the first sketch." He fetched a wooden chair that had a cushioned seat.

He'd convinced her of his intents, but Mocha remained curious. "You never sketched me before. Why aren't you painting?"

Because he couldn't render her as he used to, when all she supplied was the outline, and the colors came from what he saw with his third eye. Because that eye couldn't separate the spectrum into its endless varieties, because every attempt wrecked him mentally and physically. Because, in contrast, seeing things in black-and-white wasn't painful. But he couldn't tell her those things.

"Some objects are better sketched" was his unimaginative lie, but it apparently sufficed. Soon the busy scratch of pencil on paper was all that broke the silence, as Mocha posed for the man who had bailed her out of jail years before.

It had been in the winter, and Eugene was at a red light when Mocha rammed his car from the rear, the bald tires of her jalopy no match for the icy road. Mocha and Eugene were exchanging driver's licenses when a squad car stopped to investigate. Mocha had outstanding tickets, was driving on a suspended license, had expired plates, and she had no insurance. Mocha ended up in the backseat of the squad car.

She was locked up less than an hour. When they released her, the "white boy" who had paid her bail was still waiting. Grateful but suspicious, she asked him what his angle was. He told her that after being struck by her car he had been struck by her beauty. He told her that he was an artist and that she could repay the bail by posing for him.

Back then Mocha was living hand-to-mouth. The year before, a fast-talking, flashy-dressing Ben Yeager had convinced her to leave Norwalk, Connecticut, and let his Ear-Love Studios make her a recording star. Unfortunately, a week after Mocha cut her "demo," Yeager died in a freak accident.

Eugene finished the first sketch. Two curved lines represented the waist to upper thigh, but Mocha's mound was rendered in exacting detail: delicate shading rode along the inner thighs, while thin, masterful pencil strokes faithfully reproduced her forest in all its variety—silky in some areas, wiry in others; bushy in some areas, sparse in others. He showed it to Mocha, announcing, "Behold what gave birth to mankind."

Mocha gazed for moments before speaking. "You are one talented son of a gun. That thing looks real enough to make a pervert take a sniff."

"Well, the Museum of Afro-American History will just have to post armed guards around it," he said, "because that's where the sketches will be exhibited."

"You're lying, aren't you? The museum is not about to exhibit drawings of my coochie. Tell me you're lying."

"I'm serious. I got juice with the museum," he boasted. "So does this look like porn to you?"

"Not at all," she admitted, then said, as suggestingly as jokingly, "I've been told before that my stuff down there is good, but this is the first time I've realized that it's a work of art, too."

"And I promise you," pledged Eugene, "that it will be on exhibit. You can count on it." Eugene started walking toward the living quarters, to his stereo equipment, saying en route, "Let's listen to some Anita Baker." Mocha's singing voice had a lot of Anita's deep, throaty seductiveness, and while Eugene resumed sketching, Mocha sang duets with her favorite recording artist. Two sketches later, he declared, "We'll call it quits for today."

Shortly thereafter, Mocha was standing clothed, with a check in her hand. The amount was too generous, but typical of how Eugene had always treated her. Mocha knew that what she was about to do was token, maybe a little dishonest, since she would have to fake it; but she wanted to do something for Eugene. She looked him squarely in the face and said, "The more I think about what you told me about the dagger and its history, the more I realize how interesting the whole thing is." The appreciative sparkle in his eyes gave her the motivation to take it further. "Tell me more."

TWENTY-ONE

"What happened to the mirrors?" Mocha Springwell stepped out of Eugene's bathroom. "How's a girl supposed to pretty herself around here?"

She smiled pleasantly. In contrast to the modeling session a couple of days earlier, this one had gone without incident: no snatching of daggers, no slamming of cabinet doors.

Eugene said, "I tossed them. Mirrors are a bad influence on an artist."

They all were gone: from the bedroom dresser; from the bathroom cabinet; even the handheld one that had hung on a hook in the bathroom. In each case, what remained was the empty frame.

"Huh?"

"They only reflect the outside. An artist should be about capturing what's below the surface. Being surrounded by mirrors corrupts that ability."

Mocha said, "Half of the time you leave me wondering where in the world you get such notions."

"I have my own philosophy."

"And it's one of a kind. That's for sure."

"Don't make fun of a brother," he said. He noticed Mocha's broad smile. "What are you grinning about?"

"Oh, I was remembering a time when hearing you refer to yourself as 'a brother' sounded so weird to me. But not anymore."

"See? You were suffering from 'mirroritis.' "

"I'm starting to understand you," she said. "That's scary."

"You think I'm crazy, don't you?"

"No. I think you're . . . ," she began, and after a moment's pause, "a dynamic brother."

He was already wearing paint-speckled jeans, but now he had the peacock's pride to go along with the colors. "Really, Moe?"

"Really."

"You don't know how good you just made me feel."

"And now that I'm in a confessing mood and all, I might as well tell you this other thing." She put a finger on his chest and traced slow circles. "I like you, Gene. And you know what way I'm talking about. I've felt this way for a while."

"Are you saying—"

She put a finger to his lips. "I'm not finished. You've never tried to put a move on me, and, I admit, I've wondered whether you simply weren't interested, or had somebody else, or whether you are . . ."

"Gay?"

"A lot of artists are."

"I'm straight. I never made a move because I didn't want to give you an excuse to stop modeling for me. And, here, all this time . . ." He raised his hands, palms up, and shrugged.

"We could have been getting down to business," said Mocha. "But that's the past. What now?"

They faced off for some pulse-quickening seconds—a tender type of "C'mon, make the first move. I dare ya." Then Eugene pulled her hand to him and flattened it against his chest. She felt the thumping of his heart keeping measure with her own throbs. Their lips touched and retreated a couple of times before settling into that first lingering kiss. It was followed by a random assortment of pecks, nibbles, and tongue-darting. Mostly the pace was slow and deliberate, each of them savoring the flavor and their shared rising passion. Bodies pressed and swayed, then hands were called into play. Eugene's roamed everywhere, eventually going under her dress. Once again his focus was the area between her legs, but this time not because he was sketching her. He cupped her firmly there, and she widened her stance in accommodation. He brushed the pubic hair with his palm, gently, the way a breeze does the top of a wheat field. And when he started twirling his index finger in it, he discovered it was moist with her arousal.

He continued to tease and arouse her, until Mocha thrust her hips forward and took his fingers inside her. Eugene felt Mocha tugging at his belt, unfastening it, and arched his back and stared at the ceiling. She fumbled into his briefs and withdrew his penis, which she caressed and stroked. She paused and extended her arms above her head. He pulled her dress up and off, as she writhed to assist him. In a moment Eugene had his clothes off as well. Refusing to break their tight embrace, they waddled to the bed, collapsing into a playful roll.

"What about protection?" Eugene asked.

"I'm not on birth control. Got a rubber?"

"Yes."

"I don't want to spoil the mood with talk of commitment, Gene, but I hope this is not a one-nighter. I could grow to love you."

"And I already love you."

"Gene, please. You don't have to say that now. Not if you really—"

His sudden, long kiss prevented her from finishing the sentence. "But I do mean it. I want you to be my Nubian queen."

Their lovemaking was extended, uninhibited, and gratifying. Afterward, they lay together, breathing hard: Mocha staring at the high ceiling, Eugene's head resting on her breasts. "Your Nubian queen?" she panted, recalling his comment.

"Believe it, Your Highness."

"I like the sound of that." She interlocked her fingers and stretched her arms. "I really, really like the sound of that."

TWENTY-TWO

Eugene paused outside the door. Each time he came to his office tucked in the administrative section of the Museum of Afro-American History, he was stopped short by the nameplate that hung there: "Mr. Eugene Shaw, Artist in Residence."

The largest museum in the world dedicated to African American culture, it was a brand-new construction, sprawling majestically within Detroit's Cultural Center, a cluster of museums and related cultural institutions. Nothing short of state of the art, it housed a 350-seat theater, a restaurant, a gift store, and a research library, in addition to exhibition halls, classrooms, multipurpose areas, and offices. And at its center was a stadium-size rotunda that was crowned by a skydome.

Financed by municipal bonds, the museum was owned by the city of Detroit and governed by a board of trustees appointed by the mayor. A political pawn from its conception, the museum spawned even more factions that bickered over such issues as the racial composition of the board, blacks' participation in the museum's design and construction, and the nature of the exhibits. Even the grand opening, scheduled for the week before the primary election in August, was politically driven. Mayor Clay would preside over opening ceremonies, which, incidentally, would be attended by the president of the United States, along with black dignitaries from around the world. It was the kind of photo opportunity that an incumbent relied on.

The museum's collection wasn't entirely devoted to art. All aspects of African American culture were represented in photos, letters, books, clothes, tools, inventions, and other artifacts. The museum board and staff were advised by a team of scholars, historians, and researchers. On occasion, Eugene consulted with them, whether just for his own knowledge or specifically in relation to art he was creating or evaluating for the museum's acquisition.

Eugene's journey to artist in residence had been along a twisting road that had its starting point in childhood. After Larkin O'Neal's murder, the guilt-ridden Eugene became reclusive, banishing himself to his room, even refusing most interaction with Isaac and Gertrude. He began to pass the solitude by doodling, which matured into drawings. By the time the family moved to Detroit, Isaac had taken note of his son's budding talents. The morose themes of Eugene's art, however, caused Isaac concern. A house engulfed by flames, occupants screaming from windows, was a recurrent theme, as were depictions of a boy in a coffin. What was odd about the latter—Isaac's being an undertaker notwithstanding—was that the boy was always sitting up in the coffin, looking angry, pointing an accusing finger at another boy standing to the side.

It was obvious to Isaac that the burning house was the family home that was torched in Bent Fork, and he deduced that the boy in the coffin was Larkin. He further deduced that the standing boy was Eugene, although he didn't know the full story. Not only had Eugene not told Isaac that he knew him to be his biological father, he also hadn't told him that Jimmy Lee Polk had spared his life only because he mistook him for white.

Isaac's every attempt to get the young Eugene to discuss his art was stonewalled. More than that, the boy took to destroying his works upon completion so that they wouldn't be discovered during Isaac's frequent searches of his room. Nonetheless, Isaac continued to encounter Eugene's works through his schoolteachers, who from time to time confiscated certain ones to discuss with him. The teachers' comments invariably addressed not the obvious talent but the disturbing subject matter, which by then had evolved into racial themes: brown-crayoned characters under various attacks from "flesh"-colored characters.

When Eugene was ten, Isaac placed him in psychiatric counseling. Dr. Travis Grandville, a black man whose wife Isaac had buried, conducted weekly sessions with Eugene over the next two years. He never was able to crack Eugene's shell surrounding events in Alabama, and eventually abandoned those efforts in favor of a strategy to get the boy to create art that had more levity.

And, gradually, over a course of two years of therapy, Eugene's art did lighten—or, at least, what he permitted others to see. All the while his talent for portraits was burgeoning, and he occasionally presented his teachers with flattering portraits, drawn mostly from memory.

Eugene's high school and college years were spent in New York City on full art scholarships. By the time he was twenty-two, the art community had embraced him and he was that rare artist earning critical acclaim and significant dollars. Years passed: exhibitions, commissioned works, travel. But unresolved issues pulled at him, irresistibly, as the change of season bids the migratory bird to return home. So, after essentially having been away since his early teens, three years earlier he had come back to Detroit.

He was twenty-seven, still a young man, when he returned. His first major undertaking was to set himself up in his own studio, which he accomplished with the purchase of the building in the Warehouse District. Detroit has a sizable community of collectors of Afro art, and its appetite for Eugene's work seemed insatiable.

Eugene didn't come back charging New York prices, either. And he did other things to ingratiate himself to the community as a whole. He donated art to such unlikely places of exhibition as shelters for battered women, police precincts, and unemployment offices. Additionally, he was generous with his time to young people, giving drawing exhibitions and talks to schools and to nearly any community group that asked.

And two years ago—before ground had been broken—when the Museum of Afro-American History began its search for an artist in residence, Eugene's reputation and many charitable acts in the community made him a front-runner. When he received the congratulatory call from Executive Director Martha Chenault, he celebrated by skipping wildly throughout his studio, the dreadlocks he favored then lashing around his head.

As the grand opening approached, preparations made increasing demands on Eugene's time. As much as he hated to, he had to pry himself from Mocha's arms earlier that morning to do some additional sketches. Now, his work at home completed, he stood with

Martha Chenault in the museum's main exhibition area. Empty crates lay open like raided treasure chests, and the two stepped carefully to avoid slipping on straw and other packing material cast about the floor. Workmen carried, slid, pushed, and hung objects into place, while others busied themselves with final touch-ups, nailing, drilling, gluing, and painting.

"You did it," said Eugene. He held his arms wide to indicate the width of the space he was talking about. "This is the perfect place for the video information station."

"I didn't have any problems getting the board to authorize the system. Another one of your ideas has come to fruition."

"I just try to help where I can."

"I just wish half the people involved were half as helpful as you. Come. I want to show you something." Eugene lagged behind Martha. Having recently turned thirty-six, she was an inch or two shorter and a pound or two heavier than average, but she carried herself with the air of a woman secure in the knowledge that people respected her. Her shiny black hair cascaded past her shoulders in thick jumbo braids, framing a face that was plump but that glowed with an inner illumination that immediately drew people to her. Her penciled brows were arched above green contact lenses.

She led him to the main lobby at the entrance of the building. "DA DAAA!" she exclaimed. She flung an arm out, the long sleeves of her mud cloth kaftan rising up to reveal a cowrie shell bracelet. She directed his attention to a wall that had a three-by-four built-in display inset. Inside was a bronze sheet with a relief of Eugene's face at the top. Below that was his name. The copy celebrated him as the first artist in residence, provided a biographical sketch, and praised his contributions to the museum.

"I'm embarrassed," Eugene said.

"You're way too modest."

"This is good work. Who did it?"

"Just never you mind."

"Did you do this, Martha?"

"What did I just say?"

"Did you do this?"

"Yes. Now, what of it?"

"Take off the boxing gloves, lady. I just want to say thanks."

"You're welcome. Now let's go." She was off again, sashaying at a clip that kept her a few feet in front.

"Lead, and I shall follow," promised Eugene.

Martha halted in her tracks, and Eugene almost collided with her.

"Maybe you should wear brake lights," Eugene suggested.

"I'm sorry. This is not our destination, but I just can't seem to pass this way without stopping to marvel."

They were in the rotunda, which was capped by a dome bigger than the one on the State Capitol Building, except this one was made of glass. A mirror finish covered the top of the dome and dripped uniformly down the sides. The optical qualities of the material allowed a viewer to look through it at the sky. Martha gazed up at the dome four stories above. "Look at us," she said, craning her neck at their reflections.

"Uh-huh."

"You're not looking. So what that you've seen it before. It's still inspiring."

"Sure is," he said, casting a quick, humoring glance upward.

"The way you're shunning your image is like you're hard to look at or something," she said. "And we both know better."

"Weren't we on our way somewhere?"

"I get the hint, Mr. Subtle." She resumed walking. "We're going to the storage area by the dock. Some of the canvases from Africa are arriving in terrible condition."

"The packaging in some of those countries is a flat-out joke."

"Beautiful paintings, Eugene. Ruined."

"Flights get canceled on a minute's notice," said Eugene, evidencing knowledge gained through his travels. "Some airports don't have storage facilities, so a package can sit exposed to the elements for days."

"What should we do?"

"I don't know. Maybe a packaging expert can go over there and teach modern techniques."

"I'll propose it." She halted, less abruptly than before. "There's no need for us to go to the docks, since you already know what the problem looks like. Let's go to my office instead. I need to discuss something with you."

Martha and Eugene took the stairs to her office. Offices had been moved into despite the work that remained to be done throughout the building. The offices were on the uppermost levels.

Martha's office was spacious. A pair of black leather armchairs were angled in front of a large desk. A matching couch was against the wall, to the right of the door. A round meeting table and four chairs were the other main furnishings. The walls were beige, the rug a burnt orange. The window faced west, and the late-afternoon rays streamed through the gaps between the closed vertical blinds.

By habit she started for her desk. She pulled back her upholstered roller chair but decided against it. "Talking behind a desk is so formal," she said to Eugene, who'd chosen a chair. "Let's take the couch."

"I'm okay right here," he said, rising even as he spoke. "But if you insist."

"Ah, this is better," Martha said, now on the couch. "Been on my feet all day." She shifted into business gear. "About the Mother of Mankind series. The committee nixed it."

"They can't," Eugene bellowed. "What's wrong with those people."

"Lamont Sherwood is behind the decision," said Martha, referring to the board of directors member who chaired the art committee.

"He has to reverse himself, then."

"I wish that—" Martha started to say apologetically, but she was interrupted by an increasingly agitated Eugene.

"He can't get away with this. I've given and given to this museum and asked for nothing. Plus I've been one of its biggest financial patrons. Talk to him, Martha."

"God knows I've tried. First over the phone and then at his home. He's adamant."

"He's ignorant, is what he is. What about going to the other committee members?"

"Eugene, I've spoken with each. How do you suppose I learned that it's Sherwood who's leading the charge? No one else voiced the objection that he did."

"That it's pornographic?" Eugene surmised.

"I warned you the series might ruffle some feathers."

"How does he get away with forcing his views on the committee?" Eugene's chest had begun to heave and his expression had started to harden.

"Sherwood has donated big to the museum, just as you have. He's also a substantial fund-raiser for the mayor, so he's well connected. And he's the type of man who will put up a fight even when others aren't willing. Megan Knox spoke for a number of board members when she told me that she had better things to do than lock horns with Sherwood."

"This shit is wrong," said Eugene, whom Martha had never heard curse. "I can't let that Oreo get away with this."

"Did you say 'Oreo'?"

Eugene seemed to calm a bit. "I—I take it back. But the man's misguided."

"Eugene, I wouldn't advise going to war over this."

Eugene jumped to his feet as though he'd sat on a hot coal. Martha jerked back in surprise. She said nothing as he stomped to the window. He yanked the blinds open. For moments he gazed out in silence. He spoke with his back to her. "Take the DIA," he said, pointing to the Detroit Institute of Arts next door. "There's nudity depicted all through the place."

"In defense of Sherwood," said Martha, lowering her voice for every decibel that Eugene raised his, "he's concerned about maintaining a family image at the museum."

"Bullshit. Families go to the DIA all the time."

"Don't beat me up," protested Martha. "I'm on your side. I knew from the way you raved about them that the drawings meant something special to you. I did what I could to get him to see our viewpoint."

"I'll go over his damn head and take it up with Dr. Bowersox."

"He's vacationing overseas," Martha said of the chairman of the board, "and won't be back until mid-September. By then all the exhibits have to be in place, as you know. Come sit back down." She patted the couch. "Please."

Eugene plopped on the couch. "Get Sherwood on the phone."

"Calm down first."

"I just want to reason with the man."

"What about displaying the drawings elsewhere in the museum—in the office section, for instance?"

"Why not use them for bathroom wallpaper?"

"I'm not trying to insult you, Eugene. Just trying to come to a compromise."

"No compromise," Eugene shouted, slamming fist into palm.

"What in the world is wrong with you?" Martha was becoming unnerved. She watched as Eugene crossed his arms and started to rock.

"All or nothing," he said.

"Meaning?"

"Either the series is exhibited or none of my works is exhibited."

"You don't—"

"Plus, I'm ready to resign."

"Who's the model, Eugene?" Martha's intuition had kicked in.

"What's that got to do with anything?"

"Don't answer a question with a question. She has something to do with this, doesn't she?"

"Mocha is her name," he said, seemingly relieved. "I promised her the drawings would be exhibited."

"Is she special to you?"

"I want to marry her."

Sounding a hint of disappointment, Martha said, "Lucky gal."

"You looked frightened a while ago. I wasn't going to grab you by the throat, you know."

"You had me wondering."

Eugene rose, this time in a normal fashion. "I've taken up enough of your time," he said as he opened the door.

"What do you plan to do?"

"Never you mind," Eugene said in a manner that Martha didn't find comforting. "Never you mind."

TWENTY-THREE

Precious got out of the taxi and began the walk up the dirt path that led to the farm she had once lived on with her parents. She had arrived in Bent Fork earlier that day by bus. Now a half moon was the lone source of light. Precious inhaled deeply and smiled at the familiar smell of the countryside. As she walked, dirt dusted her cheap canvas shoes and collected in her pants cuffs.

The wire fence that Porter had built along the road was gone, and she was seized with regret that the mammoth willow that guarded the front acres—the "boggy man tree," as she and Annie had named it—was a slumped silhouette of nakedness, a victim of blight. At least the fields were cultivated, although she would argue to anyone that they had looked more robust when her father worked them. When she reached a sharp bend in the path, she got her first glimpse of the house, nestled in the night like a checkpoint at the border between the lands of past and present. There was light—and therefore occupants? But she knew nothing of them.

Whoever the present residents were they did not keep the place up as Porter and Hattie Jones had. Missing were the flower beds that used to ring the house. The front steps were in disrepair and the lowest tread was broken. What little paint remained on the one-level, wood-frame house had peeled and blistered, like a terminal case of sunburn. Precious's bedroom window was broken. The front lawn had succumbed to weeds, and there was a blown-out tire lying about.

Maybe the condition of the homestead had something to do with the death a few years back of Sam Parsons, whom Precious remembered as a real stickler about maintenance. Precious had learned of his passing from a fellow inmate who had befriended her because they were both from Green County.

The story went that one summer night Sam ranted up and down the main streets of the black section of Bent Fork, proclaiming that all his runaway slaves had better return to their quarters immediately or they'd be tied to the post and whipped. The locals contented themselves with catcalls and some hurled items, none of which broke Sam's spell. He wandered in front of a car, affording the driver no opportunity to avoid him. The toxicology report revealed no alcohol or drugs in his system.

It was the latest in what the town's folks referred to as the "Parsons Curse." They said that the genes of that clan were cross-wired and that every generation produced a wacko, the only variable being the age at which it struck. Sam's grandfather, for example, died from ingesting lye, believing that it would cure his constipation.

But whatever the reason for the neglect, Precious had another destination in mind. She headed for the shelter in back that her father had used as a storage shed and where he repaired farm equipment. It was in worse shape than the house. She went through a door that was hanging off its hinges. She was barely inside when she stepped into a pile of dog shit. She slid the soiled sole of her shoe back and forth and scraped off most of the smelly gook, then quickly strode to a floorboard that had once been covered by a disabled tractor. But the tractor was gone and the board, which used to be unnailed, was fastened in place. Precious and Annie had named this location "The Safe," their secret stash for personal items. The tractor had hidden it from unauthorized eyes, and only the girls had reason to venture under the tractor.

Precious's eyes had adjusted to the darkness enough for her to make out a rusty chisel lying on the floor. It wasn't the proper tool, but it would have to do. She gouged at the wood around the nails at one end of the board until she could slip the chisel under their heads and pry them up. Then she slipped her fingers under that end of the board and pulled. Some nails along the side of the board gave way before the board splintered. It was rotted, like much of the surroundings.

Precious dropped to her knees, ignoring the pain of impact, and frantically poked her hand around the Safe. At first, nothing. But as she reached farther—actually into the space covered by an adjacent board—she touched something. But that's all that she could do; it was too far to grab. With the chisel she scooted the item forward, then wrapped a hand around it. She knew from touch what it was; knew that it was what she had hoped to find. It was the other confidant, or, as Annie referred to her, "Miss Dee."

Precious had remembered that Miss Dee had been with Annie when she made that fateful visit. Annie always took Dee whenever she traveled from home. But Dee wasn't with Annie when Precious took that last look out the window. She couldn't have been, because Annie was bidding good-bye to Precious by gesturing with both hands. Why Dee was missing had to do with why Precious saw Annie walking across the yard toward the gate, cutting an angle that was consistent with having come from around the back of the house, consistent with having come from the shelter. Triumphantly, Precious raised Annie's diary from the Safe and kissed its moldy cover.

"Stand up, bitch!" demanded a voice from behind.

Precious yanked her head so suddenly in the direction of the voice that she toppled from her kneeling position and onto her rear end. She found herself looking up the nostrils of a shotgun.

"I said stand the fuck up," said the voice at the trigger end, "or I'll blow your goddamn head off right where you be."

"Easy, lady," pleaded Precious, her hands held high and apart. "I wasn't trying to steal or nothing like that, I—"

"Shut up, bitch. If I have to tell you again to stand, it'll be the last thing you ever hear."

"Lady, you got to listen to me," said Precious as she stood, careful not to do anything that might be misinterpreted as a sudden move. "This here's just some old diary, left long before y'all ever moved here. Like I say, I ain't stealing nothing. This all I come for. Don't kill me over it."

The woman holding the shotgun was average height like Precious, but stockier. She wore a nightgown, robe, slippers, and a headful of rollers. She was the color of a paper sack. "I think you one of Dorsey's bitches, that's what I think." She adjusted the aim so that it was between Precious's eyes. "Come to get something you left behind, did you? Don't think that I don't know he bring his bitches back here to fuck. If he told you to sneak here tonight, you the fool, 'cause he got his drunk ass in town. Probably with somebody else."

"Lady, I don't know no Dorsey. If you just let me walk away from here, I swear on my dead mama's grave that you will never see or hear tell of me again."

"Now that I done got a good look at you, I take back what I said you being one of Dorsey's bitches. Dorsey don't like no nappy-headed bitches."

"I'm only here for this book."

"Hold up that goddamn thing so I can see it."

Precious complied. "A diary. That's all. Thirty years old."

"How come you here for it?"

"It's mine. I lived up the road when I was a girl, and hid it here one day. All's in here is memories that don't mean nothing to nobody 'cept me."

"You a lie. Toss it here, and be cute at your own risk."

"Why don't I just put it on the floor and push it to you. That way . . ." She stopped talking and did it when the woman signaled her approval with a head gesture.

"I'll just hold on to this. For all I know, it might hold the whereabouts of something valuable hidden on this chickenshit farm. One thing's for damn sure: there's a reason you're so hot and bothered over it, and it ain't 'cause of no childhood memories."

"What you gonna do with me?" asked Precious, hands still raised.

"You gonna git your ass away from here, and if you ever come back I'll blow you away like I should've done already."

Just then the mutt whose handiwork Precious had stepped in earlier was using his huge head to widen the door. When he had wedged a large enough opening he barreled through, straight for Precious. Barking, growling, and snapping, he alternately lunged and retreated as Precious stomped and kicked.

"Lucifer, heel," shouted the woman. "Dog, git your ass to the house."

By the time the woman had redirected her glance to Precious, she was upon her, and they were in a tussle over the gun. Each was trying to wrest the gun from the other, and the bigger woman's heft had Precious wagging from side to side. All the while, Lucifer was circling the two women, barking nonstop, unable to distinguish long enough which part of the dervish was his master. The gun pointed up, down, sideways. Then one barrel went off, blowing a hole in the roof, followed shortly by the other barrel, blowing another hole in the roof. The explosions were too much for Lucifer, who turned tail and scurried out the door, yelping.

Precious thought of something that made her angry over not having thought of it before. She bit into the woman's hand, so hard that Lucifer would have been hard-pressed to do better. The woman exclaimed in agony, and in reflex took that hand from the barrel to shake the pain out of it. With a yank powered by desperation, Precious took possession of the gun. Both barrels were empty, so Precious swung it overhand like an ax, raining down blows on the old woman. She smashed her in the head with the first swing, knocking her to the floor, and followed up with more as the woman curled her body and covered her bleeding head with her arms. The woman pleaded for mercy.

Precious stopped swinging. She scooped up the diary, which had fallen during the scuffle. Holding the gun above her head, ready to crack Lucifer's skull should he reappear, she backed cautiously to the door. Once outside, she flung the gun, then broke into a sprint, back up the dirt path, until she collapsed from exhaustion. She lay for a moment, her lungs aflame, pain knotting the muscles of her slender legs. But she had the diary.

It was close to dawn when she locked herself into the seedy motel room. The bathroom reeked of urine and the sheets weren't clean, but those were the least of her concerns. Soon thereafter, Dee was violating every confidence that Annie ever placed in her. Dee told all that she knew about Annie: who the father was, the circumstances under which Annie became pregnant, whom Annie planned to see the day that she disappeared.

TWENTY-FOUR

Lamont Sherwood wondered what his wife had forgotten as he descended the stairs to answer the side door. She had burst out of the house minutes earlier, still buttoning, zipping, and gulping coffee, late for opening her dress shop. But when Sherwood, who'd left his bifocals upstairs, peered through the door window, it was Eugene he saw. For the previous three days, Eugene had monitored Mrs. Sherwood's morning departures and knew when Mr. Sherwood would be home alone.

Eugene was wearing a T-shirt, jogging pants, a cap, and wraparound sunglasses; thus disguised, he didn't stand out from other runners who hoofed around this pricey neighborhood that abutted the Palmer Park Golf Course.

Eugene stood facing the door, careful to keep his back to traffic along this private street. When their glances did meet, Eugene raised his hands in a thumbs-up salute, like someone giving the secret signal to get into an after-hours joint.

The thick, painted, oak door swung open, then the cast-iron screen door, and Eugene quickly slid inside.

"My man, Eugene Shaw," greeted Sherwood. He was in pajama bottoms, his flat, sagging chest sprouting coils of white hair. "This is a surprise. And I don't necessarily like surprises."

"Hello, Mr. Sherwood. Sorry for dropping by unannounced."

"It's not good manners. I'm sure your mama taught you better." After the chastisement, Sherwood offered his outstretched palm, which Eugene clasped, and they performed a ritualistic black man's handshake. Before locking the screen door, Sherwood looked out onto the driveway. "Where's your car?"

"At the park. I'm mixing business with exercise."

"So what's up?"

"It's about my Mother of Mankind drawings."

"I figured as much," said Sherwood, a spry sixty-five. He got straight to the point. "The drawings are too explicit. That's all there is to it. I would offer you a seat, but you won't be staying."

Eugene decided to give him a fair chance. "That's okay, I don't mind standing. Look, Mr. Sherwood, I make you for a reasonable man. All I ask is that you let me say what I came to say. Fifteen minutes, tops. Is that too much to ask, considering all I've done for the museum?"

"I have to admit, you've put in the work."

"So can I make my pitch?"

"Keep talking," said Sherman as he walked away to lean against the kitchen sink. "I can see the wall clock better from here."

"In the first place, pornography is explicit. We're talking about art here."

"We can argue labels all day"—the somewhat thin man ran his hand over his thinning hair—"but what we're talking about is a woman's privates."

"Right. But I did a little homework and found that nudity is involved in other works that the museum will exhibit."

"How many are close-up views between a woman's legs, though? Nudity is not the issue. In your sketches, the rest of the body is not even shown."

"You have to understand the concept," said Eugene. "I am honoring the black woman as the mother of all mankind. I can't think of a higher tribute, can you?"

"There's got to be better ways of doing that."

"Not if you see my point that mankind emerged from this passageway. Showing it in its natural beauty can't be pornographic."

"You're talking artsy shit, and I understand where you're coming from. But the layperson is not that sophisticated. Know what that person would see? Pussy and that's all." A lewd smile played on Sherwood's face, then he said, "If it makes you feel any better, you did a bang-up job on those drawings. Just between you and me, they got me to wondering what it would be like to fuck the model. You did use a model, didn't you?"

Mocha's tongue-in-cheek warning about how perverts might react to the drawings resonated in Eugene's mind. He now had determined that Sherwood was bombastic, crude, and ignorant. And it infuriated Eugene that he was reduced to currying favor from the old fool. Sherwood had disrespected the concept behind the drawings, and by extension had disrespected all black women. Worse, Sherwood had disrespected Mocha. And Sherwood had disrespected Eugene through lascivious references to the woman Eugene loved.

Eugene felt the heat of anger rising. He consciously vented, wanting to give Sherwood the benefit of the doubt—and another opportunity to save himself.

Masking his thoughts and emotions, Eugene said, "The model is someone I've used many times." Then, in hopes of warding off additional suicidal comments from Sherwood, he added, "And she's a class act in every way. Somebody who deserves respect."

"I really don't give a flying fuck if she's Mother Teresa," said Sherwood. "It still doesn't solve the problem I have with your drawings. I plan to march hundreds of children through that museum. Many of them horny boys who will be walking around with their little peckers saluting in their pants. Many of them hot-in-the-drawers girls who don't need to be reminded of their sexuality. And it's all going to fall on my bald-ass head when angry, uptight parents take their children out of my schools." Sherwood was president of Excell Education Systems, an empire of day-care centers, private K–12 schools, and adult education centers. He was semiretired, having left the day-to-day operations to his three sons.

"Now I understand better," said Eugene, outwardly still very much in control. Now Sherwood had exposed himself as a hypocrite, too, a man who placed his own interests before those of his people. The outcome of this meeting was looking more and more certain. Eugene raised the bottom of his T-shirt just enough to slip a hand into his pocket and touch the item he'd brought. Now he had to subtly reduce the distance between himself and Sherwood, for when it came time to strike, he would have to be close to Sherwood, practically upon him.

"I explained all of this to Martha Chenault," said Sherwood.

"I guess I didn't get the full understanding from her."

"That's probably because she has other things on her mind when it comes to you."

"Why do you say that?" asked Eugene, pretending interest and stepping closer to Sherwood.

"You're not blind, or you wouldn't be able to paint and draw. But go ahead and pretend that you don't know what I'm talking about. The woman pleaded so passionately on your behalf, I got the impression that you were doing something with her pussy, and I don't mean drawing, either."

"Not yet." Eugene smiled slyly, then slid closer yet to Sherwood, who obviously liked tantalizing conversation. "Think I should do her, Mr. Sherwood? I bet you were a terror in your day."

"This is still my day," bragged Sherwood. "I remarried a few years ago. Got me a young gal, and she'd be the first to say that I keep her satisfied. Man, I had her running late this morning because I touched her up."

"I'm sure you take care of plenty of business."

"Damn tooting. And nobody better mistake me for some feeble old man. I'm strong. I'll fuck you up."

"I believe you, Mr. Sherwood."

The old man's expression softened. "You're all right with me, Eugene. I've been messing with you since you got here and you been taking it in stride. Too bad it can't help you."

Too bad far more than Sherwood could suspect. At this point, they were standing close enough to touch each other. Eugene trained an unblinking stare on Sherwood. Eugene's vision began to blur and his temples began to throb. When his eyes did close, it was too long for a normal blink.

"Something the matter?" asked Sherwood.

"Had a pain shoot through my side. From too much jogging, probably."

"Then be sure to walk when you go back to your car." Then Sherwood, ever the master of diplomacy, said, "And it's about time you started that journey." Sherwood was doing everything except snatching the dagger from its hiding place and burying it in his own heart.

But, moments earlier, while Eugene had his eyes closed, a vision had come to him: an epiphany, vivid and developed. And just by the thinnest of margins, the compulsion to disclose it to Sherwood won out over the compulsion to kill him. "I have an idea how we can protect the children."

"What you been holding back for? You better spit it out. Quick. And it better be good."

Eugene said, "It's simple, really. We make it a curtained exhibit, and outside it we post a sign that warns that it might be inappropriate for viewing by minors. Adults with children can steer clear if they choose. Problem solved."

"I don't know," said Sherwood, not wanting to concede that something he had been so insistent about could have such a simple solution.

Eugene, the salesman, continued, "It could work for other exhibits, too. For example, photos of civil rights demonstrators under attack by police and dogs, and of lynchings, and of burnings might be too intense for children. You can even present the idea as yours. I have no problem with that."

"I still don't know," hedged Sherwood, enjoying having the upper hand, particularly since Eugene looked so much like a white man. "You're Isaac Shaw's son," he said, intentionally diverting the conversation.

"Yes."

"By adoption."

"Right."

"Which one of your parents was white?"

"Father." Eugene, his discomfort growing, said, "Can we get back to—"

Sherwood cut him off. "I give you all the credit in the world."

"For what?"

"Some black folks will talk your ear off, bragging about being part Indian, or part white, or part Shetland pony—anything that keeps them from simply being black. You're not that way."

"No, I'm not," said Eugene dryly. He wished that Sherwood had not given him that compliment. It would be easier to do what might have to be done if Sherwood continued to come across as one-dimensional. Plus, Eugene already had had a difficult enough time justifying to himself that the deed would be consistent with the mission.

"Speaking of Isaac, how's his campaign going?" asked Sherwood, completely unaware of the emotions he was stirring.

"I don't get into politics. Too dirty."

"But you do support your father."

"Of course."

"Because a man who doesn't stand behind his family . . ."

"I support him." Eugene wanted out of the discussion. "What about your own family, Mr. Sherwood? You mentioned a wife. Any kids?"

Suddenly Sherwood's eyelids lifted like released window shades. "What's today?" And after Eugene told him, Sherwood said, "My anniversary is tomorrow. Good God Almighty. I would have forgotten it."

"About the drawings, Mr. Sherwood."

"Man, I don't have the time now. I have to go get something for my wife." Sherwood rose.

"Can we agree to—"

"I said later, man." Sherwood waved his hand in the direction of the door. "Get on out of here."

"All you need to—"

"Look," said Sherwood, obviously irritated, "don't try my patience or I'll veto the idea right now. You should feel lucky that I'm willing to think about it. And I would appreciate it if you never drop by again unannounced."

"Sorry," said Eugene. "Real sorry." He crept slowly toward the door. The entire time, he looked into the impatient face of Sherwood. The older man broke the eye contact when he turned his back and started the trek across the kitchen. Eugene followed.

Again Eugene stole his hand under his T-shirt, resting a palm on top of the dagger's handle. His fist was about to close around it, but his arm was yanked away and he felt himself stumbling into a faster walk. Sherwood had spun about, grabbed him by the arm, and was hurrying him toward the door. The oldster was surprisingly strong.

"Maybe you didn't hear me. It's an anniversary gift I have to go get, not a Christmas gift," Sherwood said en route. "So I don't have until December." At the door he swung Eugene around so that they faced. He started unlocking the door as he continued to talk. "You can have your drawings and curtains. I'll get it past the board. Just get out." He grabbed Eugene, by the other arm this time, and Eugene's exit was quickened with a push in the back. Through the screen Sherwood said, "I owe you for reminding me about my anniversary. You saved my life."

TWENTY-FIVE

For a while after his parents divorced, Kyle Cunningham harbored hopes for their reconciliation and regarded Mary as an obstacle. He was twelve then. Mary had to get past a shoulder hunched in defense to plant that first kiss on Kyle's cheek. And their first hug was like embracing a statue. But to Mary's credit, she understood the reason for the resistance and just kept dispensing love and patience. Even now, years after they bonded, she looked at him sometimes and recalled the first time that he surprised her with a big hug and kiss.

And before Mary's daughter Gazelle straightened out, she had been a package of problems wrapped in an attitude, grappling with hormones, acne, boys, and frightened at the prospect of "growing into her mother." On top of all that, she had baggage from an absent father who had been followed by a self-absorbed stepfather. Then there had been Mary's boyfriends, none of whom, before Cliff, she'd ever liked. But as Mary had done with Kyle, Cliff used loving perseverance to win Gazelle's affection.

The night before the family reunion picnic, Mary, Cliff, and the kids were gathered in the basement. Since dinner, Cliff had been hosting a retrospective on the early black action films. He had a video library that included classics such as *Shaft*, *Super Fly*, and *Cotton Comes to Harlem*. He was kneeling at a shelf, running his fingers along a row of videos, about to decide which one he would show next.

Gazelle, slapping her knees as she stood, said, "That's all the polyester and big Afros I can take for one evening. I'm going upstairs." Tall, curvaceous, and long-haired, she resembled her mother in the eyes, mouth, and hips.

"Don't wimp out on us, Gazelle," said Cliff. "The marathon is just getting started."

"Better wake up Sleeping Beauty, then," Gazelle said, referring to her mother. "Make her watch them with you." Mary had dozed off, legs jackknifed to the side, her head on an armrest. "I'm going out this evening."

"I can count on you, though, can't I, Kyle?"

"I'm going to have to rain check you, Dad. Me and Jamall have dates with a pair of foxes. We're going to play laser tag tonight."

Mary stirred, but didn't open her eyes or move her head, even as she yawned the question. "Where?"

Kyle answered, "In Troy."

"Behave yourselves out there," warned Mary. "They'll throw you in jail just for the practice."

"I promise we'll be good."

"What time will you be back, Gazelle?" Mary asked, still reclined.

"Who said I'm coming back tonight?"

"Girl, don't play with me."

"Mama, I'm grown." Gazelle's smile revealed that she was being more mischievous than defiant.

"And I'm growner. So what time?"

"Tell her, Gazelle," advised Kyle, "while there's still time to avoid the 'whose roof is this?' lecture."

"I should be back by three or something. It'll be before dawn."

"And what about you, Luke Skywalker?"

"Put me down for the same time."

Cliff joined in. "Have those girls in by— How old are they?"

"Sixteen."

"Both?"

"Mine is seventeen."

"Have them in by two, earlier if their folks tell you. And don't bring my car back on empty."

"You know why they're sweating us about the time, don't you, Gazelle?" Kyle raised the back of his hand to the side of his face to shield from his parents the big wink he shot at her.

"You know I do," assured Gazelle.

"Then let me in on it," said Cliff.

"You want us out of the house so that you two can get your sex groove on," Kyle said, "and you don't want to be on the lookout."

"I did not hear what I just heard," said Mary. Her eyes were open now, and she was sitting upright.

Cliff had his argument at the ready. "Then why would I ask you to stay for more videos?"

"We're hip to the reverse psychology, Dad."

"Yeah," said Gazelle. "Kicking us out would be too obvious. So you run us away with the videos. Clever."

"When we're out of the house, Gazelle, they don't have to scream into the pillows," Kyle teased. The youngsters slapped a high five.

"Who are these people, Cliff? I know I didn't have any part in raising them." Mary had been ambushed by this sudden change of conversation and was struggling not to appear embarrassed, but she was just light-complexioned enough to show some reddening in the cheeks.

"We'll stop picking with you," said Gazelle. "I think it's kind of sweet that old folks still want to get it on."

"Tell us, Dad, when you and Mary first met, did she put you on hold for a long time, or did you go for the gusto right away?"

"Well . . ." was all Cliff said, but the sly grin was open to interpretation.

"Careful what you say," Mary told Cliff, remembering the sex they had on their first date.

"I'm not ashamed to say that I had to really wine and dine her. It was a bona fide courtship. Take a lesson, son," Cliff said, putting his arm around Mary and drawing her to his shoulder, "when you know the woman is worth it, don't shortchange her."

"That's so sweet, honey," said Mary. She turned her gaze on her daughter while snuggling closer to Cliff. "Gazelle, they say that you have to kiss some frogs before you find your prince. I regret that you saw some of mine hop by. But one of my fondest wishes for you is that you end up with as much of a prince as I have."

The mushiness was putting ideas in Cliff's head. "You kids shouldn't spend a Friday night looking at old movies. Get out of here and enjoy yourself."

"I wonder why the sudden change," said a mischievous Kyle. "I'm gone already." He went behind the sectional and wrapped his arms about Mary's neck and kissed her on the cheek. "Love you."

"Love you, too."

"See ya later," said Cliff. He bent back his elbow, and Kyle grasped his hand in farewell.

"Love you, Dad." He couldn't resist adding, "Don't wear Mary out, Dad."

"You rascal," said an embarrassed Mary, grabbing a pillow and hurling it at Kyle.

"I've invited Shane to the picnic," said Gazelle of the young man who was taking her out that night. "I hope you don't mind if I don't bring him downstairs when he gets here."

"Poor Shane," said Kyle. "Recruited for everything because he's the only guy who'll date you."

"Here's what I have to say to you." Gazelle punched Kyle in the shoulder.

"Oww. Help me, Dad. Mary and Gazelle are abusing me."

"You have a sick son," Gazelle told Cliff. "And I don't have time to fool with him." She was about to go upstairs. To the grown-ups she said, "Love you both," and blew kisses to them.

"Love you, young lady," returned Cliff.

"Me, too," said Mary.

The kids went upstairs. Soon thereafter Kyle could be heard backing out of the driveway, and it was about fifteen minutes afterward that Shane came for Gazelle. Mary had spent the time tidying the basement. Cliff read the latest *Sports Illustrated.* He bounced slightly as Mary flopped down beside him.

"They've sure grown up, haven't they," commented Cliff.

"You know it. That Kyle is a pistol."

"He is, but when you think about what some of these boys are doing nowadays—drugs, gangs, and the like—I'll take him."

"Me, too. Any day."

"And Gazelle has come a long way," said Cliff.

"To say the least. There was a time when she and I couldn't agree on the color of an orange. I'll always love you for sticking in there, whittling that log on her shoulder to a chip, and then knocking that chip off." Mary pressed her palm to her eye to contain the tears, but one squeezed its escape from the inside corner. She sniffed in recovery, then changed the subject. "I feel giddy over the picnic. It'll be wonderful to see so many family members. I'm looking to have a great time."

Cliff said, "If tomorrow is as hot as today was, we can save on charcoal. Just lay the meat on the grill and let the sun cook it."

Mary rested her head on Cliff's shoulder. She relished the time that the four of them interacted as a family. It triggered her nurturing instincts. It added to her sense of well-being. "Do you love me, Cliff? I mean really, really love me?"

"I really, really, really, really love you," he answered.

"Do you ever say to yourself that you deserve better than me? Be honest."

"How many times do I have to say it, sugar? I didn't marry you out of charity, and I don't stay with you for that reason, either."

"Maybe I need to see a shrink, then. Sometimes, when I'm acting up—and you know what I'm taking about—I find myself wondering whether I'm subconsciously pushing you away. If I don't deserve you, and you someday realize that and leave, maybe I'll be able to survive if I can tell myself that I chased you away."

"What's this all about, Mary?"

"I don't know. I've just been thinking. Maybe it's because of tomorrow."

"I know that family isn't always easy. You know what they say about being able to pick your friends but not your family."

"Except you and Kyle."

"What do you mean?"

"When I picked you, I got a best friend and a family."

"See there. Shows that those damn fools don't know everything."

"That's right."

Cliff slapped his palm against a sofa cushion and said, "I guess we should count our blessings a little more often." He kissed her on the forehead.

"I agree. Do you want to stay down here and watch another video?" But before he answered, she added suggestively, "Or might you have something else in mind?"

"Decisions. Decisions. A little while ago, I was ready for my favorite actress."

"Pam Grier," said Mary somewhat begrudgingly.

"Coffy, Foxy Brown, Sheba Baby," said Cliff, reciting some of Pam's title roles. "She was one sexy, gun-toting mama."

"Just hold on, mister," said Mary with some indignation. "What about *this* sexy, gun-toting mama?"

Cliff had to clean it up quickly, so without reference to the gun he said, "When it comes to sexy, you register off the scale."

"So what does Pam have that I don't? Besides a bigger Afro. Should I run upstairs and throw on one of my wigs from my days in Vice Squad?"

"That won't be necessary." Cliff stroked his chin and let spread a sly grin. "Maybe the question is, what do you have that Pam doesn't? The answer is cuffs."

"Come to think of it, she never played a cop in any of her roles."

"Cuffs," repeated Cliff. He sighed, as if pining for a lost love.

"Feeling a little kinky tonight, are we, Cliff?"

"That's a leading question," Cliff whispered into her ear. "And let me show you what it's leading to."

Since he was at her ear already, he started there. He sucked the lobe a few seconds. His tongue traced the rim, then the crevices. Mary slid down to where the couch provided neck support, and squirmed and arched and gyrated. She leaned her head to the side, offering her neck to her Dracula. He took nipping bites along its entire length, like her neck was a buttered ear of corn. And she squirmed and arched and gyrated some more.

Her eyes were shut and her head was turned from him, so she patted around until she found him. But he removed her hand by grabbing her wrist. Then he grabbed the other one, locking her into a position of arms raised and separated. With her thus restrained, he raised himself a little to kiss her, but she playfully made her mouth a moving target by turning her head away. He caught her anyway, clamping his mouth on hers, trying to insert his tongue past her pursed lips. Throughout, she jerked her wrists against his hold. And when her resistance had worked its magic, had ratcheted her excitement to unbearable, she yielded into a cavernous kiss and a boa's embrace.

Cliff released her wrists and trailed his hands along her thighs. Her shorts were large enough for his hand to shoot up to her panties. And when he pressed his hand dead center, her secretions had already soaked through. "Wait a second, honey," she said, then performed the feat of removing shorts and panties while remaining seated. Next she shamelessly opened her legs as far as her hip sockets would allow.

Cliff put his fingers back to work, strumming, parting, polishing, pulling, inserting. And he went back to speaking into her ear. "Where are those cuffs?"

"Thought you had forgotten."

"No way."

"Upstairs."

"Let's go."

"Any other toys you want to play with, little boy?"

"Let's just lay everything out, like a surgeon does, and then pick what we need to operate."

She pulled back from him to cast him in her lustful gaze. There was nothing else to say, only to do. He rose and guided her up by the hand. They were almost halfway up the stairs when Mary pulled away. "Forgot something, babe," she said, and returned to snatch her shorts and panties.

"Incriminating evidence," said Cliff, now at the top of the stairs.

Mary took the stairs with sassy, springy bounds. About midway up, she paused and looked down over her shoulder. "Eat your heart out, Pam," she said.

TWENTY-SIX

The barbecue grills were arranged in a big circle and loaded down with meats, fish, and vegetables. The grills were made from steel drums, and had been brought to the park in a pickup truck. Whenever one of the cooks would lift a cover, billowy smoke signals would be released, seasoning the air and communicating that the Kingsley family reunion picnic was in full force.

The official count was seventy-six, all wearing yellow printed T-shirts. On the front of the shirts was a majestic tree in crowning foliage, bearing fruit in the form of hearts. Arching above the tree, in bold blue, was "KINGSLEY Family Reunion Picnic," and under the tree "August 2, 1997." On the back of the shirts was an outline of mitten-shaped Michigan, with "THE MOTOR CITY" stretched across the top. A star pinpointed Detroit's southeast location below the thumb.

Three-month-old Page was the youngest Kingsley there, looking every bit like a little chocolate Buddha; Booker T., a hundred and two, legally blind and cantankerous as ever, was the oldest. And every stage of life in between was represented. They had come together, as they did every other year: from immediate family to those three or four times removed; from blood relations to in-laws; from spouses to significant others to present flings.

The Kingsleys' roots were in South Carolina. From there they had radiated to other parts of the country—spokes from a hub—but Michigan, specifically Detroit, was where the largest contingent of them had come. The magnet had been jobs in the automotive, steel, and related manufacturing industries; jobs that paid wages unattainable back home; jobs that required no special skills; jobs that a worker could raise a family on.

Mary's father, Joe, was a teenager when he came to Detroit. After finishing high school he did factory work for several years before joining the police force. It catapulted him to a position of prestige among his relatives, similar to what's bestowed on a family's first collegian. Now sixty-eight, Joe was considered the patriarch of the Detroit Kingsleys. His two older brothers and most of the family members who were already living in Detroit at his arrival were dead.

Presently, Joe had secluded himself under one of three roofed shelters that the Kingsleys had reserved at Metropolitan State Park, about a twenty-minute drive from Detroit. He was silently rehearsing. Under each shelter were tables placed end to end, ready to accommodate the hungry. Picnickers roamed among the shelters, jiving, laughing, playing, and bonding. Joe looked out toward a nearby lake at family members churning about in paddleboats. But the less sensible played volleyball, softball, and basketball in the insistent heat. The sky was a cloudless blue and sunshine washed over everything—apparent omens that nature itself was nodding favorably upon this gathering. And Joe kept rehearsing.

Across the way, two folding tables for playing cards had been set up in a corner of one of the shelters. The game was bid whist—the rise 'n' fly variety: the winner of a hand remains seated; the loser gets up. Mary and Cliff had been kicking butt for a series of hands. From the time she'd arrived at the picnic grounds, Mary had been having a grand old time. She had known she would. Moments before, it had seemed that the Cunninghams's winning streak had run its course, but the opposition blundered. Mary added insult to injury by unleashing her trademark laugh, reverberating and raucous.

Mary's cousin Donna was irked by Mary's send-off. "Explain something to me, Cliff," said Donna. "How do you put up with that awful laugh?"

"Music to my ears," Cliff said with a sweeping smile. "I love seeing my baby happy."

"Ha! I guess he told you. Don't get petty just because your little aces didn't turn. We finessed right around them, didn't we, Cliff?" Mary asked tauntingly, even rising to high-five with Cliff. "Now fly," she told Donna, "so that maybe some real competition can sit down."

"That's all right," Donna said while rising, "your butt is not glued to that seat. You'll be up sooner or later."

Mary and Donna loved each other, and no one misinterpreted this good-natured needling. The way they played the game, the psychological sparring was as much a part of strategy as deciding which card to play. To this group, bid whist was not bid whist without talking shit, nor without talking about whatever. Indeed, it was customary for topics to be shuffled as freely as the cards. And at some point, Detroit's image came to the top of the deck.

"I used to dread when it was Detroit's turn to host the reunion," said Rosie from South Carolina, standing on the sidelines awaiting her turn to sit. She and her husband had two daughters who were surgeons and a third who was a congresswoman. They owned lots of farmland and lived comfortably. "All I heard about back then was crime and killing. For the life of me, I didn't know why everybody didn't pack up and move somewhere civilized. I must say, though, that things have gotten better."

"Detroit has seen some hard times," said Cliff. "But that can be said for so many other cities. Look at New York. It wasn't that long ago that it had to be saved from bankruptcy."

"That's right," concluded Mary. "Somebody correct me if I'm wrong, but in all Kingsley reunions held here, everybody always managed to escape with their lives."

Rosie said, "Don't be defensive because you're the police, Mary. You know me; I'll speak the truth even if it kills somebody."

"I wasn't being defensive. And I'm certainly not going to get upset over anything. Not today. I've having too good a time."

"If you ask me," continued Rosie, "living got worse after black people took over Detroit."

"Don't say anything that reflects badly on your intelligence," warned Mary, smiling.

"Once white people left, Detroit was almost run into the ground," said Rosie, speaking like a historian.

"That talk doesn't surprise me, coming from you," Mary told Rosie. "We know you worship those white-owned canning companies who buy your crops."

"Don't let it get too ugly, ladies," Cliff requested. "Everyone's here to have a good time."

But Rosie hadn't had her last say. "Then inform your wife that she didn't write the book on acting black."

Cliff, not wanting to be drawn into the discussion, nevertheless felt obliged to defend Mary. "She didn't imply that at all."

Mary played a card, then raked in the book she'd won, before speaking again. "Skin color is not determined by acting."

"You know what I mean," said Rosie. "Culture."

"Without asking your definition of 'culture,' " said Mary, "I'd be the last person to say that every black person has to think and behave the same. Take this reunion, for example. We're all relatives, but look at how different we can be. I grant you that some of us have an identity problem." Mary paused long enough to trump an ace, which always gave her satisfaction. "I grant you that some of us wallow in self-hatred. Still, there's too much of the pot calling the kettle not black enough."

"I'm with Mary," said Donna, who had taken a seat at another card table. "I'm not about to go out and kill a white person to prove myself to some of these superblacks."

"Good thing," said Mary, "because you might have to start with some relatives."

It had come down to the last card. Her opponents' hopes were dashed when Cliff won the book. "Damn!" exclaimed one of the defeated. "So close."

Mary sent them packing with "If it's being close that you're counting on, you ought to play horseshoes." She was grateful for the interruption and was counting on the conversation's taking a different turn.

After the next pigeons were seated, Mary was shuffling the cards when Jamilla said, "Girl, your hands look like a man's. What's up with that?"

Mary couldn't react quickly enough to suppress the self-consciousness that stabbed her. Still, she owed Jamilla a debt of thanks for changing the subject. With sweet restraint, she asked Jamilla, "Anything else you care to mention?"

Jamilla, no less tactless, said, "It's those veins. Looks like phone cords under your skin. You have high blood pressure?"

"No, it comes from exercising."

"Doing what?"

"This." Mary performed some rapid closing and opening of her hands, then moved her fingers as if she were strumming an invisible harp. "Doctor's orders. I have arthritis."

"You should ask him to put you on medication, because the exercise is doing a number on your mitts."

Mary knew that she could have told Jamilla that the doctor also had her on a prescription. And that she quilted to add strength and nimbleness to her fingers. But she decided not to waste further explanation on Jamilla. Besides, she told herself, Jamilla was busy arranging her cards, and she wasn't the type who could do two things at the same time. But Jamilla's card partner, Clarence, didn't trust her to refrain from further thoughtless remarks. He led the conversation into another area. Mary might have preferred that the focus remain on her hands.

"I understand that you and Cliff are thinking about opening a dance studio," he said.

Cliff provided the update. "We're still awaiting word from the Small Business Administration on our loan application. I'm trying not to get too anxious, because I know that the process can take months. We should know something before much longer."

As Cliff spoke, Mary was readying herself. She hoped that he wouldn't say anything that committed her, anything that she would have to correct for the public record.

Suddenly Jamilla shrieked. "Wheee! We made it." Addressing Mary and Cliff, she said, "You two may get up now and stretch your legs."

"I was ready to eat anyway," said Mary. "Come on, Cliff. Let's fix our plates." But the food would have to wait, because even as they rose, there came her father's voice, amplified by a bullhorn.

"May I have your attention. I said, may I have your attention." Joe Kingsley was standing about equal distance from all the shelters, as if he had plotted that spot on a grid. The volleyball and softball halted, but the basketball continued for a couple more trips up and down the court, until one of the players noticed a circle forming around Joe. The music stopped. The lake frolickers remained unaware. Most who were seated remained so, but Mary walked over to join the circle.

"On behalf of all us Detroit and Michigan folks, I want to welcome everybody to the Kingsley family reunion of 1997." He paused until the cheering died. It was tradition for someone from the host city to address the gathering. Comments were supposed to be short and sweet, a cross between a welcoming and a pep talk. Joe's comments, however, were a departure.

With every sentence more somber than the one before, he resumed. "When a man gets up in age like me, he thinks about passing the torch. Who knows, the next time the reunion is here, I may be dead and buried. But I can never pass the torch to my son. Most of you know that thirty summers ago, I lost Junior. He was murdered in the riots of '67. Murdered with no more thought than you give to putting a rabid dog out of his misery."

Although this was not stuff that went well with a picnic, the sight of Joe's tears, the quivering in his voice, and the poignancy of his tale kept listeners attuned. And none more so than Mary. These were the most explicitly spoken words she had heard from her father regarding Junior's death. But the unexpressed is not necessarily the uncommunicated, and for three decades she had felt that his intended message was to blame her.

It wasn't mistreatment in the traditional sense that Mary had endured, but a degree of withdrawal by her father that was just as affecting. Before Junior's death, Joe had always been a sure source of hugs, kisses, and encouragement. From the time of her birth, he had given generously of the most precious of fatherly gifts: time. After Junior's death, Joe was a provider, a damn good one, but just a provider. The transformation left Mary convinced that her father had no real affection for her. She starved for the attention she had known. And she longed for relief from the guilt that consumed her.

As Mary listened to her father address the gathering, perspiration from her brow stung her eyes, but it wasn't due to the heat. Cliff walked up and wrapped his arms around her from behind. His timing was perfect, because she felt weak in the knees.

Joe continued his homage to Junior: an anecdote here and there; talk of dreams never to be realized; a pledge to forever hold him dear in memory. Even after that, he wasn't through.

"Junior was one of more than forty who died in the riots. And there's the public perception that they died in the act of vandalizing, looting, burning, or other criminal activity. Maybe some did, but not my son. Junior was no criminal. Yet he was shot down in the streets like he was a rabid dog. By a policeman. And as hard as I tried to get that man convicted, I failed. It's been the biggest failure of my life. But I've never given up on getting my son some measure of justice. Not long ago, I started an organization called the Survivors' Network. What the members have in common is that we lost a loved one in the riots, and we don't accept the official account of how our loved one died."

At this point Mary felt fatherlessly adrift. Cliff still had his arms around her from the back, his hands against her midsection. She clamped her hands over his and squeezed them, trying to anchor herself. Unintentionally, the pressure she applied was viselike, causing Cliff to grimace. But he felt even greater pain for her. He knew how much her relationship with her father had influenced her life, for she had told him her history—not the entire book at once, but by chapter, sometimes by paragraph, sometimes only by sentence.

Joe Kingsley lowered the bullhorn momentarily to collect himself. He had arrived at the closing. He began again. "The riots exposed a lot that was wrong with Detroit back then, and a lot has been corrected since. It changed the city forever. It's part of Detroit's history, every statistic. But they shouldn't list the loss of life the same way they do the number of buildings burned—just a number. I want a plaque in City Hall that lists the names of all who died. It doesn't have to glorify them. It doesn't have to say how they died. Just give them a name. They were human beings. I might fail in this attempt, too. But I'll never let it rest for as long as I'm alive." Joe was spent. He got out "Thank's for listening to a rambling old man" before he broke down and had to be comforted by Sophie.

Mary stood as though rooted to the spot. Her father's words had drained her. Cliff led her to a seat, fixed her a plate of food, and did what he could to get her back in a festive mood before she waved him away.

It didn't take long for the other picnickers to revert to gaiety. Later, Rufus, Joe's baby brother from St. Louis, issued a loud, drunken challenge. "Where is that Mary Kingsley? I say, where you at, gal?" He shaded his eyes with one hand and looked around as though he were searching the horizon. "Somebody git her so we can dance. I'll show her who's the real hoofer." Rufus walked with a cane, the result of an industrial accident and a botched knee replacement.

The challenge went unanswered. And it was just as well, because by that time Mary was as drunk as Rufus. Mary didn't even qualify as a social drinker. When she wanted to put on pretenses she would sip on a rum and Coke that was mostly the latter. But after her father's talk, she reversed the proportions. Four times.

Cliff was playing chess when Kyle came over, dripping sweat from playing basketball, and whispered, "Dad, I think you ought to see about Mary." He made his way to the court, where Mary was cheering each basket made and each one missed. When he reached her, she was prancing in a circle, head down, singing, one arm held up as if she were the Statue of Liberty.

"Easy, baby." Cliff gently lowered her arm, then held her by the shoulders to steady her.

Mary smiled up at him, her eyelids half-lowered shades. "Cliff? Did I tell you that I love you today? I think I did. I don't remember. Anyhow, I love you, Cliff. You love me? Huh?"

Cliff had to tighten his grip to keep her from weaving. "You know I do."

"Then that's all that matters. What I care who else don't. I'm grown, shit. Wanna dance, sugar?"

"Not now. Let's go home."

Mary released a loud, high-pitched hiccup. It made her head spring back. "I know you think I'm drunk. Don't you, Cliff? But I'm not."

"Yes, you are. Now, either you walk with me to the car, or I'll carry you."

"If my baby wants to go home, that's all right with me. But I'm not drunk. And I can walk to the car on my own." She straightened, then lifted her head proudly. The simple gesture threw her off balance.

Cliff held her by an elbow and escorted her to the car. He opened the passenger door and was about to help her in when she vomited.

Unable to further lie about being drunk, she asked, "You mad at me?"

"No."

"Ashamed?"

"No."

"My dad hates me, Cliff."

"That's not true, Mary."

Mary leaned back and turned her head toward the still-thriving celebration. She bit her bottom lip to try to stay her stubborn tears. Soon sleep would claim her for the ride home.

TWENTY-SEVEN

Eugene's office was the least utilized of all those inside the Museum of Afro-American History. Mostly his time was spent darting through the building, attending to whatever he could justify as coming under his duties as artist in residence. Sometimes he was at the receiving dock checking on art from overseas. Sometimes he was directing the hanging of art in the galleries. Never, however, did he work in his studio inside the museum; his creativity flowed best at home. And in every visit to the museum, Eugene spent part of the time as a nomadic sponge, wandering about, soaking up knowledge about African Americans.

Occasionally he'd have to endure the confinement of an office, typically Martha Chenault's, typically for conference purposes. He'd spent the day sitting through a series of meetings. Now, hours after Martha and the rest of the staff had left for the day, he remained, his mind knotted in worry—in his own office, of all places. Martha wanted an update on the art they'd commissioned him to create before the grand opening. She didn't have to remind him that—irony of ironies—Lamont Sherwood had requested that Eugene do the work.

But Eugene had not been cured of the affliction that was robbing him of his mind's eye to visualize colors. If anything, it had gotten worse. He chastised himself that he couldn't have painted his fingernails without spiraling into weakness and nausea. Soon the public, the entire world, would know that he was an impotent impersonation of his former self. It'll be so obvious as to convert even the most art-illiterate into jeering critics. He paced back and forth in his office like a caged animal. He cursed himself for having not killed Sherwood when he had the chance.

By the most optimistic projections, the museum was running a photo-finish race with its scheduled opening date. Although first visitors might be spared from having to lend a hand with last-minute cleanup inside the museum, landscaping and other grounds work was expected to be unfinished. The time Eugene had left seemed about as long as a brush stroke. His imagination needed a jump start—as in yesterday.

Eugene went downstairs to the main exhibition area. It was close to 8:00 P.M. and the work crews had left. He went to the exhibit on the Middle Passage, the name historians give to the transatlantic journey of abducted Africans destined for slavery. The centerpiece was a replica of the holding deck of a slave ship. A dozen life-size figures lay in the inhumane arrangement of that era: naked, shackled, supine, shoulder-to-shoulder—human sardines. The figures were life-size from having been cast from body molds of real people by a company that specialized in the process. One of the figures was a mold of Eugene, who had jumped at the opportunity to volunteer.

Now Eugene stood at the exhibit studying the mold of himself, as he had done many times. And as always, he was fascinated by what he saw: his body, done in black. But this visit to the exhibit would be somewhat different. He went onto the deck. He stepped across some of the figures and stepped on others—the spacing was so tight—to get next to his plaster alter ego. He picked it up, carried it off the deck, and set it down. Then he returned to the vacated spot.

Eugene took off his loafers. Next he pulled his polo shirt over his head, baring his torso. He unfastened his pants, and they fell around his ankles, after which he stepped one foot out of them, then used the other foot to hurl them off the exhibit. He pulled off his under-shorts and threw them toward the pants. Then, naked, Eugene lay down among the human cargo.

He closed his eyes and tried to imagine what the journey must have been like. The nonstop cries. Lying in one's own vomit and waste and that of fellow sufferers. Turning one's head to the side and meeting the blank stare of someone who had expired and would become shark food. The constant, disorienting motion of the sea. He tried to imagine how it could have been possible for any slave to have arrived ashore sane.

And after a while the drained battery of his imagination seemed to be receiving a boost. He actually could hear the vile voice of a crewman, thundering commands at him. If only Eugene could emancipate himself from the shackles, he would marshal the strength to spring on his tormentor and rip out his throat and heart. But the shackles were unyielding. He had to lie helpless. The crewman continued to make cruel sport of Eugene by barking taunts and even prodding him with something sharp against his sore, bare feet.

"Hey, you!" shouted a security guard, using his nightstick to get a rise from an entranced Eugene. "What in hell do you think you're doing?"

TWENTY-EIGHT

Eugene felt like hurling his palette at the man who was modeling for him; instead, he hammered the air in a single motion of frustration. Once again his model had moved, this time by rotating slightly, enough that Eugene's angle of vision was altered. Eugene stomped to his model. He clamped his hands on the man's shoulders, fingertips digging in like claws, and repositioned him. When Eugene did speak, it was through clenched teeth, but it was nonetheless a shout. "Keep your ass still." Eugene's foul mood was understandable. He was working against a suffocating deadline and with an unprofessional model.

At least Mocha wasn't around to witness the depths to which he'd descended. Though they were living together now, she was away for the weekend visiting friends in Connecticut. Eugene had to take advantage of her absence, had to work fast and furiously. He didn't have the time or the patience to fool around with someone who couldn't hold a simple pose.

Then again, Willie was a wino. Most of the time he couldn't stand straight without staggering. Willie was thin, subsisting mostly on a liquid diet. He was a little shorter than average. He was dark-complexioned, had thick, bushy hair and a full beard. He was only forty years old, but his bad habits had made him look at least another fifteen years older.

Willie frequently spent time in the Warehouse District, along the riverside park, sometimes on a bench, or, when temperatures dictated, under a tree. He was never without a brown paper bag, crimped at the top, its shape easily giving away the identity of its contents. Willie used to have ambitions of being a merchant marine, and the hours whiled away each day watching ships was how he clutched to those dreams. Willie knew Eugene, although not by name. Willie always addressed Eugene as "Mr. Charlie"; Willie addressed all the white men that he accosted for handouts as "Mr. Charlie." A good panhandler might not remember what day it is but can demonstrate remarkable recall for the faces of the generous. And Eugene had never refused him, even forking over a twenty-dollar bill at times. So when Eugene told Willie that he had a job for him, one that would take only some hours, Willie didn't discuss payment, confident that this "Mr. Charlie" would take good care of him.

Now the two were in Eugene's building. Willie had followed instructions precisely: walk across the park; go the two blocks to Eugene's street; come through the alley to the back of the building. After having let Willie in, Eugene took nervous glances up and down the alley. Deserted. Great. No one must know that he had been reduced to such desperate measures.

Mocha had made Eugene move his studio downstairs. She wanted a space where Eugene's work would not intrude on the rest of their lives, a space where she and Eugene had each other to themselves. She had also banished to the downstairs space Eugene's mementos that depicted Jim Crow, segregation, and oppression. They were too dispiriting for the mirthful ambience that she wanted for their living quarters. Mocha was the unchallenged decision maker as to decor. Eugene wanted to keep her happy, for he loved his Nubian queen. But she'd be back tomorrow. And this sad business with Willie must be completed by then. Besides, the shelf life on Willie was running out. No time to waste.

To his credit, Eugene had tried to prevent the present state of affairs. First he had gone to Sherwood and made an impassioned appeal for a sketching—a rendering in charcoal. Bullheaded Sherwood, however, was adamant that it would have to be a painting.

Sherwood had presented to the board of directors and to the art committee Eugene's idea of curtained exhibits. He'd taken full credit for the idea. When it went over well his ego took command, and in the next moment he was proposing an expansion of the idea: a painting, but one with a theme intense enough to qualify. Sherwood decided what that theme would be.

Eugene's backup strategy had been to work from photographs; however, the ones available were black-and-white. They had proved helpful in drawing the outlines, but Eugene had to supply the color. And that was the brick wall that he crashed headfirst into. In the attempts that he made, the pain and pressure were as if every artery supplying his brain had developed an embolism. Several times his stomach's contents came geysering forth, once splattering the canvas he was working on. He regarded the added color as an improvement over what he'd been able to accomplish with paint.

He had no alternative but to concede that he needed a three-dimensional, in-living-color model. Then he would perform the artistically brain-dead task of faithfully reproducing what he saw. To Eugene it was on the order of paint-by-numbers. Whom should he recruit as the model, though? There were definite considerations to weigh. Reluctantly, regretfully, he decided on Willie. But sentimentality aside, and regardless of Eugene's disgrace, he was at least doing Willie a favor. He had given Willie the dignity of doing something in counterbalance to a misspent life. Willie was making a contribution to his people. Willie was posing for posterity. That is, if he'd only be still—for, damn him, he'd just turned again. Daggers shot from Eugene's eyes, and Willie settled into stillness.

Lynching, the putting to death of a presumed offender, especially by hanging, by a mob acting without legal authority, got its name from William Lynch, a justice of the peace in colonial Virginia who set up unofficial tribunals that tried suspects and administered instant punishment to the convicted. As inherently barbarous and bestial as the practice is, it's a singular abomination in the collective consciousness of black Americans, because of the shameful period when lynching was an accepted brand of justice for them. So when Sherwood sought a theme that was part of black American history and also emotionally wrenching enough for a curtained exhibit, the old southerner thought of lynching.

As Eugene continued painting Willie, he was insulted by the ease with which he could, with a dab and stir of his brush, re-create Willie's chromatic persona. But what else would one expect? After all, as colorful as the world was, it was drab compared to combinations that Eugene could invent. Stress on *could*, as in used to. Past tense, Eugene reminded himself.

So undemanding was the present task that Eugene turned his concentration to devising plots to disguise the poor quality of the painting. Or maybe, in lightning-bolt fashion, his third eye would regain its vision and he could exchange this ponderous pace for the energetic one that used to be his trademark. Fat chance. The odds of his being struck by a real lightning bolt were better. But if the miracle of restored sight were to happen, he wouldn't need Willie any longer. He could cut Willie down.

He could cut Willie down from the steel cross-beam in the roof where Willie dangled limp and lifeless, a rope around his neck, his hands tied behind his back. Willie hung suspended like a grotesque piñata. An apt analogy to an extent, for Eugene was without vision, blindfolded in a way, and the art was the prize contained in Willie. There was, however, a distinction: Willie, the piñata, had been stricken *before* being hanged. Eugene had clubbed the unsuspecting wino with a two-by-four piece of lumber. It had opened a gushing gash on one side of Willie's head. And on several occasions already, the rope had allowed Willie's corpse to rotate enough so that the wounded side was exposed to Eugene's view, as if by such action Willie were saying, *Take a good look at what you did.* But Eugene had persevered through the interruptions imposed by his inexperienced model, and was close to completion of a work that he wished he could disown. Soon Willie would come down.

In a remote corner, Eugene had used a sledgehammer to break up a section of the cement floor. Underneath was unobstructed earth. Excellent location for Willie's grave. The headstone would be newly laid cement. There was just enough time to get it all done before Mocha's return tomorrow. She was such a fastidious housekeeper, and although she pretty much left the first floor to Eugene, he couldn't take any chance of annoying her. He didn't want to give his Nubian queen any reason for regretting having moved in with him. And most of all, he didn't want to give her any reason for leaving.

TWENTY-NINE

A quartet played jazz as cool as the night was hot. A lavish refreshment station replete with ice sculptures, fountain, and basketfuls of breads, flowers, and gourds accommodated appetites from dainty to hearty, and the bar was stocked to slake any size thirst. Politicians, power brokers, community leaders, the rich, the not so rich, celebrities, and just plain citizens mixed and mingled under a glass dome painted midnight blue by the sky, at the Grand Opening Party of the Museum of Afro-American History.

"Unless the pollsters don't know what they're talking about, it'll be you and me after the primary," Mayor Randal Clay said to Isaac Shaw.

"I promise you won't be bored," said Isaac. "Uh, your bow tie is a little slanted."

"Thanks." Clay steered the bow tie to horizontal, then fastened the jacket of his tuxedo. "Boredom can have its benefits at my age. Excitement is bad for the ticker. A boring, old-fashioned landslide would suit me just fine."

"Okay. That's what you'll get."

Clay emitted a short chuckle that cut off into a wry smile. He lifted his glass of champagne in salute. "I got a feeling you don't mean that the way I'd like you to."

"I'm sorry, Your Honor," said a woman in a full-length, silver formal gown, turning around to face Clay. Although she apologized, it had been Clay who had accidentally elbowed her in the back when he lowered his saluting arm.

"My fault totally," Clay said, then applied the frosting: "And you look stunning."

With the momentary distraction over, Clay returned his attention to Isaac. But just then Clay spotted a photographer who was maneuvering toward them through the elegantly attired throng. So Clay hurriedly said to Isaac, "Gotta go," and quickly left his side. People in Clay's path yielded to him, giving him the advantage over his shutterbug tracker, who could manage only stop-and-go progress. Clay was fleeing without being obvious, and the photographer continued the pursuit none the wiser; when finally cornered, the quarry was in the company of others with whom he didn't mind sharing a frame. No sense being photographed with Isaac, his likely opponent, when a picture could convey the impression of equals.

"Mayor Clay," said the photographer, who courteously had refrained from calling out during the chase. He was stumpy, middle-aged, and light-skinned. "Larry Catrell, with the *Michigan Monitor.*"

"How you doing, Larry?" said Clay, and extended his hand to the photographer, who worked for the weekly that was the largest black-owned newspaper in the nation. Catrell was a recent hire, but Clay knew whom he was addressing. "Need a picture?"

"Yes, sir."

"How about one with my friends here." Showing that he wasn't asking permission, Clay immediately stepped between two richly dark men from Kenya who were garbed in stately outfits that were unmistakably African. The ends of the sandwich smiled broadly as they were hugged into a tighter fit by the mayor's long arms.

"Good, now hold it," directed Catrell, then the flash went off. The huddle was about to dissolve when he asked, "One more?"

"Sure thing," said Clay, "that is, if my friends would be so kind."

"Of course," said the older one, whose gray woolly hair showed from under his woven hat.

"It is an honor," claimed the other.

After the second shot, Catrell wrote down the names of the Africans for caption purposes, then the big-game hunter was off again.

Clay rewarded his two pawns with a minute's more conversation, after which he resumed working the crowd in accordance with his style of politicking—dodging some people and intercepting others, toward the objective of keeping purely chance encounters to a minimum.

Earlier in the day, Mayor Clay had had a publicity field day at the museum's ribbon-cutting ceremony. The governor, both Michigan senators, and other elected state officials attended, their presence made obligatory by that of the president of the United States. Air Force One had since winged the president back to Washington, but not before he delivered a speech commending Detroit "for its vision in building the largest museum dedicated to the many positive contributions made by people of African descent in the building and shaping of this nation." The mayoral primary was later in the month, and Clay was banking that the publicity would bolster his support among black voters.

Isaac Shaw was at the night's gala intent on forcing Clay to share some of the limelight. On the lapel of his tuxedo, he wore a big campaign button promoting himself. And it was producing the desired result, prompting others to initiate the conversation on politics, thereby relieving Isaac of being seen as cornering people against their wills.

John Kalabrosos had come with the same motives as Isaac, apparently. The button that the perennial candidate wore had no year on it, just "Kalabrosos for Mayor," and could have been a leftover from any of his three previous runs. But, unlike Isaac, Kalabrosos was aggressively campaigning: pumping people's arms, offering buttons, and causing many suddenly to remember an urgent phone call that had to be made or something else that demanded immediate attention.

Congressman Andrew Galliger sported no campaign button; however, he did have a carnation pinned to his lapel, typical of the little touches of style and elegance he was known for. Well into his sixties, Galliger had the appearance and carriage of someone who had lived well all his life. Women liked his looks, and his wit and glibness gave him confidence in any cocktail-party setting. His low standings in the mayoral polls, despite high approval ratings, had pundits disagreeing as to the causes. Some predicted that a last-minute surge would sweep him to victory in the primary. But whatever anxiety Galliger might have felt over his chances was not evident this evening; he moved about leisurely, leaving people charmed in his wake.

Impossible to lose among the crowd was the tree-topper mayor, and it was with a tinge of envy and resentment that Isaac watched Clay pose for another photo shoot. This time a circle had been cleared in the middle of the rotunda, and when the sounds and flashes from a bevy of cameras ceased, the mayor and the museum executive director, Martha Chenault, embraced to the applause of the crowd.

Gertrude Shaw had been backed toward a wall as the clearing was formed for Clay and Chenault. She would not have watched the shoot even if her attention had not been captured by the object she was still studying when the crowd closed back in. Gertrude was uncomfortable in these types of settings. She was always self-conscious of the image she projected: Did she sound sufficiently learned? Did her discontent with her life show through? She had spent a considerable part of the evening hiding in the ladies' rest room. Aware of her tendencies, Isaac had held her hand in a captive grip to keep her at his side upon their arrival and as he made pleasantries and introductions with the crowd. After that he released her, as one might a homing pigeon that is resentful of captivity but nonetheless a slave to instinct.

And sure enough, she did return, but for a specific purpose. She wanted to show him what she had been studying. He followed her. "Did you know this was here?" asked Gertrude. Her gown was black velvet from the waist down. The top was cross-hatched in red, green, and yellow, done up in beads and sequins. Her arms were bare, and the front and back of the gown plunged modestly. She wore a pearl necklace.

"Not until I saw it earlier this evening," said Isaac of the bronze relief of Eugene made by Martha Chenault. "Good likeness."

"Then why didn't you tell me about it? You know I would have wanted to see it."

"How could I," said Isaac, speaking low and moving his mouth only a little more than a bad ventriloquist, "when you're nowhere to be found most of the time. Stay out of hiding and you can see whatever there is in here."

"I didn't come here to be talked down to like that."

"Gertrude, I wish you wouldn't." He dropped his voice lower. His smile was for the benefit of observers, whom he was trying to get a feel for by furtively darting his eyes. "You have more class than to make a needless scene."

"Save the false flattery, Isaac Shaw. And I'll have you know that I have too much respect for myself than to give these people a show."

Isaac tried to buy more insurance by saying, "I apologize for not mentioning Eugene's face. But understand, I had no ulterior motives. It's just that I have a lot on my mind."

"So much that you can't find pride in something that honors your own son? Does your selfishness know no end?"

The insurance didn't seem to be working. Isaac's next tactic reflected his desperation. "Tell you what, Gertrude, if it'll put you in a good mood, I'll go over to Eugene and congratulate him."

"Not without me, you won't."

"It goes without saying that I meant the two of us," said Isaac. With an exaggerated craning of his neck and rotation of his head, he indicated to Gertrude that he was scanning for Eugene. "Where is he? I saw him and Mocha in front of the band not long ago." He kept Gertrude within his peripheral vision, noting whether the expression she'd been wearing was softening.

Isaac's brow furrowed in irritation when he spotted Eugene and the mayor having a conversation. By appearances, it was an involved one. They were standing close, speaking confidentially. Clay had relaxed, and he was even punctuating a comment here and there with a hand on Eugene's shoulder. No frowns on either man. Isaac wished that he had a profile view of them; for, even being able to lip-read a single word might ease his anxiety. Or it could add to it mightily. What disastrous scenario was taking form?

"Well, do you see him?" asked Gertrude.

"Yes, actually. He's busy, though. Let's not bother him now. I'm sure that sometime during the evening he'll have a few spare moments."

Gertrude usually was quick to suspect motives behind much of what Isaac said, but his response seemed plausible given Eugene's involvement with the museum. "Okay, then," she said. "I'm going to eat a few bites. You be sure to come get me or bring him to me when he's free."

"I sure will," said Isaac, thankful to be able to return to his fretting.

Eugene and Clay were still at it. And observations that Isaac had made earlier in the evening about Eugene now took on added and worrisome emphasis. Yes, Eugene was dressed formally, but his new haircut was the most striking aspect of his appearance: very corporate, very Caucasian. Odd for *brotherman* Eugene. And well out of earshot, Isaac wondered in what voice Eugene was speaking, for he had more than one. His natural—if that word could be applied to anything about Eugene—voice was devoid of an ethnic stamp. But the memory was still fresh with Isaac of when Eugene, as a boy, purposely spoke with an affect meant to be identifiably black. It used to cause Isaac such grief. And as Isaac continued to observe the much too long conversation between Eugene and Clay, his present angst reminded him anew of how mercurial and how much the chameleon his son was.

A stately widow walked up to Isaac. He had supplied funeral services for her husband. Isaac had difficulty feigning interest in her as he sought to maintain eye contact yet steal glances at his son and opponent.

Fortunately Mocha saved Isaac from the balancing act. He saw her excuse herself into the conversation and lead Eugene away by the elbow. He noted how willingly and attentively Eugene followed. Isaac knew that Eugene and Mocha were living together. What he didn't know was that Mocha had pulled Eugene away from Clay because she wasn't feeling well and wanted to go home. Neither did he know that Mocha almost hadn't come to the gala because of nausea. She'd told Eugene it was probably a stomach virus and that she'd be fine. She wanted to see the Mother of Mankind exhibit. Eugene had proudly shown it to her but couldn't bring himself to view the painting of Willie that was close by.

Isaac didn't know any such particulars, but he sensed from the way that they made for the exit, with Eugene shaking hands en route, that they were leaving the building. And while hoping that nothing was seriously wrong, he was glad to see them go.

Even as Eugene and Mocha were parting, the fashionably late still were arriving. More people to network with. More potential votes. So, for the time being, Isaac suspended his anxieties over the mystery dialogue and resolved to spend the rest of the evening competing against Clay. But another potential obstacle was headed his way in the person of Gertrude, who was carrying a plate of hors d'oeuvres and fruits.

"Is Eugene still busy?" she wanted to know.

"I think he and Mocha had to leave."

Concern immediately filled Gertrude's eyes. "What's wrong?"

"I don't know. But I think it had something to do with Mocha. Eugene seemed fine."

"So you didn't speak to him?"

"No."

"That's just wonderful," Gertrude said coldly. "The boy didn't get congratulated by his own family."

Isaac spoke almost meekly, so as not to inflame her further. "I hope you're not about to blame me for that, Gertrude."

"And why not? As soon as you saw that tribute to Eugene, you should have found him and told him you were proud of him. But that's never been your style. Always at arm's length. Your own son. Disgusting."

Isaac sensed that the ill feelings between them were escalating, so, thinking quickly, he said, "When we leave here, we'll go to their home and see what's going on." Gertrude turned her head away, and Isaac sweetened his suggestion with "We'll make a stop first and buy some champagne to take over there. It'll be a real celebration." Lastly he added what he hoped would win her over: "A celebration among family."

There was no way that Gertrude would decline such an invitation. Nevertheless, it didn't wholly placate her. Eugene had not received his deserved recognition at this function. She took matters into her own hands. "Oh, Mayor Clay," she called to the man who had been trying to inch his way into eavesdropping range. Clay, the bachelor, would have loved proof that the Shaw marriage was stormy. "Please step here a minute."

As he was being summoned, Clay took steps in another direction so that he could reverse himself in pretense that he was responding to Gertrude's voice. "Mrs. Shaw, you look stunning," said Clay, getting more mileage out of that line than a compact car coasting downhill. "Is there something I can do for you?"

"I wasn't sure whether you know it, but this young man," she said, running a finger down the slope of the nose of the bronze Eugene, "is our son."

Clay overreacted to Gertrude's pride-infused face and concluded that it was best that he not remain; otherwise, he might draw others and give his rival a positive forum. He gave Eugene's likeness a short, intense look. He read the inscription. "No, I wasn't aware," said Clay. Looking at Isaac, he added with a smile, "You're dressed like a penguin, but I bet you're proud as a peacock." With a nod of his head, he excused himself and scurried away.

The episode left Isaac with a quickened pulse. Everything about it told him that Clay did not recognize that the bronze image was that of the young man with whom he'd had a lengthy conversation a short while before. And Clay was a hard-nosed politician—remembering faces was his forte. Isaac's pulse quickened further, but not from having dodged a bullet. It stemmed from knowledge about Eugene that only Isaac possessed, knowledge that caused him to ponder the seemingly illogical question of how many sons he really had. And how it would ultimately play out that whatever the number, they could be so different that they could go unidentified by a professional observer. Earlier, the question of what Eugene and Clay were discussing had had Isaac occupied and unnerved, but not as much as the one that presently gripped his mind: Who, exactly, was Eugene Shaw?

THIRTY

The early returns for the mayoral primary had been so definitive that the winners already had been projected, and it was still an hour before the late-evening news. The November election would pit Mayor Randal Clay against the second-place finisher, Isaac Shaw.

Isaac, scheduled to face the media, was receiving last-minute coaching from his campaign manager, Earl Ogden. Shaw, Gertrude, and Ogden were in the administrative building at the Everlasting Memorial Cemetery, Detroit's largest boneyard. It was the designated campaign headquarters, a stunt concocted by Ogden, who had coined Shaw's campaign slogan "Bury the past or it'll bury us."

That there was so much ground to make up and almost no time in which to do it didn't cramp Isaac's legs in tense fear, for he knew he would be powered by a special fuel—a high-octane mix of guilt and faith.

Becoming mayor was how Isaac hoped to quell the guilt that burned in him like typhoid. A successful business built on personal service had not done it, nor had community activism. His guilt demons laughed at such exorcism. How could they not when Annie Parsons lay secretly buried; Porter Jones, falsely convicted, had been killed in prison; Eugene floundered in a state of disequilibrium; and his marriage to Gertrude was a sham. They were all threads of a spider's web, and whenever his thoughts landed on one it started the others vibrating.

Isaac considered himself a devout Christian, and he was obsessed with how he might cancel the reservation that hell was holding for him. A start might be to bare his sins to the world, but whenever he weighed that catharsis of the soul against its consequences to the flesh, he couldn't do it. Redemption would have to come by other means. What if he could do the most good for the most people? Detroit had a million citizens. To substantively improve their lot had to be worth something by heaven's bookkeeping.

Isaac's preoccupation with his own mortality had produced a persistent fantasy. In it, he was on his deathbed, Eugene and Gertrude at his side professing love and forgiveness. He died, leaving throngs of mourners, grateful for the ways that he touched their lives. He ascended to heaven, where he was welcomed by the Almighty himself.

While Isaac, Ogden, and Gertrude remained cloistered inside the administrative building, the rest of the supporters, along with the media, were outside. A tent—one that reminded Isaac of the big church revivals from his youth—had been pitched next to the building. There was outdoor lighting and the tent was festooned inside and out with balloons, pennants, and banners. Folding chairs provided seating. Tables held food and drink. A steel drum band played.

Isaac was scheduled to go before the cameras after a live shot from the mayor's headquarters. Ogden had told Isaac to think of all of this activity coming together with the precision of a catered event—like food, he said, news is best served hot and while the public is hungry for it. Meanwhile, Shaw workers were feeding the media tasty comments about the candidate, campaign, and message. Plus, reporters were going smorgasbord, piling a plate with tidbits drawn from the spectacle of a cemetery serving as an election headquarters.

"How much longer?" asked Isaac.

Ogden glanced at his watch and answered, "About another half hour."

"I mean for this rehearsal."

"Like I said, another half hour."

"It'll have to be shorter. I need to talk to my wife in private."

"Then we'll speed it up," said Ogden. "Let's go over one more time the—"

"No," said Isaac with assertion. "This is overkill." He told Ogden, "Shoo," and flicked his wrists, gesturing Ogden toward the door.

"Keep track of the time" was Ogden's departing comment.

Ogden went out into a caressingly comfortable evening. The summer of '97, hot-tempered in its youth, seemed to be mellowing in its middle age. The week's forecast for no rain had allowed Isaac's organizers to proceed with the outdoor plans.

During the time that Ogden had spent preparing Isaac, Gertrude had sat dutifully quiet, occasionally looking up from one of several magazines that bored her more than their discussions. After Isaac said that he wanted to speak with her privately, she had been all pretense; the pages kept turning, the eyes kept scanning, but she wasn't reading. She was scheming. She had seen the exuberance in Isaac and knew that he wanted her to share it. That placed her in a position of power, and she was deciding how to exploit it.

Isaac closed the door to the room. Then he spun to face Gertrude, who was now on her feet. He clinched his elbows to his sides and pressed his clasped hands against his chin. For a moment he held that pose and visualized . . . something most pleasant, from his expression. Then, as if realizing that the visualization was a foregone conclusion, he punched fist into palm, twice, sounding loud claps.

"It's within reach, Gertrude. Within reach. You're going to live in the mayor's mansion and be first lady of the Motor City."

"I'm nobody's expert on politics," confessed Gertrude, "but didn't Clay get twice the votes?"

"That won't be the case in November."

"If Earl Ogden told you that you can fly, you'd go running for the nearest cliff to jump off of."

Isaac said, "Earl, Smerl. No denying that he's had a hand in my victory, but never underestimate my smarts. I'm the one in control of this campaign."

"Going head-to-head against the mayor will take big money, Isaac. Clay probably wipes his butt with it."

"The money will come. I raised more than the other challengers, didn't I? Now, as I rise in the polls, it'll flow in. That's politics, Gertrude."

"I don't mean to be negative, but—"

"Then don't. You haven't said one supportive thing all evening. This is for you, too, Gertrude. I'd say more for you than for me."

"Oh really?" Gertrude sniffed in disbelief.

"Don't you want this? It can make up for so much."

"Like what?"

"Don't play games, Gertrude. You want acceptance and approval that you feel you haven't received."

"Wrong, Isaac. I *know* I haven't received. And if you win, what's going to happen? Will I suddenly become worthy in the eyes of your folks?"

"I broke from my family. You know that. It was one of the sacrifices I made for us."

"Spare me, Isaac. You don't sacrifice. You make others do it. At most, you might tolerate an occasional inconvenience. That doesn't qualify you as a saint."

"I'm anything but a saint, and we both know it. Still, there is decency in me, Gertrude, and I want you to benefit from it."

"To think," said Gertrude with a note of incredulity, "I've spent my whole adult life with you, Isaac Shaw."

"And I've provided for you the whole time."

"And you think that was enough? My soul has withered. I'm a prune inside. And you're the cause."

"Where is your Christian nature, Gertrude? Forgiveness is divine."

"What reasons do I have to forgive? You did me wrong, and I just don't mean with some other woman."

"I've been faithful since my stumble, Gertrude. Totally."

"You did me wrong because you stole the pleasure I used to feel whenever I looked at you. That night you confessed to being Eugene's father, if you had only done what I asked, showed me that nothing was too big a sacrifice for your family, you would have won my soul forever. Instead, you looked after yourself and said the hell with me and Eugene."

"That's not how it was, and why are we reopening wounds?"

"Reopening? They never closed, let alone healed."

"We haven't discussed this in years, Gertrude."

"*Gertrude, Gertrude.* You make me hate the sound of my own name. Where are the endearments? I can't recall the last time that you called me 'sweetheart,' 'darling'—anything other than Gertrude. You are without warmth, Isaac Shaw."

"How would you know? It's like you keep a bucket of ice water close by, always ready to douse any warmth I try to show."

"And you never call Eugene *son.* Your own flesh and blood. You robbed that boy, and all the fancy schooling and material things you gave him don't make up for it."

"You're intent on punishing me. That'll never change."

"You're blind, man. After all this time, you still think it's all about you. You can't see that it's me I'm punishing. And I deserve punishment for being part of the damnable lie that we live. The more I dislike you, the easier it is to dislike myself; the more I punish you, the more I punish myself. When I let you force your hypocrisy on me, I became no better than you. So any disgust I have for you, you better believe that I have it for myself, as well."

Gertrude took some steps backward and dropped into the armchair she'd sat in earlier, a fighter returning to the corner after a slugfest of a round. She parried his attempts at eye contact, head turned away, eyes at the floor—not a message that said she was ready to exit with him to face the crowd.

"Keep track of the time," Ogden had said. Show time was almost at hand, and this tête-à-tête had gone all wrong. And what if he had less time than he thought? What if Clay was uncharacteristically brief, and Ogden came through the door within the next few seconds and announced that the cameras were ready to roll? Isaac could feel his vitality ooze like the sap from a tapped maple.

Mayor Clay was divorced, and Isaac's strategy was to package himself, in contrast, as happily married. And as it is for any magician, carrying off an illusion is easier with an attractive assistant who is in on the deception. But here they were, about to go on stage, and she wasn't showing any willingness to climb into her costume.

But Isaac and Gertrude Shaw had been strange bedfellows *before* politics entered the fray; furthermore, long before the campaign, Isaac had had an element of the politician in him. The Shaws, then, were not thrashing about in totally unfamiliar waters, a truth that Isaac grasped without conscious thought. The situation might be salvageable.

"Look at me, Gertrude. Please."

"I'm looking at you. Now what?"

"Do you love me? I'm talking about no matter how slight."

"That's the last question you should be asking me now."

"But I'm asking."

"Whatever the answer, your timing is flawed. I can't remember the last time it's been important enough for you to ask. I refuse to answer."

"Then I'll ask something else. Do you want to destroy me?"

"Yes."

"Why?"

"That's not how I meant it. If I had the power, I would destroy some things about you so that I could live with you with a clear conscience."

"Those things are as much of me as my heart, brain, and blood. You can't remove them and expect the patient to live."

"That's our tragedy."

"What I just told you, you already knew. Yet you've stayed all these years, Gertrude, and continue to stay."

"Let me guess. You're going to tell me why."

"No, I'm not. But if ours has been a marriage of convenience, it must have been a good marriage of convenience. Whatever has kept you in it has been just that—enough to keep you in it. Do you know what I'm trying to say? I don't care whether your reasons for staying have been personal, selfish, evil, or something else. I'm asking you to see whether they can be served by helping me win this campaign. Don't look at it as something for me, Gertrude."

"Help you win," said Gertrude in summary.

"It's on a silver platter, begging to be taken."

"And all I have to do is what I've been doing all along: living a lie. What a bargain." Gertrude shook her head sadly.

"I'm going to clear things with Eugene somewhere down the line, but first things first."

"Your idea of what should be first is different from mine, needless to say."

"Now might not be the best time anyway. His behavior can be so odd. His mind seems to drift off. It's like he's in a trance sometimes. Then he snaps out of it. What are you, in denial?"

"No. I grant you that he seems preoccupied at times, but that doesn't—"

"I think he might still need professional help."

Gertrude was unnerved by the thought. "It could simply be overwork, trying to do too many things at once. I don't even rule out that it's love that's got him daydreaming. Anybody can tell that he's swept for that girl, Mocha. I think you're making excuses."

"Do you think Eugene does drugs, Gertrude?"

"Heavens, no."

"I don't think so either. And let's be grateful to be able to rule that out. But don't eliminate other possibilities just because they disturb you. You've seen enough to know that Eugene might have a problem."

"What if I'm willing to entertain that possibility. What do you suggest be done?" Gertrude's willingness to place Eugene's interests first was causing her to forsake the upper hand.

"We hold off from telling him the whole truth about his parents." Isaac saw Gertrude's face contort in resentment, and he quickly added, "But only temporarily. I don't want to be too dramatic, but I have buried many an emotionally disturbed person who killed himself."

Now Gertrude was unnerved beyond containment. She was at the point of defeat. "This is what you love to do to me. Exploit my weaknesses. You know how much I love Eugene and wouldn't want to do anything to hurt him."

"This isn't exploiting you. I'm speaking what I believe. Maybe whatever's wrong with Eugene is hereditary."

"From your side?"

"It's possible, although I don't know of any instances."

"And, of course, you know nothing about his mother's side."

"How could I?"

"Then what should we do?"

"It's a delicate subject, for sure. But if I see any more signs, I'll have to find some way to suggest that he see someone."

"I should do it," said Gertrude. "I think he would take it better coming from me."

"Probably so. But be tactful. You know how he is. He might think like many a black person when it comes to that kind of help."

"And what is that?"

"Distrust. The police and psychiatrists—they both can get you locked up, one by declaring you a criminal, the other by declaring you crazy."

The door swung open. Ogden, realizing the force he had used, lunged for the knob but wasn't quick enough to prevent the door from banging into the wall.

"Quarantine over," Ogden announced.

"A few more minutes," said Isaac.

"Not if you plan on live coverage," Ogden countered. "Clay ran a little long. Now or never."

Isaac stood in anxious silence, awaiting Gertrude's reaction. Seconds passed sluggishly, and Isaac was certain that Ogden would soon know that something was amiss.

"Then it's now," said Gertrude suddenly, causing Isaac's eyelids to hoist in surprise. "What's there to think about?" She sprang from her chair and was the first to meet Ogden at the door.

Well, the opening trick of the magic act had fooled Ogden, and he was no rube. "That's my girl," he said cheerfully.

A lectern sprouting microphones was stationed center front outside the tent. Cameramen stood with equipment shouldered like missile launchers, light beams on, although there was enough area lighting to read the fine print on a used-car contract. The crowd had been informed, so the music had ceased and most had gathered near the podium.

One, however, took another trip into the tent for food. She had been eating the entire time. She looked a tad underfed. Her clothes were cheap and looked as if today wasn't the first time they'd been worn since their last washing. Earlier in the evening, she had bumped into Mocha, causing Mocha to spill water on her slacks. Eugene immediately began dabbing with a napkin, too busy to register the woman, who had uttered a one-word apology and beaten a retreat. In fact, none of the parties had reason to give further thought to the incident. Not Eugene. Not Mocha. Not Precious Jones.

THIRTY-ONE

It was just before the start of the day shift, and the few early arrivals were either settling in or pouring a first cup of coffee. Mary went to Frank's desk and dropped a file on it. The echoing thud suggested its weight. Frank was reading the sports section, holding it open in front of his face. The gust billowed the paper inward. He lowered it, revealing a face contorted by annoyance.

"The Cookie Cutter file," Mary announced. "You need to get up on it."

"Again? How many times do we have to go over the same thing?"

"The file's gotten bigger since the last time, from both our investigating."

"Any big breaks?" asked Frank.

"No."

"Then take it back to your desk. I'll get to it sometime this week."

That was not what Mary wanted to hear. "See here, Frank, why can't you be the type of pain that goes into remission once in a while?"

The display of crabbiness caught even Frank by surprise. "What's wrong with you? Things must not be going so well at home. That's no reason to take it out on your underlings, O, mighty squad leader mine."

Her disposition got no sweeter. "Save it, Frank."

"Something wrong in the marriage, Mary?"

"No, there's nothing— None of your business."

"My mama never worked a day outside the house, and she and Pop are still married. Old Italian-immigrant morals. There's a lot to be said for—"

"Will you shut the hell up long enough for me to tell you something?"

Frank was taking mischievous pleasure in the exchange, but he said, "What?"

"There's something up. Might prove to be nothing. Might prove to be everything. We don't have lots of time to prepare."

"Mary, could you be a little more mysterious? Like, maybe, write it in secret code and in invisible ink?"

"All right smart-ass. Here it is. A conference is coming to town and our boy might strike again."

"What kind of conference? NAACP? National Association for the Advancement of Cookie People?"

"You're a disgusting piece of—"

"Hey, hey. Lighten up, Mary. Not that you were ever warm and cuddly, but since you've become squad leader you've been really uptight. I'm no bigot. And you need to stop being so guarded about this case."

"I don't know what you're talking about."

"You act like I don't know anything about the hang-ups black people have."

Mary's look was most skeptical. "And, of course, you're an expert."

"As much as the next person, likely more. I interact with blacks all the time. I work with them. I arrest them. I interrogate them. I'd have to be a moron not to have learned something."

To Mary, Frank's words were demeaning and akin to how a zoologist who's spent years studying gorillas might speak of the knowledge gained. Yet missing in his delivery was that arrogant tone present whenever he was being intentionally insulting. It occurred to her that maybe this was the best he could be. "Have it your way, Soul Man. Now, about this file."

But Frank wasn't ready. "You're making fun of me, like a white man can't have soul. I'll tell you something, Mary. My uncle Joey was one of the early musicians at Motown Records. Backed up all their big artists. And you think the Temptations had some dance steps? Forget about it. You should have seen my uncle."

Mary shook her head, trying to remember at what point she'd lost control. She was his senior partner and his squad leader, but she was having a hair-pulling time trying to rein him in. "The file, Frank."

"You already know everything that's in there, correct?"

"Yes."

"Then leave it on my desk. I'm literate. I don't need you to read to me."

Mary considered it a victory of sorts and said, "Fine." And she should have left it at that. "Who knows, maybe you'll increase your already vast knowledge of the plight of black people."

"Don't give me a sob speech. I swear. You people think that you hold the copyrights on discrimination."

Mary should have walked away. Should have. *"You people? You people?"* She felt a vein in her neck get plump.

"That's right. What am I supposed to say, 'we people'? So sensitive. Well, don't cry on my shoulder. I'm Italian. You think I ain't had to deal with stereotypes of being Mafia? Look at me. I'm a cop with the same last name as the Godfather, for crying out loud. Give me a break."

Mary began playing an imaginary violin, swaying her head and humming. When she finished her number she said, "I'm willing to make a deal right about now. I'm not going to say another word to you. I'm going back to my desk, if you'll dive into that file."

"It's a deal," agreed Frank. "But you still haven't told me the name of the conference. Trying to hold out on this white boy?"

Mary snorted in exasperation. "American Black Conservatives," she said.

THIRTY-TWO

Eugene Shaw passed right by Frank Corleone, who was masquerading as an employee of the Ambrosia Hotel. Eugene went to a house phone. He picked up the receiver and told the hotel operator, "Please send someone immediately to clean the Venus Suite."

"I'll connect you to housekeeping," came the reply.

He repeated his request after being connected.

"We'll be making the rounds in about an hour."

"I want it done now, please."

"Yes, sir."

"Now?"

"Yes, sir."

"Thanks."

"You're welcome."

Felicia Wells was founder and president of American Black Conservatives, a membership organization that had as its stated mission: "To encourage and promote social and political policies that emphasize a philosophy of self-help, initiative, and responsibility by blacks, as the means of partaking of the limitless bounty of the American Dream." While Eugene spoke on the phone, Felicia was in the conference area of the hotel, presiding over the opening of her two-day conference.

Felicia was a lawyer turned lobbyist turned activist. She was from an upper-middle-class family from Virginia, her father having been a horse breeder. She was well known throughout Washington, D.C., where she had spent all of her professional life, and was increasingly receiving national exposure. At forty-seven, she was tall and full-figured, but not fat. She spoke in a husky, folksy voice remindful of the great Pearl Bailey. She was as dark as a blackberry, which made the gray in her hair appear greater in amount than it was. She wore eyeglasses thick enough to give a bat 20/20. She had arrived in Detroit the day before and given a press conference. Eugene had sat in the lobby of the hotel, just off the conference room where Felicia Wells held court. It was decision time.

"Why Detroit to host the conference?" one local reporter had asked.

"Detroit's a natural choice. It's the largest predominantly black city in the country. There's a large and prosperous black middle class here. And blacks wield power in government and the private sector. Detroit can be the model for urban America, if it's led by the right vision."

"*Right,* as in the political right?" that same reporter had asked in follow-up.

"*Right,* as in being the right and sensible course. There are no political affiliation requirements for membership in American Black Conservatives."

"Why is Governor Blocker getting an award at your luncheon tomorrow?" an out-of-towner had wanted to know.

"In Howard Blocker, Michigan has a governor whose policies are beneficial to black people."

"Does that include his welfare reform and opposition to affirmative action?"

"Yes."

"Ms. Wells, do you see yourself at odds with the civil rights movement?" a wire service reporter had asked. "Some of its leaders have called your organization misguided."

"I'm part of the civil rights movement. Always have been and always will be. People can share a destination but differ on what road to take."

"Whom do you support in Detroit's mayoral race?"

"The fact that both candidates are black underscores my previous remarks about Detroit being a place of opportunity and empowerment for us. But if by support you mean—"

"Who do you think would be the better mayor?" the same voice asked.

"Mayor Clay has attracted lots of investment, but he might be too dependent on help from Washington, and I am concerned about his continued support for outdated programs of entitlement. But I would like to see a little more conservatism in Isaac Shaw's message. Beyond those comments, this outsider will remain neutral."

Eugene waited five minutes after talking with housekeeping before heading for the elevator. He rode to the top floor. Down the hall he saw the maid's cart and the maid, just before she disappeared into the suite. She had an armful of sheets, indicating that a bedroom was her first stop.

Eugene walked a little past the door, did an about-face, and returned. He peeked inside the room and heard the sharp snap of a sheet; with the maid busy making the bed, he slipped into the hallway closet next to the door. He inadvertently jingled some coat hangers as he settled against the wall, but the maid apparently didn't hear. From his hiding place, he strained his ears to map the maid's whereabouts. At some point he heard the thump of plates, the clink of glasses, and the clang of pots and knew that the maid was tidying the kitchen. He recognized the rush of a faucet, could even hear the sinks and counters being scrubbed. Eventually there came the drone of a vacuum cleaner, first faintly, then stronger as the maid worked her way to the front. Finally he heard the door slam, as if he were being locked in a vault, sealing off his escape from his own dark intents.

Eugene slid open the closet door. It was mirrored and operated along a track on the floor. But before emerging, he extended a leg and touched the carpet with the tip of his shoe, gingerly, as one uses a toe to test the temperature of bath water. He lifted his leg, then touched down again, this time with the ball of the foot. Then he applied pressure with the full sole, lifted, and examined. Nothing. Satisfied that the carpet wouldn't hold the impression from his shoes. He stepped out. He closed the closet.

Eugene had jumped inside so quickly that he hadn't noticed that the door was mirrored. Standing there in a gray pin-striped suit, dress shirt, tie, and tasseled loafers, he considered himself once again to be in complete disguise. Even so, the mirror bothered him. He hated mirrors, hated their refusal to lie. But he didn't turn away this time. He spied on his reflection with detached voyeurism, like a clinician observing through a one-way mirror. He watched as the other person withdrew a dagger from inside his jacket and slowly, caressingly, ritualistically, examined it. From every angle. Up close. Arm's length. Then, hypnotically, the other person returned it to hiding, unaware that Eugene had seen his every move.

Charlie "Bubba" Polk's murder had taught this other person the satisfaction derived from a stabbing weapon. He later discovered the dagger in Africa. So by the time he took on the mission, fate had predetermined the instrument of retribution.

Downstairs, at the conference, waiters and waitresses hustled, refilling water glasses and coffee cups. All wore black uniforms that looked like modified tuxedos: black pants with a satin stripe down the legs, double-breasted jacket that was waist-length, and band-collar white shirt. One waitress, in particular, studied the attendees, not knowing exactly what she was looking for but hoping that she would recognize it if she saw it. Her jacket was oversized intentionally, so that her gun holster wouldn't be obvious. Mary's name tag read "Joanne."

When Felicia announced a short midmorning break, Mary went to the lobby area to find Frank. "You're dressed dapper," she told the always natty Frank. But she was complaining, not complimenting. "And here I am looking like a butch Hazel the maid."

"You're the one who wanted to be inside the conference," countered Frank. "Why, I don't know, because it's being taped anyway."

"Any developments out here?" Mary asked.

"Nothing suspicious. And you?"

"The same. But I don't make too much of that, because I still say that the killer is someone who doesn't look the part."

Frank said, "A crowd might not be his thing. Remember that the two victims were alone." He turned flippant with "Most killers are shy souls that don't like to work in front of an audience."

"No shit, Sherlock? And here I was thinking they tap you on the shoulder and say, 'Excuse me. May I get past? I'd like to kill that person in front of you.' " Then she got serious. "Crowds don't necessarily spook this killer. Livingstone was murdered at the Yacht Club and there were plenty of people in the vicinity. Kincaid got his in the parking lot and people were in the building. This killer strikes when the victim is separated from the herd, sure. But that doesn't mean he requires absolute isolation."

As they were speaking, Frank continued to dart his eyes, maintaining surveillance. He pointed and gestured to keep up the pretense that the two of them were discussing the room's arrangements. "Assuming the killer thought Livingstone and Kincaid were Oreos, there's still the question of why he picked those two."

"I don't know," Mary admitted.

"It would be nice if you did," said Frank dryly. "Then we'd know whether there's anything to your theory that he might be attracted to this conference because he sees it as one big cookie jar of Oreos."

Mary said, "Yeah, well, if I could read minds, I wouldn't waste it being a cop. I'd join the carnival and make a fortune guessing people's ages."

Next Frank told Mary, "Instead of making with the quips, you ought to be taking mental notes. I can teach you plenty about undercover work and surveillance."

Mary knew that Frank was bragging about the years he had worked in the Narcotics unit before he transferred to Homicide. He'd earned a reputation as fearless and having close to a photographic memory.

She looked at her watch. "I'll keep that in mind, Professor. They'll be restarting in a bit. I'll talk to you at the lunch break."

The partitions between two adjacent conference halls had been removed to make one hall large enough to contain the hundreds in attendance. A third conference hall had been set up for the awards luncheon. The last speaker before lunch was Cameron Sowell, a thirty-year-old former gang member with a glass eye. His presentation, "You Don't Have to Join the Army to Be All That You Can Be," chronicled how he had overcome obstacles to build an empire of fast-food franchises in inner cities around the country.

About ninety percent of the audience was black and about equally divided with respect to gender. They had come from around the country. Some were well-to-do—even wealthy—but many were of modest means. There was a scattering of young faces among an otherwise middle-aged and older crowd.

Throughout the morning some in the audience reacted to the television and news cameras: adjusting clothing, assuming attentive poses, turning to the preferred side. With some, it took utmost willpower to resist the temptation to wave. Not Felicia Wells, though;

she strutted back to the lectern with the nonchalance of someone about to perform something that is second nature.

She wore a bone-colored, double-breasted, silk suit with pleated pants, in a relaxed cut that accommodated the fullness of her bosom and hips. The red blouse was sheer. The black spiked heels looked as though they stood a fifty-fifty chance of puncturing the floor or snapping under the load they carried. The diamond and ruby pin on her lapel was a gift from her fiancé, a trader in foreign currencies.

"It just makes my heart sing and my spirit rise that things are going so wonderfully well," she said. "Let's have another well-deserved round of applause for all our speakers this morning." Compliance was immediate and so rousing that she had to raise her hand to quiet them so that she could continue. "When I started ABC five years ago, I was convinced that there were many others like myself who knew that 'black conservative' is not a contradiction in terms. Thank you for proving me right."

The applause resumed. "We'll reconvene at two o'clock. For those attending the awards luncheon, it's next door. But however you spend your lunch break, make it positive."

Chairs slid noisily along the floor as attendees pushed away from rows of tables and started filing out. Those headed next door had paid fifty dollars for a choice among chicken breast, salmon, and tenderloin steak. Not long afterward, the soups and salads had been eaten and the main course was on its way.

Governor Blocker, referring to the empty chair to his left, spoke to the others seated at his table. "Anyone know where Felicia is?" he asked.

"She said that she had to make a quick phone call," said Cameron Sowell. "I would have figured that she would be back by now."

Blocker wiped his mouth with his napkin. He was an old-looking fifty-two, lined and balding. He was as wide as he was tall, but it would be inaccurate to describe him as rotund. He was square: no roundness, no contours, just wide and flat. His beady eyes were forever zipping about the room, like those of a diver in shark-infested waters, and it was evidently difficult for him to turn his stump of a neck. "So you're saying that she . . ."

"Went to her room," Sowell said. "She said she was going to her room."

THIRTY-THREE

"Who are you?" asked Felicia Wells, her voice reflecting more surprise than fear. She had entered her suite, engaged the locks, turned around, and seen Eugene walking into view from somewhere in back. He hadn't heard her enter. He hadn't expected her until hours later, and even then, he could only hope that she would be by herself.

"Don't be rattled, Ms. Wells. I'm Ed Farley and I work for the hotel." Eugene's modulated tone belied the surprise he felt. He actually had known someone by that name, a popular black youngster in high school, and it simply had popped into his mind. He offered a handshake, stepping toward her.

Felicia aimed a finger at him and said, "Stop. Stay there. Farley, is it?"

"Yes."

"Why are you in my suite, Mr. Farley?"

"Evaluating the maid's work. We wanted to make sure that everything was in order for the reception you're hosting tonight."

"You give this attention to everybody?"

"You're far too modest, Ms. Wells. You're renting a luxury suite and have filled dozens of other rooms. You're more than entitled to special attention."

"I'd like to see some hotel ID, Mr. Farley."

"No problem."

"Photo."

"Coming right up."

He patted the left side of his chest, pretending that he was checking for something in the inside pocket of his jacket. Then, with both hands, he repeated the pretense on the jacket's outer pockets and on his front and back pants pockets.

He wasn't producing the goods quickly enough for Felicia's peace of mind. She took a step backward, making contact with the door. With her hand behind her back and still facing Eugene, she unlocked the doorknob. She still had the dead bolt and the chain to contend with. They were higher on the door and she couldn't undo them and avoid detection. She needed some delaying tactics.

"Maybe you rushed out this morning and forgot it," suggested Felicia. "Call the front desk and ask for someone to come here and vouch for you." The phone sat on a desk, far into the interior of the suite. If he went—whether for an actual or faked call—she would make her escape. If Mr. Farley turned out to be legitimate, she could apologize later.

Eugene didn't so much as glance in the direction of the phone, but performed a few more pats as if she had not spoken at all. He knew that she suspected. The right hand went from patting to reaching inside his jacket. Out came the dagger against his chest.

Felicia's breath left her in a quick, audible expulsion. She pressed herself harder against the door, as if, by osmosis, she could permeate through to the other side. When she replenished her breath with a jerky, nasal intake, she faced the decision of what to do with it. Speak? Scream?

"Quiet," instructed Eugene, his right index finger to his lips. "Believe me, Ms. Wells, it's not in your best interest to yell or unlock the door."

The taste of fear, metallic and salty, bloomed inside her mouth. She swallowed several times before speaking. "Whoever you are," said Felicia, "I can forget that I ever laid eyes on you if you let me leave right now."

"Can't."

"What in the name of God do you want?"

"I'm not a robber." He lowered the dagger to waist height. Reading something in Felicia's expression, he said, "And I certainly am not a rapist."

"Then what—"

"I'm here to talk. That's all."

"Whatever about?"

"Let's sit." He extended his hand in invitation toward the couch, his head bowed slightly.

"No, thank you," said Felicia, a little of her characteristic assertiveness coming out of hiding. "I prefer to stand here and for you to remain where you are."

"I think that I'm in a position to insist."

"If all you want to do is talk, it shouldn't make a difference."

"We'll split the difference. We'll sit in kitchen chairs, where we are now. You get them."

"I'd rather not."

"I promise not to close the distance as you get the chairs. Every step you take forward, I'll take one backward, and vice versa. You have my word." He didn't sound as if he was negotiating when he said, "It's my final offer."

It was a hesitant, synchronized choreography. When it was completed, they sat facing each other, chess opponents at a very long imaginary table.

"And now?" said Felicia.

"Now I'll get straight to the point." Eugene didn't blink for moments as his gaze seemed to pierce through Felicia. He looked into her fear-widened eyes. "You're an Oreo, Ms. Wells."

She'd never before had that specific epithet flung in her face, although she had endured its various synonyms: Aunt Jemima, sellout, house nigger. Indignation reared but was held in check by fear, although the latter did yield some space for confusion. "I don't understand any of this," she admitted. "I disagree with your charge. But why would it mean anything to you, one way or the other?"

"It wouldn't if you were a nobody. But you're in the spotlight. You could be mistaken for a role model. That makes you dangerous."

"Dangerous to whom, young man?"

"To black people."

"What does that have to do—" She didn't finish her question, because she'd been startled by Eugene's sudden movement. Although he remained seated, he had jerked his back away from the chair rest and his torso was angled menacingly toward her.

He barked loud and angrily, "Are you that stupid? The obvious answer is"—he slapped his chest for emphasis—"that I'm black."

"My goodness—I—I see." Felicia was stammering not from the revelation but from her realization that she had pushed a button, and that he probably had as many as a telephone. She had to be careful not to further agitate him.

"My father is black and my mother is white. By society's rules, that makes me black, doesn't it? And that's fine with me."

"It's your right to define yourself however you choose." Felicia worried whether she sounded patronizing or humoring. She braced for his reaction.

"I am black."

"Understood," said Felicia. "But you're absolutely wrong about me, young man. I beg you to please leave. I won't report you to the authorities."

"It's not me that I'm concerned about. My people are what's important. And the mission. Whatever happens to me, happens."

Felicia was disheartened and further frightened by his words and tone, perceiving them to be those of an unstable person with a martyr complex. Could any appeal to logic be effective? Her mind raced, and she decided her next approach. She held her mouth open but didn't speak immediately. She gathered the words on her tongue, then coached them forward, one by one, tentatively. "So far you've established that you're black and that I'm an Oreo in your eyes. Do I have that much right?"

"Totally."

Felicia took a fortifying deep breath. "I assume that your beef is not just with me, personally, but with me as the head of American Black Conservatives. Right?"

"Right again."

"Okay." She paused to summon her most sincere-sounding voice. "So what would it take for you to declare this a misunderstanding that we both can walk away from?"

Eugene had not expected that question. Rather, he had thought that Felicia would defend her philosophy steadfastly, making what he had come to do easier. But as he had been with Kincaid and Livingstone, he was obliged to be fair with Felicia Wells and give her every reasonable opportunity to save herself.

"Convince me that you're no Oreo," he said simply.

It was a concession and a reprieve; however, she exhibited no sign of relief. For one thing, she was being told to prove a negative, and more than that, the young man before her still impressed her as someone on the edge of reality, unpredictable and volatile.

Oh, how much she wished that the police would rush in, and before they escorted him away in handcuffs, would permit her to give him a piece of her mind. How dare he terrorize her the way he had. How did he find the nerve to call her an Oreo when there he sat, looking like the all-American boy. Had he looked as black as his rhetoric, he probably could not have roamed the hotel freely enough to have gotten into her suite. It was obvious that he had wanted her to mistake him for white when she had entered the suite unexpectedly. He was an impostor and a hypocrite. Probably had never been called a nigger once in his entire life. He could pass for white and for some reason it had him fucked up in the head. But how dare he terrorize her as he had. She wished that she could tell the arresting officers, *Lock up his crazy ass. And I'm definitely pressing charges.*

Felicia Wells turned her head to the side and rubbed a palm across a cheek. Then she looked at the palm and, in reference to her color, said, "See? It doesn't come off. I'm black. I know that. I can't hide it. And I don't try."

Eugene countered with "We can both see that you're black on the outside. It's your creamy white filling that's the problem."

"I'm a proud, strong, black woman and I love my people with all my heart." There was a pleading quality to her voice.

"Then why do you support so many causes against the interests of black people?"

"Like what?"

"Lots of stuff that I'd group together as conservative bullshit." His voice rose an octave in agitation as he went on to say, "Conservatives have a stake in the status quo. Therefore, they want things to stay as they are. Black people aren't vested in a system designed to keep them second class. But you and your organization don't seem to understand that."

Felicia tried to speak with some enthusiasm, to suggest that they had hit upon the problem and that the solution was self-evident. "The misunderstanding is over what I'm conservative about. I'm not conservative about racism or discrimination. I'm conservative about certain principles, young man. Strong family, work ethic, faith in God, respect for life. What's wrong with that?"

"Nothing at all. The Ku Klux Klan preach the same things all the time."

"How can you possibly compare me with the KKK?"

"I wasn't. Just making a point. Principles are interpreted through political filters. This country was founded on the principle that all men are created equal. Unfortunately, at the time, we were slaves and not considered men."

"Fair enough," said Felicia, conceding his point. "I'll speak to my political beliefs. Minimum taxation. Small government. Excellent schools. And hear me good—removal of all barriers to going as far as your talents and drive can take you."

"How come you're against affirmative action?"

"It's like welfare, a dependency. It saps initiative. That's my honest belief. We are not intellectually inferior. Yet the minds of our young are being poisoned with the belief that they can't compete without crutches. The reason I don't believe in affirmative action is that I do believe in my people."

"I see your opposition to affirmative action as giving comfort to the enemy. Handing them an excuse to say, 'See there? Even their own kind agrees with us.' But whether you are our own kind is the question before us, isn't it, Ms. Wells? By the way, are you a Republican?"

Lying about something that he might already know could set him off, so instead Felicia asked, "Why should it make a difference? This country is run by a two-party system. To argue that blacks should be involved with only one is to cut our participation in the system by half."

Felicia's fantasy of being rescued popped back into her head. Oh, how she would revel at a chance to scream her indignations at this Malcolm X wanna-be. What twisted gall he had to have her defend her conservatism when there he sat looking like he had just come from a meeting of the John Birch Society. But wait. Maybe she had made a dent in his lunacy.

In a distant, nostalgic, confiding voice, Eugene said, "When I was a kid, I had this black friend named Larkin. He used to say that nothing was going to stand in his way of becoming president of the United States."

"So where is Larkin today?"

"Dead."

"How sad. What happened?"

"Killed in an accident."

"Larkin embodied the principles I was talking about. Too bad we lost him. We can never have too many Larkins."

"I don't want to talk about Larkin." The tone was sullen but insistent. "Don't say another damn word about him."

Felicia had witnessed yet another sudden mood swing. She felt like a snake charmer, but soon she'd run out of breath for playing the flute that kept the deadly cobra in hypnotic sway, or more specifically, run out of questions and responses. A venomous strike was inevitable if she didn't think of something quick and effective.

"Aren't you forgetting the time?" she asked.

"Time?"

"I'm expecting some people, and they'll be here soon. You should leave. You really should. I can forget this entire incident."

"If you were expecting somebody, you would have said that earlier. You lied."

"All right. The truth is that I came to make some calls before lunch. Any second, someone will call—probably come up here—to see why I haven't returned."

"Now, that story I believe. So I suppose we ought to wrap this up. I have to decide what I'm going to do with you."

That sounded like cobra talk, and it pushed her to a new height of fear and desperation. "The only thing you should think of doing with me is leaving me alone by walking out of here this very second. Anything else and you're going to be in more trouble than you ever dreamed of."

"Please. Be quiet. I need to think." His head went into his hands and his eyes narrowed in apparent pain, but he kept speaking. Fast sentences. Pregnant pauses in between. "I don't want to hurt you, Ms. Wells. I don't want to hurt anybody. I never did. I kind of like you, Ms. Wells. But my mission, I have to be true to my mission. Too late to save Larkin, though. I'm sorry, Larkin." Eugene's voice trailed off, and by the end of his comments he was mumbling through trembling lips. He spoke something else, but it was verbal mush.

Felicia watched as Eugene broke the eye contact they had maintained. She watched his eyes glaze over. She was witnessing some type of transformation, one that she couldn't count on being favorable to her. His hand, still clutching the dagger, rested on his lap. If she were to spring up to undo the chain and bolt, would he recover in time to stop her? And would deadly consequences be certain if she waited to see who, or what, emerged from this trance? She decided that inaction was the worst of her alternatives.

Quicker than one would expect someone her size to move, she catapulted from the chair, whisked it above her head, and charged at Eugene.

THIRTY-FOUR

The rapid, anxious pounding on the door went unanswered.

"Give me the card," said Mary to Drew Ramsey, head of hotel security.

Mary inserted the card into the door slot, then extracted it. The green dot lit up, indicating that the card had performed its function. She twisted the door handle and began to push. The door opened only halfway. Something was blocking it.

Frank had his gun drawn. Mary circled to the back of him. He counted silently, then stuck his head inside the door, sweeping his aim across his field of vision. In the process, he got a glimpse of what the door stop was. He pulled his head back. "It's Wells," he said with resignation. "She's wasted, from the looks of it. Cover me."

Mary drew her weapon. "I got your back, Frank." To Ramsey she said, "Call EMS, but no one else."

Frank again swept his aim around his field of vision, then darted into the suite, stopping against a wall for cover. From there, another sweep, this one of the hallway leading to the back. He could see that all the rooms were open, but he could not see whether a killer lurked in one. With Frank guarding against someone emerging from the back of the suite, Mary entered and checked Felicia's pulse. None. She then took a position behind Frank.

"I'm going across," he whispered, referring to the width of the hallway. They counted with nods of their heads: one, two, three, then Mary provided the cover as Frank somersaulted across.

"Police," shouted Mary. "Come out now with your hands up."

No response. With nerve-wracking uncertainty, they searched the suite room by room. Then their weapons went back into concealment. The killer had performed a vanishing act.

"Cookie monster?" asked Frank after they returned to Felicia's body.

"None other than."

Felicia lay on her left side, curved like a thick comma. She lay in blood, plenty, if the smell was any indicator; but exactly how much couldn't be seen, because the carpet absorbed some and her body obscured yet more. Her bladder, which had been filled by a morning of coffee drinking, had involuntarily emptied. Her head rested on her left arm, which was extended palm up. The cookie lay exposed in it.

"You do anything other than check the pulse?" asked Frank.

"That's how she was, except if contact with the door moved her."

"Can't tell too much about the wounds without moving her," Frank said. He was standing straddled over the body, back bent, hands on his knees, studying the upper body, which seemed to be the source of the blood. Felicia's eyes, not fully closed, were drowsy slits. "But it's no doubt that they're on the side that she's lying on."

"We know what has to be done, so there is no sense in stalling," said Mary.

"I took the point in the sweep," said Frank, reminding her that he went first while she provided cover. "It's time for you to put your life on the line."

"I'd rather undergo a pelvic examination from Edward Scissorhands," she said, evidencing her dread over the task that awaited.

"Too bad. Get on with it."

"How about a coin toss?"

"Hell, no."

"Come on, Frank. Please?"

"Tails," he said as she let a quarter fly.

"Heads," she announced gaily. "And no two out of three, either."

"I won't welsh." Frank bitingly added, "One of us has to have balls." Then he asked, "Am I supposed to do this by telepathy? You know I can't use the phone of a crime scene."

"Sorry. I don't know what I was thinking." She dug into her pants pocket and retrieved a cell phone. She tossed it. "Catch."

"You were thinking about how you made out like a bandit." He flipped the phone open, but before dialing wanted to get in some more grumbling. "The killer strikes right under our noses, and I get stuck with having to call Inspector Newberry and explain how the fuck it happened. He's going to chew my ass like a gumball. At least matters can't get any worse."

"Hush, Frank. My mama always said that when you say something like that you invite fate to prove you wrong."

As if on cue, the phone rang. They looked stupidly at each other through the first several rings, before Frank whipped out a handkerchief. He draped it over the receiver and picked it up. "Hello?" The message was brief. He hung up. "That was Ramsey. The governor demands to know the deal and is on his way up here."

Mary gave Frank a hard, lecturing look before saying, "Is there any other way you want to jinx us?"

THIRTY-FIVE

Mayor Randal Clay's phone buzzed rudely and its red button flashed, signaling that it was his secretary.

"Governor Blocker on line three," she said.

Clay switched over and said, "The mayor."

"Felicia Wells has been murdered in her suite."

Clay swallowed hard. "Oh, my God. How?"

"I don't know. Two Detroit detectives are working the suite, and refused entry to me and my bodyguards."

"How did you find out?"

"From the head of hotel security. He went to the suite with the detectives and heard them say that Felicia Wells was in there dead. He thought I might be in danger."

"I ought to get off the phone, Governor, and start making some inquiries."

"Not so fast. There's something afoot here."

"Excuse me?"

"I'm not a mushroom, so don't keep me in the dark and feed me shit. I do know a little about police operations." As the former Oakland County prosecutor, Governor Blocker would not be easy to deceive. "This hotel was a stakeout."

Clay feigned ignorance. "I don't follow."

"The detectives were undercover. The female was a waitress at the conference. She even served me coffee."

"You're over there, I'm not," said Clay. "So I'm in no position to confirm or deny anything you say."

"Felicia was a personal friend, and I will learn the circumstances of her death. You can bank on that. And if her death was preventable, somebody's going to answer."

"Preventable how?"

"By warning her of whatever danger your police department seems to have known about."

"I really must get off the phone, Governor, I hope with your understanding."

"Go ahead, but don't plan to rest your vocal cords. The media were covering this conference. You have a ready-made feeding frenzy on your hands. It ought to do wonders for Detroit's future conference bookings—and your voter-approval rating."

Blocker hung up with a slam of the receiver. In contrast, Clay lowered his receiver slowly, recalling the day of his reelection committee meeting, when Chief Cornelius Upton told him of the murders of Kincaid and Livingstone. They had spent hours discussing the potential impact of a sensationalized case on the election. They hatched a strategy: no disclosure of the connection between the two murders; aggressive efforts to close the case quickly; no paper trail of communications with the mayor.

Since that meeting with Upton, Clay had periodically been updated by the chief. He even knew of the plan to stake out the American Black Conservatives conference. In addition to having been kept apprised, Clay had been constantly reminded of a killer on the loose, because of the added security that had been assigned to him. Clay was nervous about his own safety, even though he liked to think that no one could consider him an Oreo.

The cookie calling card had not been divulged to the media in either the Kincaid or the Livingstone murder. They withheld that key detail to nail a suspect who demonstrated that knowledge and eliminate the usual oddball assortment of confessors who showed up at the precinct house. With nothing connecting them, neither murder had remained a lead story for long. Each eventually receded from the headlines and into the netherworld of statistics. With this third murder in the lap of the media, everything might be strung together like beads. And Governor Blocker was now in the mix. But none of that was the immediate problem. That distinction went to getting a reliable appraisal of the situation at the hotel before the hordes descended. No sooner had he hung up from talking to Blocker than he jerked the receiver back up and punched his secretary's button.

"Get me Chief Upton. Now. And don't stop trying until you do. Call his pager if he's not at headquarters."

"Yes, sir. Three media people have been on hold since you were talking with the governor. And two camera crews are here requesting interviews with you, sir."

"No interviews and no calls except from the chief."

"I understand, sir." All she understood was that some type of crisis was under way. And that was all she needed to understand to do the job Clay wanted from her. "I'll handle it," she assured.

A minute later, she buzzed Clay to announce that Chief Upton was on line two. He switched over. "Where are you?"

"At headquarters," said Upton.

"I suppose you know."

"Yes."

"Well?"

"I just finished getting briefed by Inspector Newberry. His information was called in by the detectives at the scene. All indications are that it was the same killer. Newberry left for the hotel with a crime-scene crew."

"I don't want any of your officers blabbing about shit."

"They know not to make comments to the media."

"How much was hotel security told?" asked Clay.

"Next to nothing. They were informed of the stakeout but were told that its nature was classified."

"They know nothing about serial murders?"

"That's right."

"Get over here."

"I was going to do that anyway," said Upton, "before going to the hotel. You might want to make an appearance, too."

"I'm going to have to, if only to offset the damage that the governor is probably over there doing."

"He was barred from the crime scene," said Upton, "so he might not be in good humor over that. But how much harm can he do?"

"Don't sell him short, with his Detroit-bashing ass. Get here."

Chief Cornelius Upton used his gate card to enter the underground lot where City Hall honchos parked. The pair of security guards whose duty it was to protect the lot saluted. Upton made a wide swing and parked next to the mayor's limo. One of the two elevators was the private one that the mayor takes straight up to his office. Upton announced himself by intercom and the elevator was sent down to him.

When the chief exited the elevator, Clay was sitting at his desk staring out his window.

"We guessed right," Upton told Clay by way of greeting.

"Not right enough," said Clay. He rose and walked to Upton. They shook hands. "But later for that. We need a game plan."

Under intense time pressure, Clay and Upton debated furiously about what disclosures should be made, until Clay pulled rank and said, "I've made up my mind. We'll play this my way." He rose and got his suit jacket out of the closet. "I'm ordering you not to say anything about a serial killer or that Wells's murder is connected to anything else. Say that there will be an aggressive investigation but it won't be conducted in the media."

"And you expect the media to go quietly into the night?"

"What I expect is to soon be able to announce that the killer is in custody," Clay said. "Get my drift?" He stepped into the elevator, and Upton followed.

THIRTY-SIX

Three days after Felicia Wells's murder, Mary and Frank watched the couple they'd come to meet emerge from the jetway at Detroit Metropolitan Airport. The four knew one another from faxed photos, but there was no agile way around introductions.

"Special Agents Brian Hobbs and Abigail Cox," said the man, who'd spent half of his fifty-eight years with the FBI, the last eighteen in the Investigative Support Unit, which specializes in serial crimes. He was almost tall, fit, youthful-looking, and had a luxuriant head of chestnut hair that he kept meticulously dyed. His front teeth were as big as piano keys, and accordingly, his lips always were slightly parted. He wore a polyester-blend navy suit that was unwrinkled from the plane ride. The top button of his white shirt was unfastened and his solid brown tie hung loosely like a noose. His brown wing tips were scuffed.

"Welcome to Detroit," said Mary. "We're Mary Cunningham and Frank Corleone." A round of handshakes followed.

Speaking to the agents, Frank said, "She's Mary, in case you were having problems solving that one."

Hobbs smiled knowingly at Cox. "I'm picking up on some negative vibes," he said, dating himself by his phrasing.

Frank looked mockingly surprised. "No negativity here. Say, are the shades department-issued," he asked, referring to Hobbs's ultradark sunglasses, "or do you know somebody in the CIA?"

Like a mother embarrassed by the public misbehavior of her child, Mary said, *"Frrrank."*

"No, it's okay," said Hobbs. "Let him vent. We're used to resentment from local law-enforcement officers who regard us as interlopers. Let him get his cheap shots out of his system. Then maybe we can get down to brass tacks."

Cox spoke up. "There's no need for territorial disputes, Officer Corleone. The jurisdiction remains yours. We're only a resource. We're here to help you." She was thirty-six, and a former Ph.D. candidate in psychology who left Stanford University to join the unit. She was five feet six and 140 pounds, distributed in ways that reflected her fondness for aerobics. She had the face and color of a black mannequin. Her straight hair was parted in the middle, combed down, with the ends flipped up around her shoulders. She wore a gray, pin-striped, skirted suit with white blouse and black pumps.

"Let's go," Frank said with authority. "Can I carry your bag, Ms. Cox?"

"No, but thank you."

As they walked, Frank said to Hobbs, "Here's a little joke we tell at headquarters. What does FBI stand for?"

"I'll bite," said Hobbs. "Tell me."

"Forever Butting In."

"Nice" was Hobbs's compliment. "Here's one. Why does Detroit spend less on gasoline than any other police department?"

"Let's hear it," said Frank.

"No cop has to drive more than a block to find a crime scene."

Mary and Abigail Cox gave each other a bonding look. Then the two women quickened their strides and walked a few paces ahead, not wishing to be sprayed by the pissing contest. The men seemed to understand and suspended their flexing for the rest of the walk.

The foursome exited into saunalike humidity and piled into the unmarked car in front of the terminal. Hobbs slid into the backseat without concern. Cox, noticing the seat's condition, chose to sit on the *Wall Street Journal* that she had brought off the plane.

Hobbs and Cox had come to Detroit by invitation from Chief Cornelius Upton. They had flown in from FBI headquarters in Quantico, Virginia. With three murders and possibly counting, efforts had to be stepped up before something yanked away the blanket of secrecy protecting the mayor. The involvement of the FBI was relatively low-risk, because the Bureau more times than not operated outside the public's purview.

When Frank got onto the Edsel Ford Freeway, Hobbs began to earn his plane fare. "The killer hasn't taken his act on the road," he said. "We've cross-referenced national data, and no other cases fit the profile."

"Okay, he's a homebody," said Frank. "What else you got?"

Before Hobbs could answer, Mary injected a question, one that acknowledged the short span of time since materials had been expressed and faxed. "How much of the case have you been able to review?"

"Practically all," claimed Hobbs. "I finished up on the plane. The materials were well written and well organized. That made it a lot easier. I commend you, Lieutenant Cunningham."

Mary grinned like the Cheshire Cat with gas. "Hear that, Frank? I got praised by the FBI."

"Try to contain yourself."

Hobbs saved her from having to retaliate by resuming his answers. "I believe that the most important part of a case file is the coroner's findings, because the victim's body is the most revealing piece of evidence. It can hold the answers to the Big Three."

"*One*, what happened; *two*, why did it happen that way; and *three*, who has the profile to have done it," contributed Cox, following what would prove to be their style: equal parts recitation and conversation.

"We got us a suspicion about number one," said Frank. "Three people were stabbed to death, and an Oreo cookie was left with each body. We kind of think that's what happened."

Hobbs ignored the sarcasm. "True. But Kincaid and Livingstone suffered multiple wounds, Wells only one. Differences can be as telling as similarities."

"What do you make of it?" asked Mary.

With no apology in his voice, Hobbs said, "I don't know at this point."

But Cox added, "Serial killers can be so ritualistic as to kill with the same number of wounds each time, because that number is symbolic—obviously not the case here. Or the different number of wounds might simply reflect variables such as rage or how much time he had."

Frank said, "Mary and me can come up with the 'maybe this and maybe that' all day long. I thought you're supposed to tell us what's what."

"It's wearing thin, Frank," said Mary.

At that time, Frank was slowing the car in response to the traffic that was coming to a crawl. "Uh-oh. What's this ahead?" he said.

"Maybe a clunker overheating and blocking a lane," said Mary.

Hobbs left the traffic conditions for Frank to deal with and continued his explanation. "I agree with your theory, Lieutenant Cunningham, that the killer doesn't have an alarming appearance. Maybe all the victims gave him access."

"Probably not Wells," said Frank. "Somebody—I bet the killer—ordered the suite cleaned. Housekeeping remembers that it was a man. He could have sneaked in during the cleaning. A Boy Scout could earn his explorer's badge in that suite, it's so big. Plenty of possible hiding places."

"It's possible," admitted Hobbs.

With self-satisfaction directed at the agents and Mary, Frank gloatingly said, "So much for the ironclad theory about Joe Average."

"Unfortunately for you, Detective Corleone," said Cox.

"Meaning what?" asked Frank.

"You, personally, were staked out at the lobby and hotel entrance," Cox answered. "If the killer were suspicious-looking, how'd he get past you coming or going?"

"Please," Mary implored. "Don't get him started about what a great undercover man he is."

Proving that it was too late, Frank said, "Not to mention my memory for faces. I could probably recognize the obstetrician that slapped my naked ass." Suddenly he slapped the top of the steering wheel in frustration. "Shit, this freeway has turned into a parking lot."

"The killer is black," said Hobbs, retaking the lead.

"I've gone back and forth on that one," said Mary, "never feeling one hundred percent sure."

Hobbs said, "I stake my reputation on it. A white killer would make a sensational plot twist, but that's Hollywood. The reality is that blacks are mostly murdered by blacks. The Oreo thing is no smoke screen. Hatemongers, like the white supremacists, wouldn't operate on that motive. And I know of no case in the annals of a white killing a black for being a sellout. Oh, the killer is black all right."

Frank craned his neck, trying to see the cause of the slowdown, but a beer truck in front of him blocked his view. "What about age, occupation—shit like that?"

Cox got back into the conversation. "Serial killers usually are between twenty-five and thirty-five years old. Since this killer struck on a weekend, a weekday, by night, and by day, he's probably unemployed, underemployed, self-employed, or rotates shifts."

Frank said, "Hmmm. Rotates shifts. Could be a cop."

"And the killer is likely personable and conversational, at least up to the point that he kills," Cox added.

The traffic had slowed to a prolonged stop. "Drive the shoulder," Mary suggested to Frank.

"Good idea." He started the slow process of cutting across the right lane, prompting angry honks from a couple of motorists who didn't want to make way.

"Turn on your flashers," Mary said. "Let them know we're cops."

"I'll be damned," said Frank, angered and embarrassed when the flashers didn't work.

"You don't have a roof attachment, I suppose," Hobbs commented.

"You suppose correctly" was Frank's reply.

Without announcing her plans, Mary opened the door of the stationary car. She played traffic cop, showing her badge and signaling cars to stay put while Frank maneuvered onto the shoulder. It wasn't long before they reached the jackknifed trailer that was the cause of the tieup. Traffic flowed beyond that. By that time, the conversation had gotten to the weapon.

"I believe that it symbolizes something to the killer," Mary said after they had discussed the fact that it wasn't a conventional weapon.

"No doubt one of the pieces to the puzzle," agreed Hobbs.

"How far are we now from downtown?" Cox wanted to know.

"You're too old for the 'Are we there yet?' bit," Frank said. He adjusted the rearview mirror to catch her reaction, and momentarily locked gazes with her dark brown eyes. Her perfume was riding the currents of the air conditioning.

"About five minutes," Mary said.

Frank said, "Tell me, Agent Cox, have you ever arrested a serial killer?"

"No. As I explained earlier, we help in all phases leading up to the arrest. The arrest itself is usually done by the local authorities." Then, as if to establish her credentials, she said, "I've interviewed dozens of serial killers, though."

"Are interviews the bases for the profiling that you do?" Mary had angled her torso so she could face the two agents.

"To a large degree, yes," answered Hobbs. "We've built an extensive database. It's what enables us to help you construct a profile, narrowing your search to the likely suspects."

Cox shifted to reposition the newspaper under her. Frank watched her in the mirror. "Need to go to the bathroom, Agent Cox? Is that why you're in a hurry?"

"I apologize," Mary told Cox, who hadn't dignified Frank's juvenile antics with a response.

"For those of you experiencing the thrill for the first time," announced Frank, "we are now in downtown Detroit." He drove several blocks before pulling in front of the Ambrosia Hotel. "Hey, agents, bet you never had your lodging and the crime scene at the same place before."

"This is a first," Hobbs said. "But functional."

"Sure you don't want me to carry your bag?" asked Frank.

"If you like."

"I wasn't talking to you," he told Hobbs.

"No," declined Cox, "I'll manage."

"If chivalry is dead," said Mary, "you're damn sure trying to perform mouth-to-mouth, Frank."

"I want to ask my profiling experts one more thing before we go in," Frank said. "Are we dealing with a crazy bastard, or what?"

"How are you defining 'crazy'?" Cox asked.

"Like, you know, innocent by reason of insanity."

"Or even guilty but insane, and therefore off to the loony farm instead of the big house," said Mary.

"Then no," said Hobbs. "Bastard? Maybe. But crazy? Definitely not."

"Agent Hobbs believes that no one can be a serial killer and crazy at the same time," explained Cox. "I don't agree."

Hobbs stated his philosophy. "A crazy person is unable to distinguish between right and wrong. If the killer can't distinguish between right and wrong, why does he avoid capture? Every serial killer is twisted, some purely evil, so I'll go along with sicko, wacko, psycho—terms like that. But crazy as in not realizing the consequences of actions? Never."

"You have sixty seconds for rebuttal, Agent Cox," said moderator Mary.

"The insane reside in their own world," Cox began. "An insane person's belief of right and wrong as they apply to his acts can be topsy-turvy."

"Topsy-turvy," interrupted Frank. "At last, some real technical jargon."

"If this killer *is* insane, to him, what he's doing is right; getting caught and stopped is wrong." Cox began to struggle with her door handle, which wouldn't yield.

"I've heard this before, as you can imagine," said Hobbs, who had just opened his door. "Agent Cox also believes that a person can be selectively insane and not across-the-board insane."

"I believe that up until a person loses all contact with reality, he could be farther gone in some areas than others," she corrected. Then she asked Hobbs, "Would you come around and open my door?"

"Well, I suppose if you two agreed on everything, then one of you would be unnecessary," Mary said.

"I think there's something to what you say," Frank told Cox. "Nobody reported a maniac running amok before any of the killings. So, in addition to his milquetoast appearance, he's normal-acting up to the time his thing takes over."

"His thing?" said Cox. "I see that you know a little technical jargon yourself." She was sliding across the seat to go out the other door, carefully keeping the newspaper under her. Hobbs had not been able to open her door.

After waving off an advancing parking valet, Frank got out of the car, leaving it illegally parked. Together they walked through the hotel's automatic doors. A full agenda awaited the four. After the agents checked into their rooms, they would visit the Venus Suite, which was still sealed and guarded. The next stop would be the Wayne County Morgue to view Felicia's body and talk to the coroner. Then it would be off to police headquarters, where Chief Upton and Inspector Newberry waited.

As Hobbs and Cox registered at the front desk, Mary and Frank huddled to the side.

"What do you think, Mary?"

"About Hobbs and Cox?"

"Naw, Siskel and Ebert. Who do you suppose I'm talking about?"

"They might not do us any good, but as long as they don't do us any harm, I'll tolerate them."

"What about their theories?"

"Well," said Mary, "half of them are probably bullshit. The only problem . . ."

"We don't know which half."

THIRTY-SEVEN

An annual event, the Police Officers' Field Day was both a fundraiser and a morale-raiser. But with the specter of a serial killer on the loose, Mary's thoughts were very far away from the event, which had marked a significant turning point in her life.

It was traditional for merchants to donate prizes for the cops at each precinct who sold the most tickets to the Police Officers' Field Day. Several years before, Mary, who was working in Homicide at the time, placed second among officers at headquarters. Her prize: dance lessons at a studio. She didn't start redeeming her coupons right away, and during the interim months, she tried several times to make a gift of them, but no takers. One time she held the coupons twisted in her hands, about to rip them in two, so much did she associate them with dark, tormenting memories. But the coupons were given a last-second reprieve and banished to the back of a dresser drawer.

They stayed there until Mary experienced a harrowing period when she was a wishbone pulled by work and mothering. In particular, Gazelle, in her early teens, was such a hellion that Mary almost regretted not having had a headache the night the girl was conceived. With Gazelle at her grandparents' for the weekend and Mary desperate for a diversion, she redeemed the first coupon.

She had the option of divvying up the coupons however she chose, and to help her decide, the studio gave her demonstrations of the dances taught there. The waltz was first. Next came the flamenco. The fox-trot followed. Then the tango. There were some after that—

wasted time and energy, it turned out, because she had decided. The tango had bewitched her, similar to how, as a girl, she had been smitten by ballet.

Maybe in the hauntingly sensual tango she saw the intrigue and intimacy that she wished for in a relationship. She had come to the studio by herself—the three years since her second divorce had been a series of miscues, and she was on a hiatus from dating. Still, she was thinking, *My, my, my,* when the instructor paired her with a certain newcomer. "Hi," her new partner had said, "Remember me? Cliff Cunningham?"

Cliff, unlike Mary, had no formal background in dance, but he proved to Mary that he had only one left foot. In his day, he had made the nightclub circuit, and before then, in college, his Kappa Alpha Psi fraternity brothers nicknamed him "Fred Astaire" for his smoothness, especially on those slow, dreamy tunes.

They became partners on and off the dance floor, through the court-ship, the engagement, and now, into the marriage. Their progress curve as dancers was steep, and a year and a half ago, they stopped ignoring the urgings of friends and started competing. It took time to learn the intricacies, like the many ways to play to the judges and audience. But that first trophy did come—third place—and since then their fireplace mantel had become crammed with other awards.

Now the biggest competition they'd ever entered was coming up: the Tango Championship of Southeast Michigan. Mary and Cliff had taken first place at one of the regional qualifying contests. Cliff assigned a lot of importance to winning the Southeast, envision-ing the massive trophy displayed at the studio they were going to open. Surely it would persuade prospective customers to sign up. Additionally, the publicity from winning would be great advance advertising. He'd make sure that the writers mentioned that the Cunninghams soon would open their own studio.

But they were not getting in the practice necessary to have a reason-able shot at winning. As the cliché goes "It takes *two* to tango." Mary tried to convince herself that her workload was the culprit, stealing her time and energy; however, she knew in her heart that there were ele-ments of avoidance and sabotage in her lack of preparation.

Several days after the Felicia Wells murder, as she prepared to go to work, her guilt was pricking her like bad acupuncture. It was difficult to reconcile how she could love Cliff so much yet treat him so unfairly. Didn't he have a right to know that she'd pursued promotions, even as she was misleading him with hopes that she might resign and join him in running the studio? And didn't he deserve a partner who, if she didn't share in his dream, at least didn't conspire against it? In an effort to assuage the guilt, she resolved to herself that she would come home that evening, prepare a romantic dinner, and then put in a long, devoted practice.

She went out the front door. Her eyes swept the porch for something that wasn't there. Annoyed, she descended the steps and hunted among the hedges until she found the folded, bagged newspaper that the carrier had flung with poor aim. A slug had crawled underneath and was adhering to the bag with its slime. Disgusted, Mary shook off the slug, and in the process the newspaper spilled out onto the sidewalk. The headline stunned her: "Serial Killer Prowling City?" The subheading read: "Source says Clay knew but withheld information."

Mary stood as rooted as the hedges and read the entire article, her heart drumming. The cited source was that well-known blabbermouth, Anonymous. The article did not emphatically claim that a serial killer was on the loose but made a compelling case for that possibility. It mentioned that Wells, Livingstone, and Kincaid had died from stab wounds inflicted by a peculiar type of blade and that autopsy reports would verify it. Mary was aware that such information had not been officially released to the media. The article reminded that on occasion, all three victims had had their blackness questioned. And—this was the clincher—it mentioned that an Oreo cookie was found on each body, indicative of the killer's motive. Mary would have found it sensational reading if she didn't know the amount of truth it contained.

When Felicia Wells was murdered, Governor Blocker's statement that the hotel had been staked out made the newshounds smell a story; however, Clay's administration sent them sniffing along a false trail. The red herring used was the rumor that Felicia had received threats in other cities, and that the Detroit police had taken precautionary measures. Thus was invented the specter of an out-of-town stalker having come to Detroit and done the deed. And thus for the most part the media was diverted from looking for connections with other murders. Now the campaign of misdirection, like a pyramid of tin cans, was under threat of having a corner yanked away.

Mary folded the paper in half and got into her Ford Explorer. Before turning the ignition, she sat trying to predict the reception that awaited her at headquarters. The fact that she'd not received a call that morning from the brass didn't necessarily bode well for her. Clay, Upton, and Newberry probably were busy deciding the size of the tray on which they would serve her head. To be convicted in absentia is just what she would expect from them. After all, hadn't she preached with an evangelist's fervor about the public's right to know?

But she was innocent, and she would assert her innocence against all accusers. Nonetheless, the shit had hit the fan: enough shit to choke a sewer; enough fan to cool a skyscraper. And now with this leak, another ton of pressure had been heaped on the pile. Mary and Frank would have to carry the weight. The understaffing problem in Homicide, coupled with the recent developments, would bring things closer to critical mass. Mary didn't want to speculate about what would happen next. But before the morning sun rose much higher in the east, Detroit would be abuzz over the story, and national focus would follow.

From all indications, it was a sure bet that dinner and practice would be placed on indefinite hold.

THIRTY-EIGHT

The dishwasher had gargled noisily as Eugene and Mocha grappled with her blockbuster announcement. Eugene had been elated; Mocha fearful. Throughout the morning he had wiped her tears and offered every reassurance he could devise. In between, he had asked twice, and she had said "No" each time, insisting that they should consider the obvious alternatives. But he lovingly wore her down, a heavy sigh and a worried smile her signs of surrender. He asked a third time:

"Ms. Mocha Diane Springwell?"

"Yes, Mr. Eugene No-Middle-Name Shaw?"

"Will you marry me?"

"The knee thing, baby. Do the knee thing."

"Will you marry me?" he repeated, this time kneeling.

"Yes!"

She threw her arms open, an invitation for him to rise into her clutches; but on the way up, he wrapped his arms around her hips and lifted her off her feet. She took the merry-go-round ride with girlish glee. Three revolutions. Then he set her on the kitchen counter. They hugged, the silence speaking for itself. He pried himself from her embrace just enough to find her mouth. His kisses were a roaming series of pecks, and she determined their landings, shifting her head to catch some on the upper lip, shifting to catch some on the lower, shifting to catch some squarely. Then she arranged her mouth into a pout.

"My stomach is going to be sticking out like a beach ball."

He unzipped her jeans. Then he crept a hand underneath her blouse and against her belly, where he made slow, soothing circles that grew in circumference from just below her breasts to just inside her panties. "When this tummy is no longer as flat as a board, you'll still be beautiful."

"You say that now, but we'll see how you look at me months from now." Then she frowned and said, "And stretch marks are not sexy."

"Yours will be."

"What's that sly grin about, Gene?" she asked, noting his expression.

"I've always heard that sex with a pregnant woman is the bomb."

"Oh, yeah? You been getting it for weeks on end and haven't noticed any difference."

"Says who? I just didn't know the cause, that's all."

Mocha could not pinpoint the exact occasion that she got pregnant. She and Eugene practiced birth control with contraceptive foam; but obviously their practice hadn't made perfect, probably because of their penchant for spontaneity. There were times, for example, when they'd come home and get straight to business, shedding clothes at the door and getting only as far as the living room floor. At some point he'd withdraw so that she could insert the foam, but by then some semen already might have seeped. Mocha's menstruations had always come like clockwork, and she had not seen her period since she had become sexually involved with Eugene.

"Talk your sweet jive, while you can. But know this right now: when I suffer, you'll suffer," Mocha said.

"Like for instance."

"Well, every time I puke from morning sickness, I'm going to rush to you for a kiss—without rinsing my mouth, brushing my teeth, or nothing."

"Don't bring your yuck mouth my way."

"That's what was wrong with me the evening of the museum party. Your dumb butt never suspected, did you?"

"Sure didn't. It wasn't morning, for one thing."

"That's just the name for it, silly. It can hit any time of the day. I swear, all men know about a woman's body is where to stick it in."

"And we wouldn't know that much," confessed Eugene, "if we didn't have several choices."

"Forever the comedian, huh?" Then she threatened, "I'll fix you." She shot both hands to his throat. His tongue hung out, his eyes rolled up, he gagged. But they couldn't sustain the farce, and both broke into laughter.

Mocha's face turned solemn. "I'm still scared, baby."

"Don't be. Everything is going to be wonderful. I promise."

"I don't want you to resent me or feel entrapped."

"How could you even think that, Moe? You didn't get pregnant by yourself. I could have been a lot more careful. You're my Nubian queen and you're going to give me an heir. Know what I think? Subconsciously we both wanted it to happen."

"Maybe. What I do know is that I love you more than I've ever loved anybody."

"And?" Eugene coaxed.

"And I want to have your baby. Forgive me for not telling you as soon as I found out."

"There's nothing to forgive. And I'll always love you for not choosing abortion."

Shame registered in Mocha's voice when she admitted, "I thought about it. God forgive me, I did. But I couldn't do it and deny you your right to participate in the decision."

"You'll never regret it, Moe. Not ever."

Mocha got down from the counter after kissing his forehead and mussing his hair. She turned her back and leaned against him for support. She was smiling broadly, gazing upward, lost in pleasant imaginings. "I wonder what our baby will look like."

"Like a miniature person, what else?"

Mocha slapped his arm playfully. "You know what I mean. How much will it look like me. How much like you. What color will it be."

"Black." Eugene's tone was sharp.

"Gene, don't start no mess with me." She pried open his arms and turned to face him. "It's a natural thing for a black couple to wonder about. I meant nothing by it."

"I might have overreacted a little," Eugene said.

"I won't tolerate you making our child color-struck."

"Do I get down on both knees, or can I just say I'm sorry?"

"I forgive you, especially since you've chilled compared to how bad you used to be."

"I let you put your mirrors up. Don't forget that."

"True, although sometimes I still catch you avoiding them."

"I just want our baby to have some color."

"It will. Your cream and my coffee will blend beautifully."

Eugene wanted to change the focus, but in no way the subject. He reached for Mocha, and she gave him her hand. He reeled her into an embrace. "We need a house," he declared, "with a big backyard."

"Oh, Gene." Mocha was glowing. "Marriage, family, house—you're serving up the All-American Dream."

"If that's what you want to call it."

"Gene, you're blowing me away with all this, but I'm loving every second. Where will we live?"

"You choose. I just want to provide for my wife and child."

"When can we start looking?"

"Is immediately soon enough?"

Mocha answered by doing a sassy little jig—waving her arms above her head and switching from side to side. She stopped for more decision making. "If it's a girl, I want to name her Courtney."

"Damn, baby. How about LaShanda, Moyesha, or even Darlene—a real name for a sister."

"There you go being the comedian again. When I was a little girl, Courtney was my favorite doll, and I've always loved that name. When I dress our little girl in frilly dresses, do her hair in bows and ribbons, she'll be my Courtney again."

"Courtney is a lovely name, Moe."

"And if it's a boy, Eugene Jr."

"Nix that. I prefer something else."

"What?"

"Larkin."

Mocha didn't ask the reason behind Eugene's preference. She was too much in rapture to care. But Eugene was busy thinking about how he could further show his love for this woman who had changed his entire existence. It came to him. It would be quite the sacrifice. But he vowed to himself to do it—even if it killed him.

THIRTY-NINE

Malik Kenyatta was dressed regally in African garb; pants, top, and hat of the same white satinlike cloth, brocaded in gold and silver. He wore an ivory necklace, gold bracelets, and gold rings. Mary was interviewing him in his office, located in the back of his store, The Motherland.

Kenyatta sat atop the corner of a massive mahogany desk and Mary sat in a high-backed chair upholstered in zebra hide. From the walls, tribal masks spied through vacant eyes. Carved wooden statues of tribal warriors stood posted around the room like ebony dwarfs. Instead of a door, a curtain of strung beads hung, and the jumbled smells of incense, oils, and essences from out front invaded freely.

The West Side store sold books, art, jewelry, fashions, cards, and gifts and was the largest of its kind in the state. It also had a food counter where tea, coffee, and sweets were served. It had a customer base as diversified as the reasons for which people seek out things that are Afrocentric. Mary was there because The Motherland also was a meeting place where blacks of varying philosophical stripes discussed the issues of the day.

Kenyatta reached around and from a carousel of pipes on his desk selected one with monkeys carved in its bowl. Mary watched as he packed and lit the pipe. The aromatic smoke swirled through his full beard and tangled with the room's redolence.

After almost a half hour of answering questions, Kenyatta hadn't yielded any information of value. He had said he knew of no individual or group that he thought might be behind the Oreo murders.

"Looks like I won't suffer writer's cramp around here," said Mary, tapping the point of her pen against her pad, then flipping the cover closed.

"So shoot me for not solving your case for you."

"I shouldn't sound ungrateful," Mary said. "Thanks for your time."

"Don't mention it. Anything else? Of an official nature, I mean."

"Yeah," said Mary, "since you asked. What about your own little group?"

Kenyatta stood, and as if he hadn't heard the last question, said, "I'm sorry, I'm forgetting my manners. Can I offer you something? I have some sweet potato tarts." He took a bag from a small refrigerator in a corner. He held it pinched between thumb and index finger and swung it side to side, as if it were an amulet and he were a magician putting Mary under hypnosis.

Mary first shook her head in refusal, then said, "I'll try one."

"One of the sisters baked them last night," commented Kenyatta.

"Scrumptious," she said after her first bite. "Maybe you didn't hear me the first time. What about your own little group?"

Malik Kenyatta was leader of The Children of the Ashanti, a group professing devotion to African culture and traditions. He had formed the group twelve years before. Back then he was Roosevelt Foley, a thirty-three-year-old electrician. His group now numbered around 150, about half longtime followers, the other half of the come-and-go type. A variety of professions were represented within the ranks of The Children of the Ashanti, among them medicine, law, business, education, skilled trades, and craftsmen. Kenyatta's vision was a group that was as self-reliant as possible, providing internally the products and services needed by its members, much like a storied African village.

Oddly enough, Kenyatta, a.k.a. Foley, had never set foot on African soil until several years after the group's formation. And his concept of Africa had been quite naive, idealizing it more as one land than the vast, diversified, and divided continent that it is. It had taken several trips to the continent for him to appreciate that African nations had as many political, social, and cultural differences among them as did European nations, Asian nations, South American nations, et cetera. But by then Kenyatta had an investment in the concept of a monolithic Africa, so he didn't let his education change his preachings.

"The Children of the Ashanti are nonviolent," professed Kenyatta, "but you know that as well as anyone. Now, can we call this the end of official business?" He walked to where she sat and rested one hand on the curved back of her chair. Mary found herself admiring his sandals. They had individual loops for each toe, and she bet herself that they were custom-made. She lifted her gaze, pausing momentarily at his belly, slightly round like the earliest stage of pregnancy, before encountering his brown eyes, which were shades lighter than his face. His smile was a taunt, as though he held secrets.

"You say that like there's some unofficial business to tend to."

"Is there?"

"No."

"Sure?"

"I don't have to convince you."

"I don't know. Just seems to me that I was a long shot in this investigation and that you might have other reasons for being here."

"Such as?"

"You tell me."

"I already have."

"Then allow me some unofficial chitchat. How's your marriage going?"

"Heavenly." Mary got up, but Kenyatta stepped around in front of her. "You're in my way, Roosevelt." She clamped her hands on her waist, slid a foot forward, and looked him down and up before her head settled into a combative tilt.

"Sorry," he said while moving aside and ignoring that she had intentionally called him by his "slave name." "I didn't mean to run you off by mentioning marriage."

"Who's running, Roosevelt? I'm leaving here knowing almost less than I did when I came. There's no reason to waste any more of my time—or yours."

"I see you're still holding grudges."

"That's not true."

"You won't call me by my true name. I know what that's all about, Mary. I know your little spiteful ways. I was married to you."

Mary had met Foley in 1986, the last years that she was a patrol cop. He was driving his work truck when she stopped him for making an illegal left turn. He argued—truthfully—that he couldn't read the traffic sign prohibiting the turn because it had been bombed with snowballs. Still, Mary's precinct captain had been riding her about the meager number of tickets she'd been writing, and besides, this Roosevelt Foley had a smug confidence that intrigued and annoyed her at the same time. Still, to issue a ticket under such conditions wasn't fair.

She was about to send him on his way with a warning, but he didn't know when to shut his big mouth. He told her that instead of paying for a ticket, he could use that money for a nice hotel room for the two of them. That's when Mary whipped out her book. And her conscience didn't bother her as she handed him the ticket. A judge dismissed it after Mary admitted in court the condition of the sign. The dating started the next week, after she returned a call he made to her at the precinct. They married the next year and divorced two years later.

"Whose definition of marriage are you using, Roosevelt, mine or yours?"

"Don't continue being a victim of the white man's brainwashing, Mary."

"I'm not going to be suckered into that discussion. Call it brainwashing if you want. The fact is that I agreed to be your only wife. Not one of them."

"Our ancestry says that a man can have more than one wife, especially if he takes care of all of them."

"I don't need anybody to take care of me. Not materially. Anyway, they're not legally your wives."

"There you go again, using white society's standards. It's too bad that—"

"It's too bad that I didn't haul ass the first time you mentioned multiple wives."

"You still can't see that your hang-ups reflect a lack of knowledge of self. A strong black woman knows who she is and her role in the natural order."

"Rhetoric. Just bullshitting rhetoric."

"I told you you're holding grudges."

"I told you I'm not. You opened the door to this discussion."

"This is the first time we've discussed this since we separated, and it's clear that the years haven't changed things. Yet I honestly believe that if you hadn't jumped ship so soon, you would have grown to appreciate the arrangement. Now it's all water under the bridge."

"You got that right," said Mary. "I'm leaving now."

It's unusual for a cop to be happy that a lead turned out dry; it's also unusual for a lead to be an ex-spouse. Roosevelt certainly wasn't the Cookie Cutter; furthermore, he knew nothing, least of all the convoluted path that had brought Mary to his establishment.

Four pieces of straw collected on the aft deck of Livingstone's yacht had started it. To the evidence technician the straw had been insignificant, but to Mary it seemed oddly isolated, its presence begging an explanation. The Michigan State Police laboratory report said that the straw was of tropical origin and maybe was used as packing material. If it fell from the killer—maybe as he jumped aboard or moved about the yacht—how did he first come into contact with it? If, indeed, it was packing material, it could have gotten on him while he unpacked something. The logical step was to suspect the killer worked with things that are imported from somewhere that packs with straw. Nine pages of people and organizations with import licenses were received from Lansing, the state capital. Kenyatta was on that list. Oreo killings and an Afrocentric shop—a match?

Hardly, as it turned out; Kenyatta hadn't changed. His focus was monetary, not militant. But something's only a waste of time when it's spent at the sacrifice of something better. And nothing better was in the offing, with Mary figuratively and literally clutching at straws.

"Stay a minute. There's no reason for you to act like we're enemies," Kenyatta said.

"I don't consider us enemies."

"Good. Tell me about Gazelle. I haven't seen my stepdaughter since she was a girl."

"Gazelle's at Michigan State. She wants to be a veterinarian."

"She will be if she's any way as strong-headed as she was as a child. So what do you think of the place? It's a lot different from that little hole-in-the-wall I started out with, huh?"

"Careful, you're going to throw your shoulder out of joint, patting yourself on the back so hard." Mary smiled, but her body remained tense, expectant.

Kenyatta decided to do something about that. He grasped her

wrists and gently unfolded her arms. Next he converted the contact to hand holding. "You're wearing the years well, Mary. Seeing you reminds me all over again how much of a beautiful black sister you are."

"I don't believe it," she said in a shame-on-you tone. "You're trying to come on to me."

"Why wouldn't you believe it?" He raised her hands to a palms-together, prayer position, then rubbed the backs of her hands. "We still got the chemistry."

"Yeah, you're nitro and I'm glycerin."

"Mary, Mary, quite contrary. Don't be like that." Kenyatta narrowed his eyes seductively.

"Oh, no. Anything but the bedroom eyes," pleaded Mary. She turned her head and shielded her eyes with a forearm, a melodrama designed to mock.

"Playacting can't cover up the fact that we had a good sex life. Don't you remember?"

"If I don't, I suppose you want to give me a refresher course."

"I know you haven't forgotten. Look at this big, handsome desk. All you have to do is hop up there, raise your dress, and pull back your panties—that is, if you're wearing any in this heat."

"For old times' sake?" asked Mary.

"For old times' sake."

"What about privacy? That's not exactly a door, you know."

"I'll tell Azania," he said, nodding his head in the direction of the woman working out front, "that I'm not to be disturbed. She won't come back here, and it's off-limits to the customers. Anyway, the risk of discovery adds to the excitement. What about those times we did it in public places?"

"And what about your harem? No telling what number it's at now. What would they think?"

"I have three wives in spirit and flesh, and there is no jealousy among them. As for you, Mary, in my heart, you'll always be my wife."

"Don't overdo it. Too much sugar spoils a meal. If you want to fuck me, come right out and say it. I'm a big girl."

"Then let's deal on that basis," said Kenyatta eagerly.

"What basis?"

"Lovemaking."

Mary corrected him. "Fucking."

"Then fucking."

"So ask."

"Let's fuck, Mary."

Beaming a wicked smile, Mary said, "Not in this lifetime, but you're more than welcome to go fuck yourself." She yanked her hands from his and began her exit.

"False pride, Mary," Kenyatta called after her. "You know you didn't come here just to ask me questions. Be honest. There's something else you want."

Mary had pulled aside the beads, but she didn't go through. She stopped and then turned to face Kenyatta. "You're right. Who am I trying to fool?" she said. "I know my weakness, and I'm not going to fight it."

She walked past Kenyatta and toward the desk. She swept aside the pipe carousel and tobacco canister as Kenyatta pulled the waist drawstring of his pants. She plopped her butt on the desktop. She leaned back and stretched her arms behind her. Then, the bag of tarts in hand, she jumped down. As she went through the beads, she stuck her head back in for a parting comment. She held up the bag and said, "Like I told you, these are scrumptious. Thanks," and she stretched the syllables when she added, *"Roosevelt."*

FORTY

The color photo IDs lay scattered on Martha Chenault's desk, like playing cards sprung from the hands of an inept dealer. Mary began sliding them around with a finger—randomly, it seemed to Martha at first, until Mary's intent became clear. Mary was grouping the black males.

Mary had arrived at the Museum of Afro-American History through a maze of false starts and bureaucratic delays, all because of some straw. The same list that had named her ex-husband Malik Kenyatta as an importer also listed the City of Detroit. But how was that importing splintered among the various city departments? She ran into the quagmire of there being no central clearinghouse for such information. She ended up going down a list of city departments, inquiring of each whether it imported, what it imported, and from where. Without exception, she never got useful information on the first call, always told that her request would have to go through channels and that someone would get back to her. And Mary had not followed up tenaciously, because she was not gung ho that the straw was worth a ton of effort; plus, there were other leads and other cases that demanded her time.

Matters changed after the Oreo murders story broke. The pressure being applied didn't allow any potential evidence to be minimized. When word got to Mayor Clay that the investigation was being stalled by slow response, he wielded big scissors to cut through red tape. A special coordinator was appointed to aid the police. The requests went to the coordinator, who channeled them to the proper departments and then rode those departments for timely responses. Among the information generated: the Museum of Afro-American History, owned by Detroit, had done the most importing from tropical regions over the past several months.

Before Mary ended up in Martha's office reviewing ID cards, she had searched the museum's storage area, crouching, crawling, peeping, and peering. She prospected intermixed debris that was flattened under crates, scrunched into corners, and lying in the open, for gold in the form of straw like that found on Livingstone's yacht. When she got done, she had a palmful of samples and slacks with very dirty knees.

"Are you sure that you can't tell me any more than you have?" asked Martha, who had gotten only vague responses regarding Mary's interest in museum employees.

"Not at this time," said Mary. "Is this all of the ID cards?"

"Thirty-six," answered Martha. "The entire staff, part-time as well as full. Everyone is required to wear ID. These are duplicates."

"Who's responsible for putting items in storage?"

"Alvin Blondell, dock foreman." Martha tapped his card in Mary's grouping of black males, smudging his face with her fingerprint.

"Who works for him?"

The pair of photos Martha fingered next were in the black grouping as well. "These two, hired two weeks before the museum opened."

"I'm interested in people who were working at least as far back as June."

"You should have said so. Blondell was our only dockworker then. He put museum deliveries into storage. Back then the builders and tradespeople also received delivery of their materials, but they handled that themselves and they didn't have access to our security storage area."

"Was it also Blondell's job to move things out of storage and into exhibition?"

"If it was something big, the tradespeople moved it, but Blondell oversaw them."

"Was he responsible for opening the shipments?"

"Sometimes fragile items had to be inspected upon arrival to see if they were damaged. He did a lot of that."

"But was he the only staffer who should have been in the storage area?"

"Not by a long shot. I, for one, went down whenever something arrived that I had particular interest in. There were even times when I hand-carried items back up to my office."

"So it was security storage in name only," said Mary.

"You make it sound worse than it was, Lieutenant Cunningham. We had closed-circuit cameras, like we do now. Also, staff had to sign in with Alvin to get into security storage. And we had computerized tracking. If a shipment didn't come in when it was supposed to, we followed up. All our shipments were accounted for."

"Why was Blondell the only dockworker?"

"Back then the museum was all receiving and no shipping, and one person could do the job. But not now. For example, we will ship items after we're through exhibiting them. We hired people who know how to crate and handle museum pieces."

"From his picture, Mr. Blondell looks to be a bit up in age."

"Late fifties, or around there."

"And slight of build."

"I'm guessing five-eight, a hundred and fifty pounds."

Mary waved her hand over the photos she had grouped. "Are any of these fellas big or tall?"

"Let me think."

Mary interrupted Martha's cogitations to point to a photo. "By his thick neck, he looks like he could be a big boy."

"Kevin Wilson. Security guard. Over six feet, two hundred pounds, give or take. He's been with us since before the opening."

"Is he ever around the storage area?"

"Sure, but he's not involved in handling deliveries."

"Clean-cut, good-looking young man," commented Mary. "Good talker, I bet."

"I suppose."

"Why don't any other cards say 'Security Guard'?"

"Kevin is the only one on the museum's payroll. The other guards work for a security firm that's under contract with us."

Mary pored over the photos some more. Eleven faces to consider against the profile of the killer: black, young, conservative-looking, articulate. Six seemed older than forty. Two others had attention-getting hair. Of the other three, Wilson was the best fit, plus he had access to the storage area.

Martha took advantage of the pause in questioning to say, "I assume the straw you collected holds some significance. But be informed that before our grand opening, when exhibits were being assembled, debris was everywhere, and not just in the dock area."

"I'll keep that in mind. Is Mr. Wilson in today?"

"Yes. He should be making rounds now."

"That's all for now," said Mary. "Magnificent building."

"It's a gem, isn't it? I'll give you some brochures. First let me put away these IDs." The IDs, along with duplicate keys, were kept in what resembled a fuse box attached to the wall in Martha's office, but she chose the expediency of raking them into her center drawer, to be transferred later. Martha cupped her hand and sent Mary's group of cards flying, like rafts shooting Niagara Falls. Next the others—women and whites, or so Mary had believed. The ID card of Eugene Shaw landed on top and was still sliding as Martha shoved the drawer closed.

"The promotional brochure gives the layout of the place and describes our permanent exhibits. The other one is a schedule of rotating exhibits that will be here over the coming months. I expect your patronage and for you to tell all your friends."

"You can count on it." Mary opened a brochure. "Says here that an exhibit on quilts is coming."

"That exhibit will include works from the community. Do you quilt?"

"I do."

"You might think about submitting something."

"I'm not that good. I only took it up to keep my fingers nimble. Arthritis."

"Should you change your mind, you have all the information you need right there," said Martha. "Now, if you don't mind, Lieutenant Cunningham, I have matters to attend to before the museum opens for the day."

"I've already left."

Mary went downstairs. As she scanned for Wilson, the exhibits beckoned her to halt and learn; instead, she absorbed on the go, peripheral vision taxed to the limit, some views finished with backward glances. She asked every staffer that she encountered about Wilson, until she was told that he'd been spotted heading toward the dock area. That's where she found him, outside the security storage area. Her view was of his back. He wore gray dress slacks and a red sports jacket, the uniform of museum staffers. He jingled a ring of keys, apparently in search of a particular one. He found it, inserted it, and unlocked the gate. He had slid it open and was about to step inside the security area when Mary asked, "Kevin Wilson?"

"That's me," Wilson replied. Recovering from having been startled, he tugged his lapels and rotated his broad shoulders to adjust the fit of his jacket.

"Lieutenant Mary Cunningham," she said, displaying the shield that hung from her neck. "I'd like to—"

Wilson had size and speed, a combination that sent Mary flying when he knocked her aside. She landed squarely on her tailbone, and in the span of a few seconds pain converted to numbness, then back to pain. Momentum made her seated position brief, as the back of her head slammed the floor. More pain. Throbbing. Disorienting. She willed herself to her feet, and her first steps were wobbles. She went down on one knee. She drew her gun. Then she got up. She started running back into the exhibit area. She whipped her neck wildly in all directions, looking for him, the pain rattling around her head like marbles in a blender. No Wilson.

She heard fists banging against the thick glass of the front entrance doors. It was Frank. He'd been out on leads and had come by on the chance of catching Mary. He'd seen her with gun in hand, looking dazed. Now Mary was maniacally pointing, and he correctly interpreted that she was telling him to cover the back door.

Frank ran to the side of the building and saw Wilson pounding pavement. Wilson's head start was insurmountable, at least by foot. Frank sprinted back to the front where his car was. Next came the squeal of peeling tires as Frank careened onto the side street. To Wilson's advantage, Frank was going the wrong way on a one-way street. One swerve too many, and he jumped the curb and ran into a tree. When the engine wouldn't restart, Frank took up the chase on foot.

After about fifty yards, Frank hit top stride. His form was a bit tight for maximum efficiency—too much straining of the neck muscles, for example—but Wilson had worse form and already was becoming winded. Frank considered drawing his weapon, but didn't because he didn't know who this guy was or what he had done. Besides, the only target the guy was offering was his back.

"Police. Halt!"

Wilson rotated his thick neck and saw that Frank wasn't pointing a weapon at him, so he kept running.

"Police. Halt!"

The second time was no more effective than the first. All it did was leave Frank a bit more winded.

Frank kept gaining. Closer. Closer. Until he was close enough. He focused on Wilson's legs, sizing them up for the tackle. He told himself to aim for the lower portion, between knee and ankle. If Frank had been a car, he would have been running on fumes; still, he thought he had enough left in his tank. He opened his arms like a fisherman lying about the size of his catch, and for a while looked ungainly running that way. He closed in to where he could hear Wilson's panting. Then he flung himself. He closed his arms tightly, but what he snared was air before he wrapped himself in his own bear hug and flopped onto the concrete sidewalk. Facedown, he attempted to push up, but something gave in his right arm and he rolled onto his back, writhing. He never saw Wilson cut the corner. On his walk back, he met up with Mary.

"Frank, you all right?"

"I'll live, but this motherfucker is broken," he said, looking down on the arm he held against his body.

"I think that was the Cookie Cutter," Mary said.

"Shit." Frank's face contorted in pain as he lowered his arm. "Let's go to the car and put out the APB." The arm slipped a little. "Jesus, Mary, and Joseph. Hurts like a son of a bitch."

In a guardedly admiring tone, Mary said, "Nice chase, but did you have to make it so dramatic?"

"Look who's talking. Bloody Mary herself."

Mary balled her hand into a fist and threatened to punch his arm. "Is there anything I can do?"

"Yeah, help me make up a good lie about how I broke it."

"For what? You have nothing to be ashamed of."

Frank looked down at his lizard shoes. "Scuffed to hell. Might as well throw them away." Examining his arm, he said, "Damn sport coat's ruined, too. Five hundred dollars down the drain."

When they got back to the museum, Martha and others had gathered outside. You can't bolt through a place, as Wilson had done, or rush around with gun in hand as Mary had done, without garnering a lot of attention. The police had been called, and two patrol cars had arrived. Mary fast-stepped to the one in front and said something to the driver.

She opened the passenger door for Frank and supported him by his good arm so that he wouldn't have to plop onto the seat. The next moment he was on his way to the hospital.

"I've tried not to be inquisitive," said Martha, obviously about to reverse her ways, "but what was that all about?"

"I'll know for sure," answered Mary, "once we have Mr. Wilson."

"You know a lot of ways to say nothing, Lieutenant Cunningham." Martha turned to reenter the building.

"Don't be insulted," said Mary. "It's just policy. But I do need to talk to you."

"About Kevin?"

"Actually, no. It's personal. You might say very personal."

"Let's go back to my office, then," said Martha.

FORTY-ONE

Later that afternoon, Frank returned to the squad room from the hospital, his arm cocked inside a cast that extended to his armpit. He had two breaks in the forearm: one about midway, the other close to the elbow. His ruined sport coat was draped over his shoulders, and the blood from his scraped knees had dried on his pants; however, despite his tattered appearance and the pain, his expression was proud and cocksure, like that of a returning veteran of war. Frank knew that Mayor Clay had called a press conference and announced that a suspect in the serial killings was in custody. Frank didn't know all the details of the capture, but he'd made a contribution and gotten injured in the process, so he expected some recognition from his coworkers. Soon after entering he had an audience-in-the-round, but he wasn't ready to answer their questions. He wanted Mary to be there to witness his time in the limelight, and she was at her desk with a young black woman.

Promising his audience that he'd be with them in a minute, he sauntered to the back of the room. "How long you gonna be?" he asked Mary.

"Don't know," Mary said. Then she said to the woman, "This is my partner, Frank Corleone. He's working the case with me." Addressing Frank again, she said, "Pull up a chair."

"No," protested the woman. She wore sunglasses that hid most of her upper face and a big straw hat that was pulled tightly over her head. Some alarm had left her voice when she added, "There's nothing more I want to say." She rose from the chair.

"Please, Ms.," urged Mary. "Just a few more questions. If you'd prefer it be between just the two of us—"

The woman cut in with "I'm leaving." She stepped quickly around Frank, avoiding eye contact with him and the others in her path to the door.

Frank watched the woman exit, then asked Mary, "What's with her? Did I run her away?"

"It's possible that she's leery of white men, although I don't believe I would have gotten much more out of her even if you hadn't come over."

"Tell me about it later," said Frank. "People want to hear about me and Wilson. I want you to cosign for me. And feel free to fill in any exciting details that I forget."

"Yeah, right." Then Mary lowered her voice to a confidential level and said, "But first you ought to know the latest. I'll sum it up this way: Kevin Wilson is a stealer, not a killer." She proceeded to explain.

Wilson had been nabbed within minutes after eluding Frank. A motorist saw him discard his red jacket, duck into an alley, and go through the back door of a bowling establishment. Thinking it odd behavior, the motorist hailed a flashing patrol car. Wilson was at a phone trying to make arrangements for a pickup when two officers aimed their weapons and commanded his surrender. He complied without further incident.

During the interrogation he offered solid alibis for all the murders, but he wouldn't say why he had fled. That answer was supplied by a search of his apartment. Boxes addressed to the museum were recovered. Kevin Wilson was a thief who had been heisting from the museum and fencing to unscrupulous collectors. The museum had been receiving unsolicited contributions that were not part of the computerized tracking list. Wilson would skim such items out of storage after time passed and it appeared that the museum had no record of them. Mary guessed that Wilson had to have had a partner. Alvin Blondell, dock foreman, was arrested and sang sweetly. Case closed.

Frank said, "Wilson is a lucky son of a bitch, because I almost shot him. Now I got a broken wing because of a common thief. I ought to snatch him out of lockup and whip his ass with one arm."

"Hey, Frank," shouted a member of the audience, "we don't intend on staying past quitting time to hear about what happened."

Before responding, Frank asked Mary in a hurried undertone, "Do they know?"

"Nah."

Then Frank bellowed across the room, "Mary and me are discussing work. You should try it sometime."

No longer in a position to brag about bravely chasing a serial killer, Frank got the hoped-for reply. "The hell with you," said the spokesman as the group dispersed.

Now that she had Frank to herself, Mary said, "You shouldn't have told the officers who took you to the hospital that Wilson was the serial killer."

Frank's rebuttal was "I was only repeating what you told me."

"I know."

"Then why you trying to break my balls?"

Mary said, "It started a chain reaction. Word got around the hospital, the media got wind of it, the mayor was asked to confirm that the killer's identity was known, and the mayor called headquarters." She paused. Frank didn't seem lost, so she continued. "The mayor was told how the investigation led to Wilson and that it looked promising. But the press conference was all his doing."

"He's running scared because he's dropping in the polls," said Frank. "But it's his own damn fault that he jumped the gun."

"You get no argument from me," Mary said. "But he's sticking the blame to us, like we set him up or something. Anyway, it's thrown another log on a fire that was already blazing under our asses."

Frank said, "He's not going to be embarrassed twice. The next thing he runs with has to be airtight."

Mary chose that time to return to a subject. "The woman who rushed out of here was attacked earlier this summer by a white man she brought home from the African American ethnic festival. They got hot and heavy and then a little kinky. She let him tie her to the bed. But when she told him she had a thing for white men, he went ape shit. He gagged her, put a knife to her throat, whacked off her hair, and smeared her with cream and powder before leaving the place with her still tied up. And get this, Frank—he called her an Oreo."

Frank said, "And she thinks her guy might be our guy?"

"She said the possibility occurred to her when the media broke the story."

"Why did she wait?" asked Frank.

"Shame. She believes that her reputation and job would be in jeopardy if her behavior were made public. She said she has no intentions of bringing charges. She wouldn't even give me her name," Mary said of Najah Harlan.

"Then why did she come forth?"

"To warn that the killer might be white."

"She could have phoned in."

"True. Maybe it was an act of courage that she felt she had to do in person."

Frank's dark eyes burned with interest. "Did she give his name?"

"She couldn't remember. Maybe her mind has blocked it out."

"Did she at least give a description?"

"White, sandy hair, good-looking, somewhat tall, in good shape, and late twenties to early thirties." Mary noticed that Frank's face was crunched in an expression of deep thought, causing her to ask, "What's on your mind?"

"There was a white guy of that description who was standing outside with museum staffers when we walked back. I noticed him because I'd seen him before."

"Where?"

"He was at the Ambrosia Hotel the day Felicia Wells was murdered."

Mary's eyes widened. "At the ABC conference?"

"I can't say whether he attended. I remember he used a house phone in the lobby. Had on a suit and tie. Gray."

"Are you sure?"

"Positive. When I recognized him today, I didn't think of him as a suspect. Why should I, when he didn't fit the profile? To tell you the truth, I didn't give him a second thought. He could've been at the hotel that day for some other reason."

"And I'm not about to guess at that reason," said Mary, and Frank understood her perfectly.

FORTY-TWO

An evening breeze, hot and clammy as dogs' breath, panted against the back of Mary's neck as she rang the intercom at the front entrance of Eugene's building. She waited a few moments without getting a response. She rang a second time. Frank—broken arm and all—stood alongside her.

As they waited, Frank pulled out a vial of pain pills but struggled with the safety cap. Wishing to assist, Mary tried to wrest the vial from him, but Frank fended her off. With stubborn pride, he removed the cap and shook a couple of pills into his mouth. They stuck momentarily on his dry tongue before he swallowed them without a chaser. His face wrinkled in reaction to their dusty, bitter taste. Mary tried the intercom a third time.

"Who is it?" The voice followed a connecting click and sounded impatient.

"Is this Eugene Shaw?" asked Mary. Prior to their arrival, she had phoned Martha Chenault to learn the identity of Frank's "white guy."

"I asked who is it."

"Police," Frank shouted. "We're Detectives Cunningham and Corleone."

"Mr. Shaw?" asked Mary.

"Yes. What do you want?"

"To speak to you," said Mary.

"About what?"

Frank gruffly answered, "An investigation. Let us in."

The buzzer hummed in a loud, short burst, admitting the cops. Eugene had changed into studio attire since earlier in the day when Frank chased Kevin Wilson. He was standing at the intercom, wiping paint off his hands with a cloth that was stiff and spotted from prior use. He circled in front of his visitors, stopping at a conversational distance. In a voice marked with civility, he said, "I'll save you some time, since I know why you're here. I can't help you."

"Why do you think we're here?" asked Frank dryly.

"I recognize your names and faces from this morning. Other than his name and the fact that I know now that he worked at the museum, I don't know anything about Kevin Wilson." Eugene's lips met in a curve that was neither a frown nor a smile, like a midway rest from which he might continue in either direction, as called for.

"Then maybe you can help us, after all," said Frank, "because that's not why we're here."

Eugene's eyes shifted in surprise. "Then why are you here?"

"We're investigating the murder of Felicia Wells," said Mary, "at the Ambrosia Hotel."

"You were at the hotel that day," testified Frank. "We want to ask you some questions."

"In hopes that you saw something that can help us out," Mary was quick to add.

Eugene put a hand to his throbbing head. He took a deep breath, hoping to quell the nausea in his stomach. He'd been painting when they rang. He was in the finishing stages of something that had proceeded very slowly, something that he'd been able to work on only in short spurts and not even every day, so debilitating were the effects. But he had the most noble of reasons for the self-imposed torture: love. On the day that he had learned that Mocha was pregnant, he had committed to a most fitting tribute. And he was going to complete it, even if it killed him. No, he was anything but at his best; however, two cops had landed on his doorstep, and despite the fog swirling in his mind, he didn't buy their stated reasons for being there. Whatever it took, he'd have to summon the reserves to deal with them.

"So you want to talk to me as a potential witness?"

"That's right," said Mary.

"What is it that you think I might have seen?"

Mary said, "Oh, I don't know. Anybody—or anything, for that

matter—that seemed out of place. While you're thinking, let's warm up with some easier ones, starting with why you were at the Ambrosia that day."

"A meeting."

"What kind and with whom?" she asked.

"Business. Days before, I got a call from a man who said he was coming to Detroit and wanted to buy some of my art."

"Give us a name," said Frank.

"Don't remember."

"What did he buy?" asked Frank.

"Nothing. If he had, I more likely would remember his name."

"Where was he from?" Mary resumed.

"New York, I believe."

"What room was your guy from New York, who didn't buy anything, in?" Frank asked.

"What reason would I have for recalling that?"

"Floor, then," pressed Frank.

"You got me again."

"No idea?"

"None."

"Describe him," Frank said.

"Black man, sixty or around there."

"Why was there no deal?" was how Mary reentered the questioning.

"When I called him later, he had checked out of the hotel. I don't know, maybe the murder made him nervous about staying there."

"Seems to me," said Frank, "that it would have made more sense meeting here if he wanted to buy your art."

"That was the plan for later on in the day," said Eugene. "He didn't know his way around Detroit, so I was to pick him up and bring him here."

"Exactly when did you arrive at the Ambrosia and when did you leave?" Mary asked.

"I only remember that it was a morning meeting that lasted less than an hour."

"Could you—" began Mary.

"I left before noon. I remember reading that the Wells woman was murdered after that time."

"Did you spend time anywhere other than his room?" Mary asked.

"No."

"You arrived, went to the room, had the meeting, then left the hotel," Mary summarized.

"Yes."

Frank jumped back in. "Who did you tell about the meeting? Maybe that person remembers the man's name."

"No one. But I assume you've checked the guest list, and if you've talked to all of them, you've talked to my guy."

"Without commenting on who we've talked to, what would you say if I told you that nobody has claimed to have been with you?" bluffed Frank.

"I wouldn't necessarily feel I had to say anything." His tag team interrogators didn't have him facedown and slapping the mat in surrender. He got bold a bit. "Just by coincidence, I was at the hotel that day. Nothing more or less. Now, excuse me, I was in the middle of some work when you rang."

Mary and Frank had to pretend that they were too dense to understand that they had been told to get the fuck out. They both sensed it was time for the separation routine. Mary stayed with Eugene as Frank walked to a wall to examine some hangings.

"Did you know Ms. Wells?" asked Mary, for now the designated questioner.

"Not at all."

"Never met her?"

"Never."

"Did you know of her? I'm talking about before her death."

"No." Eugene cut a furtive glance at Frank, who was making his way along the wall toward the studio area.

"I just thought you might."

"Why?"

"The media announced she was coming to Detroit. Plus, she did a press conference after she got here."

"I don't pay much attention to the media." Eugene had virtually remained planted, arms folded, throughout all the questioning. But now he made a few steps in Frank's direction, stopped, then called out, "I'd appreciate it if you didn't go into the studio. I don't want anything accidentally knocked over."

"Don't worry," said Frank, halting short of the area, "this cast is not the result of clumsiness."

"Just the same, my studio is private." Each of his last several responses sounded less hospitable than the preceding. Definitely, Mary and Frank had overstayed their welcome.

"Do you consider yourself politically active, Mr. Shaw?" asked Mary. She wanted to reclaim his attention and give Frank time to explore the reason for Eugene's edginess.

"Huh?" Eugene said, eyelids fluttering. Mary observed that his response wasn't indicative of not having understood the question, but of not having heard the question. She sensed that Mr. Eugene Shaw's mind was in a very different place than his body.

Mary pressed on. "Are you politically active?"

"Uh, no." He was eyeing Frank.

"What about socially active? For example, are there certain causes that you support or sympathize with?"

Eugene looked at her and frowned. "Yes. I suppose."

"Felicia Wells was known as an activist. What do you think of her politics?"

That question jerked Eugene into focus. He shifted more of his gaze on Mary, but out of the corner of his eye kept watch on Frank. "What am I, a suspect?"

"Why would you think that?" Mary put on an expression to go along with the incredulous tone of her voice. To declare him a suspect would place legal limits on how his answers could be used against him. "Suspect? The word never came out of my mouth."

"I don't know what the woman's politics were, and I don't give a rat's turd." Unfounded discourtesy. It signified a crack in his armor. Having to think so hard while still recovering was taking a toll. Mary knew that Frank's snooping was getting to him.

"I take it, then, that you decline to answer."

"I did answer."

Using his good arm, Frank made a sweeping motion with a pointed finger, tracing around the room at the posters, signs, and other memorabilia. "This whole place gives the answer. I'd say you're heavy into a black-struggle thing, my friend." He read no objections in Mary's eyes, so he continued with "Felica Wells's critics said the opposite about her."

"Is Detective Corleone correct, Mr. Shaw?" Mary asked.

Eugene didn't answer; however, the long inhalation, then exhalation—both audible—and the darting eyes spoke something.

"Too bad you never met," said Frank. "You could have taught her a thing or two about being black. Might have saved her life, no disrespect intended for the dead."

"I admire how your art portrays blacks so positively," said Mary, in counterbalance to Frank.

Eugene's silence continued. It magnified the whirl of the industrial fan that was running in the studio. Yet there was still the smell of oils and chemicals about the place, because there were no windows or other escapes. It was as though the smells had amassed and were surfing the currents around the room—leaving and returning, leaving and returning.

"Then again," said Frank, "white boy that I am, maybe I don't understand what makes a person," he made quotation gestures with his fingers, " 'black.' Take my partner. She's into tango dancing. Can't get on *Soul Train* with that. Does that make her an Oreo? What do you say, my friend?"

"I want you to leave." Eugene's brow was knitted.

Mary and Frank could not legally refuse Eugene's demand. Both were certain that Eugene would never admit them again without an arrest warrant or search warrant, neither of which they presently had the goods to justify. They had to go for broke.

"As you wish," said Mary agreeably. "May I use your rest room upstairs?"

"No," came the inhospitable reply. "There's one down here." He pointed at an open door.

"Thanks." Mary flashed a glance at Frank, wishing him better luck.

While Eugene watched Mary close the door behind her, Frank strolled toward the studio. It drew Eugene's attention, and this time, free of Mary, he stepped hurriedly toward Frank, who stopped and faced him, uncertain of his intent. "I asked you very nicely to stay out of my studio." Eugene's voice was sharp, his expression stony.

"I forgot. You own this place?"

"I do."

"And you live upstairs?"

"Yes."

"By yourself? Look, I'm just trying to make conversation until she comes out, that's all."

"No."

"Shacking, huh?"

"My fiancée lives here." Mocha was upstairs. She slept a lot nowadays. But what if she were to come downstairs and get caught up in the interrogation? The thought occurred to him for the first time, and it made him even more light-headed.

Mary emerged, and seeing both men next to the studio, she headed there instead of for the door. Eugene would have walked toward her if not for Frank, who showed no inclination to move.

"I need to make a pit stop myself," said Frank, "as well as take my pain pills." He didn't start immediately for the john, but dug his hand into his pocket and fished for a couple of seconds. Intentionally, his hand withdrew forcefully and the vial went sailing from his hand and into the studio. The vial rolled from sight under the chaise lounge on which Eugene's models sometimes posed.

"I'll get it," said Eugene in an urgent trot, but Frank was a step ahead and reached the lounge first.

While Eugene dropped to his knees and made swipes under the lounge, Frank was glancing frantically about, as was Mary. Almost simultaneously, their attentions locked on the same thing: the canvas Eugene had been working on when they arrived. They were still fixed on it when Eugene lifted his head after having snared the pills.

"Here." Eugene tossed the pills to Frank. "Get out."

"Looks like a self-portrait, if you allow for the obvious exception," said Frank, studying the canvas as if he were going to bid on it. "Is the woman your fiancée?"

"You've been told to leave."

"That's an interesting-looking object you're holding in your hand," continued Frank, referring to what was depicted on the canvas. "Mind if I see the real thing?"

"Get out. Now!" His voice was a quivering shout. His tense arms were held down straight against his body and ended in tight fists, looking suitably like exclamation points, punctuating his outburst.

"Have you ever met Xavier Livingstone? Have you ever been at the Detroit Yacht Club?" Mary asked in rapid fire.

"Did you know Thomas Kincaid, the talk-show guy who was murdered?" asked Frank. "Like to use the public phones in the neighborhood, do you? Speaking of which, let's hear your best *Boyz N the Hood* voice."

"You'll hear from my lawyer for refusing to leave after I told you."

"We're gone," said Mary, walking away.

"Yeah," said Frank, "we'll save you the legal fees. You might need them later on."

They came out of the fan-cooled building and were pounced upon by the heat, as if it had been waiting in ambush for them.

"He's our guy," said Frank.

"No doubt about it," Mary said. "But like you once told me, I'd prefer a confession over your certainty. And he knows that we know. Let's pray that it's enough to keep him inactive while we make the case."

She felt a fat globule of perspiration course down her spine, leaving a wet trail. An icy, wet trail. Matters had tumbled so quickly after she'd seen the painting that now she was having a delayed reaction to having come face-to-face with the Cookie Cutter. She shivered in the hot night air. Although she and Frank had been armed, and Eugene obviously had not been, she couldn't shake the sensation of having escaped mortal danger. She'd observed his mercurial behavior, alternatingly slack and animated. She'd seen him go from conversational to confrontational. She'd seen his eyes, alternatingly flashing and impenetrable. His image was stamped on her mind. And all at once, every mental picture she'd ever had of the killer—many reenacting the murders—stampeded back. She assigned Eugene's image to them. It fit. She rubbed her arms to warm herself, as though she'd been knifed by an arctic blast.

Inside, Eugene was staring vacantly at the painting that had arrested the attention of Mary and Frank. It was of himself and Mocha. It pictured them in tribal garb, he as a Nubian king seated on a throne and Mocha as the Nubian queen, standing beside him with a hand rested on his shoulder. Eugene's skin was painted dark—darker than Mocha's—and in his upheld hand was the dagger.

FORTY-THREE

Isaac Shaw had seen Precious Jones only once before, at the funeral of her mother, Hattie; therefore, it was impossible for him to have suspected that the woman in his office was the same girl thirty hellish years older.

Her cheap dress was a size too large and was bunched around a tightly drawn belt. The dainty pink of the dress didn't soften the squareness of her frame or the entrenched lines of her face. The bow on one of the black patent leather pumps was crooked. In contrast, his custom-tailored suit looked fresh from the cleaners, the white shirt was as crisp as cold lettuce, and the designer tie splashed colorfully to his waist. His shoes had a mirror shine.

It wasn't easy catching the busy, hard-campaigning candidate these days. The lead that Mayor Clay held immediately after the primary had been like a big pie, with Isaac able only to nibble the crust; however, since the Cookie Cutter exposé, he was taking bites. Can't do that while staying in seclusion, he told himself; have to get out there and shake hands, kiss babies.

On three previous occasions, Precious had missed Isaac when she showed up unscheduled. All three times, she told his receptionist that her business was confidential. She neither made an appointment nor left a telephone number. She did give a phony name.

"Welcome, Ms. Rollins. How may I be of service?"

Isaac remained standing after having risen when Precious was ushered in by the receptionist. A pair of chairs were angled in front of the desk, and Precious obeyed his gesture and sat in the left one.

He reseated himself, rested his palms on the desk, and awaited her reply.

Precious didn't answer right away. She avoided eye contact, and bounced an uneasy glance around Isaac's office, which had been redecorated in modern politics. Behind his desk, an American flag draped from a vertical pole, and a brass eagle perched on the shiny metal ball that crowned it. The desk looked executive enough— thick reference volumes sandwiched between handsome bookends, and a fountain pen station suitable for signing the most official documents. Gone was the swivel chair, by Earl Ogden's advice: during an interview, absentminded motion distracts from the speaker. Gone were the flowers with their propensity to wilt, replaced by thriving hanging plants. A long painting of the Detroit skyline hung center wall.

"I'm a proud person, Mr. Shaw. Never been one who expects something for nothing."

"If it's cost you're worried about, don't be. We'll give your loved one a decent yet affordable burial."

"That ain't it. Truth is, Mr. Shaw, I need me a job."

"I see. My administrator handles hiring, Ms. Rollins. Her name is—"

"I'm from Bent Fork, Alabama, same as you. You buried plenty of my folks. I'll work my fingers to the bone if given half the chance."

"I vaguely remember some Rollins, but it's been so long. You're saying we have a kinship, being from the same place and all."

"That's how I see it. Because of that, I'd give you my best and then some. I'll tell you something else, too. I'm proud of the fine reputation you done built up here. Running for mayor. That's really something. And I know you gonna do a fine job after you win."

"I appreciate that talk, Ms. Rollins."

"Savannah."

"You're the first person from home I've come across in ages. What sort of work did you have in mind, Savannah?"

"I ain't particularly educated, as you might tell. So I can't be picky. What I had in mind was housekeeping. I'll make sure that a speck of dust never settles around here. This here's a big place, and I can keep it swept, mopped, scrubbed, vacuumed, and polished from roof to basement. I hope you ain't forgot how us old Alabama gals can put in a day's work. After work, I'll even pass out your campaign flyers and buttons."

"Do you have a car, Savannah?"

"No, sir, Mr. Shaw. But just like the bus got me here today, it'll keep getting me here."

"How long have you been in Detroit?"

"Couple weeks."

"Why did you come?"

"Promise you won't laugh. I came to get me a job in the factory making cars. Only, come to learn that there ain't any. Come to learn that they laying people off up here. Giving the jobs to machines."

"So why haven't you—"

"Gone back home? To what?"

"Family, for one thing."

"My mama died last year. Never knowed my daddy. I got some half brothers and half sisters, but we never was what you call close. I divorced a trifling nigger some years back. Basically, it's been just myself for a good while now."

"Still, why stay in Detroit, even if you don't go back to Bent Fork?"

"Might as well try this town out. Don't have no money to be wandering about like Moses in the desert, anyhow."

"Detroit's a good town." Isaac Shaw's billboard-practiced smile spread across his face.

"And it's going to be a lot better, once you take over, Mr. Shaw."

"If you're half the worker that you are the flatterer, Savannah, I ought to consider hiring you."

Precious was being stabbed by hunger pains, as if her stomach were devouring its own lining. She tensed to muzzle the rumblings. The effort weakened her further, as did merely sitting. During the conversation, she had been a tire with a slow leak; now, taking encouragement from Isaac's last comment, she sat more erect, as if just given a jet of air. Meals were a luxury. The austerity had started with the discovery of Annie Parsons's diary. After weeks of overtime washing dishes and saving like a miser in the Great Depression, she quit her job by simply not showing up anymore.

The fake identification and the fake Social Security card put a crack in her nest egg, even though a prison crony got her a discount. She invested in a few new clothes. She bought a one-way bus ticket. And when she rolled into the Detroit terminal, a thin envelope inside her purse contained every dollar that she had to her name.

Carrying a battered suitcase that she counterbalanced by leaning like a hunchback, she went along the chain of taxis, asking each driver to name a nearby hotel with cheap weekly rates. One place was mentioned more than once, and that's what she chose. It was in the Cass Corridor, Detroit's Hell's Kitchen. In the Corridor, the merely downtrodden are the well-to-do, compared to the hundreds of homeless entrapped there. It's a pocket of poverty where drug trafficking, prostitution, money laundering, and food-stamp fraud are main enterprises. Precious checked into a dilapidated structure misnamed The Majestic Hotel.

"Where are you staying?"

"This side of town. My place is small but clean. I aim to find something bigger once I get myself situated."

"Do you have a phone?"

"I'm trying to scrape up the deposit so I can get one."

"Then how would I let you know my decision?"

"I'll call you, unless you make the decision before I leave."

"That's a little pushy."

"I need work, Mr. Shaw."

"So you've said."

There was a bench warrant with her name on it for having left Alabama. Parole violation would send her back to prison to finish out her original sentence and probably tack on additional time. To her a return to prison was a daunting thought, but worth the risk, because she had decided that she could not conduct her revenge from out of state. And she wasn't working on borrowed time; it was stolen.

"You keep up with news back home?"

"Not like I used to. What's Bent Fork like these days?"

"Still country, like me."

"How are race relations?"

"White folks still run everything."

"And what about—"

"Like the Parsons family."

"Huh?"

"The Parsons family still runs Bent Fork, is what I was saying. You remember them, don't you, Mr. Shaw?"

"Of course."

"Heard about old man Sam gitting killed?"

"Yes, I did."

"Miss Charlotte is still alive. Their boy is a judge on the county bench, and the rest of them Parsons is still into banking and anything else that can turn a dollar. I never could stand any of them. What about you?"

"Never had contact with any of them."

"See there? Prime example of what I been saying. You a good man. Won't even bad-mouth people who deserve it."

Isaac let the conversation fall silent for seconds as he mulled over Precious. A "Shaw for Mayor" lawn sign was being peppered outside by an alternating sprinkler, one of a platoon of sharpshooters hatching the yard with its cross fire. He tapped his fingers on the desk, keeping beat with the sound coming through the window.

This was the largest and newest of the Shaw Funeral Homes, and it served as central control of the empire. Its bricks were the cheerful red of a country schoolhouse. Pillars like giant tree trunks of alabaster propped up a second-story balcony. Windows featured prominently in the scheme. The main chapel could accommodate three hundred people, and there were three smaller chapels.

"I seen you in this room a number of times—in the papers, on television, and whatnot," resumed Precious. "With all them newspeople trampling through here, the place should be kept spic 'n' span all the time. Not to say that the place don't look presentable, mind you, but I could make it look better."

"Like how?"

"I can see the dust on top of that picture frame from here. And this here chair I'm sitting in should be polished. You might say that them's little things. But what are reporters gonna report about after they done covered everything that's worthwhile? They gonna fill space and time with petty stuff that could make you look bad. It's unnecessary."

"Keep talking. I'm smiling only because of a thought I'm having."

"Let's say that your office is kept spotless. Since that ain't no news, they gonna make some excuse to see other parts of the place. They gonna keep snooping until they discover something bad. This whole place got to stay its best."

"You sound like my campaign manager. That's what I was smiling at."

"Then I must be making sense to you."

"I'm not saying that you're not."

"People coming through here on funeral business. You can't wait 'til you close to clean up behind them. I tell you, Mr. Shaw, I won't even let ashes rest in a tray."

"I do have a cleaning lady that comes at night. But you're talking about keeping the place in showroom condition around the clock during the campaign. I can see real advantages to that. I should have seen it before. Did you live inside Bent Fork, Ms. Rollins?"

"I did after I got grown. I grew up on a little spread."

"It could make for a good feeling inside to know I've helped somebody from my hometown. After all, we're put on this earth to do good."

"You saying what I think you saying?"

"I'm asking—when can you start?"

FORTY-FOUR

Inspector Newberry rushed the caller off the phone to resume discussions with the group seated in his office. "Sorry for the interruption," he said to Mary, Frank, Abigail Cox, and Brian Hobbs. Then Newberry addressed the FBI agents, who had flown in that morning. "I appreciate you catching the first flight out after my call. We know where our rabbit is. We're hoping you can help us flush him out of his warren."

"We'll give you our best efforts," promised Hobbs. "Who's your suspect?"

"The name's Eugene Shaw," said Frank. "Artist in residence for the Afro-American Museum. Mary and me were at his studio in the building where he lives. There's your black museum. Don't misunderstand me. Having racial pride is a beautiful thing, but with Shaw, it's a motive to kill."

Mary injected an important piece of information with "To look at Eugene Shaw, you'd swear he is white."

"I did, the first time I saw him," said Frank.

"And the second time, too," reminded Mary.

Feeling the need to vindicate himself, Frank said to Mary, "There was no reason for me to suspect Shaw, not when you and Hobbs had me looking for a black man."

Mary owned up by saying, "True. But at least we were right about the killer not having a threatening appearance."

Hobbs quickly reminded them, "We were also right about the killer being black. It's just that you can't tell from looking at him."

Cox asked, "Is Shaw biracial?"

"What we know for sure," said Mary, "is that he's the adopted son of Isaac Shaw, a black businessman who's running for mayor. The director of the museum told me that Eugene claims that his mother is white."

Evidencing new insights, Frank said, "I never gave much thought before to the distinction between race and color. It's tricky. We got all these terms flying around this room—white, black, biracial—tell you the truth, I'm not sure what to call Eugene Shaw."

Mary simplified it. "Try killer."

Hobbs said, "I didn't think this case could get more politically charged, but I was wrong, given who his father is. Have you interviewed the candidate?"

"Not yet," Mary answered. "Eugene Shaw's only been our suspect since yesterday."

"There's more to it than that," said Newberry to the FBI agents. "Before we go running to Isaac Shaw, telling him that his son is a serial killer, we better have more than we do now." Referring to Kevin Wilson, he continued, "We've already been burned with a wrongly accused suspect. If we ever get Shaw to trial, his attorney will remind the jury of that. For now I don't want the media to know that Eugene Shaw is our suspect. Not until we have a case that won't crumble."

Hobbs asked, "Did you discover who leaked the story, by the way?"

"No," said Newberry. "But I'm satisfied that it was neither Mary nor Frank." Newberry directed his gaze at his two detectives. "Update the agents on how you fingered Shaw as a suspect."

Mary did most of the narrating about how the straw led to Eugene and ultimately the painting. Eventually she got to the description of the dagger. "It was wavy, and had a snake's head at the top of the handle."

"And you believe the dagger in the painting is the murder weapon," Cox stated.

"Positive," said Frank. "We described it to the coroner, who agreed that it could have inflicted the wounds."

"Unfortunately," said Newberry, "the painting is not the murder weapon. We have to find the real article."

"You don't even know if there is a real article," interjected Hobbs. "The dagger could be a creation of his mind, like the melting clock in a Salvador Dalí painting."

"Point made," said Newberry, "but we're going with the odds. I am concerned, however, that he might have discarded the dagger."

"I doubt it," said Cox. "The dagger symbolizes something very meaningful to him. He might have it hidden, but he still has it."

Frank jumped back in. "Like Mary said, he painted himself dark-skinned." He made eye contact with Cox, then said, "You're the psychologist, but I say Shaw has a slight identity crisis."

Cox maintained eye contact with Frank while she said, "What Detective Corleone means is that Shaw is homicidally psychotic from a fixation on blackness and a complex about his color."

"You said all that, Frank?" asked Mary, for the first time realizing that there was a flirtatious attraction between Frank and Cox that had showed indications since their initial meeting.

"You heard the lady," Frank said, laughing.

Hobbs addressed Cox: "I'll go along with 'psychotic' as long as it doesn't mean insanity beyond accountability."

Cox declined to debate. Instead she asked, "What's known about the woman in the painting?"

Mary recited, "Mocha Diane Springwell. Shaw told Frank that she's his fiancée. They live together. Dark-skinned, twenty-four, no criminal record, works at Victoria's Secret. We don't think she's involved or that she knows about his sideline, but we haven't decided how to fold her into the investigation."

"If he's a ticking time bomb," said Hobbs, "she stands a good chance of being around when he explodes, since she lives with him. She should be put on alert, even if she refuses to believe or refuses to help the investigation."

"That's one of your better suggestions," Frank told Hobbs.

"Inspector," said Hobbs, reacting to Frank's nettling, "are you so short on manpower that you retain officers with broken arms?"

"He's officially on medical," said Newberry. "Maybe he likes your company, Agent Hobbs."

"Or somebody else's," instigated Mary, under her breath.

"What did you say, Mary?" Newberry asked.

"Nothing."

Newberry smoothed the furrows from his brow momentarily before they deepened. "We have no weapon, no witnesses, and no physical evidence such as prints or blood tying Shaw to a murder."

Mary added, "And no confession, although I'm not holding my breath for one. I called Shaw this morning, requesting another interview, and he told me to go take a flying leap."

"So," resumed Newberry, "we want the Bureau's wisdom."

"Is Shaw under round-the-clock surveillance?" asked Cox.

Newberry answered indirectly. "We're undermanned already."

"Would probably be wasted effort anyway," said Hobbs, "if he doesn't kill by a time pattern. A killer who knows he's under suspicion usually will either lay low or make a game of it. Which type is Shaw?"

Cox leaned forward and looked at Frank, then at her colleague. "Tormenting the police is not his objective. There have been no taunting messages, no bragging phone calls. By his logic, he's pursuing a cause."

"Is he insane?" Newberry asked Cox.

"Hold on—" But this time Hobbs wasn't allowed to finish.

"I know your opinion," said Newberry to Hobbs. "I want to hear hers."

"He's no raving lunatic, but that doesn't rule out a psychotic disorder." Cox conveyed another bit of information. "Just in case this ends in a barricaded situation, keep in mind that sometimes they commit suicide rather than be captured, probably because they automatically face a life sentence or capital punishment."

"What do you suppose sets him off?" asked Newberry.

"People who he thinks are Oreos," said Frank.

"It's more complicated than that," assured Cox as she turned to face Frank.

"Give me a theory," requested Newberry.

Cox responded, "I believe that he decides his victims in accordance with a reference."

"Like a formula?" asked Mary.

"More like an authority. Perhaps a person, although not necessarily. The victims weren't Oreos merely by his decree, but as judged by this authority that he holds in high regard."

"Still," said Frank, "how does a victim come to Shaw's attention in the first place?"

Mary slid to the edge of her seat and said, "Let's not overlook a simple theory. All three victims were controversial and had received media coverage not long before their deaths."

"Let's combine the two," said Cox. She recited Mary's theory. "Victims come to Shaw's attention through public channels, and—"

Mary broke in, returning the favor by reciting Cox's theory, "Then he measures them against the authority, to decide whether they are Oreos that have to be dealt with."

Newberry pulled at his lower lip before saying, "Stay tuned. The next murder could come as soon as tomorrow's headline."

FORTY-FIVE

"Here's to a beautiful, healthy grandchild," proposed Mocha, who had engineered the gathering. Four glasses clinked in a toast, Isaac's a bit more than the others because he was relieved that the evening might end without incident. They were in public; an embarrassment could find its way into the media and cut into the slim lead that he'd built over Mayor Randal Clay that very week. Isaac had wanted the gathering to be at his home and would have settled for Eugene's; however, he and Gertrude were the invitees, and Gertrude had made their attendance a condition for her continued appearances on the campaign trail.

"Hear, hear," chimed Isaac.

"I'll drink to that," said an ebullient Gertrude.

Eugene was silent. Mocha, as planned, had announced the pregnancy, but there were other announcements that Eugene had promised her he would make. When everyone was seated again, he spoke without forewarning, as with any decent ambush. Seated opposite Isaac at a round dinner table, he told him, "I was awake that night you confessed that you're my biological father." His tone was more detached than angry.

Isaac had reserved a separate room in the pricey Wilshire Restaurant, not enough privacy to muzzle the explosion that seemed imminent. The waiter entered, not knowing that as he poured their refills the prevailing calm was a charade. Once the waiter exited, Isaac tried to ward off a spectacle. "Let's leave and discuss this in private."

"Relax," advised Eugene. "No one's going to cause a scene. I couldn't bring Moe into a nest of lies. She knows the family secret. We've discussed it for days and decided for our child's sake that things have to be resolved."

"You've been hiding the same secret from each other," said Mocha to the clan of which she'd soon become a member. "And everyone has suffered. Our child must not be lied to about phony bloodlines."

"The lie took on a life of its own," said Isaac. "I take the blame." He looked Eugene unflinchingly in the eyes and said, "I've always loved you as my son and wanted the best for you."

Gertrude, who'd always envisioned this moment, hadn't been caught totally unprepared. She found her voice, and spoke the words that she'd had in her mind for years: "And so have I, Eugene. Forgive me, won't you, for my part in the deceit. The temptation is to say we did it for your protection, but that's a hollow claim. We were protecting ourselves just as much—from the world's condemnation. Our priorities were misassigned. Our moral compass was broken. Now a blessed grandbaby can emancipate us."

"That was lovely, Mrs. Shaw," said Mocha. Then she told Eugene, "I'm going to speak for you a minute, if that's all right." After he didn't protest she said, "It means everything to Gene to hear those words from both of you. All his life, he's felt you were ashamed of him, and he didn't want to deepen that shame by letting on that he knew the truth."

With loving admiration, Gertrude told Mocha, "Only you could have gotten us to this point. No one has ever influenced him like you do. It'll be a joy having you in the family."

Mocha said, "Thanks. Together, we three can correct his sense of being disowned."

Eugene decided to speak for himself for a while. Tapping the bridge of his nose with a finger, he looked at Isaac and said, "And maybe someday I won't hate this as much." He'd told Mocha the story: high school prom, car crash, date died, new nose for him. "You should have told the surgeon to give my nose its original look. I'm not asking you to admit it, but you believed that the nose identified me too much as a Shaw. I can have it undone, but why bother when I can't undo Carol's death?"

Her voice still reflective of that painful episode, Gertrude explained to Mocha, "Carol was his high school sweetheart. Eugene hadn't had his driver's license for long when the accident happened. The other driver was proven at fault. Eugene blames himself."

"She shouldn't have been my date," said Eugene dourly. "All her friends told her not to go to the prom with 'Casper.' "

"Looking at you," said Gertrude, "you resemble her, Mocha." She saw Mocha's response and fell silent.

Isaac felt obliged to comment, fearing that Eugene might turn volatile with resentment. "Motives can have more than one facet, son. I come from a family background that believed the more one looked a certain way—"

Eugene interrupted. "Don't talk around it. Say it. White."

Isaac accepted the challenge. "The more one looked white, the better one's chances in life. Old habits and old beliefs die hard, Eugene. I'm so sorry for the pain when what I wanted to do was make your life easier."

"When I was a boy, you told me all the time to be proud that I'm black. You were a hypocrite."

"I understand how you can say that, but I was trying to give you the best of both worlds."

"Instead, I got stuck between them."

Mocha interceded. "Gene, you promised me that this was going to be a reconciliation. Don't turn it into a public flogging." To Isaac she said, "Things would be so much simpler if he would accept the white half of himself, Mr. Shaw. He's no less human because of it."

The words almost lodged in Gertrude's throat when she said, "I wish we knew more about your mother and her folks, Eugene. People you could see and talk with. Would make it easier to accept that we're all just flesh and blood, no one any more human than the other."

"Don't build false hopes of that, Gertrude," said Isaac, "when it's clear she doesn't want to be found."

Gertrude countered with "That was then. Times in the South are different now. I'm not suggesting that you run off looking for her, Eugene. But just like it seemed this day of truth would never come, you might know your real mama someday."

"You are my real mother," Eugene said.

Gertrude, her spirits lighter than helium, said, "You dear, sweet boy. I'd do anything in this world for you."

"We both would," said Isaac. "But the fact remains that half our grandchild's gene pool is unknown." With that as a prelude, he said, "Eugene, you ought to get a complete physical."

"For what?"

"To see what you're passing on to your child. By complete I mean everything. Physical . . ." Isaac tried to will himself not to pause, but he couldn't, "and psychological."

Eugene flared his rebuilt nostrils, like a bull readying to charge. He'd become instantly angry and defensive as he recalled his psychiatric sessions in childhood. That, plus the battle of denial that he had been waging of late that something might be amiss. "You're saying that I'm crazy."

Eugene bolted upright without first sufficiently pushing his chair from the table. Mocha had to cradle her glass to keep it from spilling. Feeling the chair still against his legs, he back-kicked and sent the chair flying.

The waiter had returned just in time to witness the outburst. He froze, not knowing how to pretend that he hadn't seen anything. Isaac waved him away.

"See, here," Isaac said with paternal disapproval.

"No, you see here," shot back Eugene.

"No, you see here." It wasn't an echo. Mocha was wearing a most irritated expression. "Your father makes perfect sense. He's putting the interest of our child first, which is more than you seem to be doing. You've spoiled the evening. Take me home."

Eugene was panic-stricken. He had to make things right with Mocha, and quick. "I apologize," he said to all. "I've got to let the past go for the sake of the future." He lifted his glass. "Before our champagne gets flat, another toast." With uncertainty, the others joined. Eugene winked slyly at Isaac and proposed the toast: "Bury the old or it will bury us."

FORTY-SIX

Isaac Shaw had told Precious Jones to stay after closing because a camera crew was coming the next morning and he wanted the place in tip-top condition.

Isaac activated the security alarm. From the wall safe he retrieved the envelope that had arrived by mail yesterday. He already had torn it open; he hadn't owned a letter opener since that day Annie Parsons used one to slice his hand. The torn, jagged pattern of the tear reminded him of the jaws of a trap, even more so when he compressed the sides, causing those jaws to gape threateningly. A trap, indeed. He inverted the envelope and shook out its contents, then watched the four sheets do a crisscrossing glide to his desk. He stared down at them, intensely and penetratingly, as though his vision could ignite them. When he gathered them, they quivered in his hands, betraying his nervousness.

Precious Jones was in the main chapel, vacuuming. She directed the vacuum cleaner in long, overlapping pushes and pulls. When she felt contact, she screamed. "Sweet Lord, Mr. Shaw," she said, pressing her palm over her heart, "you almost sent me to my maker, come tapping me on the shoulder like that." She noticed that Isaac was holding one hand behind his back. "I don't know why they ain't invented a silent vacuum by now. I didn't hear you come in. I'm still a little jumpy working around the dead. Thought one of these here bodies had got up out its coffin."

"The dead can't harm anyone. If only the same could be said for the living."

"Come to think of it, everybody who ever done me dirt had a heartbeat," said Precious. Isaac's stern expression caused her to ask, "Something the matter?" She looked at the chapel doors that she had left open. They were now closed.

Isaac's elbow began to angle outward, slowly drawing the hidden hand into view. "You shouldn't have used my copier," he said, holding out the sheets for view but not for transfer. He was barely audible above the vacuum, just as he wanted. "It makes this dark streak along the left. I've been meaning to get it fixed."

Suddenly Precious had three hearts—in the chest, throat, and between the ears—all pounding in synch. Nevertheless, she spoke defiantly. "I've seen your adopted son come through here. *Adopted,* my ass. I knew right off you two is blood. But I seen somebody else in his face. His mama. How did you make Annie Parsons disappear?"

"Your name's not Savannah Rollins. Who are you?"

"Never you mind. Just don't you try nothing cute with me. Especially since you don't know the whereabouts of the diary them pages was copied out of."

"I have no intentions of harming you." Isaac stepped back as a disarming gesture. "Actually, I'm hopeful that we can come to an arrangement."

"Arrangement?! You no-conscious, motherfuckin' son of a bitch." She spewed the venomous words, yet they felt so inadequate. She wanted to strike, kick, and bite. She shut off the vacuum. Realizing her disadvantage, however, she maintained her distance. "The only arrangement I'm interested in is having you pay."

"Pay for what?"

"Let me out of here," she said, ignoring the question.

"What's stopping you?"

"Move aside."

Isaac said, "I'll go you one better and go first." He left the chapel and walked to the main entrance. He felt Precious's distrusting eyes as he unlocked the front door and swung it open.

"Push the screen door, so I know it's unlocked," directed Precious, standing a hall length away.

He did, and it was. He then stationed himself in a far corner. It took him out of Precious's field of vision. He couldn't see her either, as she fearfully crept along. So that she could judge his location, he called out to her, "I'm over here in the corner."

"Stay there." She scurried and peeked around the corner. He hadn't moved. She paced quickly toward the door. She held one arm extended in front of her as a guide, and kept her gaze fixed backward on him. She made contact with the screen door. She pushed. It resisted. She felt for the knob, determined not to take her eyes off Isaac. She found it, and with a turn of the wrist, she opened the door and held it ajar. She had her escape hatch, but she didn't dive headfirst through it. Isaac kept watch from his corner. That was what was wrong with the picture. He was making no attempt to stop her. "What you got up your dirty, lowdown sleeve?" asked Precious, still standing in the doorway.

"You demanded to leave, and I've obeyed."

Precious's voice was filled with disdain and incredulity. "You saying you got no plans past letting me walk out of here, even though I know about you and Annie? Before I believe that, I'll believe that Satan is my savior."

"If you walk out now, you only postpone the inevitable," Isaac said dispassionately. "It's obvious that you want the final resolution to be just between us. Otherwise, you would have gotten others involved by now, such as the law or the Parsons family."

"Is that some kind of confession?"

"What am I supposed to confess to, besides receipt of the childish scribbling you mailed me?"

"That's what Annie was—a child—when you got her pregnant. That's what she still was when she came back to see you and ain't been heard from since."

"You're accusing me of being responsible for her disappearance?"

"I know you're behind it. Annie would never stay hid and let a innocent man get blamed for her murder."

"How do you know that your father didn't kill her?" Isaac's eyes narrowed as she struggled to hide her surprise. He made her efforts futile when he said, "Answer me, Precious Jones."

Her eyes widened involuntarily. He knew her identity. What else did he know? Had he already contacted Alabama authorities to come whisk her back to prison? What would become of her revenge?

It hadn't been a great challenge for Isaac to deduce who the so-called Savannah Rollins really was. Many pieces fit. Yet a piece or two remained missing, like why hadn't Precious shown up before? His cunning told him that she was hiding something. He could identify with that. A fake identity might mean that she was trying to bury the past. He could identify with that, too. And her blunder with the copying machine suggested that she was no genius. Isaac had assessed the situation and concluded that the chances were good that he was dealing with a dim-witted fugitive.

"Any trouble here, Ms.?" came a voice, close and unexpected.

Precious spun her head into the blinding glare of a flashlight.

"Identify yourself" was the disembodied request, for she couldn't see the cop, or that he had his hand on his holster.

"Police?" asked Precious. She looked away from the light and tried to blink her vision into returning.

"Yes. Are you alone?"

"No, she's not, Officer. I'm Isaac Shaw, the owner. What's the problem?" Isaac was at the door now, in back of Precious.

"Seems your silent alarm went off to the precinct," said the cop, who recognized the mayoral candidate.

"Saw the lady in the door, so we were just asking the routine questions," came a different voice, that of the cop's partner, who had stepped from the side of the door and into view, behind the first officer.

"My fault," said Isaac. "I forgot to disengage the alarm, and my employee, Ms. Rollins, set it off preparing to leave. I apologize."

"We're glad that's all it was, Mr. Shaw," said the first officer, who had put away the flashlight.

"We were discussing a few things," explained Isaac, "and not mindful of the alarm, right, Ms. Rollins?"

"Uh-huh." Precious licked her lips and nodded.

"Well, the alarm is still going, so would you do something about it?" said the cop in back.

"Immediately," said Isaac. "Do you mind stepping back inside, Ms. Rollins, so that we can finish our discussion?"

Without saying anything, Precious reentered. Isaac locked the screen door, then closed the inside door. The cops already had turned away and headed for their patrol car. Isaac went to his office and attended to the alarm. He returned to find Precious still at the door. She looked defeated.

"Mind if I call you Precious?" he asked. "It's a nice name."

"It don't matter what you know about me. I ain't scared of you. Not now. Though you be the Devil incarnate. You gonna be brought down. I'd give my life to have a hand in it, but some way or another, you gonna be brought down."

"So far," said Isaac, "all you have is that Eugene is my son. Okay, I committed adultery. My family knows that. If it became public, it might hurt my chances for becoming mayor. Then again, maybe not. Either way, I don't think that's what you're after. You want a much bigger tumble for me. And you can't get it from proving that I'm Eugene's father. You could by proving that Annie Parsons was his mother and that I killed her. But you can't prove that. Where's the body?"

"You done away with her body. A minute ago, you spoke about her like she was dead when you said I couldn't prove that Annie was the mother. *Was*."

"Figure of speech."

"You a damn lie. You know she's dead, 'cause you killed her. Most likely cremated her or some shit like that."

Isaac said, "Annie Parsons was not right in the mind. You know about the Parsons Curse. What she wrote in her diary was delusional. Dead? Annie Parsons could be alive somewhere in an asylum. Sam Parsons was ashamed of her anyway. That's why he let her have you as a friend. Or maybe she ran away, after which the Curse got her so bad that she doesn't know who she is."

"Or maybe you killed her. Of all the 'maybes,' that's the one I'd bet my life on."

"Even if what you say is true, the proof is gone forever. Other than make wild accusations, what can you do? Nothing." Isaac straightened his tie, his tone casual, as though he were speaking to a child.

"Keep thinking that, you bastard, all the way to when you fall from your high-and-mighty horse."

"Do you want to kill me? You've had chances."

"Maybe I will. Or maybe you'll kill me, only a lot sloppier than how you done Annie, and they catch you and send you to jail for life. I wouldn't mind dying for that cause. You killed me a lifetime ago, anyway."

Isaac raised his right hand and swore, "If I ever killed anyone, may God strike me down this very second."

Although no lightning bolt struck Isaac, Precious wasn't sold. "You killed my father, a kind, decent man."

"Not so."

"Yes you did, every bit as much as whoever strangled him, 'cause he never should have gone to jail."

"I agree he should not have gone to jail. I didn't send him. The system did, and you know it. There was never enough evidence to convict Porter. The system sacrificed him rather than let the case go unsolved. And Sam Parsons ran the system."

"You're the Devil, and I won't let you confuse me. No system made Annie vanish. Sam Parsons didn't, neither."

"That's true, but I don't hear you claiming that they played no part in poor Porter's death." After a loud silence by Precious, Isaac said, "You know they did."

"Don't make too much of my silence. I don't have to let you know everything I'm thinking."

"They made you a witness for the prosecution. What kind of system and what kind of family would force a child to testify against her own father?" Isaac stood next to the American flag in his office, smiling slightly at the irony.

"Shut your filthy-ass mouth." Precious was shivering. "I didn't testify against my father."

"You didn't mean to, I know. Everyone knew that, just like everyone knew how it was used against him. I'm sure you've thought about it a million times."

"No," she said, wanting to clamp her hands over her ears. "Ain't gone be no making me doubt what I know for myself. You the cause of everything that happened."

"It's convenient for you to place all the blame on me, because you're powerless against the system and the Parsons family. But you hate them both. You don't trust the system, especially the police. And, however you acquired the diary, you haven't shared it with the Parsons family. For the sake of argument, let's say that I owe you something. Well, so do—"

"For the sake of argument?!"

"For the sake of argument. What I was about to say was, so do others. But they are not willing to offer you anything."

"Unlike you."

"You spoke about me paying. I spoke about an arrangement. What if—again for the sake of argument—I were to offer you something?"

"Like what?"

"Money."

"I'd tell you what you can—"

"A half million dollars, cash."

"I'd rather die poor."

"I'll say it again: I haven't killed anybody, and you can never prove that I did. That aside, you lost your father, and no one has ever compensated you. My offer is a measure of justice. The money can mean a new life, especially if you can't go back to the old one." His last remark was designed to play on her uncertainty about how much of her past he knew.

"Hell no." But it sounded weak.

"Think about it," he said, unnervingly businesslike. "I'm going to flip the alarm so you can leave." He left to attend to that task. She had a barbed greeting for him upon his return.

"I hate your fucking guts."

He stepped toward her, and she retreated. "I accept that, but don't let it blind you."

"It ain't over."

"It's late," said Isaac. "Dangerous waiting for a bus this time of night." He pulled some folded money from his pants pocket and peeled off a bill. "Here's a hundred. Flag a cab."

"Shove it up your ass."

"I owe you for time worked. I don't guess you'll be coming back to work, so let's settle now." More bills came off the roll, too much for the stated purpose. He slipped the cab money and wages in the pocket of her smock. "Stand on the corner and hand it out to strangers if you like. It's up to you."

"Let me out of here," she demanded. But the money stayed in her pocket. "You turn my stomach."

"A half million," Isaac repeated. He opened the inside door, then held open the screen door.

"Kiss my ass" was her good-bye.

A gamble the size of Michigan had just gone into the night. Isaac had played it as best as he knew how. He leaned his back against the door, solid oak, and could smell the polish that Precious had recently applied. He braced himself for the fallout.

FORTY-SEVEN

In an abandoned junkyard in northwest Detroit, plainclothes cops Starsky and Andy were conducting an interrogation. Andy launched a knuckle missile at the nose of a cowering Ricky Powell, but it was intercepted in midflight by Starsky, his big hand engulfing Andy's fist like a five-tentacled octopus.

"Not in the face," admonished Starsky, wanting to avoid evidence of the beating they were giving Powell.

Andy nodded compliance, and when Starsky let go, shot a mean uppercut to Powell's midsection, folding him over.

"That's more like it," approved Starsky.

"You'd think there would be at least one damn tree in this yard," complained Andy, who preferred shade when working outdoors. He slapped his palm against the back of his itching neck and raked his fingers across it. Dirt and sweat made body mud that caked under his fingernails. It was early September, but it was as hot as July. "I'm out here getting sunstroke because of you, motherfucker," he told Powell. Expressing his displeasure differently, Andy straightened Powell just enough to dig another uppercut into his gut.

Starsky and Andy were their nicknames, unaffectionately taken from the television shows *Starsky and Hutch* and *Amos 'n' Andy*. Starsky, white, fifty-three, looked like a quarterback long retired and gone to seed. Andy, black, forty-seven, looked like one of the verticals of a goalpost. Powell, twenty-four, wheezed and coughed, trying to collect air into his lungs. When he had enough to plead, he said, "How many times I got to tell y'all? I ain't done nothing. If you want to question me, take me to the station. I got my rights."

"I got your rights," mocked Andy, shaking his right fist, "and your lefts." He shook his left. Then he delivered a right-left combination to Powell's kidneys.

Starsky pushed his bean-pole partner aside and said, "You hit like a faggot." He yanked Powell upright by the back of his collar. "See here, burr head, playtime is over. Either you roll over, or I swear to God, we waste your ass, right here."

Starsky and Andy were certain that Powell had robbed a wig shop by pistol-whipping its elderly Korean owners and making off with money, some wigs, and packaged hair. These were wily, street-savvy cops whose quirky investigative trails frequently produced results. They had thought to canvass area beauty shops and learned that a particular woman came in for a weave, the interesting part being that she supplied the hair herself. When they interrogated the woman, she gave up Powell as the one who had given her the hair, along with a wig. There were no tags or other identification to prove that the items came from the Korean shop. Then again, how many Romeos hand out fake hair to their girlfriends? It was too much of a coincidence, but Starsky and Andy knew that they needed substance, otherwise the prosecutor's office would pass on this one. Hence this little detour en route to the station.

But if Powell had a confession in him, it needed more coaxing to come to the surface. Bent double from the pain, he looked up defiantly and said, "I'm innocent."

Powell already had absorbed considerable punishment, and they couldn't heap much more without risking having him wear the evidence. And they didn't want to release Powell so that he could round up and destroy the other gifts he might have given. Starsky decided that it was time for a last-ditch ploy. It didn't always work, but it had a decent batting average.

Starsky pulled up his pants leg, which hid an ankle holster and a .22-caliber. He freed the gun and emptied the bullets. Next he pulled out his shirttails and polished the bullets. Then he wiped the gun thoroughly. His actions were mysteriously slow, and all the while he smiled devilishly at Powell, who was watching with panicky fascination. Starsky explained his peculiar behavior when he told

Powell, "Got to make sure your prints are the only ones found."
Then, to Andy, he said, "You know what to do."

Powell stiffened as Andy gripped him by the handcuffs and the
back of his collar and tried to force him downward. "Hey, wait.
Don't. You can't—" Powell shut up to channel his strength into remaining upright. He had a hard body and was doing a good job re-
sisting Andy. But when Starsky pounced, Powell was forced to his
knees and then slammed face forward onto the ground. Powell inhaled dust and spit out some dirt, bitter and gritty.

"Stay down, nigger," Andy commanded, his knee in Powell's back.

Starsky grabbed Powell's right hand. Powell resisted by making a
tight fist. Starsky pried the fingers with such force that Powell had
to relent or have them broken. With one hand Starsky clamped Powell's fingers, and with the other he pressed the bullets and then the
gun handle against Powell's fingertips. Facedown, Powell couldn't
see, but he knew what was happening. His mind, however, fought
desperately not to believe why it was happening.

Starsky and Andy stood up. "On your feet, motherfucker,"
barked Andy.

Powell labored upright, then had to watch Starsky's next moves.

Starsky reloaded the .22, again handling bullets and gun with his
shirttails. He held the gun between thumb and index finger and replaced it in the ankle holster. Starsky pulled Powell into a brotherly
one-armed shoulder hug. Then the big cop made a high, sweeping
arch with his other arm and looked skyward, like a visionary. "Try
to imagine this, Sambo," he told Powell. "Me and my partner plead
self-defense for killing you when you pointed a gun at us."

Powell's mind made fitful starts and stalls, like a lawn mower
with a bad spark plug. "This is a bluff, right? It's got to be." But
Powell wasn't completely convinced of his own words. Like many
who lived inside the Precinct 8 area, Powell knew Starsky and
Andy, at least by reputation. They were known, feared, even de-
spised, for their style of law enforcement. Powell wondered if they
were capable of carrying out the threat, and if it was worth his life to
bet against them.

As Powell pondered what to say, Andy broke in with "Either you
confess to something we know you did, or else we kill your punk
ass. Either way, you're out of commission. You choose."

"Look, Ricky," Starsky said in a softened tone, "what we want is for you to tell us what you did with the take. Names. Addresses. And while you're at it, tell us where the gun is. The shit ain't worth dying over."

Without warning, Andy yanked his .38 revolver from his shoulder holster and quickly squeezed off two rounds.

"What the—" Starsky, completely surprised, was looking in all directions at once, to see whether the shots would summon the curious to the junkyard, which was enclosed by a high wooden fence, blocking view from the outside. An opening left by a missing slat had been their entrance. "Have you lost your fucking mind?"

"I can't stand no goddamn rats," Andy said. "Motherfuckers scare me shitless."

"Your wife's greasy cooking got your brain so slippery that thoughts slide off," said Starsky, confident now that the shots had not disturbed the outside world.

"When I was a boy in the projects, my baby sister was eaten alive by rats," said Andy, holding the gun down at his side. "I'm the one who discovered her. Face all gone. She wasn't even a year old. I still have nightmares sometimes. I got what you call a . . . ." He fumbled for the word, his curled index finger tapping his lips.

"Phobia?" stuttered Powell. He had been facing Andy when he drew and fired. Powell had thought that Andy was aiming at him and had started to pee on himself, but he cut off the flow before he wet through his pants. He still was clenching his thigh muscles tightly.

"Who asked you, motherfucker?" Andy's voice rose in indignation.

"That's sad about your sister," offered Starsky. "But rats in a junkyard are like flies in a shithouse. They come with the territory."

"Fuck that," Andy said. "They better keep their damn distance, because I'll blast their asses." As if to back up his irrational threat, Andy didn't reholster his gun but stuck it down in the front of his pants.

"Don't accidentally blow your dick off," advised Starsky. Then he returned his attention to Powell. "Well, bright boy, what's it going to be?"

That two shots could be fired without causing a stir had decided it for Powell. He was isolated and at their mercy, of which they had none. The world was a junkyard, where rusted-out cars without tires and doors lay in repose like elephants at a burial ground, a world populated by just the three of them—oh, and the rats—and Powell was a much bigger, slower, and closer target than the rodents. "I confess."

Pretending to be hard of hearing, Starsky, head cocked, hand cupping his ear, asked, "What did you say?"

"I said, I confess."

"Start singing," Starsky said. "Hurry up, we got crime waves to fight."

Powell, frightened for his life, confessed as Andy scratched down the details in a notepad. He had divided the merchandise among three girlfriends and his mother. Aside from the $113 in his pocket, he had blown the money. And the gun had been nothing other than a BB pistol borrowed from his friend, Quincy Franklin.

Starsky planned to tell whoever was on turnkey to deny Powell any phone calls, at least until they completed the roundup. And of course he and Andy would deny, even in court, having taken Powell to the junkyard.

"Can we go to the station now?" asked Powell. The fact that he was asking to be taken to jail said everything about what he thought of his present surroundings.

"What's your hurry?" returned Andy. "Better enjoy the great outdoors while you can. You won't see it for a while. It's prison this time, brother."

"Maybe for the rest of your life," said Starsky. "That whipping you put on old Chop Sticks sent him into a coma. You're looking at life if he dies."

"At least you'll be alive," said Andy, "if you want to call getting butt-fucked nightly, living."

Powell had never been to prison, just jail, and the thought made his asshole tighten. But he had more immediate concerns, like avoiding a signed confession; like getting a lawyer; like how to get the recipients of the wigs to lie for him; like a score of other things he couldn't think of then but might later when he was safe in a cell.

"Take this piece of shit to the car, partner," Starsky said. With a powerful push, he sent Powell stumbling backward toward Andy.

Powell's fear-weakened knees didn't react fast enough, and he was about to fall when Andy caught him, merely as a reflex action. Next it was Andy who was stumbling backward; a .38 bullet from his own weapon had spiraled into his gut. Although his hand was clamped over the wound, as if to trap the bullet inside, it already had blasted through his intestine and liver and had exited through his back.

Starsky caught a bullet in the groin as he took Powell down with a flying tackle, then two more in the chest, after which the gun was dry clicking. But Powell didn't need those two shots spent on the rats; Starsky lay on him, the cop's life leaking onto him.

Powell's strength was so sapped that he rolled from under Starsky instead of pushing him off. On his knees, he retrieved Starsky's keys and uncuffed himself. He took Starsky's .38 from its belt holster. Then Ricardo Ruben Powell slipped through the fence.

FORTY-EIGHT

Mary did a vertical, sideways limbo dance, careful not to snag her linen pants as she went through the opening in the fence. Milling around the junkyard was a typical cast of characters: cops, technicians, and medicos, with Chief Upton making a guest appearance. The covered bodies of Starsky and Andy lay where Ricky Powell had left them.

Upton stood his ground, since rank dictated that Mary come to him. As squad leader for Special Assignments, Mary automatically was involved in the investigation of any shooting by or of a police officer, even if only in a supervisory capacity. In fact, Mary had sent Jewel Ralston and her partner, Larry Flanders, to the scene. Shortly thereafter, Mary got a call from Upton, ordering her to the scene as well. She learned why after she'd walked over and greeted him.

"There could be a link with the serial killer. It's my understanding that the black officer had a reputation as an Oreo, so to speak."

Mary asked Upton, "Was a cookie found on the body?"

"No, but that doesn't rule it out. There was a crowd by the time the first officers arrived. Somebody could have disturbed the scene. Or birds could have eaten it." Upton added, "Or maybe rats. This *is* a junkyard."

"Still," said Mary, "my guy didn't operate by chance. He made sure that the cookie had to be discovered along with the body."

Mary asked other questions of Upton, his answers leaving her convinced that the cop killings weren't the handiwork of the Cookie Cutter. None of the other victims had been killed along with someone else. None had been shot. She wanted to tell the chief that he was wasting her time. Still, discretion dictated that she go through the motions—though not too long in this heat. Already, Upton's forehead wore beads of sweat, like an outbreak of liquid chicken pox. "I'll poke around," she told Upton.

"You do that. I'm going outside," said Upton, nodding his head toward the other side of the fence, "and speak to the jackals." A chief is expected to show a sense of personal loss and outrage whenever one of his own is killed. Inspector Newberry might have put in an appearance, too, had he not been out of town at a seminar.

While awaiting an official statement, some reporters had been taking statements from the crowd. Starsky's and Andy's seemingly abandoned police car had caused curiosity to get the better of caution, and a few locals had dared to take a peek inside the yard. The news quickly spread, and a crowd assembled. And now some were telling the media the type of cops Starsky and Andy were. There was no air of mourning within the crowd.

Mary went to the bodies, both covered with sheets, and asked whoever wished to answer, "Which one is which?"

A young uniform cop, a short bodybuilder, spoke up. He had his cap tucked under his arm, and his shaved head glistened in the sun. He pointed to the body closer to Mary and said, "That's the black guy."

"The man's mama gave him a name," said Mary. "I don't care what type of person he was, he's dead now. Besides, he was a cop. Call him by his name."

"Jarvis Landrum," said the miniature muscle man. "Landrum had a wife and six kids."

"Thank you," said Mary, bending to raise the sheet. "Let's have a look at you, Jarvis."

Jarvis Landrum was light-skinned with a handlebar mustache. His face was cratered by acne. His hair was greasy Jeri curls that had trapped a lot of the dirt that was stirred when he fell. His eyes were closed. His right hand still was held over his wound, and his lower shirt and upper trousers were blood-soaked. Mary knew at a glance that Eugene Shaw hadn't done this. She lowered the sheet.

Larry Flanders said, "They might have had somebody in custody, or were making an arrest, because cuffs and keys were lying between them."

Mary asked, "What about the murder weapon?"

It was Ralston who said, "The black—I mean, Landrum's .38 was found empty at the scene. It might be the murder weapon. The wounds look like they might have been caused by such a caliber. The other guy's gun is missing. We assume the killer has it, although who knows who might have taken something before we arrived. Both victims were shot close range."

Flanders pulled up Starsky's pants leg, showing Mary the .22 in the ankle holster. "If the killer has the service weapon, he must not have known about this little number."

Mary summarized the working theory. "A killer somehow gets one cop's gun, shoots both, gets away, and it happened in a junkyard."

"Unless you can come up with something better," challenged Ralston.

"I wasn't ridiculing it," said Mary. "Run with it, it's all yours. Do a good job, because there are a lot of questions begging for answers. Me, I'm getting back to headquarters." She started for the fence, then stopped in midstride, head hung, hands on waist. She couldn't do it—that is, be lazy. She might as well finish the formalities. She pivoted on her toes and went to Starsky.

"Was that a tango step, Mary?" asked Flanders.

Mary ignored him and lifted Starsky's sheet. He was lying on his front and the one eye that could be seen was as wide open as a fish's. His hair was blond, not much gray, but it was thin on top and the hairline was receding. His beer belly flowed out to the side. Mary looked over at the group. "Hell, he took one in the groin."

"You see it for yourself," said Flanders, wincing.

Mary said to Starsky, "You got it worse than your partner." She looked back at the group. "He fought with the shooter."

"Why do you say that?" asked Ralston.

"You know how kids lie on their backs in the snow, wave their limbs like they're doing jumping jacks, and make snow angels? Look at the ground under him. He's lying in a dirt angel. And look at this mark," she said, pointing to a grooved arc. "That was made by the heel of a gym shoe." Then she put it together for Ralston and Flanders. "The shooter was on his back with this guy on top of him. Jarvis had to have been the first one shot." Referring back to Starsky, she said, "Scraped knees. Another sign of a struggle. Yeah, I'd say Jarvis was shot, then his partner attacked the shooter."

"The killer could have rolled him over on his stomach. Good way to go through his back pockets," said Ralston.

"Not likely," countered Mary. "Look at the exit wounds in his back. The blood would have made the dirt stick if he'd spent any time lying on his back. And if he had been on his side, the blood would have run down instead of spreading in a circle. He fell face forward, and that's how he remained."

The EMS workers had not been interested in Mary's dissertation, and took advantage of her pause. They almost pushed her aside as they moved in to lift Starsky onto the stretcher. They had already removed Andy.

Mary closed her eyes, placed her fingertips to her temples, and fought off dizziness; the moment had caught up to her. She had put on a fine performance; the others suspected nothing. "Wait," she called to the EMS workers.

She uncovered Starsky's face one last time. She was faintly aware of one of the uniformed officers speaking to her, saying something about the man she was viewing, perhaps giving his name and other details. But she wasn't tuned in. The voice sounded distorted and ever so slow, similar to when the plug is pulled on a phonograph and the album drags to a stop. Mary's mind was on a long trek back across the years.

Sure, Starsky looked a lot worse for wear; decades of boozing and womanizing will do that to a man. It didn't matter, though; she would have known him anywhere, under any conditions: The cop who had shot and killed her brother, Junior, thirty years before. The cop who had stamped the Nike scar above her mouth that had served as a constant reminder ever since.

Mary lowered the sheet back over the face of Reed Carson.

FORTY-NINE

After Ricky Powell left the junkyard, he walked more than a mile, flagged a cab, rode to a drop-off point, then walked more than two miles—his objective to reach his hideout without laying a traceable route.

Now, hours later, he was slouched in an armchair that was dirty and faintly smelled of sour milk. Continuously, he had pondered his thorny situation, but solutions were hiding out themselves. A big problem, in itself, was that he didn't know the exact extent of his problems: what could he be connected to? Maybe that would change, because it was time for the early-evening news. He got up and switched on the television. It had a coat-hanger antenna and the VHF knob was broken off. A pair of pliers rested on top of the set, to be used for switching channels. The set took its time warming up before the picture appeared in pastels. Powell was the lead story, named as a fugitive suspect in the murder of two police officers.

But it's a shame what passes for news reporting nowadays. Where were the salient details? What were the police holding? Had he, for example, been seen leaving the scene? How can someone be expected to map a strategy within such an informational void? Powell sank dejectedly into his soiled throne. He began remembering little things, like what he had touched: handcuffs, key, .22 pistol, bullets—all of which he'd left behind in his panic. And there were Andy's notes. How damning were they? The panic he'd felt at the junkyard had tracked him to his hideout, and now had busted in like a pillaging home invader. He had never owned a car, and all the public means out of town certainly were staked out. No, he wasn't in custody, but that was a technicality; he was as trapped as a rat at the bottom of a barrel, with room to run in circles but nothing more. Powell racked his brain in feverish, lurching thought, and by the start of the second hour of local news had decided upon a scheme.

His phone call surprised the television station's telephone operator, who required convincing that it really was Powell on the line. In minutes Joe O'Shannon, lead anchor, was announcing that a live, on-the-air interview of Ricky Powell was about to happen.

"I didn't murder those police. It was self-defense. They tried to beat a bogus confession out of me, and were about to kill me for refusing. Why you suppose they had me in that yard instead of at the station?"

In Detroit, O'Shannon was the dean of news anchors. An aging, feisty Irishman with white hair that looked as if it could scrub pots, he was as notorious for his two-fisted-drinking, barroom-brawling lifestyle as for his cagey, opinionated delivery of the news. "Ricky, tell the viewers how you managed to defend yourself against two armed officers."

"I ain't got the time to explain. For all I know, this call could be traced. I will say this, though: everybody knew that them cops was dirty."

"Ricky, how about surrendering? High-profile lawyers would stand in line to represent you."

"I'm scared, because I'm sure the cops don't want to take me in alive. Sure as I'm talking to you, they got a hit out on me. All they concerned with is that two of theirs is dead and they want to cover up all the circumstances. I'm innocent. But I'm black and poor, too. What chance I got against the system? I gotta go." Click.

The snowball had started its roll down the mountain. The enterprising Ricky Powell had presented himself to the public as an innocent target running from a renegade police department bent on silencing him. It was insurance that might restrict itchy trigger fingers once the cops inevitably caught up with him. Afterward, it might be the foundation to a jury's reasonable doubt that would release him back to the streets. He felt more calm already. And in the meanwhile he would not venture from his hideout, would avoid capture as long as he could. He was certain that he'd be denied bail and would be jailed while he manipulated the system. Might as well savor each day of freedom, Ricky decided.

His concentration was broken by a child's crying. Powell cupped his mouth and shouted to his host, who was in a back room, "Stick a goddamn bottle in her mouth. I'm trying to think. And then fix me something to eat."

FIFTY

One roach—a big female with an egg case—outraced the others in a mad scramble for crevices along the sink counter. They sensed the hurried approach of an intruder. He opened the doors of the cabinet under the sink. One door leaned off its hinge. More roaches scattered. Some, ironically, leaped from a can of Black Flag spray. A plastic pail was three-quarters full from leaky plumbing. The cabinet's floor was rotting. The area was small, yet he swept his vision around it repeatedly before accepting the obvious: there was no place under there to hide what he was looking for.

The doorless cabinets above the sink had no shelves and contained plastic plates, paper cups, two small pots, canned goods, and a box of cornflakes, arranged in an orderly fashion on newspaper. He took everything down, even looked inside the box of flakes. Checked under the newspaper, too. He replaced everything hurriedly, accidentally knocking to the floor a hot plate and a skillet. A dried-out sausage patty, entombed in grease, was dislodged on impact and sent sliding like the hockey puck it resembled. He put back the plate and skillet, but with a kick of the patty scored a goal under the bed.

The small refrigerator was clean but bare except for a fried pork chop, an open can of beans, and water in a soft drink bottle. There was no table on which to eat. The linoleum floor cover was worn through in a number of spots but had been mopped well. So much for the kitchen.

. . .

A thorough check of the living room produced nothing of value, as did the bedroom. The only closet contained a couple of items on hooks and a few on hangers. He rifled through every pocket, coming up with a stick of gum, coins, a grocery receipt, and lint. And there was nothing in the lone pair of work shoes. He retrieved a particular garment and laid it on the bed; he had to make good the lie he had told.

He cast his gaze about the place, hoping for an oversight; however, with kitchen, bedroom, and living room being just one unpartitioned area, and each containing next to nothing, he was left disheartened by his own thoroughness. That left the bath, the only separate room.

The bathtub badly needed caulking. The sink had a rust spot where the porcelain had been eroded by a dripping hot water faucet. The medicine cabinet creaked as he swung it open: a bar of soap, pink antacid, toothpaste, and a toothbrush wrapped in toilet tissue to keep the roaches from sucking on it. The toilet was bowl and tank. He lifted the top of the tank. A square plastic container with a pry-off lid floated inside. He fished it out and opened it. He was snapped from his euphoria by a sudden voice coming from the front.

"Anybody in here?" the voice inquired.

The successful hunter quickly flushed the toilet. It swooshed noisily. He stuffed his prize inside the front of his pants, tightened his belt, then buttoned his jacket to complete the concealment. Company had arrived, and he headed in its direction.

"Still here. I had to use the bathroom."

"Don't mean to hurry you, Mr. Shaw," said the new arrival, scratching stubble that could sand bark off a tree. "I thought you might have left, and I come to lock the joint back."

Larry Griffin stood with his hands in the pockets of his dull-gray trousers, fumbling with keys and loose change.

"This is what she'll have to wear," Isaac said, scooping the garment that he had laid on the bed. "It was the only halfway decent thing in the closet."

"She wasn't much on fashion," commented Griffin. "I'd only see her coming and going. Always by herself."

"As it turned out," said Isaac, "she didn't keep to herself enough."

"It happens around here. Nobody can deny that. That's how this area is. This ain't the Ritz, but I do the best I can. I believe in evicting problem people. But I never snoop."

Griffin waved off a fly with his right hand.

Isaac had the garment, a pink dress, draped over his palm. He raised and lowered his palm a few times, as if he were trying to guess the garment's weight. It was a ruse to set up his exit. "Since I have what I came for, I'll get out of here. You're a busy man."

"Nowhere near as busy as you, Mr. Shaw. And I don't mind saying that I don't get to talk to many people of your caliber. Not around here. It was a pleasure making your acquaintance." Griffin's boot licking had been bought with the twenty-dollar bill Isaac had given him.

Isaac shook Griffin's extended hand. "Same here. I appreciate the cooperation."

"With you supplying a funeral for free, it was the least I could do. Even the misguided deserve a decent burial."

"So true," said Isaac as he walked toward the door.

A concern hit Griffin, and he stepped quickly to catch up with Isaac. "What should I do with the rest of her belongings?"

Isaac went through the door and stopped in the hall while Griffin locked the apartment. "What's hers?"

"The furniture belongs to the joint," said Griffin.

"Leave that decision to her folks," said Isaac, reaching into his pocket. "Box up the stuff and wait for word." He handed Griffin two more twenties.

"Sure thing, Mr. Shaw." He tucked the bills away.

"That about it?" asked Isaac.

"Can't think of anything else. Sure is a shame, though."

"Thanks again for your cooperation." Isaac started down the narrow, dirty hall, where the air hung with cabbage, incense, and smoke other than from cigarettes, and where honky-tonk music blared from apartment 4D.

"I better see you to the door," said Griffin. "The way you're dressed could make you a target. It don't matter to vultures that it's broad daylight."

Even without such an escort, Isaac would have walked confidently. Easy to do when one lives a charmed life. Isaac felt almost invincible. Yes, his sins were mighty, but he had a plan of atonement. And fate, destiny—God?—was paving the way. Precious Jones was dead and he had Annie Parsons's diary. Add that to leading in the mayor's race, having reconciled with Eugene, and having rekindled his marriage.

Nights before, Precious had stormed from the funeral home, leaving Isaac to obsess over her next move. And for days that's what he had done, for Precious was completely incommunicado. She had gone after Isaac with a half-baked scheme, hoping to panic him into mistakes that her proximity would allow her to exploit. But Isaac had shown her that she didn't know the meaning of *exploit*, not like he did. She left that night confused and reeling because what he'd done was rip her another asshole, then offer her a fortune to get it sewn up.

Isaac and Griffin descended the stairs, the tired old boards creaking in complaint. Most of the steps had slopes of dirt in their corners, and debris was on every landing. Isaac made certain not to touch the banister. Twice the men had to form a single file for two-way traffic: once for a whiskey-soaked young guy who managed to brush Isaac despite being given a wide path, and once for an old woman toting a bag of empty cans and bottles.

The day before, Isaac's hearse driver had gone to the morgue to pick up a car-accident victim. The driver phoned the news to Isaac: the new cleaning woman was undergoing an autopsy. He spotted Precious on an examining table when he walked past it to get to the refrigerated vault where the scheduled pickup lay. She still resembled herself enough in the face to cause the driver to do a double take even before he examined the toe tag, which read, "Savannah Rollins." But even the driver's trained eye might not have recognized her before she had undergone the Y incision that opens the torso so that the internal organs can be removed. Most of the bloating had subsided with the release of the cavity gases, and it was easier to ascertain that she had been a slender woman. Who knows whether Isaac otherwise would have found out about her death. But that's the point: that's how things work out when one lives a charmed life.

Isaac knew that no family would come forth to claim the body of "Savannah Rollins." Since corpses were fingerprinted, she might eventually be identified, but the authorities would have to run a check; they don't always, choosing the lazy way and relying on identification documents. But even if the tag was one day changed to read "Precious Jones," the matter might never end up on Isaac's doorsteps. If it ever did, he'd say that she was just someone who worked for him, and only for a brief while. He'd express shock and dismay over her tragic death.

Griffin was no big risk. He probably already had given the police a statement, which likely amounted to knowing nothing about the woman's background. If he were to be subsequently interviewed and mentioned Isaac's visit, big deal. Isaac would say that he was unable to follow through on his plans to give his employee a free funeral because he never received authorization from the family. Anyway, how much time could someone reasonably expect him to devote to something like that when he was in the thick of a mayoral race? It seemed certain that poor Precious was slated ultimately for a pauper's burial at the county's expense.

The night that she died, the same night that Isaac dismantled her, she'd gone back to the Majestic, but had made a stop and a purchase before going to her apartment. Shortly thereafter, she was dead from an overdose of heroin. She hadn't shot up in years, not since she went cold turkey in prison. And although the Majestic and the area was rife with drug use, she had abstained. That was before reality became unbearable. Days later, accelerated by summer heat, the smell of death had prompted Griffin to use his passkey. It was not a suicide, just one of those instances wherein the rush was too much too soon.

Isaac would never know all of the details, and he didn't want to. That way he could absolve himself from being a causal factor. She had been an addict and had paid with her life, is how he rationalized it.

Isaac stepped through the front door of the Majestic and the world transformed from the dinginess of underlighting to the radiance of an unblocked sun. He glanced about. No cameras, reporters, or gawkers. He loaned a good thought to Precious: *May she rest in peace.* He told himself that he meant it.

FIFTY-ONE

The inspiration came to Mary in an epiphany, and she spent her entire day off work and most of the night making the quilt. The next day she took it to Martha Chenault at the museum. Martha's reaction exceeded Mary's most unchecked hopes.

"Let me show you where it'll be displayed," said Martha. They left her office and went downstairs to the rotunda.

"Here?" asked Mary. She looked around. To her left the main entrance doors led to where she was standing. To her right the reception, information, and ticket counters formed a large horseshoe in the center of which they now stood. Light poured through the glass dome above them.

"Yep," confirmed Martha, her eyes trained on the wall above the head of the young man working the reception counter. She moved aside, letting a family step forward and pay for admission. "After the museum closes, I'll get some workers to hang it."

"I'm so tickled. I really owe you, Martha."

"I'm not doing it for you. The minute I saw that quilt, I knew this was the place for it. It captures the concept of the museum, and I want it on permanent display."

"I'm still grateful to you."

"Save your gratitude. I'll accept it if I'm able to pull off the favor you asked."

"How's it coming?"

"I'm working on it." Returning to the subject, Martha said, "A lot of groups slugged it out over what this museum should be about.

Some wanted to make it an assault on white guilt. Others said keep it positive and prideful. And there was every position in between. We don't all think alike, act alike, look alike, and that's why I love that quilt."

Mary shifted her weight from foot to foot, feeling a mixture of pleasure and guilt. She was thrilled that Martha loved the quilt, but felt guilty for not telling her that Eugene was a suspected murderer. Like Mocha, Martha was regularly in his company. But Mary was under the closest thing to a gag order and Martha was not on the need-to-know list. Mary kept her guilt at bay by rationalizing that Martha's affiliation with the museum shielded her from being branded an Oreo. That didn't make the cookie-cutter mentality any less oner-ous to her. She'd transferred some of those feelings into her quilt's design.

Lying neatly folded on the table in Martha's office was the quilt and its message for the ages. Two faces, frontal views, overlapping like Venn diagrams. Clearly discernible as male and female. Afro features. Yet the faces were rendered in patches of so many different colors, patterns, and materials, all against a white background that thrust the faces forward in contrast. And under the faces, in flowing script, this message: *We are a quilt.*

FIFTY-TWO

Three days after Ricky Powell killed Starsky and Andy, Mary cruised by a house for first impressions. She looked for signs that the occupants were hunkered down: drawn curtains despite sunshine; neglected lawn; garbage cans not at the curb on a pickup day. But there was nothing overtly suspicious about the one-story, two-bedroom, vinyl-siding frame house that Brenda Giles rented.

The Detroit Police Officers Association had announced a $10,000 reward for information leading to the capture and conviction of Powell. The police force was reeling under negative publicity about unexplained circumstances of the shooting, alleged outlaw practices within the department, and having a contract out on Powell.

Choosing to do what he could to soothe the public, Chief Upton promised that Powell would be brought in alive and that a no-holds-barred investigation would be conducted. The reward triggered a landslide of leads—too many for Jewel Ralston and Larry Flanders to handle in a timely fashion. So they were dealt out among the rest of the members of Special Assignments, like cards from a deck that might not contain aces.

Mary's lead had been supplied by Quincy Franklin. Flanders and Ralston had interviewed him the day of the shootings, and although he admitted knowing Powell, he pleaded ignorance as to why his name was in Andy's notepad and why the word "gun" had been written next to it. Yesterday, having heard about the reward, he had come to headquarters with a newfound sense of civic responsibility.

"He might be here," Franklin had said, unfolding a piece of paper containing an address. "A woman named Brenda Giles lives there. I introduced her to Ricky, and she been sweating me about him ever since. You know, trying to get me to hook them up. I let Ricky know she had the hots for him, but I didn't know if he made a move. Anyway, the same day the officers was shot, I dropped by to see if she knew Ricky was wanted and all, 'cause she don't have a phone. She didn't let me in. She might have been busy, like she claimed. But it was something about the look on her face when I mentioned Ricky."

Mary parked a block down from Giles's house to prevent a lookout from giving Ricky time to flee. Additionally, she approached from the direction opposite the largest front window—in this case, a picture window that stretched half the width of the house. She had noted that there was no second door on either side, so it must be in the back.

She went up the front walk to the door, stepping around a tricycle. The doorbell was missing. She flapped her arm against her side for the reassuring feel of her gun under her blazer, and prepared to knock. But first there came noises—a woman's voice, actually. Mary thought that she recognized the type of noises coming from the side of the house. She lowered her hand from the knock position and went around to a side window.

Like the other side windows, this one was striped with permanently affixed burglar bars. The screenless window was raised about a foot. For a few seconds Mary stood flattened against the house, immediately to the side of the window, before lowering to one knee and then inching up her head to steal a look.

Ricky Powell and Brenda Giles were having forceful, sweaty, and determined sex. Giles was on all fours, at the edge of a double bed that had no headboard and only a dingy white fitted sheet on it. Powell was standing, ramming her doggy-style, her ass and his groin repeatedly slamming together in wet slaps. Giles grimaced lewdly, her eyes closed tight. For his part, Powell began to sound off, unintelligibles mostly: hissing inhalations intermingled with "uh-uhs" and some "oooh babys." When Giles chimed in again with her assortment of moans, groans, and pleadings, they had a hot duet going on, until he took solo. "What's my name? Say my name. Say my name."

"Ricky," panted Giles.

Mary drew her weapon with her right hand. With her left she retrieved her handcuffs. Stealthily she draped the cuffs around the intersection of a vertical and horizontal bar. Then, peering under the

window, she drew a bead on Powell. Although all during their performance the lovebirds had faced away from the window, Mary had
easily made out Powell in profile.

"I say what's my name?" Powell repeated.

"Ricky Powell," Mary obliged him. "Police. Freeze." Instantly
the irony of that command occurred to her, and for one insane moment she almost laughed.

Startled as though suddenly in free fall, Powell yanked out of
Giles. He lost his balance and fell seated onto the bed, his glistening
penis erect as the Washington Monument. His attention was riveted
on Mary's 9mm Glock, which was aimed like a sound-seeking can-
non that was locked onto his hammering heartbeat. Giles had been a
second slower to react; she had collapsed onto her stomach and
rolled over to a half-supine position, supporting herself on elbows.
Both remained fixed as statues.

"Hands up, both of you. Don't make me kill you. Who else is in
the house?"

"My baby. She's asleep in the other bedroom," said Giles with
the utmost nervousness. "Don't shoot. Look, I'm raising my hands
as I sit up." And so she did, slowly. She was young, the color of
honey, Powell's height, slender, and slightly bowlegged. She had an
oval face dominated by large, slanted eyes.

Mary raised the window to the top, maintaining aim on Powell. The
musky smell from vigorous sex met her. "Move only when I tell you
and how I tell you. You first, Ricky. Stand and turn your back to me."

He did.

"Hold back your left arm."

He did.

"Now step back towards me—slow—and don't look at me. I'm cuffing you to these bars." She told Giles, "And you're next, girlfriend."

But before Powell started moving backward, a toddler scampered
in, rubbing sleep from her eyes. She scaled the mattress, then dove
onto her mother's lap.

In a blur, Powell snatched the child from her mother and spun to
face Mary. He held her under her armpits and up against his chest,
ducking his head as best he could behind the girl's back, using her
for a shield. He started backing out of the room.

It was like dueling one's reflection in the mirror. Mary angled
from side to side, trying to see around the baby and reset her aim on

Powell, but he matched her every move, holding the screaming child in front of him and obstructing Mary's view.

It took seconds for Giles to recover from the shock. She sprang to her daughter. In between her attempts to wrest her from Powell's clutches, she swung at him with her fists, screaming frantically for him to release the child. Her heroics weren't doing Mary any good, though, for now Powell was being shielded by the child and Giles. When Powell got to the door he released the baby, pushing her forcefully into her mother's arms. Then he was out of Mary's sight. Giles disappeared, too.

"Shit," Mary said, and kicked the house. She thought about whether Powell had Starsky's gun. What were Powell and Giles going to do? Whatever it might be, she knew that she should not remain at the window.

There came a loud rattling at the back door. She tucked herself into a head-lowered position and ran to investigate. She halted at the corner and trained her gun at the door. More rattling. Too much; too loud; too obvious. Decoy.

She backpedaled a couple of steps, then whirled around and darted for the front, again stopping at a corner. She stooped to one knee for steadier aim. An oak tree, taller than the house itself, was closer to the door and could provide cover. She debated whether she would have time to reach it before Powell made a dash through the door. So far the front door was still, but Mary was sure that it had been Giles at the back door making like a poltergeist to decoy her so that Powell could escape through the front. Mary braced herself, took a deep breath, and rushed for the tree, careful to stay low and close along the side of the house.

Mary was passing under the picture window when it exploded as Powell came flying through. He landed on her back, slamming her face into the ground. As she instinctively tried to break her fall with her hands, her fingers bent awkwardly and her gun slid free. Powell, who hadn't expected Mary when he went airborne, was struggling to his feet when she grabbed his ankle. He sent a mule kick in her direction, catching her squarely in the jaw and freeing himself. The next instant, he was sprinting away.

Mary stretched out her arm for her gun, but which one was it? She saw three. She slapped at the first phantom gun, then the next, before finally contacting cold steel. She staggered to her feet. "Halt." She attempted a repeat, but it was choked off by the blood that had collected in her mouth from the kick. Her vision still blurry, and using a two-handed aim, she pointed the barrel skyward for a warning shot. But no shot sounded, because her fingers suddenly were locked, frozen by her arthritis.

Powell tried to dart across the street. A motorist demonstrated lightning reflexes, but the tires didn't burn to a stop before Powell was given a hefty bump. Powell kept going, but not as the slashing runner he had been; he hobbled painfully across a front lawn. Just before he cut between houses he glimpsed Mary coming in full dash, gobbling the distance between them like a gunslinging Lady Pac Man. He crossed one backyard into the adjoining one, and she was so close that he heard her pounding steps, even on grass.

"Stop, Ricky. Stop."

Escape on foot was out of the question. He had to choose: surrender or . . . Or what? Something in his character that had accounted for a life devoted to irresponsible freedom dismissed the first and most logical option; another something in his character that had accounted for a life devoted to acting on impulse decided the "what." This was just one female cop; even hobbled he should be able to deal with her. He sprang off his good leg, making a side dive to the ground, while pulling Starsky's gun from the waist of his pants. Twisting on the way down to fall on his back, he landed pointing the gun. Four rapid shots splintered the morning silence.

"You stupid fuck. Why'd you make me do it? You poor, stupid fuck." Tears cascaded down Mary's face. She stomped the ground and shook her head in denial. She was a confusion of anger, disappointment, fear, and relief.

Powell couldn't answer. He lay sprawled like a chalk outline at a crime scene. His eyes stared unblinking into the sun. The holes in his bare chest overflowed like little crimson ponds.

Mary reholstered her gun, then placed a trembling finger against the side of Powell's neck. His carotid artery did not pulse. Why would it, when one of the shots had blasted a tunnel through his heart?

"You didn't have to kill him, you old-ass bitch. Why did you go and kill him?"

It was Giles closing in fast from about fifty feet away, wearing only Powell's shirt, half buttoned. She stopped so close to Mary that they could have kissed. Instead, she spit in Mary's face.

Mary pulled her fist so far back that it twisted her torso, then she uncorked a vicious right cross to Giles's jaw. The young woman fell to the ground in a heap, sobbing hysterically.

FIFTY-THREE

Of all the contestants in the Tango Championship of Southeast Michigan, only Mary had killed someone that day. At registration, Mary had protested loudly after her request for a different contestant number was denied, and Cliff had to calm her. Still, before handing the number to Cliff so that he could pin it on her back, she had given it the stare of a condemned prisoner reading a rejection letter from the governor. The Cunninghams were couple number thirteen. Mary sometimes reverted to her mother's superstitious teachings in times of stress. She and Cliff already were doomed by their lack of practice. The unlucky number was overkill. But if they were jinxed, there was no evidence yet. The first round had reduced the couples to ten. The second round had shaved them to six. After the third round, there were three finalists: the Cunninghams and two other couples.

The final round consisted of two parts: group and individual dance. The Cunninghams had completed the group portion, during which all three couples take the floor simultaneously. Now couple number thirteen stood alone on the floor, about to perform individually. They would be the sole focus of the judges and the audience seated at round tables in the Starglow Dance Hall in the Detroit suburb of Bloomfield Hills.

Mary and Cliff flashed saccharine smiles as they posed in readiness, waiting to be announced. Mary signaled to Cliff with a tug of his sleeve. He inconspicuously leaned an ear toward her to hear what she was about to whisper. "I'm thankful I'm not on my period. I won't have to hold in my gut."

Cliff nudged her playfully with the side of his hip, too subtly for anyone else to detect. Her levity was in welcome contrast to the knotted tension she'd displayed at home. In the wake of the shooting, Cliff had suggested that they not compete. Mary had argued that the competition would be therapeutic for them both. Mary knew that dancing would help her cope, that somehow the spins she performed on the dance floor were like the revolving door between police work and the rest of her life. Only when she stopped, only when she lost her point of focus would the vertigo set in.

Never prior to Ricky Powell had Mary seen the corpse of some-one whom she had killed. The convenience store robber that she shot when she was a patrol cop died en route to the hospital. The john she shot, who tried to strangle her when she was working Vice as a prostitute decoy, died days later.

But with no shirt to obscure them, Powell's gunshot wounds—round, black, angry portals, deceptively small for the massive destruc-tion of tissue, muscle, organ, and bone concealed underneath—lay exposed in all their gory glory. Two were so close they almost over-lapped, and all four were clustered within an area the size of a man's fist. Powell's blood had held Mary rapt. From each wound it flowed, first collecting in a pool, then dispersing in wiggly rivulets down his chest. The smell of blood, unmistakable and incomparable, pushed her to the verge of nausea. When she had checked his pulse he was hot and moist from the chase, but she knew that along with the blood, his body heat was draining, and he'd soon be reptilian cold.

"Somebody call 911," she had asked, zombielike, no one in par-ticular in the crowd.

"Our third and final couple," crooned the announcer, "is Clifford and Mary Cunningham, of Detroit, who will perform to 'Nuestra Luna Suerte,' translation: 'Our Lucky Moon.' "

The music of the preceding rounds was by orchestra, but each couple was required to bring their own recorded music—minimum of three minutes—for the individual performance. Like suddenly hearing one's native language in a foreign land, the familiar strains stirred Mary, made her want to communicate all the emotions roil-ing inside of her, to fully engage in the daring dialogue that is the tango.

Mary twirled outward from Cliff to a stop, grabbed his out-stretched hand, then twirled back to him. He captured her inside the frame made of his right hand held at the small of her back and his left arm held shoulder-high where his left hand cradled her right hand. Her left hand rested on his right shoulder. They stood with feet together, faces kissingly close, and gazed desirously at each other. Then Cliff stepped backward with his right foot as Mary stepped forward with her left, and their performance was under way.

Three minutes lay ahead, to be consumed not in seconds but in movements. More than enough time to prove mastery, or whatever level short of it. And more than enough time to be distracted if you'd had the kind of day that Mary had, for thoughts can be felons, experts in breaking and entering. Three minutes to keep them locked out.

The wooden parquet floor was treated with a finish that made it shiny but not slippery. Pin lights, recessed just below floor level and protected by a Plexiglas strip, framed the floor, giving it the appearance of a landing pad, or, as Mary liked to think of it, a magical pad that, itself, had the capability of flight. The room's lighting was lowered to candlelight intensity, and from overhead the Cyclopean beam from a spotlight was a death ray or a levitation ray, depending upon how a couple performed within it.

Three minutes.

"Hand it over, Mary."

The speaker had been Sergeant Westley Archibald, a precinct cop. As the ranking officer at the scene, he already had performed his duty of taking the preliminary statement of a fellow officer involved in a shooting; however, he also had the obligation to take that officer's weapon. She handed him her Glock. She was seated with Archibald in the back of a squad car. Strange, but without the accustomed heft of her gun, she experienced the illusion of weightlessness, as if she were drifting upward and about to bang her head against the car's roof. Because the tigress had been caged, spectators closed in for a closer look, and Mary remained on display until cops from the Special Assignment Squad arrived to take her downtown.

Mary and Cliff knew every note of the music they had chosen for their individual performance. Even when they weren't practicing, they often listened to it at home and in their vehicles, visualizing their steps. Often they had made love under its corrupting influence.

In "Nuestra Luna Suerte," the bandoneon, instrument of the tango, rules like a tyrant over the tamer strains of a guitar, violin, flute, and drum. The bandoneon, which resembles and is played like an accordion, expands and contracts, breathing life into a composition and into any dancers willing to sell their souls to this devil of a squeeze box. In "Nuestra Luna Suerte," the bandoneon exhales notes that drone, roll, and pulse in smoldering combinations.

And the Cunninghams came appropriately dressed for falling under the music's control. They were donned all in black, the unofficial color of the tango.

Mary's dress was hemmed in tassels, each a cat-o'-nine-tails that flogged her legs which were crosshatched in fishnet stockings, heightening the deviantly sexual aura of the dance itself. Spaghetti straps rode her bare shoulders, connecting the low-cut back with the low-cut front. Its hem varied from knee length in the back, to a cut inches above the knee in front, liberating Mary to perform the leg lifts, dips, and lunges that are too suggestive for other dances, but are signature elements of the tango.

Cliff's ensemble was pleated pants, collared shirt, tie, a satin vest, and a broad-brim hat tilted rakishly. He was a sleek, commanding, Zorro-like figure. The tango is a masquerade that grants permission to be someone far different from one's everyday self; and Cliff, the professor, conservative in many ways, loved that aspect.

Indeed, the tango is a many-splintered thing. It offers dancers endless choices of interpretation: fast or slow, flashy or demure, tender or domineering, improvisational or choreographed, brooding or gleeful. But however danced, it should be in a manner that highlights the tango's most intrinsic qualities—passion, sensuality, and intimacy.

Mary and Cliff, under the unforgiving scrutiny of the judges, went through their paces. Steps and movements combined into figures— the obligatory classics and their own variations. The music convulsed and urged them on. A pattern was soon established as it became evident that their figures, while maintaining count with the music, were increasing in complexity. The drama was mounting. It was a good thing that they were not illicit lovers, for the rapport shown on the dance floor would have betrayed them. The tango peels to the core of a couple's relationship.

To demonstrate versatility, they danced some show tango, the dazzling dervish style with vertigo-inducing spins and some linear tango, requiring them to traverse a large floor. But mostly they performed in rotary tango, dancing in a circling, weaving, wrapping fashion. Rotary requires little floor space. Rotary is closeness. Rotary is intimacy.

Rotary is ritualized stalking.

Mary kept her shoulders parallel with Cliff's, which better enabled her to follow his lead, which he communicated through movements that were clear, confident, and gliding. The resulting impression was that the light fantastic was being tripped by telepathy.

Two minutes.

"All right," the police union representative had said after reading what Mary had written. *"You ready to go over this?"*

"Yeah."

Any officer that has been involved in a shooting is taken downtown to give a written account of the incident. Until that account is given, the officer is kept in isolation, and always away from any other involved officers and material witnesses. The only person with whom the officer may confer during the isolation is a representative from the police union.

An officer who has killed someone is taken off active duty while a mandatory review process is conducted. The Special Assignments squad files an Investigator's Report, based on the officer's written account and verbal statements, along with input from any other involved parties. The report is filed with the Board of Review, a civilian body that has the responsibility of declaring whether the deadly force was justified. If the board determines the shooting was clean the officer is returned to active duty. A ruling of nonjustification subjects the officer to penalties that range from departmental reprimand to criminal charges.

Even the greenest rookie knows that there is no such thing as a shooting that generates universal agreement over all its details. Careers are at stake, even freedoms. Take nothing for granted. And never, never begin the process without the guidance of the union.

"So we're talking self-defense here," the union rep summarized.

"He tried to shoot me."

Mary felt it, Cliff felt it, and each knew that the other felt it: they were dancing their best ever, lack of practice notwithstanding. The reasons driving their individual performances were different but interrelated. Mary's was to battle the encroaching thoughts about

Powell. Thus far, total immersion into this dance competition had proven effective. But for how long? The least lapse could trip her figuratively, and maybe literally. Cliff's reason was to celebrate that death had not claimed the woman he loved. His first wife had worked for the electric company and was electrocuted while making repairs after an ice storm. It was dangerous work, and he would always feel that he should have steered her into a safer career.

Mary's and Cliff's rhythms might have been similar to those of the Afro-Argentineans, descendants of the slave trade who contributed so mightily to the evolution of the tango, giving it its name from an African word meaning "a meeting place."

Mary and Cliff were giving a dynamite performance, and the judges were taking note. The tassels were constantly in motion. The eyes remained the endpoints of one mesmerized stare. And at no time were their bodies not in some form of contact. All of this continued—became more intense, actually—as they kept track, almost to the second, of where they were in their performance and how much more they had to go.

One minute.

"I think we got a good shooting here, Mary," the rep had said. "We still need to nail down a few things."

"Like what?"

"Four shots?"

"I wasn't counting. I was just squeezing while I could, because earlier my fingers locked when I tried to get off a round."

"As you know, the public's attention was on Powell. Don't be surprised if there are claims of excessive force."

"I admit I meant to kill him. He would have killed me. What was I supposed to do, try to wing him, or better yet, shoot the gun out of his hand? To anybody offended by four shots, I say I would love to have done it with one."

Mary was at Cliff's left at one second, on his right the next. Pressed against him at one second, held purposefully away the next. Sent into spins that, if not for her returning her vision to a fixed point, would have spiraled her into dizziness.

Time to let loose with all the embellishments—hooking, swiveling, and straddling—performed with a rapidity and proximity intolerant of miscue; freeze-framing into dips and other poses, in body positions that tantalized the spectators.

Forty-five seconds.

"Brenda Giles says that you threatened to kill both of them from the start."

"She's lying."

"Says you never identified yourself."

"Damn lie."

"And that she saw you take the gun off Powell and place it to look like he had tried to shoot you."

"That heifer's brain is between her legs. She's trying to get revenge on me over that stupid fool."

There's much about the tango with which black people might identify. There's vilification, for example. The tango was damned as indecent, heathen, and uncivilized in many privileged circles. Take irrepressible as another example. The tango would not be denied, and resisted its suppressors, even when it meant being practiced in secrecy. Variety is still another example. No limit as to its shades and tones.

Thirty seconds.

"Choose how you want to ride out the review," Inspector Newberry had told Mary after she submitted her written account and answered some questions. *"Do you want to ride the desk or take vacation?"*

Experienced couples know how to sneak glances at the judges while maintaining the illusion that they are oblivious to all except themselves. Mary and Cliff had read the judges like a Dick and Jane book. They were a lock. The trophy would be theirs in scant seconds. Cliff couldn't restrain from supplying Mary with some final motivation. They were nose-to-nose and he was leading her in twirls around the floor, when he announced, "The SBA approved our loan. You'll never have to be shot at again."

The time for the finishing flourish was at hand. Cliff hoisted Mary in a one-armed sweep as she held on to his neck, knees folded, her free arm saluting the audience. He lowered her in a gentle glide. She was supposed to spin out and grab his extended hand before they took their bows. Simple. She could do it in her sleep. She missed the connection. Badly. The audience gasped in unison.

FIFTY-FOUR

Eugene had not worked on the royal couple painting since the day
that Mary and Frank had invaded his sanctum. He briefly considered destroying the incriminating evidence, but he had too much
time and spirit invested in it. But was it worth the risk? Despite constant vacillating, he hadn't been able to get past what the painting
symbolized; thus he chose to spare it. He'd spent the day applying
the finishing touches, working between bouts of debilitating, blinding headaches and vomiting. Exhausted and reeling, he'd collapsed,
able to make it upstairs but not into bed.

Eugene was awakened by the chug of the freight elevator. It had to
be Mocha; it had better be Mocha. But she wasn't due home from
work for hours. He pressed the heels of his palms into his eye sockets. The kaleidoscopic light show only irritated his already jangling
nerves. His eyes burned. His mouth was caked with the remains
of his wretching. He rose to a seated position on the couch just as
the elevator bumped to a stop. The accordion gate screeched as it
was pulled back; the latch clanked as it was unfastened; the door
grumbled as it was opened. Mocha stepped into the apartment.

She wiggled her long fingers in a greeting. She didn't pull off her
sunglasses. Her mouth was turned downward, bottom lip in the
clinch of her upper teeth. Vertical wrinkles were bunched between
her eyebrows. She beelined to the bathroom and locked it.

Eugene walked to the bathroom, slowly, the travel time spent trying to guess the cause of her strange, wordless arrival. "Moe? Anything wrong?"

"Not now, Gene. I need a minute."

He prepared for her reemergence by getting a bottle of cranberry juice from the refrigerator and pouring two glasses. He carried them to the living room and was placing them onto coasters on the coffee table when Mocha came out.

From the way that she looked in her gold leather miniskirt it was impossible to detect that she was pregnant. She had shed the matching pinched-waist jacket and her black high heels. Her eyes were bloodshot. The cold water that she had splashed on her face had smudged her makeup.

"Drink something," Eugene advised, holding out her glass.

"Thank you." She emptied it in one gulp.

"Ready?"

"Yes." Her chest heaved in a preparatory deep breath. "I love you so much, Gene. I want you to know that."

"I love you double."

"Enough to tell me the truth?"

"Yes."

"I need to know. I have a right to know."

"Know what, Moe?"

"A Lieutenant Mary Cunningham came to my job today."

His eyes clapped a single blink, as if he had been surprised by a paparazzo's camera flash. "What did she say?"

"It's me who needs to ask the questions. I'm hurting. I need you to take it away."

"Moe, first sit down."

"I don't want to sit." Then her voice rose in pitch and volume, and the words tumbled from her mouth. "She spoke of a dagger and cookies. Tell me it's a horrible coincidence. That night I first posed for the Mother of Mankind sketches, when I found the dagger, when I saw the cookies in the cabinet—a night so beautiful can't be connected to something so awful. Tell me I'm right, honey. Say it. Now, damn it." She slammed her curled fists into her thighs.

"Did you tell her anything?"

"No. I told her I didn't want to talk to her. She gave me her card and said to call if I changed my mind. She suspects the wrong person. Isn't that so, Gene, baby? Tell me I'm hurting for nothing."

Eugene was momentarily adrift in the purgatory of not being able to lie, not being able to tell the truth. Mocha read the dilemma in his eyes, and she knew. Realizing what he had conveyed, he said, "Moe, you have to let me—"

"Ommmmm." She had pressed the back of a quaking fist to her lips, but the wail escaped anyway. It stretched long and guttural, before breaking up into bursts of sobs.

She collapsed onto the couch and wrapped her arms about herself. Her face twisted into a grimace of pain as she threw her head from side to side. Pounding her heels into the floor, tears streamed down her face. Shrill screams vibrated her vocal cords.

"It'll—" Eugene began. He paused as another stifled scream escaped from between Mocha's clenched jaws. "It'll be all right. Once I explain, you'll understand."

He dropped down beside her and tried to gather her in his arms. Her strength sapped, she still managed to push him away. Eugene sat and stared at her, watching her writhe in agony.

"It was mean and cruel," she charged. "You had no right, no right at all to make me love you, fill my head with fantasies that you knew would blow up in my face. You had the nerve to call your father a hypocrite. You're the one. While you were telling me all the family secrets, you neglected a few of your own." She was leaning on her side, looking over at him, her eyes red rimmed and swollen.

"That's not how it was, Moe. I swear."

"Don't lie," she shrieked. "You said you loved me enough to tell me the truth."

"And I am. I have a mission, Moe."

"Stop it! Stop it! You can't justify it. You killed people. And now the police are hunting you." Her own words made her stomach lurch, and she doubled over. "Nobody should hurt this bad. I should hate you. God, let this be a nightmare. Wake me, God. Wake me or take me."

"Moe, it's over. I promise. I'll quit the mission."

Mocha sprang upright, her eyes flashing. "You talk like you're giving up cigarettes. This is about murder, Gene. They'll jail you for the rest of your life."

"They can't prove anything, Moe." Eugene's tone was plaintive, conciliatory.

"You don't know that."

"They know I was at the Ambrosia."

"Where the Wells woman was killed?" Mocha asked in self-torture.

"And they saw our painting. That's their entire case."

"Our painting?"

"Yes. I'll show you. Don't move." He had brought the painting upstairs after finishing it and planned to surprise her with it that evening, under much more pleasant circumstances. He got up and dragged a large easel and painting from the corner. He set it in front of her. He slipped off the sheet that covered the canvas and let it slide to the floor.

Mocha stared dumbfounded at the enormous portrait and its ebony frame. Then she resumed crying, silently this time, interrupted by "Us?"

"Nubian king and his queen. This is all they've seen of the dagger. I have the real thing in safekeeping. This painting symbolizes you standing at my side, supporting the mission."

Her voice cracking, Mocha said, "Gene, look at it!"

"What do you mean?"

"Don't you see? Look at how you painted yourself."

"I still don't know what you're getting at."

Mocha rose unsteadily. She was wearing the saddest smile. She ran her fingers through his hair. Tears fell. They represented love, pain, sorrow, and now pity. "You need help, baby. Give yourself up. They'll know you were not responsible for what you did."

"I did nothing wrong. They wouldn't understand that, and I don't think you do either," he said as he pulled her hands from his hair.

"But I do. And so will they. This Lieutenant Cunningham, I trust her for some reason. I'm not sure why."

"She's turned you against me, hasn't she?" Eugene began pacing, his arms wrapped around himself.

"Impossible. I'll never stop loving you. Let's call her."

"No." His voice was emphatic. He stopped for a moment. His eyes narrowed as he stared at her before he resumed walking.

"Then let's talk to your family. Get their advice. The police will get around to them if they haven't already."

Eugene stopped and spun on his heels to face her. "My family knows nothing. Anyway, it's you that I'm most concerned about."

"Your father and mother will ask you. Will you lie?"

"They don't have to know."

"And you want me to lie, too."

"We'll be married soon. A woman can't be forced to testify against her husband."

"We can't get married under these conditions, Gene." She stomped in frustration. "I won't. Not knowing whether you'll be taken away at any time. It's no way to raise our son, either."

Eugene's eyes widened. "You said 'son.' "

Mocha buried her face into cupped hands, and her shoulders pumped up and down through another crying seizure. She felt his touch and moved away.

"So it's Larkin in there." Eugene suddenly wore a big, silly grin. He placed a hand on her abdomen. She flinched, and then, seeing Eugene's reaction, relaxed and allowed him to touch her again.

"Your father's suggestion about a complete physical reminded me that my father's sister had Down's syndrome, which can run in families, so I got a CVS to see whether our baby was normal. He is."

"CVS?"

"Chorionic villus sampling. It also tells the sex. What a fool I was, frantic about the baby's health, when all the while it's his father that's, that's . . ." Mocha's choking sobs drowned out her words.

"Don't cry, baby. The police will give up eventually and leave us alone to raise Larkin."

"Those poor victims, Gene. Don't you feel anything?"

"Of course. But I was thinking about what was best for our people."

"It's like talking to a brick wall," Mocha said, raising her gaze beseechingly to the ceiling. Suddenly she was gripped by the need to vent in a different manner, and she swiped the drinking glass from the coffee table and hurled it against the wall, where it shattered in a perfect imitation of her life.

"Don't give me that!" she shouted. "If anything, it was about what was best for you and your obsession about your color. Look at that picture. Force yourself. That is not your color, Gene. Why can't you accept the fact that you look like a white man? I'll say it again, Gene: you look like a white man."

"Watch what you say to me." A vein pulsed in Eugene's forehead and his jaw twitched uncontrollably.

"Or what? You'll kill me, too? All I ask is that you make it merciful. Clean and swift. I've already done the suffering." Mocha stood in front of him, her arms extended, ready for the cross.

For the first time during the ordeal, Eugene cried. The first tears fell intermittently, but when he broke his vacant stare, they dropped with every blink. "You're the one who needs help," he said with affection, "if you believe that I would ever harm my Nubian queen."

"Stop with the queen fantasy, Gene," she scolded. "I'm not feeding into it anymore. I realize now that it's sick. Baby, agree to get help. I'll wait for you. Me and Larkin."

"For them to let me out in time to die of old age? No, thanks. I'll miss the best years with you. I'll miss seeing Larkin grow up. My plan is better. We go on like none of this ever happened."

"No." She raised a fist, then struck down at air. "I won't turn you in. But I'll never forgive myself if you kill again or if you get killed by the police. But I'll worry about that later. For now my first priority is to get as far away from here as I can." She started toward the bedroom.

"What are you saying?" he asked with alarm.

"I'm leaving, Gene." The crying had stopped. She was more composed. She sounded resolute. "I'm leaving Detroit."

Leaving. Hearing her say that word made his head feel as if it had been caught between cymbals. At this point he was struck hard by the similarities between their conflict and the one he had overheard as a child the night he learned that Isaac was his father: secrets, followed by confession, followed by abandonment. Only, in his case he didn't think Mocha would return as Gertrude had done. Like father, like son. But maybe history could be prevented from repeating itself.

"That's the last thing you want to do, Moe." Eugene's voice was steady.

His calm unnerved her. "I'm down to the last thing, Gene. This is the best for both of us," she said. "Always remember how much I love you." She kissed him lightly on the lips, and it bore all the traits of a final good-bye. She started to pull away, but he caught her by the wrists.

His voice slow and meditative, Eugene said, "I can't let you do it, Moe. You'll see things differently if you give yourself time."

Mocha's eyes darted around the room, and she tried to tug her arm out of his grip. "Gene, let go. You're hurting me."

"You're my queen." He clamped harder as she tried to pull his thumbs back to release herself.

"Let go."

"Stop struggling. I can't let you leave me, Carol."

"Carol?"

"I misspoke. I'm sorry."

"Now I understand," said Mocha, recalling that she resembled Carol. "I've been a substitute, haven't I? If I were light-skinned you never would have looked at me. Everything is about race and color with you. Every twisted thing. Let go, Eugene."

"Larkin," said Eugene. "Think of him. Don't make me lose him twice."

"Twice?" Mocha's mind raced. Eugene's ever-stranger behavior fueled her terror, giving her enough added strength against his thumbs to free her hands. He instantly grabbed at them again. She yanked away. She whirled to dash from his reach. But the easel and the painting were there, and she turned squarely into them. Before she could react, her balance was gone. She went down hard, an arm flung over the top of the easel, a leg tangled in its legs. The framed painting was knocked free, and it and she hit the floor at about the same time. The painting was almost vertical, about to fall backward, when her face slammed into it. The frame caught her under the nose, shoving it up into her head. Death was immediate.

FIFTY-FIVE

Mary felt as if she were seated in a beanbag chair. She shifted and reshifted; trying to scoop out a pocket in which to nestle down. Despite her discomfort, this was the same chair she'd sat in for years, at the same desk, in the same squad room. The difference now was that she'd been taken off active duty while the Powell shooting underwent the review process; in other words, she was deskbound. On this first day, adjustment wasn't coming easily.

Inspector Newberry opened the squad room door. He didn't venture inside but spoke while maintaining his grip on the doorknob.

"My office," he said to Mary. "Now." He closed the door before she rose from her seat.

Once she got to his office, Newberry said, "The Investigator's Report is finished, and it clears you of wrongdoing."

"That was quick," said Mary, reflecting that only a weekend had passed since the shooting.

"Witnesses came forth to say that Powell drew on you first. Brenda Giles is nullified."

Mary wiped imaginary sweat off her brow. "Inspector, I could kiss you. I would have gone stir-crazy if I had to ride the desk for long."

"Hate to burst your bubble," said Newberry, sounding foreboding and as if he were holding a long needle. "You know that there's another part to the process."

"Sure. The report goes to the Board of Review. How can they rule other than justifiable shooting?"

"I'm certain," said Newberry, "that's exactly what they will rule. I was referring to the timing. It might not come anytime soon."

"And why not?" She already suspected the answer.

"I'm sure you didn't spend the weekend in a cave, Mary. Even if you did, you still might have heard the loud rantings of McArthur and the K-9s."

The Reverend Jeeter McArthur was founder of the K-9s. He was a man-mountain, with a belly and butt in separate zip codes. He had permed, shoulder-length hair. He wore big, tinted eyeglasses with bejeweled frames. He chose the name K-9s because by his description the members of his organization were police attack dogs—they went after the corrupt, the brutal, the unfit members of the Detroit Police Department. They had a 1-800 number for reporting police brutality and other misconduct, and advised callers on how to sue Detroit. Not surprisingly, he was no favorite at City Hall. The controversial McArthur was hailed by some as a social crusader, while others branded him a self-promoting rabble-rouser.

McArthur and the K-9s had taken a supportive stance for fugitive Powell. And after Powell was killed, their version was that he'd been executed as an act of revenge. The contract had been given to an experienced, trigger-happy assassin who'd killed other black men, a badge-toting hit woman who heartlessly went dancing afterward, a cop appropriately known within the ranks as "Bloody Mary."

Mary took another chance. "Maybe the chief would be willing to talk to the board on my behalf."

Newberry shook his head. "He wouldn't without clearing it with the mayor. And Clay might want the dust to settle a bit before you're reinstated. He's trailing Shaw in the polls and doesn't want the gap to get any wider."

"Which it might, if the public believes his police force has a review process that's a rubber stamp," translated Mary.

"You got it," said Newberry. "Politics and law enforcement are an ugly, entangled mess in this city. It's got me sick to my stomach."

Mary said, "Clay would make a quick turnaround in the polls if the public knew that Isaac Shaw's son is a murder suspect."

"You're doing what I was complaining about a second ago, mixing police work and politics. I haven't told the chief about Eugene Shaw because he'd take it straight to Clay, who'll exploit it politically. Our case against Shaw might end up no case at all after he gets through screwing it up."

"The Cookie Cutter case is what got the mayor in trouble in the first place," Mary said. "So why wouldn't he want me back on active?"

"You might have that going for you. It remains to be seen. But don't be surprised if you're pulled off the case, even if you're reinstated tomorrow. The K-9s have thrust you into the public's face. You're high-profile, Mary. Maybe a little too hot to handle. Clay might see you as a liability."

Mary's words were measured and solemn. "You're taking me off Cookie Cutter?"

"What's to take? You're on desk duty. But I'll give my word that if it happens, it won't be my doing."

Mary said, "God must be laughing himself silly over the joke he's playing on me." Mary considered the unlikely chain of events that brought her to this point: Reed Carson, a.k.a. Starsky, killed her brother; Powell killed Carson; she, of all people, killed Powell and is now being skewered by a watchdog organization to such a degree that her career might indefinitely be in suspended animation.

Newberry, unaware of Mary's history with Carson, said, "Don't be the drama queen, Mary. All of this will work itself out . . . eventually. Meanwhile, help your own cause by seeing the department psychiatrist. Have him give you a short medical leave for stress."

"Stress?"

"Work with me here, Mary. You killed a man the other day, remember? Pretend you're affected by it. It could counter the image that the K-9s are painting of you."

Mary didn't like the advice, yet she couldn't deny its logic. Anyway, hanging around, being a desk jockey and a political pawn, was more distasteful to her. "I'll do it."

"Good. All I ask is that you stay the rest of the day and brief Flanders on the Cookie Cutter case. He and Ralston will run with it while you're off."

"Will do. Inspector?"

"Yes?"

"Something's been on my mind for a while now. I'm just going to spit it out. First of all, I'm aware of your dislike for mixing politics and police work, and I know that you don't have high regard for the mayor. And I know you believe that Chief Upton has the job you should have been given, but—"

Newberry interrupted with "What became of spitting it out?"

Thus chastised, Mary asked, "Did you leak the Cookie Cutter story?"

Newberry cast the room into silence as he held her in his unrelenting gaze. Mary, who'd been seated throughout the conversation, pressed her knees together, then started clicking her heels nervously. The silence continued. Newberry was giving her plenty of time to squirm, to rethink the audacity she'd displayed; for, whatever the truth, he wasn't answerable to her. He tugged at his lower lip. Then, with evident displeasure, he said, "No. Now leave."

FIFTY-SIX

Mary's briefing of Flanders was cut short when he received a call from the hospital that a victim of blunt-force trauma had awakened from a coma. Maybe she could reveal who'd attacked her and her sister, who hadn't survived. Flanders told Mary that he would come straight back after the interview.

Shortly thereafter, Mary was slightly surprised, yet grateful, to be visited by the daughter of the Korean couple that Ricky Powell had robbed and beaten. The visit was short, however, and Mary was idle again.

Mary went through the door that connected her squad room with Squad Three. Humphrey Steward was in there alone. She did an immediate about-face before he could look up from his writing. She wasn't desperate enough to suffer his only conversation topic: his spastic colon.

Mary thought of Lyla Mallory, who worked in Squad One. They sometimes ate together. When she came to the doorway, she knew who was checking in even though his back was turned, for she had memorized him from every angle. The shock of seeing Eugene Shaw made her go tense, in preparation of drawing her gun. She patted her side to remind herself that she'd had to give up her weapon. Without noticing Mary, Eugene walked to the back of the room and disappeared into a passageway that led into the adjoining squad room.

Mary wasn't sure that her voice was with her, so she didn't at-

STERLING ANTHONY | 303

tempt to speak to the desk sergeant. She picked up his register and read that Eugene Shaw had signed in to see Peter Bridgeport. In quick, long strides, she followed Eugene's path. She had to apply the brakes in short skids to avoid bumping into Bridgeport's desk.

"Hey, slow down to seventy," Bridgeport said. He eased his lanky frame into a chair.

"Why are you here?" Mary demanded of Eugene. And to Bridgeport she said, "Hi, Pete."

"Nothing to do with you," said Eugene, standing. Her sudden presence had startled him out of his flat affect. He angled his back to her.

"Is this a reunion of some kind?" asked Bridgeport.

"Why is he here, Pete?"

"I asked first," said Bridgeport.

"Can I talk to you in private, Pete?" Mary asked. Referring to Eugene, she asked Bridgeport, "Is he restrained from leaving?"

"He's under no restraint whatsoever. Take a squat in that chair until I return, son." When he and Mary were in the passageway he said, "You want to let me in on this?"

"He's my suspect in three murders."

"Holy shit. We gotta find some way of operating around here so that the right hand knows what the left is doing. I'm working his girlfriend's case. He called—"

"Whoa, whoa, whoa," she stammered. "Mocha Springwell?"

"That's her. It was an accident."

Stunned, Mary said, "Whatever happened, Pete, it was no accident."

"Don't take that attitude with me. I do thorough work. If I say accident, Scotland Yard couldn't prove different." Bridgeport took a comb out of his back pocket and ran it through his silver hair.

"I don't want to fight with you, Pete. Just tell me what happened."

"She tripped over a painting. This guy's an artist."

Mary impatiently said, "I know. She tripped over a painting. Go on."

"She fell face forward onto a picture frame. Caught her below the nose, killing her."

"She tripped over a painting—that's his story, right?"

"Right."

"Autopsy supports it?"

"Report hasn't come back yet. But the scene supported it. We took the painting all the same. That's why he's here. He called and I told him he could come down and get it back."

"Where is it?"

"In the basement, in property lockup."

"Don't release it, Pete."

"For the sake of your case or mine?"

"Mine, since your mind's made up."

"Hell, Mary, you don't even know what painting it was."

"Then tell me."

"Him and his gal, except—"

Mary finished what he was about to say. "He's painted black."

"That's the one."

"Pete, don't give him that painting. And now that you know he's my suspect—"

"Don't change a thing. I can't prove it wasn't an accident. I won't let him have the painting, though. Three murders, you say. I took him for a wacko, but not like that."

"How?"

"The black art, the black girlfriend, he's one confused white man, Mary. Good luck with him. Let's get back in there before he starts teaching Swahili." Eugene had never taken his eyes off the doorway, and he stood up just before Bridgeport said, "No can do about the picture. It stays here for now."

"Why?"

"I'm not through with it, obviously," answered Bridgeport.

"Then how long before—"

"Look," said Bridgeport, in a tone meant to intimidate, "I'll give you a call."

For a few seconds, Eugene stared at Bridgeport, eyes squinting in anger, then said, "You do that." He glowered at Mary before starting for the passageway.

"Not through there," called Bridgeport. After Eugene halted and looked around, Bridgeport nodded at the front of the room. "Go out that door."

Mary thought that she had timed it so that Eugene would be on the elevator, but when she entered the hall he was there, leaning against the wall. "You waiting for me?" she asked. Her pulse was racing.

"You shouldn't have talked to Mocha." His voice was distant, as were his eyes.

"I didn't have a choice. So where does that leave us?" Mary nervously fingered her scar.

"That painting is invaluable to me. It's like her spirit is being locked up in this place. I came to free her. You got in my way."

"Tell me the real story how Mocha died."

"You killed her."

"I'm not going to dignify that with a denial. But don't you want to talk, Eugene? Deep down, don't you want this to end?"

"Save your weak psychology. Besides, you're off active duty. I follow the news. As for the end, it's closer than you think." He turned and walked to the elevators. A car was waiting. He entered, leaving Mary perspiring under the arms.

Mary hadn't recovered enough to redirect her eyes before Frank Corleone stepped from another elevator car.

Frank went to her and said, "I heard about the shooting. Glad you're still among the living, partner. Guess what? I spent the weekend in Washington, D.C., with Abigail Cox."

"Uh-huh," Mary said vacantly.

Frank stood before her expectantly, waiting for her to hound him for details. He followed her stare toward the elevators. "What's the matter with you, Mary? You look like you seen a ghost."

FIFTY-SEVEN

The painting at police headquarters and the drawings at the museum were the only ones missing; all other pieces that Eugene ever created of Mocha surrounded him, having been retrieved off the walls, out of closets, from trunks—wherever they had been placed or stored—and assembled in the shrine he had created.

Eugene had come straight home from police headquarters to worship, a practice that, over the past days, had taken various forms. Sometimes he had arranged the pieces chronologically, denoting evolution of style and technique. There had been times when he had arranged them by personal preference, judging them by artistic merit. In other stretches he had flipped through sketch pads, mentally retracing each drawing. No matter the activity, at some point tears would fall. Each of his senses—sight, smell, hearing, taste, and touch—had its favorite memory of her.

The Shaws had learned of Mocha's death in a phone call from Eugene. Gertrude fainted on the spot. Isaac's heart underwent palpitations. But in keeping with how he'd conveyed the tragic news, Eugene insisted that he be allowed to mourn in isolation. Still, the Shaws filled his voice mail with their pleas to see him. After their calls went unanswered, they dropped by unannounced; however, Eugene ignored the doorbell just as he had the telephone.

Isaac was determined to console his son in person. When Eugene ventured out on his way to headquarters, Isaac was waiting, a vigil he'd maintained off and on since first learning of Mocha's death. So that he could be left alone to go to headquarters, Eugene relented and went back in with Isaac.

Their meeting, even by their standards, was weird. Eugene had gone back downstairs for a minute, and when he returned, his conversation focused singularly on Isaac's political platform. And try as Isaac did to feel Eugene out on how he was holding up, Eugene kept returning the conversation to politics. Isaac, with his lifetime of experience with the myriad ways that people mourn, gave in and engaged in Eugene's chosen topic. After all, mourners are said to go through stages, and Isaac theorized that this might be Eugene's form of denial.

After a half hour, they said good-bye. Both were crying profusely: Isaac because he loved his son; Eugene because he'd been spared the unthinkable. As they stood embracing, Isaac had felt something long and hard in the back of Eugene's belt but didn't know what to make of it. Just as Mayor Randal Clay had done the night of the museum's grand opening, Isaac had passed Eugene's test.

Mocha's funeral was scheduled for the next afternoon. Mocha was survived by parents of very modest means and six younger siblings. Eugene paid to have her body flown to Connecticut. He also paid for the funeral.

Mocha hadn't been long dead, but already the surroundings that she had meticulously maintained echoed her absence. Dirty dishes and empty food containers lay around. Clothes lay wherever he had gotten out of them. The garbage smelled. Eugene smelled gamy himself, something Mary had noticed hours earlier. The stubble, so many quills days ago, had begun to lie down in some semblance of a beard.

Mocha, a son, and a dream: all were dead. The day she died, he had tried to provide her explanations and apologies. He'd been unsuccessful, of course, but that was because Mocha was so overwrought, so upset, so taken with the immediacy of the situation. Now she'd had time to calm down. Now she would listen to what he had to say. So he began again, determined to tell her everything, at least as best as he could patch together his thoughts. He spoke in a chant, mournful but fast. His head weaved and tears squeezed from the corners of closed eyes. He tried to spare no details about how things happened, why they happened. And he let her know that her brief presence had been the happiest time of his life.

Toward the finish, he told her that he would do as he'd promised and give up the mission. It was way out of control anyway. What he might have done earlier in the day, against his own father, was irrefutable proof that it was a Frankenstein's monster, lumbering amok and disdainful of its creator. Yet, he assured her, he must lure his monster to one last location. He fully expected the monster and creator to be destroyed in the same climactic scene.

After two hours, nonstop, he paused. He listened. He heard her response. She understood. Finally. More than that, she agreed with his conclusion as to how the ordeal should end. The last thing that she told him was that it was all right that he would not be able to attend her funeral. They already had said their good-byes.

FIFTY-EIGHT

Mary crept to the door of the study. She could hear Cliff's fingers steadily tapping on his computer's keyboard. Some of her confidence had wandered off. While she awaited its return, she performed one last inspection. First, the long-range: she held out her right hand, arm's length, shoulder height, wrist flexed upward, backhand facing. She craned her neck back and smiled approvingly. Now the close-up: she pulled the hand in, flipped it to palm-facing, folded the fingers, and smiled some more. Confident or not, she barged in, held out her ten trophies, and asked Cliff, "Do you like them?"

Cliff had no doubt about the answer; what he was uncertain about was how to avoid giving it. "Oh, I see you have false fingernails." They were long, painted white, and swirled in orange and blue.

"You don't like them," Mary interpreted. The gleeful pride vanished from her face, replaced by a wounded expression. She hid her hands behind her back.

"I didn't say that."

"Not in so many words."

"Give me another look."

With less confidence than before, she presented her hands.

"What made you suddenly decide to get nails?"

"You're stalling," she accused. She retracted her hands and assumed a hands-on-hips stance.

"I was just asking a simple question."

Mary made an impatient concession. "Okay. The daughter of the Korean couple that Powell robbed owns a nail salon, and she did me for free—well, almost, because I told her I couldn't accept gifts. I think they make my hands prettier." Then Mary said, "Now, be a man and tell me what you think."

Cliff's pride was pricked, and he got direct. "I don't like them. Not just yours. I don't like that type of nails, period."

"And why not?"

"They look ghetto."

Her eyebrows almost lifted off her face. "Well, well, well," she said, tossing her head from one side to the other with each "well." "Listen to Mr. Upwardly Mobile."

Cliff knew that he was being baited. "I don't have time for foolishness. Stand here and argue with yourself if you want. I'm busy with my English proficiency exam project." He positioned his fingers back on the keyboard.

"Then by all means, proceed. The world must be saved from those who talk ghetto in addition to us who wear ghetto."

"Why don't you leave the room, Mary." His words marched out like soldiers. "Cool out, before this gets more out of hand than it already has."

Mary didn't like the current state of affairs one iota. Cliff was behaving out of character, not bending over backward to coddle her. She had a suspicion as to why. "You're getting in your digs over the dance contest, aren't you?"

"Wrong," said Cliff curtly. "You messed up on purpose, regardless of how much you deny it. But I'm not nursing a grudge."

"Then why are you being such a cold fish? And I didn't mess up on purpose."

"Sure you did, as soon as I mentioned that the loan came through. You want to stay a cop, Mary, and nothing I do and say can change that." It was a difficult admission, and he became surly. "So why did you lead me by the nose when you knew your intentions all along? I at least deserve that explanation."

Mary lowered her gaze and weakly said, "I don't know." She still hadn't told him about her promotions.

"I think you do. It's your brother, your father—and now Carson's ghost is haunting us. I've tried to be understanding and supportive, but I'm wearing down. Maybe we should see a family counselor, because it doesn't appear that our issues are going to resolve themselves. Especially the career thing." He exhaled wearily, then said,

"What's so frustrating is that you make it seem like I'm obsessed with a dance studio. I'll remind you again that it was *your* idea. I would have been just as enthusiastic with any other career change as long as it took you out of harm's way. I love you so much that the thought of something happening to you makes me desperate. I even—" He guillotined his own sentence. He broke eye contact.

A realization hit Mary like a falling safe. "You even what, Cliff?"

"Forget it."

"You leaked the Cookie Cutter story, didn't you?" She'd kept him informed about the case. She should have suspected earlier.

"I'm not going to lie to you, Mary."

Her demeanor turned angry and lecturing. "You had no right. None at all. Of all the— How dare you." Momentarily outdone, she began to pace the room.

"I didn't do it to hurt you. As misguided as it might sound, I did it to protect you."

She came to an abrupt stop. She axed the air and said, "Oh, bullshit. You could have gotten me kicked off the force."

"That wasn't my intent. What I wanted was for you to get the most help possible, whether through added manpower or public tips. I guess I didn't think it through enough. I went crazy with worry. I'm truly sorry."

She knew that he was sincere. Nonetheless, he'd committed a grave trespass, and although divorcing him was out of the question, she didn't want to be too forgiving too quickly. So it was time to make an exit, sniping all the way. "I'm so ticked, I can't see straight." Then she added, "Since you brought up the subject of unresolved issues, here's one to throw on the pile: you lose one wife to a dangerous job, then you marry a cop. If you rescue me, will that make up for Jeannie?" she asked, referring to his deceased first wife by name. And after seconds of his silence, she ended with "Go back to what you were working on. I'm taking my ghetto ass upstairs."

But Cliff didn't resume working. He was too distracted. He remained in his workstation chair, swiveling back and forth along a short arc, regretting having been stupid twice—for leaking the story and for letting it slip. The phone rang insistently, but he ignored it, being in no mood for conversation. Apparently Mary was of the same mind. But the next minute the ringing started again. He still ignored it.

"I'm leaving to go to the Afro-American Museum," Mary announced from the top of the stairs. Although angry, she still extended him certain considerations.

"Isn't the place closed?"

"The director, Martha Chenault, is still there."

"You're on inactive duty," he said, as if she needed reminding.

"Martha knows that." Mary's voice had almost calmed to conversational. "She didn't want to say over the phone what she wants. I asked her for a favor, and I suspect that's what it's about."

"What time will you be back?" Cliff was fumbling for a pleasant parting.

But Mary chose to leave on lesser terms. "You don't want it to be anytime soon. Believe me." Saying nothing further, she left the house.

FIFTY-NINE

The museum's side door swung open and Mary entered, not able to see who had admitted her until Eugene pushed the door closed and faced her with his back against it. She realized instantly that she had walked into a trap. Eugene must have coerced Martha into making the call. "Where is Martha Chenault?"

Eugene's voice was without inflection, and his expression was blank except for wide eyes. "Concerned for someone else's safety when your own's in trouble. Admirable. Or selfish? Outdoors the other day, you wanted to speak to Martha about something personal. Afraid she won't be around to do you the favor?" He was all but bragging that he'd *persuaded* Martha to disclose her discussions with Mary, giving him the means for setting the trap.

"Don't try me, mister, unless you have a death wish."

"And who better to fulfill it than the infamous Bloody Mary?" said Eugene mockingly. "The scourge of black men, far and wide."

Mary, fearing that Martha was dead, was tempted to dive into a bottomless pit of guilt for not having warned her. "As a police officer, I'm asking you: Where is Martha Chenault?"

Eugene ignored the question. "You suspect that I'm a killer. Is that an example of 'it takes one to know one'? What's your body count up to now? You probably no longer keep tally."

"Martha! Martha!" Mary's summoning shouts resounded through the area, but no response. From anyone.

"Are you armed, Lieutenant Cunningham?"

Despite her fear, Mary managed a threatening tone. "Don't make me prove that I am."

"That's odd. I thought cops had to give up their guns while under review."

"You think I'm playing some type of goddamn game," said Mary. She took a step back, lowered her purse from her shoulder, then thrust a hand inside, ready to withdraw a weapon. Eugene's lips curled in amusement, and she changed her bluff to "Trying to force me to kill you, is that it? I won't be your easy way out. You're going in alive." She pulled out her cell phone, and had no sooner flipped it open than Eugene reacted.

"Drop it!" The dagger had appeared as if by sleight of hand. In one motion, he had cleared it from under his dashiki.

Mary let the phone drop and it obediently tumbled in Eugene's direction. He put it in his back pocket. With a whip action of the wrist, he signaled Mary to turn around.

"Fuck you. You're going to have to look me in the face. And get ready for a fight, you sick son of a bitch."

"You misread my intentions, Mary. I was motioning you into the main exhibit area. That's where the answers are."

"I'm not turning my back on you!"

Then he'd just have to coax her into cooperating. Eugene lunged at her with the dagger. Again. Again. In between lunges, he sliced the air with arcing swipes. Mary didn't know that his aim was intentionally off, so she leapt back repeatedly. He kept charging, carefully blocking paths of escape, rounding her up like a stray sheep, until he'd herded her onto the floor of the main exhibit. "The investigator in you will thank me," he said.

Mary was breathing through her mouth, audibly, in shallow intakes. "You're the tour guide," she said, her lungs needing a long, deep draw.

"This exhibit tells our history in America. I'll understand if you haven't toured it, since your mind was elsewhere when you visited the museum. How does being in here make you feel, Lieutenant?"

"Not counting present company?"

"Are you proud to be black, Lieutenant?"

"Yes."

"I don't believe you," he said with the condemning coldness of a hanging judge. "I was involved with this exhibit since its inception.

I know it by heart, section by section, period by period. It's so inspirational."

The realization hit Mary as pieces of the puzzle arranged themselves, magically, like computer graphics. "This museum was not conceived to be your inspiration for murder. You dishonor everything it stands for."

Eugene evidenced his disagreement with an agitated outburst. "Liar!"

Mary's shoulders jumped in startled fear. She uttered a little yelp that she hoped Eugene didn't hear. Direct challenges weren't smart. Try direct appeal. "I'm asking you to give yourself up."

"That's what Mocha said." Then his voice changed from melancholy to anger when he said, "You coached her."

"She knew that on her own."

"I didn't kill Mocha. You did by getting her involved."

Mary knew she'd better shift the discussion off herself quickly. "Why did you kill Thomas Kincaid?"

As if he'd been reminded of why they were in the main exhibit, he said, "I'll tell you." He moved toward her, and she moved back. He waltzed her to the slavery section. "We didn't have right of assembly back then," lectured Eugene. "Freedom had to be planned and discussed in secret. Communications to the masses has always been vital to our struggle. Still is. It shouldn't be abused and misused."

"Which is what Kincaid did?"

"Absolutely."

"And Xavier Livingstone?"

Eugene pointed and said, "Go over there," and Mary obeyed with backward steps, traversing eras, to a time coinciding with the Industrial Revolution. Eugene resumed speaking. "The Labor Movement gave us our first taste of equality. Labor unions are still the only political and economic power for many blacks. Livingstone was an insult, especially in Detroit."

"That leaves Felicia Wells."

"Politics account for the laws that have kept us oppressed. Every era, from colonial to present, proves it. Even today, our oppressors are legislating reversals of the gains won with blood. Ms. Wells and her organization were giving moral support to a conservative agenda bent on reenslaving us."

Mary was a captive audience to a lecture being delivered by a crazed professor whose pointer was a dagger. But was Eugene willing to let her walk from the classroom afterward? He didn't hold her in suspense for long.

Eugene said, "You'll identify with what I'm about to show you." He crossed the room, putting distance between them, but nonetheless ready to pounce if Mary so much as looked in the direction of the exit. He stopped in front of a blown-up black-and-white photo of civil-rights demonstrators being attacked by police with hoses, dogs, and nightsticks. "Police brutality against blacks goes way back. But the police aren't always outsiders." The lecture kicked into higher gear. "Oreo cops are the foreign invaders in our neighborhoods, committing war crimes against us. One executed an innocent brother and then danced on his grave. That same one killed an innocent sister—more than that—she was the mother of mankind." What might have been ramblings to someone else were being translated perfectly by Mary. "That person deserves to be made an example of more than any of the others." Then came the deadly rhetorical question "Can you guess the identity of our mystery race traitor, huh, Bloody Mary?" Class dismissed, but Mary would be staying. The dagger had been held to his side, and now he raised it waist high and pointed it at her. His wrist moved in tight circles, as if he were winding up for that first strike. His retreat into the dark realm began: the eyes glazed over; the mouth contorted; the head wobbled.

Mary was mesmerized for some seconds until she realized that she was that stupid person in the monster movies, watching the werewolf transform instead of running like hell. She bolted, her objective the side door. She didn't dare try dashing past him, so she was forced to twist and turn through the layout of exhibits. Her head start was a couple of seconds, but he knew the place better. He saw various portions of her disappear and come back into view as they both wove madly through, between, and over the exhibits. She had only a short way to go before reaching the turn leading to a straight path to the door.

Something tripped her. She fell facedown, unable to see Eugene. All she could think of was not to stay where she had landed and rolled off to the side, just as the dagger's point came down forcefully where her neck had been. She ended up seated on the floor. Using her hands and feet, she scooted backward, scurrying like a crab in reverse. He stalked her, slowly, forcing her back into the museum and in the opposite direction of the door. She scrambled to her feet. "Help! Help! Help!" The shouts tore at the lining of her dry, raw throat. And after they proved ineffective, she fared no better with "Fire! Fire! Fire!"

The guards out in the guardhouse couldn't hear her. Nor could the guard making rounds in the patrol car. But the guard stationed in the building could hear her plainly; however, he was tied up at the moment—gagged, too—in the security cage. The janitor was likewise indisposed. Eugene had taken care of every contingency: checked in at the guardhouse; come in and knocked the guard unconscious; waved the guard's gun at the janitor; and then visited Martha. One, two, three, four.

There was nothing that Mary could pick up, nothing to throw. Everything either was encased or was permanently affixed. But because she had to, she continued to snap her head around in all directions in search of something that could win her a chance to sprint for the door. He kept coming with calm, deliberate steps, so much in contrast to her frantic dashes from point to point. Through the glass wall and doors that separated the exhibit floor from the rotunda and front entrance, she spotted a potential equalizer. With speed reflective of the circumstances, she was at the front entrance, pushing against the horizontal bars that disengaged the locks. The thick twin doors remained locked. By this time she had close company, and she spun around to face him.

He knew all along that the door would be locked; but so did she. The true object of her interest stood at the side of each door. He stopped about two yards in front of her and psyched himself, and when he was sufficiently pumped, he raised the dagger above his head and charged. Mary timed her move perfectly, lifted the circular ash tray that was the lid to a trash can and threw the sand in his face.

It caught him flush. He rubbed his eyes, blew through the nose, and spit, as he slashed blindly. Mary lifted the trash can and threw it at him. It had been heavier than she guessed and she couldn't muster much force behind the throw, but it struck him in the chest, knocking him back on his heels. She snatched up the other trash can. This one, she held in front of herself and raced toward him to ram him with it. But the tray separated from the can, causing it to fall from that end, barely missing her toes.

She stooped to get another grip. By then Eugene's vision had improved to blurry, and Mary felt sharp pain as the dagger glanced off her collarbone and sank deep into her shoulder. She screamed once when it entered, again when he pulled it out. She ducked under the next downward thrust and broke into a run, wounded, bleeding, and farther than ever from the side door. Just barely into the rotunda, she felt the dagger pierce her back in the area of the right shoulder blade. She screamed.

Suddenly she detoured and dove on the reception counter. The momentum carried her across it and onto the floor. She popped up and tore down her quilt, just before he was upon her again. She held it up in defense, trying to wrap and fold it at the same time for maximum cushioning. He stabbed through the quilt, this time slashing her forearm. Then he discovered that he couldn't free the wavy dagger from the layers. For the moment, it was trapped like a corkscrew in a mattress. She tugged at the quilt with one hand and beat him in the face with the other. He pulled at the dagger and tried to ward off her strikes. His hands were slick with her blood, and the same mighty yank that freed the dagger sent it flying out to the floor. Both hurtled over the counter and after it. He reached it first, but he couldn't slow himself to avoid accidentally kicking it away. Mary got to it. He got to her. They wrestled and rolled. They ended up with her on her back and him straddling her chest, and with teeth-gritting force, he pried the dagger from her.

He adjusted his position: pressed her down by the throat and raised the dagger for the coup de grâce. She stopped flailing away at him and readied her hands, in an attempt to catch his wrist as it descended. But as he posed in readiness, she rammed a knee into his butt and got just enough of his testicles to make him drop his mouth open in a voiceless yell. Infuriated, and without premeditation, his fist collided with her jaw and she was knocked out.

Now he could finish her. Finally. He decided to go for the heart. He wrapped both hands around the dagger handle and raised it high. He was close to hyperventilating. He thought he felt a bit of his resolve drain away, so to make for a mightier strike, he reared the dagger farther and arched his back. He saw his reflection in the dome.

The image froze him. He saw his crazed expression. Moreover, it mirrored Mocha's cutting comment: *"Gene, you look like a white man."*

The past year, his mind had been a rubber band that would stretch to the fringes, then recover enough to deceive most of society; however, each stretch had left it more fatigued and more susceptible to the inevitable. This time the rubber band was stretched beyond its elasticity and snapped; what proportions were due to the oxygen-starved trauma of his birth, survivor's guilt over Larkin, the Parsons Curse, the murders, or grief over Mocha—it was impossible to say.

First order of business: those fucking mirror panels. Sleeping Beauty would stay put until he returned. Then he could do his thing without distraction. He rose. He staggered out of the rotunda, through the exhibits, and up the stairs, en route to Martha Chenault's office. He passed the janitor's closet, and the racket that Martha was creating didn't even register with his ears. Once inside the office, he took a key from the lockbox. He climbed more stairs and unlocked the door that opened to the outdoors, to the roof walkway that circled the base of the dome. A ladder, used for dome maintenance, arched from the bottom to the top of the dome. The ladder was anchored to a guide track and could be rolled anywhere around the dome. Its present position was fine for ascending to the top and breaking the shit out of those mirrored panels. A selfishly humanitarian thought came to him: concern that glass would rain down on Mary and cheat him. He thought of removing the mirrors panel by panel.

Eugene wasn't far up the ladder when both feet left the rungs and he found himself hanging on just by his hands. Mary was wrapped around his ankles, hanging like a ball and chain. Locked together, the pair spilled down the ladder. She landed on her back and Eugene landed on top, knocking the wind out of her. She locked her arms around him, for what good it did, because with one flex motion he sent her arms flying open. Then she sent them flying immediately back, her hands clamping down on his face. Driven by the survival instinct, she curved her fingers into claws, digging ten decorated acrylic nails into his flesh. Since his eyes still were open maniacally wide, some of the nails hooked into his eyeballs, cutting into the gelatinous orbs, slicing through cornea, iris, and pupil. He felt as if he were wearing contact lenses that had been soaked in sulfuric acid. He tore her hands from his face and rolled over on his hands and knees, panic-stricken, looking about but seeing nothing. He stumbled upright. He could only listen for his target.

"It's over," came her voice. "Give up."

He made a lunging stab in her direction, but Mary had the advantage of sight and sidestepped him easily. His momentum made him flip over the rail. He hung by one arm. The surprise of momentary free fall caused him to drop the weapon. It fell three stories to the ground. Eugene kicked and grabbed wildly for the rail with his other hand. He lacked the strength to pull himself high enough to hook his hand on the rail. He kept coming up short by a deadly inch, stubbing his fingertips against the side of the rail. Then Mary's hands slapped around his wrist and he felt her tugging. But he outweighed her and she was pulled past her center of gravity. She was close to going over the rail with him. Still she held on. Still she pulled. Too weak from struggle and loss of blood. Feet sliding. Still she held on. Still she pulled. Severe cramps set into her fingers, and as much as she tried, she couldn't tighten her grip further.

Her head was far over the rail and she couldn't look up, but she figured that the drumming footsteps were those of the guards. When she had returned to full consciousness, still on her back, she saw Eugene stumbling around on the roof. Still woozy, she thought about Cox's warning about killers committing suicide. She even was reminded of how Ellery chose to escape his punishment. There had been no time to go to the guardhouse, but she did call them from Martha's office.

One guard pulled her by the waist as the other one reached down to Eugene, not knowing that he couldn't see. Critical seconds lost. Eugene's fingertips gave out. He released the rail. Mary could not support his full weight, and he slipped from her grip. He fell, never uttering a sound.

SIXTY

Mary's grogginess lifted stubbornly, like a fog retreating to the sea. But Mary didn't need her full alertness to know Cliff was there. She knew from how her hand was being held. "Cliff," she said, not ready to open her eyes and struggle with focusing.

"Shhh. Don't talk. Rest."

"How long have you been here?" she asked, defying orders.

"Ever since they brought you back from surgery."

Mary pinched the bridge of her nose with thumb and forefinger and tightened her eyes. She paused—ready, set, go—and sprung her eyes wide open. After some fluttering, she could see her husband smiling warmly. Then she scanned the length of the bed to see how her bedcovers were lying. "Pull them back for me, Cliff." She lifted the top of the covers to indicate to him what she was talking about. "I want to see what's left of me."

"I checked already," he toyed. "You didn't lose anything except blood. They transfused you, then stitched you up."

"Probably with sutures as big and ugly as shoelaces. I sure won't be parading around the house naked anymore," Mary said, fishing for reassurance.

Cliff delivered. "Why punish me?" he seductively whispered into her ear.

"I don't deserve you, but I don't deserve being almost killed, either, so I guess things have a way of balancing out."

Cliff moved toward her haltingly, as if deciding on the best way to hug a porcupine; but he gathered Mary in his arms without hurting her. She assisted, holding up her arms, enduring the pain. They eased into a loose embrace. Their faces touched, and tears slid down her cheeks. After a while he guided her arms down from his neck, supporting them all the way to minimize her exertion. "I apologize for interfering in your career. Will you forgive me, Lieutenant? Or should I call you squad leader?"

"How long have you known?"

"Frank Corleone is one of the people waiting to see you."

"That big-mouth." Mary smiled and then her expression turned serious. "Please forgive me, Cliff. I handled it so badly. And I felt terrible the whole while. I'll never withhold from you again."

"You'll never lie to me?" Cliff carefully reworded her remark, placing the emphasis where it was needed.

"I can't promise all that," she said, smiling wryly.

"I didn't think so," said Cliff with good humor. "Like I said, others are waiting to see you. And I'll be back after everyone's had a visit."

After he left, Mary spent a few minutes taking in her surroundings. She didn't know what hospital, but she was in a private room. Cliff had left a beautiful floral arrangement. Turning was painful, so she was grateful that she could see much of the room, albeit in contour, in the blank screen of the television perched on its wall stand. Not many sounds: carts being wheeled down the hall; passersby talking; a nurse cackling over a joke. She heard someone walking into the room.

"Hi."

"Daddy." She didn't mean for her voice to register the surprise that it did.

"You're indestructible, girl," Joe Kingsley said, "but one of these days you're going to cause me a fatal heart attack." After that scolding, he kissed his daughter on both cheeks.

Mary patted the bed in invitation. "Sit here, Daddy."

Joe stood at her bedside, holding his hat by the brim, nervously turning it in both hands like a steering wheel. He was in suit and tie, a look he reserved for church and for "taking care of his business," as he often put it. He braced his hands on the edge of the bed and lowered himself slowly so that he wouldn't jostle Mary. "It was never the same between us after Junior died. If it's not too late, I'm here to beg your forgiveness. I've been burdened by guilt all these years over his death."

"That's foolish. I'm the one who needs forgiveness."

Joe held up his hand to quiet her. "I don't fault you. You were a child. I failed you and your mother by not being able to get justice for Junior. It drove me into a shell, and I wasn't the father you deserved or the husband your mother deserved."

Mary clutched her hand over his. "Daddy, if I could have taken Junior's place down there on the ground, I would have."

"Hold back the tears, Mary," Joe demanded, seeing that they had begun to roll, "so I can get through everything I got to say."

Joe cleared his throat and began again. "As a little girl, you used to think I could do anything. And it was wonderful to be looked up to like that. But I fell flat on my face in the biggest challenge of my life. When you looked at me, you saw a miserable failure."

"That's not true."

He held up his hand again to silence her. "For thirty long years. But God might finally be smiling on me. I didn't rejoice when Reed Carson was killed, but I didn't feel any sorrow, either. Now something much more positive has happened. Something wonderful. Junior and the others that died in the riots are going to get a memorial."

"That *is* wonderful, Daddy. More than wonderful." Mary was warmed by her father's beaming face.

"Don't you want to know the details?" Joe asked, his eyes sparkling.

"I certainly do."

"Got a call from a lady named Martha Chenault, director of the Afro-American Museum."

"The name sounds familiar. Go on, Daddy."

"She said the museum will make a memorial plaque part of the exhibit on the civil unrest of the sixties. She contacted me because I'm the head of the Survivors' Network. I asked her how she came up with the idea, and she said it was suggested by a sympathizer. I should have thought of it, instead of putting all my attention on City Hall."

"The important thing is that somebody did."

Joe's expression clouded for a moment and he stared into the hat he held in his hand. "I feel like I've finally done something for

Junior. I was hoping it might redeem me with you, if only just a tad. I didn't want to come empty-handed asking forgiveness."

"Bend down and hug me, silly old man."

He did, not perfunctorily as had been his practice, but warmly and snugly, heedless of her condition.

Mary stifled a groan and grimaced in pain.

Realizing his oversight, Joe released her as if she were radioactive. "Sorry."

"Well worth the pain," Mary said.

Joe summoned his resolve and said, "My dream was for Junior to follow in my footsteps. But if he had lived, I don't see how he could have built a more distinguished career than you have." Joe made a wide left turn with the brim of his hat. "What I'm saying in my clumsy way is that you're the best kind of cop and I'm damn proud of you. Always have been. I've been too much in a shell of self-pity to say it like it should have been said. Forgive me for that, too."

That hospital room had never witnessed so much healing over so short a time.

Her euphoria told her that nothing would serve better than a simple heartfelt reply. "I forgive you, Daddy."

EPILOGUE

It was the same ending that Mary and Cliff had attempted at the Tango Championship of Southeast Michigan, but this time they nailed it. More than that, they'd danced effortlessly the entire evening, and in front of the world's most knowledgeable judges of tango talent. It was still early, but they were dancing their way through the San Telmo section of Buenos Aires, famous for its tango bars, and they planned to hit each bar before dawn.

They'd decided that this was a great time to get away on vacation, since Mary had fully healed and would return to work soon. Cliff had made his peace with it. Instead of focusing on worst-case scenarios, he'd resigned himself to being thankful for each day they had together, never taking tomorrow for granted. The dance studio project was kaput, but they'd undertaken a more important enterprise: the building of a stronger marriage.

Back in the United States it was Thanksgiving weekend, but in Buenos Aires it was almost summer.

The mayoral election was over, and Randal Clay had won another four years. He ran unopposed on Election Day. Isaac Shaw withdrew, since he had pled guilty to a statutory rape charge, since there was no statute of limitations on such an offense in Alabama. Eugene's lawyers planned to enter an insanity plea that relied heavily on Isaac's revelations about Eugene's legacy of the Parsons Curse. To prove his claim, Isaac told where Annie was buried. There was no scientific evidence to disprove that she died in childbirth, so he escaped a murder charge. FBI Agent Abigail Cox also bolstered

Eugene's cause, offering her expert testimony that he was impaired beyond the ability to aid in his own defense. Isaac's first act of love for Eugene had been to literally breathe life into him. His last act for Eugene was to sacrifice himself on the chance that his son would be sent to an institution rather than to prison. Gertrude planned to relocate to Alabama for weekly visits to Isaac. Until then, she visited Eugene weekly.

Eugene Shaw now resided, an escapee into his own mind, in a lockdown ward at the Northville Psychiatric Hospital, a half hour's drive from Detroit. The broken leg he had suffered from the fall had mended, but not all his injuries. Mary had—as the saying goes—scratched his eyes out, with acrylic claws and mighty muscle. He was blind, but not color-blind, because, wonder of wonders, he could see colors again. Everything was no longer black and white. His third eye was more functional than ever, and this was an endless source of bliss for him. He spent his days creating finger paintings. The orderlies raved over his work, but he didn't need their fawning. He knew that each of his creations was a masterpiece.

In San Telmo, the locals, true to custom, had taken a naked nightfall and dressed it in festive lights, in some places gaudily, in other places tastefully. The air outside was warm and moist and loaded down with the smells of grilled meat and caramelized sugar, for the *porteños*—as the citizens call themselves—are lovers of beef and sweets. Mary's sweet tooth, in fact, had known no restraint since her arrival in Argentina.

An English-speaking couple joined the Cunninghams' table. Arturo was Afro-Argentinean, elderly but spry. Linda, also Afro-Argentinean, appeared to be young enough to be his daughter. After complimenting the Cunninghams on their dancing, he ordered a round of drinks for the table. Then he said to Mary, "Many women from your country have trouble finding the inner soul of the tango."

"Why?" Mary asked.

"Unwilling to yield to the full control of the man. In the tango, the man is the master, the woman his servant who must follow without questioning."

Linda cut in with "Arturo believes my generation has the same problem."

"It does," Arturo insisted. "Corrupted by the fantasy of equality of the sexes." Then he spoke to Mary. "But you, señora, I can tell that you are different."

"Tell me how I am," Mary said with a mischievous glint in her eye.

"You, señora, accept that the man must be king. And I bet you're that way off the dance floor, too."

Cliff looked away, smiling roguishly, anticipating Mary's denial.

But she sat in introspective silence for a few moments, a lifetime when measured by the speed of thought. She'd danced all her life with different partners—father, husbands, coworkers, community—with lots of missteps. Maybe what Auturo saw was her new sense of calm confidence that came with knowing the moves that were hers alone. The ones mastered through experience.

Mary released a modified version of her signature laugh. She winked at Cliff and feigned an astonished look for Auturo and confirmed "You are good, sir. Damn good."

About the Author

STERLING ANTHONY is a former professor who now works as a business consultant and is often called on to testify as an expert witness. He lives in Detroit. This is his first novel.